Liver...
Daughter

Katie Flynn is the pen name of the much-loved writer, Judy Turner, who published over ninety novels in her lifetime. Judy's unique stories were inspired by hearing family recollections of life in Liverpool during the early twentieth century, and her books went on to sell more than eight million copies. Judy passed away in January 2019, aged 82.

The legacy of Katie Flynn lives on through her daughter, Holly Flynn, who continues to write under the Katie Flynn name. Holly worked as an assistant to her mother for many years and together they co-authored a number of Katie Flynn novels, including *Christmas at Tuppenny Corner*.

Holly lives in the north east of Wales with her husband Simon and their two children. When she's not writing she enjoys walking her two lurchers, Sparky and Snoopy, in the surrounding countryside, and cooking forbidden foods such as pies, cakes and puddings! She looks forward to sharing many more Katie Flynn stories, which she and her mother devised together, with readers in the years to come.

KATIE FLYNN

Liverpool Daughter

arrow books

5 7 9 10 8 6 4

Arrow Books
20 Vauxhall Bridge Road
London SW1V 2SA

Arrow Books is part of the Penguin Random House
group of companies whose addresses can be found
at global.penguinrandomhouse.com.

Copyright © Katie Flynn 2020

Katie Flynn has asserted her right to be identified as
the author of this Work in accordance with the Copyright,
Designs and Patents Act 1988.

First published in Great Britain by Century in 2020
First published in paperback by Arrow Books in 2020

www.penguin.co.uk

A CIP catalogue record for this book is available
from the British Library.

ISBN 9781787463028

Typeset in 11.02/14.1 pt Palatino LT Pro
by Integra Software Services Pvt. Ltd, Pondicherry

Printed and bound in Great Britain by Clays Ltd, Elcograf S.p.A.

The authorised representative in the EEA is Penguin Random
House Ireland, Morrison Chambers, 32 Nassau Street,
Dublin DO2 YH68.

Acknowledgements

To all at RAF Harrowbeer.

Mum, always and forever.

Prologue

Glasgow, 1923

Matron swiftly wrapped the baby in a towel before handing the tiny bundle to the waiting nurse. 'You can take this one, Nurse McIntosh.'

Nurse McIntosh attempted to soothe the yowling baby by rocking her back and forth in her arms. She turned to leave the room when a stab of conscience made her pause. She half turned before Matron, who had anticipated the nurse's actions, spoke abruptly. 'I told you to take the baby away.'

Nurse McIntosh gave a small, reluctant nod before hurrying through the doors. She knew she shouldn't question Matron, especially after their earlier conversation.

'Your job is to assist me in delivering the baby, nothing more! What happens to it after it's born is none of your business. You were told when you started working here that you shouldn't allow yourself to get attached, and today's no different from any other ...' She wagged a warning finger as the nurse opened her mouth to object. 'We're not here to judge.'

1

'This is a bit different,' said Nurse McIntosh defensively. 'I'm only tryin' to do what's best ...'

The matron had held her hand up. 'It's not up to us to decide what's best.'

Now, Nurse McIntosh gently placed the baby on to the scales, waited for the needle to settle and made a note of the weight. She knew Matron was right; she knew, too, that having no children of her own, she was in no position to judge others. Taking the tape measure, she recorded the baby's length, noting as she did so that the baby's eyes appeared to have a hint of green deep within the blue. She took a jug and had started to fill the bath with tepid water when the door behind her burst open, startling her and causing some of the water to spill on to the floor.

It was one of the midwives who worked on the ward; she was shaking her head reprovingly. 'Haven't you bathed her yet?' Without waiting for a response she jerked her head towards the door through which she had entered. 'The Quinns are waiting to leave.'

The nurse gawped at her. 'Already? But she's only just been born, surely her mother' – she spoke the last word with contempt – 'should at least be shown how to bathe and feed her? This is her first child, after all ...'

Ignoring the question, the midwife handed over a brightly coloured patchwork blanket. 'Her parents want her wrapped in this. You knew they wouldn't be staying – their kind never do. It's somethin' you'll get used to over time. She may be your first but she won't be your last.'

Nurse McIntosh continued to fill the bath. 'I'm sorry, but I can't help feelin' a sense of responsibility ...'

The midwife relented a little. 'I know, but there's plenty of folk come through these doors who aren't fit to look after a dog, let alone a baby. You have to do the best you can whilst they're under your care, but once they leave you just have to forget they were ever here; either that or spend the rest of your days worrying over something which you can't possibly control.' She held the door open with one hand as she made to leave the room. 'Do you want me to do the handover?'

Nurse McIntosh shook her head. 'Like you say, it's somethin' I've got to get used to. I'll be fine, I promise.' The midwife nodded as she let the door swing shut behind her. The nurse gently sloshed the water over the small pink bundle, who, rather than scream her displeasure like some of them did, was gurgling with delight. 'Someone's a water baby,' she cooed. She scooped the baby girl out from the bath and on to a soft, clean towel and gently patted her dry, then expertly pinned a nappy into place before swaddling her into the blanket.

As she entered the waiting room, she glanced at the parents who were talking earnestly to one of the midwives. Sitting a short distance away was a large man whom the nurse had seen earlier that day. He had thick bushy mutton chops and his face wore the lines of a man who spent most of his life scowling; on his knees rested a long ebony cane with a large silver handle.

Her shoulders tensed as the midwife beckoned her over. 'There you are! Matron can't come because she's got a baby what's breeched, so she asked me to oversee things here.'

Nurse McIntosh hesitated. She wanted to refuse, to take the child back to the safety of the ward, but she knew it wasn't up to her. Whether Matron was present or not didn't matter: word would soon get back. She begrudgingly handed the baby over to her mother, then glanced at the man, who cast the baby a look of revulsion. Her cheeks flushed angrily. How could anyone regard an innocent baby in such a heinous fashion? Pompous, stuck-up pig of a man! She hadn't liked him when he had entered the hospital, but seeing the look of disgust on his face she now considered him utterly detestable.

The man spluttered something inaudible to the parents before slamming the swing doors so hard with the palm of his hand they continued to swing violently in his wake.

The mother glanced nervously from the doors to her husband, before turning her attention to Nurse McIntosh. 'Is she all right?'

She nodded brusquely. 'She'll want feedin'. Do you need—'

The midwife cut her off mid-sentence. 'No need to worry, nurse, I shall take over from here.'

Nurse McIntosh continued to look at the woman, who smiled lovingly at the baby now sleeping peacefully in her arms, leaned down and kissed the child softly on her forehead. 'My sweet alannah.' She glanced briefly at the nurse before turning her attention back to the small bundle in her arms. 'I know what you think of us, but we'll take good care of her ... is the lady—'

The midwife cut across the woman. 'Nurse McIntosh can't be standin' round chattin'.' Her voice shrill, she addressed the nurse directly: 'Go and see to Mrs McCarthy. She's been having great difficulty in getting her baby to latch on; I'm sure she'll appreciate a bit of help.'

Nurse McIntosh turned on her heel, and not a moment too soon as hot tears of frustration began to trickle down her cheeks. 'Stupid, stupid, stupid girl,' she muttered to herself, 'Matron warned you not to get involved, and she was right.' Wiping the tears from her cheeks, she straightened her starched apron and smoothed her hair back before entering the ward. She had wanted to be a nurse ever since she could remember and, when she visited a hospital during her initial training, she had decided that she would like to work on the maternity ward because she loved children; being a naïve young woman she had viewed the profession through rose-coloured spectacles, and had not realised that not all births went to plan. Not all babies were born alive and not all parents were worthy of having children. It had taken time, but she soon grew used to the fact that not every birth had a happy ending, and was therefore annoyed at herself for having let her feelings get the better of her.

She opened the door to the maternity ward and headed for Mrs McCarthy, reasoning that just because the Quinns lived in a wagon, it didn't mean to say that they would be incapable of looking after the child. After all, Mrs McCarthy, now on her eighth baby, was still having difficulty at getting her latest to latch on.

Chapter One

Liverpool, June 1940

Dana Quinn awoke with such a start she nearly fell off her narrow bed on to the wooden floor. Leaning up on her elbow, she stared bleary-eyed around the dark interior. Seeing nothing amiss, she focused her attention on the sounds coming from outside the brightly painted wagon. She paused; it must be another false alarm. There had been many since war had been declared and even though she strained her ears, she failed to hear the siren. Her father let out a grunting snort and Dana suspected it had been his snoring that had woken her. Snuggling down beneath her blankets, she began reflecting on the day ahead when there came a tremendous pounding against the small wooden door.

Stepping lightly across the short space between her bed and the wagon door, Dana paused for a moment, her hand on the knob. 'Who is it?'

'It's Martha Tidswell. Our Millie's got the colic and …'

Dana heard the sound of her father's feet hit the floor behind her. 'Don't just stand there, open the door.' His voice was muffled by the thick pullover he was sliding over his head. Dana opened the door to reveal a short curly-haired woman, her face white with worry. She wrung her shawl between her hands. 'Sorry to disturb you, Shane ...'

Shane Quinn, Dana's father, shook his head. 'Don't be daft, woman. Where's Millie at?'

Martha's bottom lip trembled as tears began to well. 'She's in the stable. We tried to get her outside, but she keeps tryin' to go down.' She blinked and tears trickled down her pale cheeks. 'If we lose her we lose everythin'. We can't afford another horse ...'

Shane nodded. The Tidswells were carters; without their horse they had no way of earning a living. If Millie didn't recover, they wouldn't be able to pay their rent, feed the kids ... He turned to his daughter. 'Get dressed. She's a big mare is Millie; it's goin' to take everythin' we've got to stop her goin' down.' He smiled fleetingly at Martha. 'Don't worry, queen, we'll do everythin' we can to get her right.'

Dana tucked her nightie into the waistband of her trousers at the same time as shoving her feet into her stout lace-up boots. Colleen Quinn, Dana's mother, had been listening from the bed she shared with her husband at the rear of the wagon. 'Is there owt I can do?'

Shane shook his head as he pulled his braces over his shoulders. 'Too many cooks an' all that. Best you stay here an' keep me bed warm – me and our Dana'll manage.' He pointed to a row of bottles above Dana's bed. 'Get the one for colic, then you an' Martha can go and help the others, whilst I fetch a length of hose and a rope.'

Dana traced the line of bottles with her forefinger, her lips moving as she whispered the contents of each bottle beneath her breath: 'Udder balm, black oil seed, abscess balm, colic …' Clutching the bottle to her chest, she followed Martha as fast as her legs would carry her and, within a minute or two, the two women hurtled into the open stable. Freddie Tidswell was kneeling down beside Millie's head, trying to soothe the stricken beast, who had lain so close to the stable wall she was unable to get to her feet.

'She's cast,' said Freddie, 'so mind she don't kick you by accident when she tries to get up.'

Nodding, Dana knelt down by Millie's rump. 'I'll take her by the tail.' She looked up at Martha. 'You can help, just make sure you stay to the side of me 'cos once she's free she'll be on her feet before you can blink.' Martha leaned down beside Dana and together they took a firm hold of the dock of the horse's tail. Dana looked at Freddie Tidswell, who had two clumps of the horse's mane clenched between his fists. 'Ready?'

With a short nod, he said, 'On the count of three, one, two, three …'

They hauled the mare away from the wall and in less than a second she was on her feet. Snorting, she started to strike her belly with her rear hoof.

'No you don't,' said Dana to the mare, just as her father appeared in the stable. He was holding up a length of hosepipe.

'Lift her head and keep talkin', she ain't goin' to like this,' he instructed Dana, who obeyed without hesitation. The mare's eyes rolled wildly as Shane began to thread the hose down her throat. Dana spoke in calming tones as she gazed reassuringly into the mare's eye. 'Easy girl, we're not here to harm you. Stay still so's we can get the medicine down, you'll soon start to feel better.' The horse stared back and a calmness began to descend.

'Good girl, Dana, it's easier to get it down her when she's relaxed,' said Shane as he administered the potion. When the last drop had gone he removed the pipe from the horse's throat. Keeping a tight hold of her head collar he spoke quickly. 'Let's get this one movin'; we can't afford for her to go down again.'

Dana and Shane walked Millie round until she stopped sweating and when she started to calm down he led her back into the stable. 'I don't know what she ate but a fair bit of it's come out. Keep your eye on her; if she starts sweatin' or frettin' come an' get me wi'out delay.'

Nodding, Freddie rested his hand across the top of the horse's withers. He spoke to Dana. 'If you hadn't got here when you did, it could've been a different story.' He glanced at Shane. 'You've got a good 'un there, good as most men – if not better: she knew exactly what to do, and got on wi' the job.' He pushed his hand into his trouser pocket. 'How much do I owe you?'

Shane waved a hand. 'I'll call by in a few hours, see how she's gerrin' on; we can sort summat out then.'

Freddie shook Shane firmly by the hand. 'I wish there were more like you, Shane Quinn, them others don't know what they're talkin' about.'

Placing his arm around Dana's shoulders Shane walked with her back towards their wagon. 'Quite the little heroine! Wait till I tell your mam!'

Blushing, Dana smiled shyly. 'I only did what you taught me.' A slight frown creased her forehead. 'What did Freddie mean when he said he didn't care what the others said? He wasn't talkin' about the carters, was he?'

Shane shook his head sharply. 'God no. I expect he were referrin' to them who's allus moanin' about us livin' up by the locks.'

Dana pulled a resentful face. 'What's it to them where we live? We pay us rent.'

'It's not so much about where we live, they don't like us 'cos we're not like them.'

'The carters don't have a problem with us, so why should they?' said Dana.

'The carters like us 'cos we're cheaper than the vet. Them who don't have horses don't like us 'cos we've nothin' they want and we don't choose to live the same way they do, plain and simple.'

Dana waved at her mother, who was sitting on the steps to the wagon, keeping an eye out for her husband and daughter. Colleen waved back. 'Is she …?'

Shane nodded. 'Freddie said he'd spend the rest of the night in the stable so he can keep an eye out.' He glanced up at the star-studded night sky. 'What's left of the night that is.' He ruffled the top of Dana's head. 'Time for bed!'

Dana stifled a yawn as she snuggled down beneath the sheets. It had been a hard night and her head had barely hit the pillow before she was fast asleep, only to

10

be woken what seemed like moments later by the air raid siren. Sitting up on one elbow, she was about to get out of bed when her father called out: 'It'll be another false alarm. I've said it before and I'll say it again, they shan't be botherin' us up here. If they're goin' to drop bombs on anyone it'll be them poor devils down south what'll get it. Besides, everyone knows they only bomb in the dead of night.'

Seeing her father pull the blankets up around his ears Dana lay back down. Britain had been at war with Germany for nearly a year and despite many false alarms, Liverpool had remained unaffected. When the aptly named Moaning Minnie first wailed out her warning, the Quinns had taken refuge along with many others down one of the public shelters, but as time went by, people began to believe that the phoney war, as it had become widely known, was just that, and they were better off getting a decent night's sleep in their own beds.

Try though she might, Dana found it almost impossible to fall back to sleep. It seemed like hours before her lids began to droop, only to hear the sound of the all clear. Dana peeked through the small gap in the curtains above her bed and bright sunshine pierced her eyes. Blinking, she dropped the curtain. Drat! How was it you could be awake all night, but as soon as you started to drift off … Sighing heavily, she swung her legs out of bed and fumbled around in the drawer below until her fingers found the handle of her small hand-held mirror. She grimaced at the sight of her face, still smeared with dirt from the previous night's activities. Wrapping her thickest shawl tightly

11

around her shoulders, she tiptoed down the steps of the wagon and poured some water from the bucket into a jug which she took back inside. Stripping down to her vest and knickers, she dipped her flannel into the ice-cold water and let out a small gasp as it touched her skin. She rubbed enthusiastically until every trace of dirt was gone before quickly drying herself and getting dressed into her shirt and dungarees. She gathered her long, curly, strawberry-blonde hair between her hands and twisted it tightly into a large bun, pinning it deftly into place. Now that she was ready, she went about making the tea. She collected the small stove and kettle and took them outside. Placing the Primus on the ground she pumped the stove and lit the ring. She poured some water from the container into the kettle and set it to boil; then, with nothing left to do, she sat on the steep wooden wagon steps and waited.

It was mid-June, but it was still cold in the early hours. She pulled her knees close to her chest and rested her chin on them as she waited for the steam to escape the spout.

When she had been a child she had taken it for granted that the only family she had was her mother and father, right up until one of the carters' wives had asked how many of them lived in the wagon.

'Just me and me dad and mam, they're the only family I got,' Dana had said matter-of-factly.

'Where do the rest of your family live?' the woman had asked conversationally. Seeing the confusion on Dana's face, she elaborated, 'Like your grandparents, do they live in a wagon next to yours? And your uncles and aunties, do they live nearby?'

Dana had blinked. 'I haven't got grandparents, nor aunties and uncles, it's just me, me mam and me dad ...'

Dana's father had walked in halfway through the conversation. 'Never mind standin' round gossipin' like a fishwife, you've work to do,' he had snapped before grabbing a pair of pliers and heading back outside.

Blushing, Dana followed her father, who addressed her from the corner of his mouth. 'Don't go listenin' to wimmen what's got nowt better to do wi' their time than stir up trouble for others,' he had hissed.

Dana, who was having to trot to keep up with her father, shook her head. 'She weren't causin' trouble, she were just askin' about me grandparents ...'

Shane stopped so abruptly Dana nearly cannoned into the back of him. 'Stirrin' trouble, like I said.' Placing a hand on her shoulder, he turned to look down into Dana's innocent face. 'The only family you've got is me and your mam, so if anyone else starts pokin' their nose in, tell 'em to mind their own business!'

Dana had no idea why her father had taken offence at what seemed like such an innocent question, but she knew better than to ask him when he was in a bad mood, so she waited until she got home and asked her mother whilst they prepared the evening meal.

Colleen's face had turned crimson and she placed a finger to her lips. 'What on earth makes you ask that?' Grasping Dana by the hand she led her away from the wagon and across the wasteland.

'You know Shirley?' Colleen had nodded. 'She were askin',' said Dana, a frown puckering her small forehead; when she thought about it, it made sense that her parents must have parents, and judging by the anxious look on her mother's face, Dana had hit a raw nerve. 'I told her I hadn't got any, but I do, don't I?'

Her mother drew a deep breath then gave a small nod. 'You're too bright for your own good sometimes, Dana Quinn. But best not mention it to your dad. He don't like to talk about it.'

'Talk about what?' said Dana, intrigued.

Her mother had gone on to explain that Dana came from a large family of travellers, and her father was one of six children: two boys and four girls. The girls had all gone off and married, so it was just the parents and his brother who had remained. 'Sometimes,' Colleen explained, 'families fall out and no one seems to know why. Mebbe it's all of you livin' together and gerrin' on each other's nerves, or mebbe it's a difference of opinion, but sometimes words are said what can't be unsaid, and when that happens you end up goin' separate ways, an' that's what happened with your dad.'

Dana nodded thoughtfully. 'What about your mam and dad? Why don't we ever see them?'

Colleen eyed her daughter sympathetically. 'My mam and dad died a long time ago, and, like you, I was an only child, so I've no brothers or sisters.'

'Do you reckern Dad'll ever make it up with his brother?'

Colleen shook her head. 'It's not your dad's fault they fell out, so unless his brother has a change of heart, which I very much doubt, they're destined to live their lives apart, and with his brother bein' the eldest the others followed suit and turned their backs on us.' Seeing the disappointment on her daughter's face, she smiled reassuringly at her. 'We've got each other, an' that'll never change.'

Now, as Dana sat on the steps to the wagon, she supposed her mother had been right. They might be a small family but that didn't matter as long as they had each other.

As the steam escaped the kettle Dana hopped down from her perch and removed it from the stove. Taking the kettle inside, she spooned tea leaves from the tin into the teapot and poured the water in. Dana left the tea to stew by the stove whilst she went to tend to Crystal, the large white cob which her father rode when he needed something from out of town. She untethered him from the bank that backed up against the canal path and led him over to the wagon. Picking up one of the stiffer brushes she began to methodically remove the dirt from around his feathered legs.

'You do get yourself into a mess, Crystal. Good job I'm here to take care of you,' she said as she used her fingers to break up some of the larger clumps of hardened mud. She cast her mind back to the time when she had asked her father whether she could go to school with all the other children instead of helping him with the horses.

Dana's father held a firm belief that all people, except for horse folk, were against them because they lived in a wagon. 'What can school teach you that I can't?' he said huffily, adding, 'And you don't want to be mixin' with them who reckern we're good for nothin's who take what they can and give nothin' back. If they don't say it to your face, you can see it in their eyes.' Looking at the disbelief on his daughter's face, he shook his head. 'Trouble wi' you is you don't know anythin' outside of our world, so all you see is happy, smilin' faces. You mark my words, five minutes in one of them schools and you'd soon see your old man was right: they'd look at you like you was summat off the bottom of their shoes.'

Dana, who had been fourteen at the time, had felt herself more than capable of making her own decisions.

'Couldn't I just try it for a week? It'd be nice to have friends my own age ...'

'And have all them young lads slobberin' over you?' Shane had spluttered. 'I don't think so. I can teach you all you need to know. You can stay here with me, where I can keep an eye on you, and let that be an end to it.'

In all fairness to Dana, this was a complete contradiction. 'I thought you'd said they'd treat me like summat off the bottom of their shoes ...'

Shane scowled at his daughter's persistence. 'The gels would, 'cos they'd be jealous, but the boys would be too friendly.' Dana had rolled her eyes, something that had not gone unseen by her father. 'Don't roll your eyes at me, my gel, I've seen the way some of the young carters look at you, and they wouldn't mind bendin' the rules for a gel as pretty as you.'

Dana had frowned. 'Rules? What rules?'

This time it was her father's turn to roll his eyes. 'Not to gerrinvolved with people like us. By God, their fathers would tan their hides just for lookin' at you, and believe you me they want to do a lot more than look at you!'

Dana had been intrigued to know what else the boys would like to do, but it was no use arguing, so she had given up. Her father was convinced that people saw them in a different light, without even giving her the chance to prove him wrong. 'He's probably frightened I'm goin' to make friends with the local boys and girls and want to live in a house,' Dana had reasoned to herself, 'and that's why he doesn't want me mixin' with them, 'cos he knows as well as me that they don't care where you live or what you do as long as you don't harm no one, and we ain't harmin' anyone livin' the way we do.'

This conversation had taken place a couple of years ago and her father had never swayed from his decision.

Now, her thoughts were interrupted by her mother who had opened the door to the wagon. 'Up with the lark again, our Dana? If that tea's ready me an' your da' wouldn't mind a cup.'

Laying the brush to one side Dana held her hands up to retrieve the mugs that her mother was passing down.

'You goin' with your dad to market this mornin'?'

Wiping her forehead on the back of her arm, Dana nodded. 'He reckerns I'm good when it comes to hagglin'.'

Her mother grinned. 'That's true, it's all them fellers what can't resist a pretty face.'

'So it's all right for a bunch of old men to ogle his daughter if it gets him a good price, but not schoolboys?'

Colleen nodded. 'That's different; one's business, the other ain't.' She chuckled softly. 'Besides, if any of them old fellers so much as look at you in the wrong way, your dad would soon put 'em straight.' She held her hands out to receive the two mugs of tea. 'Apple of your dad's eye, that's what you are.' She disappeared into the wagon before reappearing with a saucepan, which she proceeded to carefully carry down the steps. 'I've put the oats and milk in, all you've got to do is heat 'em up.'

Dana smiled to herself as she placed the saucepan on to the ring. Her mother was right when she referred to Dana as the apple of her father's eye. They spent nearly all their time in each other's company, either working together or fishing in the canal. 'Better'n any lad,' her father used to brag to her mother. 'Our Dana has them fish jumpin' on to her hook.' As the milk began to simmer Dana stirred the saucepan with a large wooden spoon. When it came to her father the two of them were like peas in a pod.

September 1940
Swearing loudly, Shane Quinn burst through the door to the wagon. 'They've hit one of the warehouses on Stone Road!'

Dana stared open-mouthed at the fireball in the distance. 'They've hit summat else by the looks of it, summat big ...' She was interrupted by the snorting, whinnying arrival of Crystal, who had escaped his tethered stake.

Shane walked towards the large gelding and, with his hand outstretched, he managed to clasp hold of the piece of frayed rope that was swinging from Crystal's head collar. 'Steady on, old boy, it's just those bloomin' Germans throwin' their weight about. Don't you worry, we'll get you to safety.' He stroked the horse's neck, which was wet with sweat.

Dana joined her father; speaking softly, she soothed Crystal's trembling shoulders. 'Should we go to St Martin's on Silvester Street?' said Dana, her eyes skimming the skies for signs of the enemy.

Shane shook his head. 'What for?'

'We'll be safe there. They wouldn't dare bomb a church,' said Dana, who was slightly surprised that her father had asked the question.

Shane gave a short mirthless laugh. 'They don't care what they hit.' He shook his head. 'We're better off out in the open than trapped like a rat in one of them shelters. Same goes for Crystal, but I ain't goin' to have my family used as target practice, so from now on we'll head off into the country before nightfall. They won't waste their bombs on countryside.'

Dana glanced fearfully at the night sky as she patted Crystal's neck. 'Looks like they've decided to bomb here as well as London. Do you think that means they'll start bombin' durin' daylight?'

'Nah, too much of a risk, they're harder to spot at night which is why they only bomb in the dark. They're bloomin' cowards, droppin' their bombs and runnin'

19

away.' As he finished speaking the all clear sounded. Walking towards the rear of the wagon, Shane reached down and picked up a coil of rope and gestured to Dana. 'Bring him here; I'll tether him to the back – he might feel more at ease if he's close to us. We may as well get up now, see if we can't help them poor buggers what've been hit.'

Obediently, Dana led the horse round the back of the wagon and handed him over to her father. 'Where will we stay tonight?'

Shane shrugged. 'Dunno. We're bound to find somewhere though. I might have a word with the bargees. Some of them keep their horses in fields near the canal; I'm sure they'd let us stop there overnight. They're a bit like us in a way, allus movin' from place to place.'

Dana wrinkled her brow. 'But we've lived here for as long as I can remember.'

'Before you was born me an' your mam used to travel all over. We rarely stayed in one place for more than a few nights at a time.'

'Was that when you were with the rest of the family?' said Dana, her voice slightly hesitant.

Shane grunted an inaudible reply as he walked towards the front of the wagon, adding, 'Get Crystal some water.'

The next few days saw Dana and her father starting work at daybreak, and taking the wagon into the heart of the countryside before nightfall, where they would either set up camp on the side of the road, or, if any farmers in the area needed help with their stock, Shane would offer his services in exchange for a night's stay in one of the fields.

Their plan worked flawlessly until 6 September 1940, when the unthinkable happened. Dana and her father had been tending a horse in Ashfield Street when the air raid siren sounded.

Norman McGregor, the horse's owner, leaned over the stable door as he slid back the bolts. 'I hope some bugger's set it off by accident, but I s'pose we'd better go down the shelter just in case.'

Shane shook his head. 'I ain't wastin' time down no shelter. We all know the Krauts don't do raids durin' the day. You mark my words, it's another false ala—'

The rest of his sentence was lost as they heard a sickening thud in the distance. Norman threw the stable door wide open. 'That ain't no false alarm. Best we get to an underground shelter than take our chances in a stable.'

Nodding, Shane collected his tools and left the stable.

Dana's eyes rounded. 'What about Neanor?'

Shane shook his head. 'She'll have to take her chances.'

They followed Norman over to a shelter; a warden stood in the doorway frantically waving and yelling at them to get a move on. Apologising for their late arrival, Dana sat on a narrow bench between her father and Norman. She glanced round at the worried faces, all of which looked shocked that the Luftwaffe had decided to risk a daylight bombing raid.

Dana slid her fingers through her father's as the unmistakable sound of the Luftwaffe engines passed overhead. Norman smiled reassuringly at her. 'They won't be here long, they're taking a big enough risk as it is.' He glanced at Shane. 'Where'll Colleen go?'

'She'll stay where she is. Much easier to see the planes when you're in the middle of a field, lot easier to get out the way an' all ...' Shane cast a worried eye around the walls of the shelter.

'I bet she'll be worried sick. I'll take Dana back as soon as they sound the all clear whilst you finish Neanor off,' said Norman, adding as an afterthought, 'And the Cleggs' mare of course.'

Shane shook his head. 'I'll finish Neanor but that's me lot.'

Dana frowned. 'You've still got to do—'

Shane cut her off. 'I'll not be doin' any more horses today,' he said firmly.

Dana blushed as she met the gaze of a girl around her own age who was listening with interest. The girl had an ordinary face and straight brown hair which hung limply around her shoulders. Dana watched as the girl's gaze travelled down Dana's dungarees to her stout lace-up boots covered in muck and straw. Dana tried to shuffle her feet beneath the bench, ashamed of her appearance in comparison to the other girl who wore a square-necked frock covered in the daintiest blue forget-me-nots. Dana looked enviously at the beautiful dress and the most exquisite pair of matching blue patent-leather sandals. The girl caught Dana's eye and smiled sweetly. 'I've not seen you before, do you live far from here?'

22

Knowing her father's views on people who weren't horse men, Dana glanced fleetingly at her father before answering. 'We live by Stone Street durin' the day, but we go into the country at night 'cos of the bombin'.'

The girl raised her brow in astonishment. 'The country? Where do you sleep? Surely not in the open?'

Dana shook her head; she couldn't have explained why, but she felt an urge to impress the other girl. Saying that you owned your own home and could take it wherever you wanted was far more impressive than saying you slept under a hedge. 'We own our own wagon, so we can take it wherever we want. I think we're quite lucky really, although we do offer shelter to those poor souls who have to sleep rough.' Dana was pleased with her explanation and thought it made them sound posh, so she was surprised when the other girl's lips twitched into a smirk of amusement.

'I didn't realise you lived in a wagon ...'

Dana looked round the occupants of the shelter, who were staring at her and Shane. Wishing she had never mentioned the wagon, she gave a small nod. 'Kind of, but we've allus lived in the same place, or at least I have—' The sound of the all clear cut Dana off. Grateful that their time in the shelter was at an end, Dana followed her father outside. She opened her mouth to ask if her father had changed his mind about going to do the other horses, but Shane was looking at her with disapproval.

'What did you mean, "kind of"?' We're travellers, nowt wrong wi' that, so don't ever let me hear you bein' ashamed of who we are again, is that clear?'

Embarrassed, Dana hung her head and muttered an apology. 'I didn't mean anythin' by it; I don't even know why I said it.'

''Cos you felt pressured by her fancy clothes and shoes, that's why,' said Shane gruffly, 'but you shouldn't, 'cos fancy clothes don't mean she's any better'n you, understand?'

Dana nodded. Eager to change the subject she began to walk in the direction of Ashfield Street. 'Are you sure we can't do the others today? I don't reckern they'll be back.'

Shane stood still. 'You'd best be gettin' back to your mam, tell her we're safe. I'll finish Neanor off.' He hesitated before apparently making a snap decision. 'Tell your mam to get everythin' ready, tell her we're on the move.'

Dana twisted her long strawberry-blonde curls around one finger. 'Are we goin' into the country early tonight?'

Shane called over his shoulder as he walked away. 'Tell her to be ready for when I get back.'

Turning to make her way back to Stone Street Dana muttered an apology as she almost collided with the girl she had met down the shelter.

The girl, who had been quite civil earlier, folded her arms and narrowed her eyes. 'Looks like you're on the move after all.' Her eyes swept over Dana's attire with disgust. 'Just like your sort, first sign of trouble and you're off.'

Remembering her father's words, she placed her hands on her hips and stared the other girl square in the eye. 'There's nothin' wrong with goin' into the countryside at night, makes more sense than sittin' down some smelly shelter.'

The girl, who was a tad taller, stared down her nose at Dana. 'There's a big difference between stayin' in the countryside to avoid the bombin' and runnin' away, and that's what your father's goin' to do, only you're too thick to see it.' She gave a sniff of contempt. 'They should make you stay here and fight like the rest of us, instead of scuttlin' off behind a rock like some kind of beastly insect.' She viewed Dana through narrowing eyes. 'Although I s'pose I should be sayin' good riddance to bad rubbish. Your kind don't belong here anyway.'

Dana's heart was racing. How dare this dreadful girl make such unfounded assumptions? 'What do you mean, "your kind"?' She continued without giving the other girl a chance to reply: 'I've just as much right to be here as you.'

The girl also thrust her hands against her hips and spoke through gritted teeth. 'My family have lived in Liverpool for generations, which gives me more right to be here than you. We can't up and leave whenever the fancy takes us, 'cos our house hasn't got wheels.'

It suddenly dawned on Dana that the other girl might be jealous. Dana smiled sympathetically. 'If you're scared of the bombin' – and I don't blame you if you are,' she added hastily, 'then why don't you go into the countryside at night? You'd be more than welcome to stay in the wagon with us if you didn't want to sleep rough.'

The girl's mouth hung open. 'Stay with the likes of you? I'd sooner take me chances with the Luftwaffe!'

Dana couldn't believe her ears! Was the other girl really saying she preferred the Germans? Shaking her head, she decided it was better to walk away than waste her time talking to someone who made such ridiculous statements. Dana would have liked to leave without saying another word, but she wanted to set the record straight on her family's behalf before she did, so she addressed the girl from over her shoulder. 'You're wrong about us. We love living in Liverpool, that's why we don't move around. Home is where the heart is, and my heart belongs to Liverpool. We wouldn't dream of leavin' our beloved city.'

The girl snorted angrily. 'You're a bunch of thievin' little liars who care for no one but yourselves. You'll see, this time next week Liverpool will be nothin' but a distant memory.'

Hot, angry tears shone in Dana's large green eyes. She turned back to face her adversary. 'You don't know me, or my family. If you did, you wouldn't say such horrid, hurtful things.'

The girl smiled malevolently, revealing a slight gap between her two front teeth. 'Your lot have a bad reputation; everyone knows you can't be trusted.' She laughed jeeringly at Dana. 'Even you can't trust them and you are one! Golly, how I wish I could be there to see the look on your face when they cart you off for good.'

For the first time in her life, Dana had encountered one of the people her father had spoken of. She realised now why he had warned her so fiercely, but even so she found it hard to understand how this girl could be filled with such hate. Determined not to show the effect she had had on her, Dana banished the tears which were threatening to spill, and stared the girl square in the eye. 'I pity you,' Dana said softly. 'It must be awful to be so eaten up wi' jealousy you want to make everyone else feel as miserable as you.'

Barely able to believe her ears, the other girl shrieked angrily in Dana's face as she thrust her fists down by her sides. '*You* pity *me*? *You're* the one who needs pityin'! The sooner you bugger off the better, so go on, go back to your wagon in the woods!'

Dana folded her arms. 'I'm goin' nowhere. If you want to get away from me it's you who'll have to leave ...' Leaning forward she smiled calmly at the other girl. '... and I don't live in the woods.'

The girl's mouth moved up and down wordlessly as she tried to find a damning response; she reminded Dana of the goldfish she had won at a fair when she was a child. The image caused Dana to start giggling.

'Cow!' was all the girl could manage before turning on her heel and stalking off in the opposite direction.

Dana felt a sense of satisfaction as she set off at a brisk trot. She had no idea how long the two of them had stood there but it had seemed like an eternity. She was not surprised to see her mother pacing back and forth at the top of Bevington Hill. As Dana approached, her mother wrapped her arms around her.

'Where've you been? I've been worried sick!' Looking past Dana she continued, 'Where's your father?'

Feeling guilty that she had stood arguing with the girl, Dana apologised, adding, 'He won't be long. He's goin' to finish doin' Neanor and then he'll be back.' She remembered her father's words. 'He says you're to

27

pack up ready, 'cos we're on the move, whatever that might mean.'

Pulling a face, her mother shrugged. 'Your guess is as good as mine.'

Dana eyed her mother cautiously. 'Some stupid girl thought Dad wanted to leave Liverpool.'

Her mother arched an eyebrow. 'What stupid girl?'

Dana told her mother all about the encounter, finishing with, 'She's never even met us. How can she say such awful things?'

Colleen sighed breathily. 'She's right about travellers havin' a bad reputation. Even though we're nothin' like some of them, we still get tarred with the same brush.'

'How bad can they be?' said Dana simply.

Colleen gave a half shoulder shrug. 'There's a family called the O'Reillys. They had a real nasty reputation, were renowned for nickin' anythin' and everythin', then beggarin' off in the middle of the night, leavin' the camp like a pigsty.' She grimaced. 'They'd tip their waste out on to the road or into people's gardens if they took against 'em.'

Dana, who didn't know any other travellers, was horrified. 'Crikey, no wonder she was quick to jump to conclusions.'

Colleen shook a reproving finger. 'You mustn't accept people's hate. Just because some travellers are wrong 'uns, that girl had no right to speak to you the way she did wi'out gettin' to know you first. That's the trouble with people like her: quick to curse you out, but deaf when it comes to hearin' your side.'

Dana nodded thoughtfully. 'Are there a lot of people like her?'

Her mother shrugged. 'It's hard to say. We've been here a long time, and your father's allus had a good reputation with the carters – they wouldn't hear a bad word said against us – but we never really wander outside of that world.' She squeezed Dana's arm reassuringly. 'Don't take no notice of the poisonous little beast. I bet she don't own her own home like we do, nor have a beautiful horse like Crystal.' Hearing his name, Crystal whinnied.

Dana smiled. 'You're right, I even said I thought she were jealous.' She giggled. 'She didn't like that one bit!'

Colleen smiled. 'The truth hurts. Perhaps you hit the nail on the head.'

Breaking away from her mother, Dana headed towards Crystal, determined to put the silly girl and her nonsense from her mind.

It was a good deal later when Shane returned. He tossed his cap on to the bed as he entered the wagon. In his left hand he held a bundle of papers. He handed one to Colleen and one to Dana. 'We're booked on the next ferry to Ireland.'

Dana stared at the papers in her hands. 'Why are we goin' to Ireland?'

Shane was careful to avoid his daughter's eye. 'Call it a bit of a holiday. It's been a long time since I've been home, and now seems as good a time as any.'

'But we never go on holiday,' said Dana, her voice full of suspicion.

Shane shrugged. 'They may not be runnin' ferries much longer if this keeps up, so I thought it best to get over there sharpish.'

'You said "home".' Dana kept looking from the papers in her hands to her father, who seemed intent on not making eye contact. 'But Liverpool is our home.'

'No it's not!' Shane snapped irritably. 'Ireland's our true home—'

'Well, it's not mine!' Dana said as she held the papers out towards her father. She had a sinking feeling that the girl from the shelter might have been right. 'You can take these and burn 'em 'cos I ain't goin' any-where.' She tutted underneath her breath. 'Home! I've never so much as seen a picture of Ireland.'

Shane pushed the papers back into his daughter's hands. 'Then it's high time you went. Thinkin' about it, you're right, you should've gone years ago, that way we wouldn't be in this mess.'

Dana glanced in the direction of the wagon door. 'I know you better than this, you're not the sort who runs from danger, so what's the real reason for wantin' to go to Ireland? And don't tell me you wanna go on holiday because I shan't believe you.'

For the first time since he had entered the wagon Shane stared his daughter directly in the eye; a deep line furrowed his brow. 'Why on earth do you think I want to go? You've got eyes in your head, you can see what's happenin'.' He opened the door and pointed at one of the bombed buildings. 'That's why we're leaving.'

Dana stared at the white flames which burned fiercely from the chemical company on Norfolk Street,

30

the words of the nasty girl ringing in her ears. 'Running away ...' Dana turned accusingly to her father. 'You want us to run away?'

Shane rubbed his forehead between his fingers and thumb. 'Not run away as such: I just want to keep you and your mam safe.' Closing the wagon door, he sat Dana on the small bench next to her mother. 'We're lucky, Dana, we can live anywhere we want, and seein' as me and your mam are both Irish, well, we may as well go there ...' He looked at his daughter imploringly. 'They're not at war with Ireland, Dana, we'd be safe there. It's not runnin' away, it's bein' sensible.'

Dana shook her head. 'What about the carters? All the folk who've given you work all these years? You know they can't afford proper vets, what are they meant to do wi'out you?' She stared deep into her father's eyes. 'They trusted you!' adding quietly, 'So did I.'

Shane's lips parted slightly as he stared back at his daughter. 'I can't help them, Dana, they have to stay here, but we don't. I bet they'd leave if they could.'

Dana leapt to her feet. All her life she had believed her father to be a brave, strong man, yet here he was, suggesting they run off, just like that awful girl said they would. 'What would happen if we all decided to run away? Where would we be then?'

Shane pulled an awkward face. 'This is a war between armies, luv, but they're attackin' ordinary folk. It would be better all round if we could all go and leave the forces to do their jobs.'

A small part of Dana knew her father was right. This should be war between armies, but it wasn't and no

31

matter what he said, she felt that she would be abandoning her country if she went with her parents. Folding the papers she placed them on to the bench. Taking a small hessian sack she packed her belongings, such as they were. 'What are you doing?' said Shane, his voice hoarse.

Dana shrugged. 'Packing. You and Mam can go, but I'm stayin' right here, where I belong.' She tied the top of the sack into a knot. Leaning down, she kissed her mother lightly on the forehead before making her way towards the door to the wagon.

Blocking her path with his arm, Shane shook his head. 'Don't be so bloody stupid ...' He pointed a shaking finger at her mother, who was crying softly. 'Look at what you're doin' to your mam. You're breakin' her heart.'

Dana glanced guiltily back at her mother. 'Sorry, Mam, but it don't feel right to go to Ireland.'

Colleen turned tear-brimmed eyes towards her husband. 'Shane, please!'

Shane folded his arms defiantly. 'And just where are you plannin' on goin'?'

Dana shrugged. 'I'll join one of the services or work in a factory.' She looked her father squarely in the eye; a silent tear trickled down her cheek. 'There's plenty of work about. I could even work for the carters.'

Shane shook his head. 'What with? I've got all the tools, the medicine – you've got nothing!'

She nodded. 'Looks like it'll be the services or one of the factories then.'

Colleen also leapt to her feet. 'For goodness' sake, stop it, the pair of you. You're behavin' like children ...'

She glared at Shane. 'At least one of you's got an excuse.'

Shane's eyes rounded at his wife's words. Standing to one side, he thrust the door of the wagon open. 'Fine! Off you go and best of luck to you, but remember, Dana, those who you want to defend and fight for wouldn't lift a finger to help you should the boot be on the other foot ...'

Dana heard her mother give a cry of despair as she stepped past her father and began to make her way across the wasteland. Behind her she heard her father shout out to her mother: 'Leave her, Coll, she'll soon be back, tail between her legs ...'

Colleen appeared by Dana's side; she spoke earnestly as she tried to keep up with Dana, who was striding out, her heart thumping in her chest. 'Please, luv, don't leave, not like this. Come to Ireland for a bit – you can allus come back. You must see that your father's only tryin' to look out for you.'

Without breaking pace, Dana nodded. 'Of course I do, but it doesn't change how I feel.' She stopped walking. 'I love you both dearly, but I can't leave Liverpool, it wouldn't feel right.'

Clasping Dana's hand in her own, Colleen pushed some money into Dana's palm. 'Take this. If you change your mind you can take a ferry to Ireland; we're bound to be stayin' in Drogheda, your dad knows a few of the locals and they'll not see him short of work. If you need anythin', send us a letter, but address it to Clarke's Bar in Fair Street, the landlord's an old friend of me dad's.'

Dana looked over her mother's shoulder as she hugged her goodbye. Shane was staring at them from the steps. Dana gave a small wave, but instead of returning the gesture, he backed into the wagon and closed the door behind him. Dana fought back the tears which threatened to course down her cheeks. She loved her father dearly and she couldn't bear to think she had upset him, but she had to be true to herself. Leaning back, she kissed her mother on the cheek; her voice trembling, she whispered, 'Say goodbye to Dad for me—' She stopped speaking before her emotions got the better of her.

'Goodbye, luv. If you change your mind there's a good hour or so before the ferry leaves. I'll keep an eye out for you, and if not you can allus write to us. Don't forget, it's Clarke's Bar, Fair Street, Drogheda.'

Holding up a hand to acknowledge her mother's words Dana walked away before she could change her mind.

Chapter Two

As Dana approached the last boarding house on Staple Row, she paused before knocking. So far she had been met with icy glares, slammed doors or, more often than not, both. Being a lone female traveller, Dana had expected to be welcomed with open arms, but a lot of the landladies had given her the same look as the awful girl from down the air raid shelter. Dana had studied her attire; she was still wearing her work dungarees and boots. In hindsight it would have been better if she had got changed into a skirt and blouse. She knew her hair looked neat in its bun, and her shirt and dungarees were free from holes. She brought her forearm up to her nose and gave it a tentative sniff. She shrugged; as far as she could tell she didn't smell of horses, or worse. There was no way any of these women could tell she was a traveller just by looking at her, so it had to be something else. She heaved a sigh and rapped a brief tattoo on the splintered paintwork of the large black door. Hearing the sound of approaching footsteps from the other side of the door, Dana stood up straight, adjusted the dungarees and smiled brightly. As the door opened, a girl, who Dana guessed was around the same age as herself, peered around the corner.

Dana spoke quickly. 'Hello. I'm in need of a bed for the night – have you anything available? I've got money.' She shook the coins Colleen had given her.

Nodding, the girl rubbed her nose with her forefinger. She had shoulder-length brown hair. 'We've one room left, but it's in the attic so it's a bit on the poky side. You can have a look if you like ...'

Dana smiled thankfully. 'I'm sure it'll be just fine.' She held out a hand. 'I'm Dana Quinn.'

The girl shook Dana's hand. 'Hello, Dana, I'm Patty Blackwood. Me mam's left me in charge whilst she nips out to me nan's.'

Dana hesitated. 'Will that be a problem? When she comes back, I mean. She might not want me stayin' here.'

'Can't see why not. If anythin' she'll be pleased we've a full house – that's if you decide to stay of course.' She mounted the bottom step of a large wooden staircase. 'Follow me.'

They ascended several flights before finally reaching the top floor of the house. Patty climbed a short steep set of steps which led to a small wooden door. 'Mind your head,' she called to Dana as she disappeared into the room.

Dana ducked as she stepped inside. Glancing round, she was pleasantly surprised. Patty might have thought the room small, but the bed that stood in the corner beneath the eaves was twice the size of her old one; she even had her own chest of drawers, not that she had much to put in them. On top of the drawers stood a basin and ewer.

Patty pointed under the bed. 'The gazunder's where you'd expect to find it, and I'll bring you some water up in a mo … if you want the room, that is?'

Dana nodded quickly. 'It'll do me grand …' A thought struck her. 'How much is it for the night?'

Patty screwed her lips up in thought. 'We don't tend to rent this one out much 'cos most of our customers are men and they reckern the bed's too small. How does half a crown sound?'

Dana beamed. 'Perfect.'

Patty left to fetch the water. 'Back in a mo!'

Dana placed the hessian sack down on the bed and then walked over to the small round window at the back of the room. She smiled at the view of the city below her. Peering into the distance, she tried to see if she could make out the strip of wasteland by Stone Street, but she was either too far away or in the wrong position. Hearing Patty enter the room behind her she turned back.

Patty smiled awkwardly as she placed the jug of water on to the chest of drawers. 'Me mam allus insists on payment in advance …'

Gabbling an apology, Dana fished the money out from her dungarees' pocket and handed it to Patty. 'I'm afraid I haven't got anything smaller.'

Patty shrugged. 'Not to worry, I'll get you your change …' She turned to walk down the steps, hesitated, and then turned back. 'Would you like anything to eat? I could do you a quick jam sarnie if you like?'

Dana nodded. 'That would be lovely. Just take it out of the money I gave you.'

When Patty returned, Dana had already drawn the blackout blinds on the window and lit the small candle that stood beside the ewer. She took the sandwich in one hand as she stowed her change into her pocket with the other. 'Is your mam back yet?'

Patty shook her head. 'Me nan lives right across the other side of the city. Mam goes round to visit a couple of times a week. She don't go durin' the day 'cos that's when she does the rooms, sees to the washin', all that type of thing, so I stay here whilst she goes just in case we have anyone wantin' a room, like yourself.' Patty eyed Dana's dungarees. 'How come you wear trousers?'

Dana looked down at herself. For one brief moment she considered lying, in case Patty took against her, but there was something different about Patty's demeanour which separated her from the spiteful girl in the forget-me-not dress. 'I work with me dad, lookin' after the carters' horses. You can't really do that in a skirt.'

Patty nodded dreamily. 'You lucky thing. I love horses. Do you ever get to ride?'

Dana swallowed the mouthful of jam sandwich she had just bitten into. 'Not as often as I like, we're normally too busy, but in the summertime when the evenings are long I sometimes go for a ride down the towpath, or down the beach.' With the sandwich poised to her lips, she nodded at Patty. 'What do you do, apart from help your mam, that is?'

Patty leaned against the chest of drawers. 'Nothing. The boardin' house takes up most of me time ...' She paused. 'You say you work with your dad. Don't you live with him?'

Dana shook her head. 'He's goin' back to Ireland, but I didn't want to go so I'm stayin' here. I'll either join one of the services or get work in a factory.'

'Didn't you want to go with him? I hear it's a lot safer over there than it is here.'

'It is, but this is my home.' She handed the empty plate back to Patty. 'Do you reckern you'll ever leave – the boarding house, I mean?'

'God, I hope so,' said Patty, with such conviction Dana burst out laughing.

A woman's voice called out from the bottom landing. 'Patty? Are you up there?'

Patty rolled her eyes. 'Comin', Mam.' She smiled warmly at Dana. 'See you in the mornin'. We serve breakfast 'tween six and nine in the dinin' room, bottom of the stairs, first on the left.'

Closing the door behind Patty, Dana stripped down to her vest and knickers and had a brief wash with the warm water before changing into her pyjamas and the thick seaman's socks her father had given her to keep her toes warm in bed. Blowing out the candle she snuggled beneath the blankets. As she settled down to sleep she wondered whether her parents were waiting for the ferry, or whether they were already aboard. Lying in the dark a thought occurred to her. This was the first night she had ever spent away from the wagon, let alone her parents, and she was surprised to find that the thought of being on her own didn't frighten her one bit, in fact she was rather enjoying herself. If things went awry, she knew she could join her parents in

Ireland; even though her father was angry with her now, he would soon forgive her. He never stayed cross with her for long. Dana cast her mind back to the day her mother had found her riding a Friesian stallion using a head collar and lead rein as bridle.

'Get down this minute!' she had demanded. 'How d'you expect to control a beast that size wi'out a proper bit?'

'I'll be all right, Mam, he's a softy, wouldn't harm a fly ...' came Dana's casual reply.

'I don't care. Get down or you can forget goin' to work with your dad in future,' snapped Colleen, who was beside herself with fear.

Shane, who had been seeing to another horse, came around the corner to see what the fuss was about. Seeing his daughter on the large stallion he grinned proudly up at her. 'Well! Don't you look grand? He's like putty in your hands.'

Colleen had slapped her arms down her sides. 'She shouldn't be on him, Shane! What'll happen if he bolts?'

Shane's grin broadened. 'Why would he bolt with our Dana on him? That's why she's such a good rider, she keeps the horses calm.' Standing to one side he nodded encouragingly at his daughter. 'Let's see you take him round at a trot, I bet he's a stunner.'

Lying in her attic bed Dana smiled as she remembered her mother shaking her head in despair, muttering as she walked away that Dana would end up in hospital or worse. Dana would miss her parents and knew they only had her best interests at heart, but this was her opportunity to make a life of her own.

Dana yawned. She would get a good night's sleep; then, in the morning, she would ask where she could sign on. Satisfied that things were going to go well, Dana drifted off to sleep.

Standing on the deck of the ferry which would take them across the Irish Sea, Colleen looked anxiously towards the floating bridge, but there was still no sign of Dana.

'Come and sit down next to me, Coll,' said Shane. 'Dana'll be here before long, you mark my words. She's probably makin' us sweat so's to prove her point, but she'll be here.'

Tears trickling down her cheeks, Colleen turned to face her husband. 'But what if she's not? She seemed pretty determined, and she's like you when it comes to being stubborn.'

Shane smiled reassuringly. 'She's nowhere else to go and she ain't got no money, and she's got more sense than to sleep rough in a city, that's why I never chased after her, I knew she'd *have* to come back ...'

Colleen spoke quietly, her face masked with guilt. 'She has got money. I gave her enough to tide her over ...'

Shane's mouth hung open in disbelief. 'You *what*?' He jumped up. 'How could you be so stupid, you ...' Luckily for those within earshot Shane's words were drowned out by the sound of the ferry's horn.

Tears coursed down Colleen's cheeks. 'She was determined, Shane. I reckern she'd sleep rough if she had to, and I couldn't take the risk – I thought if I gave her enough to get by for tonight and perhaps a ferry crossin' to Ireland in the mornin' ...' Colleen's shoulders shook as the enormity of her actions caught up with her.

Shaking his head, Shane took his wife in a tight embrace, kissing her cheek as he tried to soothe her woes. 'Sorry, Coll, I shouldn't've shouted – you only did what you thought right. Not to worry, we'll just ...' He had been about to say that they would disembark and make their way back to Stone Street when, to his horror, he realised they had already left the terminal.

'Stop the ferry!' yelled Shane at the top of his lungs.

A passenger standing further along the deck turned to face him, a look of alarm on his face. 'Has someone fallen overboard?'

Shane shook his head. 'It's my daughter, she's not here yet ...'

The man pulled a face. 'They won't stop the ferry for that. Is she young?'

'Sixteen, but she's never been on her own before ...'

The man shrugged. 'If she's got money she can allus catch the next 'un.'

'What if she doesn't?' said Shane, staring anxiously at the terminal, which was getting further away.

'Not a lot you can do, then. The only thing they'll stop the ferry for is if someone goes overboard ... What the—' Leaping towards Shane the man grabbed him around the waist just in time to stop Shane launching himself off the ferry. 'What the bloody hell are you playin' at? You can't just jump ship.'

Shane struggled in the man's grasp, and Colleen, who knew her husband couldn't swim, screamed for Shane to stop. Hearing Colleen's screams, two more men came to aid the first and within a few seconds they had wrestled Shane to the ground. The first man had his knee in the middle of Shane's back. 'I ain't lettin' you up unless you promise to behave.'

Shane, who was exhausted from the struggle, nodded. 'I can't swim anyway ...'

The first man turned to Colleen. 'Has he been drinkin'?'

Colleen shook her head. 'No, and I'm sorry, I promise he'll not do anythin' that silly again.'

The men backed off, but kept an eye in case Shane made another desperate attempt. Shane buried his head in his hands. 'I know it were a stupid thing to do, but it were the only thing I could think of.'

'You silly bugger, even if they did stop the ferry, you'd've drowned before they could get you out.' She shook her head. 'Dana's got money, but she's also got the address of Clarke's Bar in Drogheda. I told her to write if she changed her mind, or needed us for owt. I was pretty sure that's where we're headed?'

Shane rested his head against his wife's shoulder. 'Aye, you're right. I spoke to Donny earlier today, to see if I could secure some work; he said he'd sort summat out.' He drew a deep breath. 'Donny'll soon let us know if he hears owt.' He brightened. 'Who knows? It may do her good to get out on her own for a bit, mebbe then she'll appreciate how much we've done for her.'

Colleen smiled, relieved that her husband was finally seeing sense. 'Possibly.'

He wrapped his fingers around Colleen's hand. 'It's far better she comes to us because she wants to and not because she has to.'

Colleen kissed him softly on his rough cheek. 'You're a good man, Shane Quinn, and an even better father, but there again I allus knew you would be.'

Dana listened to the sound of the other residents as they got up and went about their business while she lay in her cosy bed in the attic. Sitting up, she wondered how many other people were staying in Eccleston House, and supposed it must be a lot as she had been listening to the sound of closing doors and footsteps descending the stairs for the past half-hour.

The church clock struck the seventh hour, so Dana swung her legs out of bed and padded over to the washstand. The water in the jug might have been cold, but it was nothing compared to the water in the wagon first thing of a morning. In the winter months, Dana would often have to break the thin surface of ice off the jug before attempting to pour it into the small metal basin. This made her think of her parents.

A pang of guilt lurched unpleasantly in her stomach as she wondered whether she had done the right thing by leaving. As she lifted the cool flannel to her face, she tried to imagine what would have happened had she convinced them to stay closer to Liverpool. Could she have persuaded the carters to go to them for treatment instead of the other way round? Shaking her head, Dana rinsed the flannel out and patted her face dry with the hand towel.

How could someone take a lame or colicky horse into the countryside for treatment? Besides, once her father had set his mind to something there was no changing it; she should know, because she was exactly the same. She sighed. There was no doubt in her mind that if she had stayed to talk them round, there would have been a frightful row and she and her father, both as hot-headed as the other, would have said things they would later regret. No. She had made the right decision by leaving before things got out of hand.

Dana plaited her hair and changed into her Sunday best: a long green skirt, which hid her boots, and a cream blouse. She nodded with satisfaction as she glanced at her reflection in the mirror hanging on the back of the bedroom door.

Making her way downstairs, Dana decided she would ask Patty if she could stay for a few more nights whilst she sorted things out. She descended the final staircase and walked along the hallway towards the dining room. Once inside, she looked round for an empty seat. She was about to walk away when one of the diners got up and left the room. Dana hurried over but the man sitting next to the empty chair glared at her, picking his workbag off the floor and dumping it on the seat. Her cheeks turning crimson, Dana looked at the diners, all of whom were taking great care not to catch her eye.

'Good morning!' called Patty from the doorway to the dining room. 'Have you come for your breakfast?'

Dana turned to face the other girl. 'It's all right, I'll get summat later.'

Patty looked past Dana at the seat where the man had placed his bag. Smiling, she beckoned Dana to follow her out of the room. 'As it's full in here, you can sit with me and me mam in the kitchen ...'

One of the men in the dining room let out a snort of contempt.

Ushering Dana past, Patty went back into the dining room; hands on hips she stared expectantly round the diners. 'Sorry, did someone say summat?'

Dana, who could see a couple of diners over Patty's left shoulder, waited to see if the man who had been rude would speak out, and was surprised when a younger man who was sitting at a full table spoke up.

'You do know what she is, don't you?' he said, flicking his eyes in Dana's direction.

'She's a woman,' said Patty bluntly.

Looking at Dana again, the man narrowed his eyes. 'She's one of them what lives in a wagon down by the locks.'

Patty folded her arms across her chest. 'And what if she is? What has that got to do with you, Neil Fletcher?'

There came a general murmuring from the assembled diners. Another man, whom Dana couldn't see, began to speak. 'Her kind'll nick all us stuff when we's at work, that's what it's got to do wi' us. I bet your mam don't know she's got someone like her livin' under her roof, does she?'

Dana froze. Patty had been kind enough to take her in; the last thing she wanted was to cause any trouble. She was about to speak out, to say she would leave, but Patty spoke first. 'No, Mam doesn't know, and neither do you, not for certain. But I'd've thought more of you, Neil Fletcher – we've got Nazis tryin' to flatten us, and all you're bothered about is who you're havin' breakfast with.'

Dana gave a small, polite cough. She smiled briefly as Patty turned to face her. 'Perhaps it'd be better if I left.'

Patty's forehead shot towards her hairline. 'Why? You ain't done nowt wrong. If they don't like it here they don't have to stay.' Turning back to the diners, she spoke through pursed lips: 'From what I recall, Neil Fletcher, you come here 'cos we were the only place what'd take you in ...' She glared at an older man who had chuckled loudly. 'You too, Bernard Griffiths!' She cast a critical eye at the rest of the diners as Bernard stopped laughing. 'In fact, most of you is only here 'cos you've worn out your welcome elsewhere, so I'd think on if I were you!' Patty continued to stare accusingly around the dining room, but it seemed no one wanted to talk. She half smiled to herself before beckoning Dana to follow her up the hallway to the back of the house. 'In there,' Patty said as she pointed to a half-open doorway.

As Dana walked into the small kitchen, a kind-looking woman with shoulder-length salt-and-pepper curly hair smiled up at her. 'Ah-ha! You must be the mysterious Dana Quinn.' She indicated to Dana to take the seat next to hers.

Nodding, Dana sat down and looked around the kitchen, which seemed to be made up of a mishmash of different furniture, as well as a large Belfast sink which sat next to an ancient-looking range. If you took all the cupboards, sideboards and cabinets out, the kitchen would be a decent-sized room.

'Cuppa tea?' said Patty.

Dana nodded. 'That'd be grand, thanks.'

Placing a mug of tea in front of Dana, Patty pushed a jug of milk towards her. 'Help yourself.' She glanced at her mother. 'I told Dana to come in here with us 'cos some of the fellers were soundin' off, sayin' that Dana lived in a wagon ...'

Dana licked her lips nervously. 'I do, or rather I did,' she said, looking up at her hosts from under her thick lashes. 'That's why I said I'd go if it'd make things easier. You've done enough for me already.'

Patty's mother sat forward eagerly. 'Can you read palms?'

Blushing, Dana shook her head. 'Sorry, but no.'

Her mother sat back, disappointed. 'Oh well, never mind.' She cocked a hopeful eyebrow. 'Tea leaves?'

Dana peered into her mug. 'I don't think so, or at least I can't see any.'

Patty rolled her eyes. 'Mam!' Shaking her head, she explained to Dana that reading someone's tea leaves was another form of fortune telling.

Dana giggled. 'You don't really believe that, do you, Mrs Blackwood?'

Mrs Blackwood grinned. 'Some say it's mumbo jumbo, others just a bit of fun; I say you never know your luck!' Her grin faded a little. 'So how come you ain't with your family?'

'Mam!' Patty began to protest, only to be waved into silence by her mother.

'My parents wanted to go back to Ireland, but I wanted to stay: it's as simple as that.'

Folding her arms, Mrs Blackwood leaned against the table. 'Why'd you decide to stay? Many would've left, given the bombin's, so why not you?'

Dana glanced defensively at the older woman. 'Because this is my home, the place where I grew up; it'd feel like I was desertin' if I left.'

Mrs Blackwood tilted her head to one side. 'Your mam and dad didn't feel that way?'

Dana, who had just taken a mouthful of tea, swallowed quickly. 'They're not bad people – Dad just wanted to keep us safe; that's why he moved us into the countryside every night, but when they did that daylight raid yesterday, Dad said we'd be better off in Ireland … It's not that he doesn't care, he does, he has many friends here, but …'

Mrs Blackwood waved her into silence. 'Your father's right: blood's thicker than water, and he should put his family first.' She eyed Dana curiously. 'I should imagine he wasn't too pleased when you up and left?'

Dana grimaced. 'He didn't take it seriously. I heard him tell me mam I'd soon be back wi' me tail between me legs.'

Mrs Blackwood drummed a tattoo on the table surface with the tips of her fingers. 'Will you?'

Trying to hide her smile, Dana shook her head. 'You'll see the devil in long johns first!'

A shriek of laughter escaped Patty's lips. 'That's a no then?'

Dana nodded. 'The apple didn't fall far from the tree when it comes to me an' me dad; we're both pig-headed, and he taught me from a young age that you have to stand on your own two feet, never ask for help from nobody.'

Mrs Blackwood's nostrils flared. 'The toast, Patty!'

Jumping up from her seat, Patty crossed over to the grill and fished out two pieces of toast, dropping them on to a plate. She picked up a knife and started to scrape the burnt bits off over the sink. 'Dana's thinkin' of joinin' up, Mam.'

Mrs Blackwood raised an admiring brow. 'Doesn't surprise me; any particular service?'

Dana shrugged. 'I don't know whether they'll want me.' She cast a meaningful glance in the direction of the dining room. 'Not everyone's keen on folk like me.'

The older woman coughed on a chuckle. 'Dana, they'll bend over backwards to have a woman like you on board.' She also glanced in the direction of the dining room. 'Don't take no notice of that lot in there, they're nowt but fishwives in trousers!' She jerked her head in the direction of Patty, who was standing behind her. 'This one wants to join up too, only I've not been happy about her goin' in on her own. She don't mind bossin' them big hairy customers of mine about, but she's a lot quieter when it comes to some of them gobby little beggars she used to go to school with.'

'I never went to school,' said Dana. 'Me dad reckoned he could teach me all I needed to know.'

'Can you read and write?' said Mrs Blackwood.

Dana nodded. 'Dad taught me. He reckoned I'd get bullied for bein' different if I went to school.' She turned to Patty. 'Did you; have any bullies in your school?'

Patty grimaced. 'Only one. Her name was Alexa, but everyone called her Lexi. Everythin' was grand until she came to our school; it all changed after that. Her father had a sweet shop in Love Lane, which was just around the corner from my old school, and Lexi used to hand out free sweets to all her pals. As you can imagine, everyone wanted to be her friend, but I'm not like that, I don't think you should be friends with someone because of what they can give you, so I didn't smarm up to her like the others, which didn't go down well with Lexi. I think she thought I were snubbin' her, so she did the same to me by not invitin' me round for tea, or to her birthday parties.' Patty placed another slice of bread under the grill. 'I reckern she used to say nasty stuff about me behind me back because the other kids started to snub me too. Pretty soon I didn't have any friends left.'

'That's awful,' said Dana.

'Lexi might've had lots of friends, but they weren't real ones; even her so-called boyfriend Clive was only with her because of what she could give him.'

'Why do you say "so-called"?' asked Dana.

Patty arched an eyebrow. 'Clive Thomas was the most handsome boy in our school; all the girls fancied him summat rotten. I'll admit I had a small crush on him, but I don't think there was a girl in our school who didn't. I was surprised when he asked her out, but who am I to judge, different strokes an' all that.' She shook her head. 'You could've knocked me down with a feather when I seen him with another girl in the cinema.'

'No!' said Dana, a slice of toast poised before her lips.

Feeling further explanation was needed Patty continued, 'I used to have a Saturday job in the cinema – it didn't pay much but I were allowed to watch the show for free once I'd finished cleanin'. One Saturday Clive come in with a bunch of his mates. I knew they'd start messin' round if they seen me so I kept out of the way until the lights dimmed. They were bein' typical boys, throwin' sweets at each other and makin' silly noises. Clive was boastin' that he'd not had to pay for his sweets, when one of his pals said he'd rather suck a boiled onion than kiss Lexi. I thought Clive would punch him on the nose, but he just laughed.'

'Rotten bugger!' said Dana, unable to help herself.

'That's not all! Just before the film started a couple of girls came in and sat in the row in front of Clive and his pals. I didn't think much of it until Clive got up from his chair and jumped on to a spare one next to one of the girls.' Patty's eyes rounded as she envisaged the scene. 'That's when he kissed her!' she said, clearly still shocked by his actions, '*and* he give her some of his sweets.'

'Filthy rotten cheat!' said Dana. 'Did you tell Lexi?'

Patty nodded hastily. 'Monday mornin' came and when we was queuin' for the bus I told her what I seen and that's when things really turned nasty.'

'Did she give him a good wallop?' said Dana hopefully.

'Did she heck as like,' snorted Patty, 'she said I were makin' it up, said I were a vicious little sneak who wanted to be just like her, and was tryin' to steal Clive by tellin' nasty lies about him.'

Dana's jaw dropped. 'What did you say?'

Patty shrugged. 'Nothin', 'cos that's when Clive and his pals come over. Lexi told him what I'd said but he denied it, sayin' I were the one who was lyin'. Lexi told everyone to steer clear of me, an' that I were a nasty little liar, and Clive agreed.' She shook her head. 'I really was on me own after that, especially after she told everyone me mam were runnin' a brothel.'

Dana could hardly believe her ears. 'What on earth made her say summat so nasty?'

'Spite,' said Mrs Blackwood. 'I reckern she knew Patty were tellin' the truth about Clive, and that made her angry; she were determined to make sure Patty kept her gob shut so she made up a vicious lie so that the parents wouldn't allow their kids to have owt to do with her.'

'Didn't you say summat to her parents?'

Mrs Blackwood nodded. 'They didn't want to know, they said it was girls bein' girls and it'd all come out in the wash.'

'I reckern they were scared to tell her off in case she threw a tantrum ...' said Patty.

'A tantrum?' echoed Dana, her eyes widening. 'Just how old is she?'

'Sixteen, same as me, but she were thirteen at the time,' said Patty. 'She's been spoiled rotten all her life. If you ask me they should've put their foot down years back.'

Dana rolled her eyes. 'My dad'd wipe the floor wi' me if I behaved like that.'

'They ain't doin' her any favours,' agreed Mrs Blackwood. 'She'll have to learn to stand on her own feet one of these days and not everyone's goin' to give her her own way. She'll have to be told "no" sooner or later.'

Dana eyed Patty thoughtfully. 'Talkin' of standin' on your own feet, why don't me an' you sign up together?'

'Yes!' gasped Patty, before looking hesitantly at her mother. 'As long as you could cope wi'out me, of course?'

Mrs Blackwood held up her hands. 'I've allus thought you should get out there and see summat of the world.' She eyed Dana shrewdly. 'You may not believe in fate and tea leaves and the like, but I do, and I reckern that's why you ended up at Eccleston House last night.'

'So that's why everyone else on Staple Row turned me away, because I was fated to come to Eccleston House.' Dana chuckled.

'Their loss!' Patty grinned, her brown eyes sparkling. 'This is goin' to be great!'

Colleen ran down the lane waving an envelope at Shane, who was wrapping a poultice around the hoof of an enormous draught horse. 'We've gorra letter, it's off our Dana, I reckernise her writin'.' Skidding to a stop she grinned at her husband as she presented him with the envelope.

Shane wiped his hands on his apron. 'Open it, woman.'

Still beaming with excitement, Colleen took the sharp little knife from her husband's toolbox, slit the envelope open and handed the letter to Shane who read it out loud.

Dear Mam and Dad,

I hope this letter finds you safe and well. An awful lot has happened to me since I saw you last, all good I might add, so try not to worry! I've been staying in Eccleston Boarding House on Staple Row, and I've become firm friends with the landlady's daughter, Patty. We both wanted to sign up so we've been to Brougham Terrace and done just that. The man said we would hear from them in a week or so and guess what? We've both been accepted into the WAAF and we're being sent to somewhere called Bridgnorth, to do our initial training. We fibbed a little bit about our age, but so do a lot of other girls so it's not a big deal, besides, I'm nearly seventeen and so is Patty.

I don't know what we'll be doing when we're trained, but we've both said we'd like to learn to drive, because you get to go all over the country, and do all sorts of interesting jobs. We're hoping to stay together but who knows! When I get posted I'll let you know where I am and you can write to me there. In the meantime you can write to me here at Eccleston House. Elaine – that's Patty's mam – said she'll pass on any letters I get.

Has Clarke's Bar got a telephone? If so you could ring me, then we could speak properly. They've said I'll get three days' leave after initial training, but that won't be long enough to get to Ireland and back, but I promise I'll come and see you as soon as I can.

Hope you're both well. Give my love to Crystal.
All my love,
Dana xxx

Shane nodded approvingly. 'She's a Quinn all right, she allus were a determined little blighter! Good job an' all, takin' off the way she did!' Relieved to hear that his daughter was safe and well he was no longer angry at her show of defiance.

Colleen frowned a little. 'Why is she goin' to this Bridgnorth place? I thought she said she wanted to stay in Liverpool?'

Placing an arm around his wife's shoulders, Shane kissed the top of her head. 'She said she wanted to stay to help with the war effort and that's what she's doin'.'

'You don't think she said it just to get away from us?'

Shane laughed. 'Course not, you daft mare. If Dana wanted to leave she wouldn't need excuses – she'd tell you straight.'

Colleen looked relieved. 'Good. I couldn't bear to think she'd left because she was unhappy.'

Shane scratched the top of his head. 'She weren't the one that left, we were, and whilst I wasn't happy with the situation at the time, I've had time to think since then, and seein' as how she were goin' to fly the nest sooner or later, it may even be for the best.' Shane began to untether the horse. 'I reckern it's far better she joined one of the services, 'cos they'll look after her, and she'll meet folk from all walks of life.'

A cheery-looking man with a balding head was making his way towards them. 'All done?'

Shane nodded. 'Make sure you keep the dressin' clean and dry.'

'You're a top feller, Shane. We've missed having the Quinns do the horses.' He hesitated. 'Will the rest of the family be comin' home?'

Shane knew full well that the man was referring to his siblings, but rather than give the man gossip to spread, he pretended to have misunderstood the question. 'We've just had a letter from our Dana, she's joined the—' He stopped speaking as the horse began to bang her hoof against the stable door.

'Oi!' yelled the older man. 'You can pack that in ...' He disappeared behind the door.

Thankful for the interruption, Shane began to pack away his tools.

'You knew folk would ask sooner or later,' said Colleen.

'We're goin' to have to come up with a plan because I'm not havin' them know the truth before our Dana, and I'm hopin' that won't be for a long time yet, if ever.'

Colleen helped her husband place his tools back into the large wooden box. 'Tell 'em that everyone's fine – they don't really want to know anyway, they're only askin' to be polite.' She shot him a warning glance. 'And as for our Dana, you're goin' to have to tell her the truth one of these days. The older she gets the more questions she asks; it's only natural she wants to know more about her family—'

'Family!' Shane snorted. 'Is that what they call themselves?'

Fearing Shane might attract unwanted attention, Colleen hushed him. 'I'm just sayin' the truth will out, and it's better comin' from us when it does.'

Calming himself, Shane picked up the toolbox in one hand and offered his free arm to his wife. 'I know, luv, and you're right, I were just hopin' that day were a long way away.'

'We didn't do anythin' wrong,' Colleen soothed. 'Just you keep that in the back of your mind.'

Shane smiled lovingly at his wife. 'I know that an' so do you. Let's hope our Dana sees it that way.'

'She will. She's got a good head on her shoulders, and that's because we've taught her well.'

Shane released a long sigh of content. 'I reckern I must be the proudest man alive!'

Colleen smiled. 'Make sure you tell her that when you write her back.'

He nodded. 'I will, luv, don't you worry.'

Chapter Three

Dana and Patty, both tired from having next to no sleep the previous night, were feeling worse for wear when they boarded the train bound for Wolverhampton at 9.30 a.m.

'It's like a big adventure, isn't it?' Patty whispered beneath her fingers. 'This train is full of strangers, all goin' off to different places, startin' new lives; some of them might win us the war, others might ...' Her voice trailed off as she drew a finger across her throat.

'Blimey, you're full of optimism!' said Dana with a chuckle. 'I hope we're the ones who win the war, and not the others.'

Patty beamed at her. 'Course we are – might even gerra medal! And bein' Waafs we're bound to meet all sorts of people. We could end up rubbin' shoulders with aircrew, mebbe even pilots ...' She gave a small gasp as she thought about this. 'We might even marry 'em!'

'Sounds like you've got it all worked out!' Dana chuckled. 'I hope mine's handsome.'

Patty rolled her eyes. 'Bound to be, you'll have the pick of the crop with that golden mane of yours, not to mention those eyes!'

'Then they'll find out who I am and ...' She spread her hands out in a theatrical manner. '... boom, that'll be the end of that!'

'If you don't tell them, and' – Patty thrust her thumb towards her chest – 'I don't tell them, how're they goin' to find out?'

Dana eyed her friend shrewdly. 'Trust me, these things have a habit of comin' out when you least expect it. That's why I intend to tell folk the truth from the start.'

'Really?' said Patty, clearly surprised. 'Are you sure that's wise? Don't you think you'd be better off hangin' fire until you get to know people first? You know how judgemental folk can be; if they find out your ...' She cast an eye around the carriage before lowering her voice: '... past they'll've made up their minds and there won't be a thing you can do to change 'em. Better they get to know you first.'

Dana pulled a face. Perhaps Patty was right. After all, who would know unless she or Patty told them? It wasn't so long ago that Dana had thought her father silly for thinking that other people judged them, but a lot of water had passed under the bridge since then and Dana knew first-hand how disapproving people could be once they knew the truth. Making her mind up, she nodded. 'I'll keep shtum for now.'

'I think it's best. After all it's nowt to do wi' anyone else.'

By the time they reached Wolverhampton the lack of sleep was taking its toll and the girls agreed they would try to get some rest on the RAF coach which would take them on the last leg of their journey. Taking their seats they rested their heads on each other to get more comfortable; they had not intended to fall asleep but were soon woken by the sergeant who had met them at the station.

'Wakey, wakey, sleepin' beauty,' he said, his voice tinged with amusement.

As Dana's eyes snapped open she heard muffled giggles escape the lips of the girls around them. Blinking, she nudged Patty awake.

'Sorry, we didn't get much sleep last night ...' she mumbled, knuckling her eyes.

'You'd better get used to it 'cos you won't get much sleep here either.' He turned to Patty. 'Sorry to disturb your nap, but it's time to get off,' he said, much to the amusement of the other women.

Blushing hotly Dana and Patty lined up outside the gate with the rest of the girls on their coach. One of them sidled up to Dana and Patty and held out a hand. She was slightly shorter than them, with fawn coloured hair and light brown eyes.

'I'm Lucy Jones. Don't worry about fallin' asleep on the coach; most of us did. I'm guessin' by your accents that you come from Liverpool, same as me?'

Dana felt her cheeks turn pink. If what Lucy said was true, why had the sergeant chosen to single her and Patty out? She shook Lucy's hand. 'Thanks, and yes we do come from Liverpool.' She hesitated, then said, 'If we weren't the only ones who fell asleep why did he pick on us?'

A girl standing behind Patty suppressed a giggle. 'I reckon it was your mate snoring fit to bust what did it.'

Patty's cheeks bloomed red and she sank her face into her hands. 'Oh, please tell me I didn't ...'

There was a ripple of light-hearted giggles. 'Don't worry, you can't help what you do in your sleep,' said a girl next to them. 'Besides, it helped break the ice as well as give us all a good chuckle. Even that grumpy-lookin' sergeant cracked a smile.' She held out a hand. 'I'm Jo, and this is Sarah. We're from Scarborough ...' As the girls shook hands a stern-looking woman in WAAF uniform ordered them to get in line.

Doing as they were told, Dana noticed how smart the woman was, all in blue; the belted waist gave her an hourglass figure and the overall appearance was far smarter than anything Dana owned. The female corporal cast a critical eye over her new recruits. 'I'm Corporal Ainsworth, and I shall be in charge of you for the next two weeks.' She produced a clipboard from beneath her arm and began reading off a list of names. When she had finished she barked an order for the girls to get in line and follow her to their billet.

As they walked, the corporal pointed out various buildings, including the sick bay, before stepping into one of about ten identical wooden huts. She waited impatiently as they filed in behind her. Dana peered around the room. There were two rows of bunk beds, one down either side. At the far end was a door, which, she later found out, led to the ablutions, and in the middle of the hut was a tall lead stove. The corporal indicated the lockers beside each of the bunks. 'You've got five minutes to choose a bed and stow your belongings; after that you're to report to sick bay.'

'But I'm not sick,' began one of the girls, only to be barked into silence by the corporal.

'Good, and that's the way we intend to keep things,' she snapped, 'You will be inspected to make sure you've got nothing contagious – the last thing we need is an epidemic, so you'll be checked for everything from flat feet to nits.' She looked expectantly round the new recruits. 'Any questions?'

There was a general shaking of heads, which seemed to please the corporal, who left the room briskly before anyone could change their minds.

Patty stared down at her own feet before glancing towards Dana's. 'Aren't everybody's feet flat?'

Dana shrugged. 'I'd've thought so – you'd look silly with round ones.'

Jo chuckled as she made her way to one of the beds. 'She means people who've got fallen arches.'

Patty plonked her bag down on the bed next to Jo's. 'Sorry, still not with you.'

'You know where the arch of your foot is?' Patty and Dana nodded. 'Well, some people don't have that, their foot is flat, hence ...'

'Flat feet!' said Dana and Patty together.

Lucy, who had chosen a bed opposite, shook her head. 'You'd think they'd've checked that before draggin' us all the way out here, wouldn't you?'

As they made their way towards the sick bay Dana turned to the others. 'How do you know if you've got nits?'

Sarah nodded in the direction of a girl with thick frizzy brown hair further up the queue. 'See her? The one who can't stop scratchin'?'

They nodded.

'Nits,' Sarah said informatively. She looked at Dana's magnificent locks. 'If I were you I'd steer well clear of her – last thing you want is a head full of creepy-crawlies!' Seeing Dana's horrified expression, Sarah broke into giggles. 'Don't worry, you won't catch 'em. They'll send her off to the nit nurse ...'

'What does she do?' said Dana, her eyes widening with horrified fascination.

'Shaves all your hair off ...' Jo began before being hushed by Sarah, who was trying to keep herself from laughing at Dana whose eyes were practically out on stalks.

'She's teasin'. They don't shave your hair off – well, not unless it's really bad – they remove them with a special steel comb.'

'I've only been in the WAAF for a few hours and I'm already learnin' new stuff,' said Dana as she watched the girl being taken to a separate room.

After the girls were announced free from infection, they were taken to the cookhouse where they were given their irons, which turned out to be a knife, fork and spoon along with a mug. 'Guard 'em with your life or starve!' said the Waaf in a no-nonsense fashion. Patty looked at the food on offer.

'What's that brown sloppy stuff?' she asked the cook behind the counter.

'Stew.'

'Blimey, looks more like soup than stew.' Dana chuckled. 'What's the point in makin' sure we're free from infection if they're goin' to kill us with the grub?'

Holding a ladle in one hand, the cook glared icily at. Dana. 'No one's forcing you to eat it.'

'I'll have one of them sandwiches,' said Patty.

The cook wandered over to the sandwiches. 'They're all cheese. Does that suit your highness?'

Nodding, Patty giggled, hissing, 'I don't think she likes you,' out of the corner of her mouth to Dana.

A couple of girls they were sharing their billet with came into the cookhouse. 'Hurry up, you two, Corp says she'll be along in five minutes to show us what's what.'

Patty stared at the stale sandwich she had in her hands. 'As if this wasn't goin' to give me enough indigestion, without havin' to bolt it down me neck.' She took a large bite out of the sandwich and spoke to Dana, her voice muffled by the bread. 'C'mon, best gerra move on.'

They arrived in their billet just ahead of the corporal, who proceeded to show the girls how to make up their beds.

Patty looked at the bed linen; she cleared her throat in order to gain the corporal's attention. 'Sorry, but I don't seem to have any sheets.'

The corporal nodded. 'Good. Nor does anyone else.' She turned her attention back to the hut in general. 'Take your biscuits ...'

'Biscuits?' said Lucy, eagerly looking around her.

The corporal picked up one of three cushions which lay on the bunk next to her. 'These are what we call biscuits, you spread them out to make a mattress.'

Once they had been shown where everything was the corporal said they were free to do whatever they wanted, as long as they didn't try to leave the camp.

'Reveille will sound—' she began.

'Sorry,' said one of the girls from the far end of the hut, 'but what's reveille?'

The corporal half smiled. 'Don't worry, you'll know it when you hear it.'

'I don't know about you,' hissed Patty under her breath, 'but I'm ready for me bed. I'm fair whacked after today.'

Dana nodded. 'Me too, and it doesn't sound as though tomorrer's goin' to be much better.'

The next morning when reveille sounded the girls went from being fast asleep to wide awake in the blink of an eye.

'I'm guessin' that's reveille,' said Patty as she half slid, half fell out of the top bunk. She glanced in the direction of the door which led to the ablutions. 'Quick, get your wash stuff, else we'll be last in the queue.'

Dana followed Patty's line of sight to where a few girls were already forming a line, wash kits tucked under their arms.

An hour later the girls were washed, dressed and ready for the day ahead. 'Flippin' heck,' breathed Dana, 'I feel like I've been put through the wringer an' it's only just gone seven!'

'I hope we don't have to spend the entire day queuein' like yesterday,' moaned Patty. 'I thought it'd be a lot more excitin' than this – we've not even had proper uniforms yet!'

Patty might have regretted her words as they received their uniforms only to be told they had to write their names in everything, from shoes to blouses, skirts and hats. Dana rotated her wrist. 'I feel like me hand's goin' to drop off.' But if they thought that was bad it was nothing compared to how they felt after they received their inoculations.

'I don't remember anyone tellin' us about this,' Patty groaned as she huddled up in her bed. 'Me arm's throbbin' fit to bust an' I feel sick as a pig.'

Things got better over the next few days and the girls began to get into a routine. As soon as reveille – or, as Patty called it, 'that bloody trumpet' – sounded the girls were up and into the ablutions before anyone else had a chance to stir.

'Get into a routine, and everythin' else will fall into place,' Patty told Lucy.

'If you plait your hair every night before you go to bed it'll be a lot easier to manage in the mornin',' said Lucy as they queued for their turn with the gas masks. 'That's what Edna used to do for me ...' She fell silent.

'Who's Edna?' said Patty.

Lucy's neck had started to turn a pale shade of pink when, much to her relief, the man at the door signalled it was her turn.

'Good luck,' said Dana as Lucy nodded to say she was ready to go in. They watched the door close behind her. Patty turned to Dana.

'Was it me, or did she look like she'd rather go into a gas chamber than explain who Edna is?'

'Nope, she definitely preferred the gas chamber!' said Dana. 'Perhaps Edna's her sister. Mebbe summat awful happened to her and she doesn't want to talk about it.'

Patty was about to reply when the man on the door to the gas chamber turned and spoke to her earnestly. 'Stand here and don't let anyone in.' He pulled his own gas mask over his face before disappearing into the chamber.

Patty obediently took her place in front of the door. 'I wonder what that's all about?'

After a few minutes the man reappeared; his face was stern when he addressed the remainder of the women who still had to go through the chamber. 'Remember to take a deep breath *before* you remove your masks and not *as* you remove them. That Waaf's lucky this was only an exercise.'

'Is she all right?' said Patty. She was eyeing the door to the chamber with dread.

The airman raised his voice so that the other women could hear what he was about to say. 'She'll be fine, but she wasn't concentrating on the matter in hand, and that's real important: you can't be thinking of anything else. That's why we drill it into you – there's no second chances if it comes to the real thing.'

Patty grimaced at Dana before heading into the chamber. When they had both completed the exercise they went to visit Lucy, who was recuperating in the sick bay.

'Wotcher,' she croaked as the girls made a beeline for her bed.

'What happened?' said Dana. Taking a chair from beside the door she sat down next to Lucy.

Lucy rolled her eyes. 'I weren't thinkin' straight when I took me mask off ...'

'Was it to do with Edna?' said Patty.

Tears brimmed in Lucy's eyes and she nodded slowly.

Dana and Patty exchanged glances. 'Don't worry,' said Dana, 'you don't have to tell us if you don't want to.'

'On the other hand,' said Patty, 'it can be good to talk about these things, get 'em out in the open as it were.' Fearing she was about to be denied a piece of gossip, she added, 'A problem shared is a problem halved.'

'I didn't want anyone to know.' Lucy sniffed. 'I thought people might take the mick out of me if they found out.'

Dana and Patty were intrigued. 'I'm sure they wouldn't,' said Dana in reassuring tones. 'People are more understanding than you think ...'

'It's different for everyone else. Even the ones from the courts are wanted, but not me.'

Patty looked perplexed. 'Who is Edna exactly?'

Lucy peered earnestly past Dana and Patty; once satisfied that no one was close by she said, 'Promise you won't tell?'

They both nodded solemnly.

'She's one of the girls that used to be in the same orphanage as me.'

'What happened to her?' said Patty.

Lucy frowned. 'Nothin', or at least I don't think it did; she left a lot sooner than me, 'cos she were older.'

Dana, who was quicker off the mark than her friend, butted in. 'I get it! You're not worried about Edna, you didn't want folk knowin' you're an orphan, am I right?'

Lucy nodded.

'I see!' said Patty as the penny finally dropped. 'Although I don't see why you're worried, it's not your fault you ended up in an orphanage.'

Lucy shrugged. 'Isn't it? There are a lot of folk who think you must be a bad 'un if your own parents didn't want you.'

Patty frowned angrily. 'What a dreadful thing to say. How could anyone blame an innocent child for the actions of their parents?'

Lucy shrugged. 'I s'pose it's just an excuse so they don't have to have owt to do wi' you. When I left I had the devil of a job findin' work, I only got the job in the Chinese laundry because I lied about me past.'

'I'm the same—' Dana began before being cut short by Lucy.

'I knew I'd seen you somewhere before! I've been rackin' me brain but I couldn't place you. It's been a few years, mind.' She eyed Dana with approval. 'I like your hair better this way ...'

'Hold on a mo,' said Patty quickly, 'I think you've got the wrong end of the stick.' She looked at Dana. 'I know we said you should keep shtum, but I don't think that's possible in this case.'

Lucy looked inquisitively at Dana, who nodded before turning to Lucy. 'I'm not an orphan, I'm a traveller.'

Lucy's mouth dropped open. 'Well, blow me down! I weren't expectin' that – not that there's anythin' wrong wi' bein' a traveller,' she said hastily, adding, 'I'm guessin' you meant we both don't want folk to know where we come from?'

'Exactly. It seems that people have the same feelin's towards travellers as they do orphans, like they reckern you're bad news.'

'I'm glad I ain't the only one with a secret,' said Lucy. 'It's awful when you think you're the odd one out. That's what I liked about bein' in the orphanage: we was all in the same boat.'

'It was a bit like that for me, 'cos we only ever mixed with the carters, and they accepted us for who we were. Dad told me other folk didn't like people like us, but I didn't really believe him till I left home.'

'Yup, it was the same in the orphanage; I hadn't got a clue that I were different from anyone else 'til I left.' She raised her eyebrows fleetingly. 'Come as quite a shock.' She looked at Patty. 'You're quiet. Are you a traveller too?'

Patty shook her head. 'Me mam runs a lodging house on Staple Row, and me dad's overseas doin' his bit for King and country, so when it comes to family I suppose you could say we're pretty average, but I know what it's like to be singled out: I had a bit of a rough time in school, none of the other kids would speak to me 'cos of one girl.'

Lucy shook her head. 'We're three different girls from three different worlds, yet we all hail from the same city and we've all got summat in common. Who'd've thought it?'

'Which section are you hopin' to get into?' said Patty.

'MT,' said Lucy. 'I'm not great with paperwork, I can't cook to save me life, and I faint at the sight of blood. I reckon MT's the only choice left.' She looked from Patty to Dana. 'How about you two?'

Patty answered for them both. 'Same as you.'

'Wouldn't it be grand if we ended up at the same station?' said Lucy. Her voice was beginning to lose its croakiness from the effects of the gas.

'It would that, but I reckern it's unlikely,' said Dana.

'I hope we do,' said Lucy. 'It's nice to have summat in common with someone.'

Patty shook her head dismissively. 'It won't happen though. We've got more chance of flyin' to the moon than endin' up on the same station.'

Lucy pulled a face. 'What were the chances that three girls like us would end up in the same trainin' camp? Not to mention wantin' to get on to the same course?'

'All I'm sayin' is I'm not gerrin' my hopes up,' said Patty, although she had everything crossed from her fingers to her toes.

The two weeks at Bridgnorth soon passed by and it was with bated breath that Lucy, Patty and Dana waited to hear their fate. The corporal who was reading from a list stopped short as he was drowned out by a collective cheer from Dana, Patty and Lucy.

'Sorry!' they said as they made their way out of the hut.

'Pwllheli!' breathed Lucy. 'I don't know where it is and I don't much care, not as long as we're together!'

'I think one of the airmen said the MT training camp was somewhere in Wales,' Dana informed her friends, 'and that certainly didn't sound English to me!'

'When I were little me mam and dad allus took me on a week's holiday to stay with me Auntie Gwen in a small village called Talacre. It was lovely and the beach was huge!' said Patty wistfully. 'Just imagine, if we end up by the sea, we could go for moonlit strolls with handsome pilots.'

'You and your handsome pilots.' Dana giggled; then she sighed as a memory of her swimming in the sea at Seaforth Sands entered her mind. 'Seaforth beach, now there's a place for a good moonlight stroll, not that you could when there's a war on, not with all the sea defences.'

'Oh yeah,' said Patty, a shade disappointed, 'I'd forgotten about that. Well, we can allus go for a moonlit stroll somewhere which isn't covered in barbed wire.'

'Are you goin' home for your three days' leave?' said Lucy.

Patty nodded. 'I promised me mam we'd go home and tell her all our news. What about you?'

Lucy shrugged. 'I didn't realise we was goin' to get any leave. I thought we'd go straight to Pwllheli. I can't go back to where I was stayin' 'cos I give up me room.' She thought about it for a moment. 'I suppose I could go to Pwllheli and see if I can stay in a B and B.'

'Why don't you come and stay with me and Dana?' said Patty cheerfully. 'You and Dana can share the attic.'

'Are you sure?' said Lucy, her eyes shining with hopeful anticipation. 'I wouldn't want to impose ...'

'Positive, and you wouldn't be an imposition, it'll be fun stayin' together wi'out havin' to do drill every two minutes!'

Dana agreed heartily. 'Not to mention bein' able to lie in and not jump out of bed 'cos some bugger's blowin' that trumpet fit to bust!'

Lucy rolled her eyes. 'Or runnin' to the lavvy before everyone hogs the loos!'

'To be able to wear normal knickers!' said Patty with such passion she caused the other girls to fall about laughing. 'Oh come on, you can't say you actually like wearin' them big bloomers?'

Lucy giggled. 'Passion-killers, that's what the fellers call 'em.'

'I'm not surprised!' said Dana. 'I rather think that might be the RAF's intention.'

'They do keep you warm though,' said Lucy thoughtfully. 'Although I should imagine they'll be a nightmare in the middle of summer.'

The corporal who had read the deployment list exited the hut. 'You lot still here? I'd've thought you'd've been chompin' at the bit to get away. Three days ain't long, you know, yet here you are gossipin', although what about I can't imagine.'

'Knickers,' said Patty absent-mindedly.

The girls hooted with laughter at the startled expression on the corporal's face. 'Not like that!' Patty added hastily. 'We were sayin' we was lookin' forward to not havin' to wear 'em.'

'Oh, I – I – very well,' said the corporal, and he left before Patty had a chance to explain.

As the corporal disappeared from view, Dana, tears rolling down her cheeks, held on to Patty's arm for support. 'You've really got to start thinkin' before you speak, Patty Blackwood.'

74

'Oh, I dunno,' said Lucy, who was giggling fit to burst and clutching a stitch in her side. 'She's given him summat to think about.'

'Thank God we're leavin' today is all I can say,' said Patty. 'I don't think I'd ever be able to look him in the face again!'

'I think he feels the same way,' said Dana, who was roaring with laughter.

Her cheeks still flushed with embarrassment, Patty headed for their billet. 'Let's get us things and get out of here before I say summat else!'

After arriving in Liverpool, some time later that same day, Patty, Dana and Lucy stood in front of Patty's wardrobe and examined the contents within. 'Trouble is,' said Patty, 'I've never been to a dance before so the only dresses I've got are me Sunday best, and most of them are too small, except for the one I allus wear and that's hardly suitable for a dance ...' She fingered the hem of the frock in question.

'Was it one of your mam's old 'uns?' said Lucy.

Patty turned to her friend, a look of dismay etched on her face. 'Is it really that bad?'

Dana suppressed a giggle. 'It's ideal for church and funerals ...'

Patty closed the doors to her wardrobe. 'I've made up me mind. I'm goin' to wear me uniform – it's better than anythin' I've got.'

'Now that's sorted all we've got to worry about is the actual dancin',' said Lucy, who had told the girls repeatedly that she had never been to a dance or been shown what to do.

'It can't be that hard,' said Patty. 'I've watched me nan and granddad as well as me mam and dad, in tea dances and stuff like that: it's easy if you're a woman 'cos the man takes the lead, all you have to do is just foller him. How hard can it be?'

Dana's jaw dropped. 'You mean we have to dance with men?' She glanced at Lucy, who was looking equally aghast.

Patty frowned at them. 'Course we do, that's the whole idea of goin' ...' She hesitated for a moment before adding, 'Who did you think we'd be dancin' with?'

'Each other!' said Dana and Lucy simultaneously.

'But there's three of us, we couldn't possibly all dance together, so at least one of us would have to sit on the side ...'

'I don't mind!' Dana quickly volunteered, before Lucy had the chance.

Patty stared at the other two. 'Don't you want to meet a feller?'

'Course I do,' said Lucy. 'But couldn't we meet him in the chippy?'

Patty glanced at Dana in appeal, who shrugged. 'I just don't want to make a fool out of meself. Couldn't you at least show us the basics before we go? It's all very well you sayin' to foller the feller, but it'd be nice to know where we were goin' before we get there.'

Patty deflated a little. 'I s'pose you're right. I'll go and get me mam – she's gone to loads of dances whereas I've only ever stood on me dad's feet ...'

'What do you mean?' said Dana as Patty made to leave the room.

Patty grinned. 'When I were little me dad used to tell me to stand on his feet and he'd dance me round the floor.'

A chuckle escaped Lucy's lips. 'Perhaps we could say that to the fellers who ask us to dance.' She put on a posh accent. 'I say, would you mind h'awfully if I stood on your feet?'

Dana and Patty broke into a fit of the giggles. 'Oh yes,' said Patty, who was trying to catch her breath, 'that would look good, wouldn't it? The three of us standin' on their toes as they whisked us round the dance floor!'

Within twenty minutes under Mrs Blackwood's tuition the girls had mastered the box step.

'What'll we do if summat a bit faster than a waltz comes on?' said Dana, who was feeling a little more enthusiastic.

'You sit down and have a drink until it's over.' Mrs Blackwood laughed. 'But I've told you over and over you're not goin' to have that problem, there's hardly any fellers at these dances, so it's more likely than not you'll end up dancin' with each other.' She wagged a finger at their forlorn expressions. 'From what I've seen, you could do with a bit of practice, especially before you go to one of the dances on camp where there really will be a few fellers to choose from and they'll have a lot more dances under their belts than the box step.' She cast an admiring eye over the girls in their uniforms. 'By heck, though, you do look grand.'

Later that evening, with their hair pinned into place and their shoes polished 'til they shone, the girls entered the Grafton. Patty gave a quiet squeal of delight. 'It's miles better than any of the places me mam and dad've taken me to.'

Lucy fidgeted with the hem of her jacket. 'It looks a bit posh ... d'you reckern we'll fit in?'

Dana nodded. 'Didn't you see the look on the cloak-room attendant's face?'

Patty shook her head. 'Why?'

'When we first walked in she was leanin' against the counter, but as soon as she seen the uniforms she stood up straight.'

'So?' said Lucy, who couldn't see what the cloak-room girl's stance had to do with anything.

'She reminded me of us whenever Sarge enters the room,' said Dana mildly.

Patty nodded. 'I know what you mean, but do you really think that's why she did it? We've only passed basic trainin' – we've not done anythin' important yet.'

'She doesn't know that,' said Lucy, who was beginning to understand. 'As far as she knows we've been in since the start of the war.'

Dana was looking at the other people in the hall as they spoke. 'What's more it looks like we're the only ones in uniform; everyone else is in civvies.'

Patty grinned. 'I feel like a proper grown-up – shall we get a drink?'

Dana nodded. 'After that we can find somewhere to sit and watch everyone else for a while, see what the protocol is, as it were.'

Nodding their approval, the girls approached the bar. Lucy and Patty were first to get served and Dana had just opened her mouth to ask for a glass of lemonade when a man gained her attention by clearing his throat.

As she turned to face him, he held up a hand to the barmaid and the young girl walked towards him. 'Yes, sir, what can I get you?'

Dana glared at the barmaid. 'Excuse me! I was here first; he's pushin' in.' She turned her glare on the man next to her. 'Which isn't very gentlemanly, I might add.'

The man appeared startled. 'I wasn't …' he began before Patty added her tuppence worth.

'You jolly well were. We were here first. Dana was the last to order her drink; me an' Lucy's already got ours.' She held her drink up to prove her point.

The man swallowed hard and Dana noticed his Adam's apple bob up and down in his throat. 'I'm not saying you weren't.'

Dana stared at him in a righteous manner. 'You admit it?'

'I had no intention of pushing in,' he said quickly, 'I wanted to buy you a drink. I'm sorry if I've caused any offence.'

Dana's face turned an instant shade of scarlet. 'Oh …' She looked at Patty and Lucy, appealing for help, but the girls shrugged their ignorance, although she noticed a grin was beginning to curve the edge of Patty's lips. She turned back to the man. 'No one's offered to buy me a drink before. I just assumed.'

He raised his eyebrows in disbelief. 'I can't believe I'm the first man to buy you a drink.' He smiled broadly at Dana, revealing a white and even set of teeth; as his face relaxed she noticed a small dimple appear in his chin.

'That's very kind of you ...' She looked at him expectantly.

He held out his hand. 'I'm Pete Robinson.'

Dana took his hand in hers and noticed how big it was compared to her own. 'I'm Dana, and these are me pals Lucy and Patty. We're on leave.'

'Would you like any drinks?' said the barmaid, who was beginning to grow impatient.

Pete raised an enquiring eyebrow at Dana, who nodded. 'Lemonade, please.'

Pete smiled at the barmaid. 'Make that two.'

The woman unscrewed the top off a bottle of R. White's and poured the drinks. Dana looked at Pete. 'So what do you do, Peter Robinson?' She glanced at his shirt and trousers. 'I can see you're not in uniform, so ...'

He ran his fingers through a short crop of thick dark hair. 'It's Pete, and believe it or not, I'm training to be a Spitfire pilot.'

Patty eyed him candidly. 'How come you're not in uniform?'

He held up his hands. 'It's not my fault. My father owns a racing stud on the Wirral and I've been staying with him these past few days. I left my uniform at my pal's so it wouldn't get dirty.'

Patty placed her hands on her hips. 'So you're a Spitfire pilot ...'

'Nearly,' Pete corrected.

'Nearly,' repeated Patty, 'and your dad owns race horses?'

He nodded. 'That's about the size of it.'

'So you're a rich handsome hero?' said Lucy, who also found the stranger's story a little remarkable.

He looked from one to the other. 'I don't know about the hero or handsome bit, but as for the rest of it, yes, although I suppose it does sound a little far-fetched, especially when I'm not in uniform.'

'A bit more than a little!' said Patty.

Pete looked at Dana. 'I can assure you I'm telling the truth.'

Dana smiled uncertainly at him. 'I'm sure you are, but we don't really know you ...'

Pete placed his drink on the bar before holding out a hand to Dana. 'In that case it's up to me to prove myself. May I have this dance?'

Hearing the band break into a waltz, Dana was so relieved it was something she knew she agreed without hesitation.

As the pair made their way to the dance floor Lucy turned to Patty. 'Looks like it's just me and you – do you fancy a turn?'

Patty nodded. 'That way we can keep an eye on that feller, make sure he's not pullin' a fast one on our Dana.'

Pete guided Dana around the floor effortlessly and as he smiled down at her, Dana noted laughter lines appearing in the corners of his eyes. Pete had said his father owned a racing stud. If there was one thing Dana knew, it was horses. She decided to test his knowledge. 'Do you have much to do with your father's horses?'

Pete nodded a little hesitantly. 'I did before I joined the RAF, but that was over a year ago, so I've not done much with them lately.'

Careful to avoid eye contact, she said, 'Have you got many geldings?'

Pete shook his head with a chuckle. 'I can see you don't know much about horses. A stud farm doesn't have geldings, it has stallions ... and mares of course.'

Dana smiled to herself. 'Are they big?'

'Depends,' he said. 'On average I'd say around sixteen hands.' He caught her eye. 'Do you like horses?'

She decided to come clean. 'I've grown up around them.'

He smiled approvingly. 'So were you giving me a little test?'

Smiling, Dana stared deep into his brown eyes. 'Does your father really own a stud farm?'

He laughed. 'I was right, you were testing me!'

Blushing, Dana gave a small nod. 'I'd be a fool to take a stranger at his word.'

Pete gently tightened his arm around her waist. 'Let me see. What can I say that would convince you?'

Dana thrummed her fingers against his back as she sought a question which would prove he was telling the truth, but could think of none, so instead she said, 'You could allus take me there ...'

'I could,' he said, 'only I'm going back to Scarborough in the morning.'

'What about your uniform?' said Dana tentatively, thinking she might have caught him out.

'I told you: I've come here straight from my father's stud. I left my uniform in my pal's house so it wouldn't get dirty.' He gazed into her eyes. 'You're far too beautiful to lie to.'

Blushing, Dana averted her gaze to the tables and chairs placed around the dance floor, when a thought struck her. 'Where's your pal? Surely you didn't come here on your own. I bet he could back you up.'

Pete cast his eyes to the ceiling. 'You're right, I didn't come here on my own; I was with my pal, only he wanted to go home because we've an early start. I was going to go with him, when I saw you.' Placing a finger beneath her chin he gently tilted it so that he could look in her eyes. 'I told him to go on without me.'

Dana wanted to believe him so much, but the more he spoke the less plausible he sounded. The man had an excuse for everything. She made up her mind. 'I'm sure you're a very nice man, but I came here with my friends and I really think I should be gettin' back to them.'

Pete slid his arm from around her waist and slipped his hand into hers. 'How about I take you out another night? Give me a chance to redeem myself?'

Dana smiled politely. 'I thought you said you were goin' to Scarborough in the mornin'?'

'I am,' said Pete. 'But there's no reason why we couldn't arrange something for a later date.'

'I don't know where I'm goin' to be three weeks from now, let alone three months,' said Dana. 'Perhaps we should say "till we meet again"?'

He nodded.

Lucy nudged Patty. 'They're comin' over,' she hissed through the side of her mouth.

'So I see,' said Patty, 'but the music's still playin'.'

'They're holdin' hands so it can't be bad news ...' Lucy stopped talking as Dana and Pete came within earshot.

Pete nodded to the two girls. 'I return your friend, unharmed.' He lifted Dana's hand in his and kissed her knuckles. 'Till we meet again!'

Dana nodded, although she very much doubted their paths would ever cross again. 'Goodbye, Pete.'

Pete bade them goodnight and headed towards the exit.

'Is that mine?' said Dana, pointing at a glass of lemonade. The girls nodded and Dana took a sip before putting it back down on the table. 'Would either of you like to dance?'

'No we wouldn't,' said Patty impatiently. 'We want to know what happened, what did he say, what did you say ...'

'We know you didn't kiss because we were watchin',' said Lucy.

Dana chuckled. 'He didn't say much, not that it matters – he's gone and I dare say I'll never see him again.' Even though Dana believed this to be true, she felt disappointed at the thought. There was something about the stranger that she found most appealing. She smiled inwardly. And it wasn't just because he was tall, dark and handsome.

Entering the small kitchen of the terraced house, Pete groaned as his pal grinned expectantly at him from his seated position by the kitchen table. 'Don't tell me Pete Robinson's finally met his match?'

Pete nodded grimly. 'Even I thought I sounded far-fetched!'

Eddie raised a chiding brow. 'I did tell you we should've come home and got changed before goin' out.'

'It would've taken too much time,' moaned Pete. 'Besides, how was I to know someone like that was going to be there? I didn't even know you had women like her in Liverpool.'

Eddie chuckled softly. 'Cheeky beggar, some of our lasses are the finest in the land.' He looked at Pete with intrigue. 'What did she say?'

Filling the kettle, Pete placed it on the stove to boil. 'She said that whilst she was sure I was a very nice man, she'd come to the dance with her friends, and she wanted to be with them.'

'Is that all?' said Eddie, who had been expecting far worse.

Pete wrinkled one nostril as he summarised the rest of her words. 'She also said she'd be a fool to believe me ...' As an afterthought, he added, 'It didn't start off too well because she thought I was trying to push in at the bar.'

Eddie shook his head. 'Never thought I'd see the day you failed to win a girl over.'

'You and me both,' said Pete. 'What's more, I may not get a chance to redeem myself.'

Eddie slapped a hand against his friend's back. 'Plenty more fish in the sea. If anybody knows that, it's you.'

Pete poured the boiling water into the teapot and stirred the contents with a teaspoon. 'She likes horses. She told me she'd grown up with them.'

Eddie eyed him inquisitively. 'She really got under your skin, didn't she?'

Pete shrugged. 'There's something about her ...'

'Did she tell you where she's from?'

Pete shook his head. 'I didn't think to ask, 'cos every time I opened my mouth, I just seemed to make things worse.'

Tilting his chair back on its legs, Eddie eyed his pal thoughtfully. Ever since Eddie had gone to work on Pete's father's racing stud as a groom, the two of them had got on like a house on fire. They both had a sense of adventure and loved anything that was deemed dangerous or life-threatening, something the ladies seemed to find irresistible in Pete, yet even though Eddie did the same daring feats, he wasn't like his pal when it came to the gift of the gab. He tapped his chin with his forefinger as he tried to think of a time when Pete had been tongue-tied around a woman, and couldn't come up with a single example. He'd always been able to woo them; half the time he didn't even have to try. Eddie wondered whether Pete was only keen on the girl in the Grafton because she'd turned him down, or whether the long-time Lothario had finally been tamed. Inside his head he tutted at his own stupidity. Since being in the RAF Pete had courted many women, both civilian and service, and he'd never got serious with any of them. Pete believed that war was too unpredictable, and you were a fool if you took a relationship seriously. There was no woman who

could tame Pete, Eddie was sure of that, but still …
'You could look her up in the Kelly's Directory next
time you're back on leave.'

'What a good idea!'

Eddie laughed. 'I do have them on occasion. What's
her name then?'

Pete's jaw dropped.

Eddie started to chuckle. 'Don't tell me you never
asked her because I shan't believe you!'

Pete shook his head. 'Her name's Dana, but I didn't
think to ask her surname …' He threw a teaspoon at
Eddie who was laughing so hard tears had formed in
his eyes.

'You – you have to be kiddin' me!' wheezed Eddie.
'Mr Smooth forgot to ask her name?'

Pete heaved a sigh. 'Prince Charming had more luck
searching for Cinderella.'

'She may be a Cinderella, but you ain't no Prince
Charming,' Eddie snorted, adding, 'Although if you'd
listened to me in the first place, you might've looked
the part in your uniform.'

'I know, I know.' Pete took a large swig of his tea.
Why on earth was he making such a fuss over her? He
had set a firm rule when war was first declared. 'Have
fun whilst you can and live each day as if it was your
last.' He liked to think he respected women enough
not to promise them something he couldn't deliver, so
he never did, instead keeping things casual, or at least
that was the plan as he saw it; however, a few women
had had different ideas and had not been pleased when
he found another companion. Still, that was hardly his
fault. He made it a rule to tell them from the start that

he wasn't in the market for anything serious. He rolled his eyes. Get a grip, Pete, he scolded himself, she's just another girl, nothing special. He drew a deep breath; she *was* something special, because unlike the other women in his life, she had turned him down. He was intrigued to see if he could change her mind. A small smile formed on his lips. He'd always liked a challenge.

Chapter Four

The gears of the Hillman Minx Dana was learning to drive squealed, crunched and ground before the corporal in charge shouted, 'For God's sake, double-declutch, woman, else you'll be learning how to put a gearbox back together!'

Grimacing apologetically, Dana slammed her foot hard down on to the clutch, released it and then pressed the clutch pedal again before finally engaging third gear. She grinned sheepishly at the corporal. 'I never forget when we start off, but once we get goin' it completely slips my mind.'

'I had noticed,' he said with feeling. 'I wouldn't mind, but half the camp can hear you, then I get it in the neck for not teaching you properly.'

'That's not fair. It's not your fault I keep forgettin'.' She glanced at him from the corner of her eye. 'Mebbe if you reminded me every time I went to change gear it'd become second nature.'

He nodded. 'We'll have to do something 'cos you won't pass the course otherwise.'

Dana gaped at him. 'But I've got to pass if I want to stay with Lucy and Patty.'

Corporal Dagnall shrugged. 'Then you're going to have to start remember—' He stopped short as Dana tried to crunch her way through the gears once more.

'Sorry!' she yelled as she tried to ram the gear lever into place.

The corporal pointed to where Lucy and Patty stood waiting for them. 'Pull over by your mates whilst this thing's still got a gearbox!'

Dana pulled over to the side and placed the car in neutral. She turned to Corporal Dagnall. 'Perhaps if we start afresh tomorrow?'

He nodded resignedly. 'I think that would be best; besides, it's time for lunch.'

'You're gettin' better,' Patty assured Dana, who was feeling downhearted. 'Me and Lucy were just sayin' as how we never heard you pullin' off earlier, and you ain't kangarooin' down the road no more neither.'

'And Dagnall didn't look as nervous when you got in this time,' said Lucy encouragingly.

Dana smiled appreciatively at her friends. 'Thanks, and I know I'm gettin' better, but Dagnall says I won't pass if I keep crunchin' the gears, and we've only got a few days left before they put us on the vans. How am I goin' to cope with summat bigger if I can't even drive a car?' As she spoke, a 30-cwt lorry drove past. The driver waved merrily at them. 'And as for one of them ...' Dana shook her head.

Patty gave Dana a reassuring squeeze as she linked arms with her friend. 'Don't worry. Like Lucy said, you've come on leaps and bounds since you first started.'

'But you two got it straight away,' said Dana miserably. 'And we've really landed on our feet here. If I don't make the grade within the next two weeks they'll put me somewhere else.'

She remembered the day they arrived some two weeks before. The girls hadn't been able to believe their eyes when they had first pulled up outside the hotel.

'The other one's got bells on!' laughed one of the Waafs as the corporal who was driving the lorry told them that this was to be their new billet.

'Don't get too excited. You'll still be expected to keep everywhere spick and span, and they've even replaced those awful hotel beds with our lovely military ones just so you'll feel at home,' said the driver as he dropped the lorry's tailgate.

'Please tell me we haven't got those awful itchy blankets too?' moaned Lucy as she jumped down from the vehicle.

He nodded. 'But they have spoilt you by giving you proper sheets.'

'They haven't really swapped the beds, have they?' said Dana, who couldn't imagine where they had managed to store the beds from the hotel, just so they could install military ones.

'Yup, but don't ask me why 'cos I ain't got a clue.' He jerked his head in the direction of one of the buildings. 'That's the Orderly Office. You're to report there; they'll tell you what's what.' With the last Waaf off the lorry he lifted the tailgate and secured it into place. ''Bye, girls.'

Now, as they made their way back to the hotel, Lucy slid her arm through Patty's. 'Me and Patty'll practise changin' gear wi' you back in our room. We can use books for pedals and my umbrella for the gear lever.'

Dana was doubtful at first, but the more she thought about it the more it seemed to make sense. 'I s'pose it's a good way to get some extra practice.'

Patty grinned. 'We'll soon have you changin' gear like a pro.'

Dana breathed a happy sigh of relief. 'Thank goodness for that, because I really enjoy drivin'. It's a lot of fun when I'm doin' it right.'

'So it's got nowt to do wi' drivin' dishy aircrew around the station?' said Lucy.

'No it hasn't!' said Dana firmly. ''Cos knowin' my luck I'll end up drivin' some fat old blighter round the countryside in the middle of the night. I want to be a driver because of the sense of freedom you get. I s'pose that's the traveller in me.'

'Talkin' of which, have you heard off your mam and dad?' said Lucy.

'They wrote the other day. I was quite surprised really ...'

'Why? Didn't you think they'd write?' said Lucy.

'I knew they'd write, but I thought they'd be whinin' at me to leave the WAAF and go to Ireland, but it was quite the reverse. Me dad said they were really proud of me, and they couldn't wait to see me behind the wheel of one of the big lorries.' She smiled as a picture of her father formed in her mind. 'Me dad's allus said I could do anythin' a man could do, if not better.' The smile faded. 'Good job he can't see me changin' gear.'

Patty stifled a giggle. 'You mean hear you changin' gear.'

Dana rolled her eyes. 'Exactly! I s'pose that's why I'm so keen to pass the course. It's not just because I want to drive, or because I want to stay wi' you two, it's 'cos I want to make me dad proud, show him I made the right decision by leavin', an' that I'm good at what I do.'

As they entered their hotel room Lucy picked up the plain ladder-backed chair and placed it into the middle of the room. 'Sit yourself down, I'll go fetch some books.'

Some time later, all three girls were roaring with laughter as Patty and Lucy sat on the bed behind Dana pretending they were in the back seat of one of the Hillmans. 'Tight turn to the left, girls.' Dana giggled. 'Hold on tight.'

Behind her, Patty and Lucy leaned as far to the left as they could without falling off the bed. 'Watch out for the potholes,' yelled Patty, who was thoroughly enjoying their game.

What the girls didn't realise was that they hadn't shut the door to their room properly and a small gathering had formed outside the door. The RAF corporal who was closest to the gap shouted, 'Watch out for the deer!'

Without thinking Dana slammed her foot hard on Lucy's copy of Agatha Christie's *Death On The Nile*, which shot across the floor.

'Steady on!' said Lucy, who had vacated the back seat in order to retrieve her book. As she bent to pick it up, movement from the gap caught her eye and she stood up to see the corporal pushing the door open with the tips of his fingers.

'Been anywhere good?' he said with a chuckle.

'Just practisin',' said Lucy before hurrying back out of view.

The corporal rapped his knuckles against the door before stepping inside. He had short-cropped blond hair and the warmest smile Dana had ever seen. 'Nice to know you're takin' the course seriously, and havin' a bit of fun whilst you're at it.' He approached the girls with an outstretched hand. 'I'm Corporal Leonard Ackerman, Lenny to me pals.' He shook each girl's hand as they introduced themselves.

'I bet we sounded like a right bunch of twits,' said Patty.

He chuckled softly. 'You certainly gave us somethin' to smile about.' He arched a single eyebrow. 'So what were you practisin'?'

'Double-declutchin',' said Dana, and before she could get any further Lenny clicked his fingers.

'I know you – I've heard you goin' round camp.'

Dana gave a small groan of dismay. 'Am I that bad?'

Shaking his head, he smiled reassuringly and Dana noticed again how his whole face seemed to light up. 'Don't worry, you'll soon get used to it, especially if you carry on practisin'. It may have given us a good giggle, but it's a damned good idea, and if you want my opinion it's a pity a lot of others don't follow suit.'

'It was my idea,' said Lucy, who was no longer feeling embarrassed.

'Well done you.' He turned his attention back to Dana. 'If you like, I could take you out for a few extra lessons in the evenin's. Me an' the lads've got shares in a Morris Oxford. It's only a two-seater, but it's ideal for learnin' in.'

Dana tried to ignore Patty, who was nudging Lucy. 'It's very kind of you to offer, but I don't think your pals would be thrilled if they knew you were thinkin' of lettin' me behind the wheel.'

He shrugged. 'We all have to start somewhere.'

Dana, who was still holding the book she had been using as a steering wheel, was about to turn him down when Lucy piped up. 'You'd be daft not to, Dana, you said yourself they won't pass you if you don't stop crunchin' the gears, and it's not often you get someone offerin' to lend you their car now, is it?'

Unable to think of another reason to turn down the offer, Dana nodded shyly. 'As long as your pals are OK with it.'

Lenny beamed down at Dana. 'I'll pick you up around six? I may not be an instructor but I know all the routes they take you on for your test, so we can practise on one of them.'

Dana found his smile infectious and grinned back at him. 'Sounds good, but if you're not an instructor what do you do?'

'I'm an engineer, but I reckon I could teach you just as well as one of the instructors.'

Dana shrugged indifferently. 'I'm game if you are! I'll see you at six.'

As Lenny left the room Dana turned to Patty and Lucy who were staring open-mouthed at her. 'You lucky sod!' said Patty. 'You've got your own personal instructor – and he's goin' to teach you the test routes!'

95

'Never mind the test routes,' said Lucy, 'Corporal Ackerman's a right bobby-dazzler, local too, by the sound of that accent.' She looked enviously at Dana. 'Some girls have all the luck.'

'I don't know whether I'd call my bad gear changin' lucky,' said Dana, 'but I s'pose if it means I get private tuition from the lovely Lenny ...'

Patty considered this for a moment. 'Do you reckon the lovely Lenny would take your pals out and teach them the routes before it comes to test day?'

Dana shrugged. 'It couldn't hurt to ask.'

Clasping her hands together Lucy jumped up and down on the spot. 'If he does, then we'll definitely pass ...' She hesitated for a moment before adding, 'He could give us all sorts of tips that could help us through. If we come out top of the class they might send us to a flying station; I imagine they only want the best to ferry the pilots to and fro.'

'Talk about bein' in the right place at the right time,' breathed Patty. 'If he hadn't seen us pretendin' to drive, we probably would never've got to speak to him.'

'It's not what you know, it's who you know, that's what my dad allus says,' said Dana as she placed the chair back by the table.

Confident in the knowledge that they were on the path to success the girls collected their irons and made their way to the hotel restaurant.

At six o'clock sharp Lenny was standing in front of the car waving to Dana. 'May as well start at the beginnin',' he said, holding out the hand crank.

Dana grimaced. 'Is it one of the evil ones?'

He shook his head with a chuckle. 'Some of them Hillmans are a bit temperamental, but you've nothin' to fear with this 'un.'

Slotting the handle into the hole, Dana pushed her cap firmly on to her head before gripping the handle in both hands and spinning it round like fury; it only took a few turns, however, before the little engine burst into life.

Lenny smiled approvingly. 'So far so good.' He held his hand out to retrieve the crank, which Dana dutifully handed over; then he opened the door to the driver's side and indicated for Dana to get in. Lenny sat in the passenger seat as Dana took her place behind the wheel. 'I hope you don't think I make it a habit to take Waafs out for extra lessons, because you're the first.'

Dana smiled gratefully. 'Let's hope you won't live to regret that decision.'

Lenny twinkled at her. 'I very much doubt it. C'mon, let's go for a drive around town, plenty of junctions and lots of gear changes' – he grinned as Dana let out a groan – 'which is just what you need; the more you do the better you'll get. Don't worry, I'll keep remindin' you to double-declutch until you get it down pat.'

An hour later Dana beamed with confidence, having only crunched the gears once, after performing an emergency stop. Seeing the look of disappointment on her face Lenny had leaned across and placed a reassuring hand on hers. 'Don't beat yourself up, I know people who've been drivin' longer than you who would've made that mistake.'

Dana had blushed a little when their hands connected and even though she knew he hadn't meant anything by it, she had enjoyed the feel of his reassuring touch.

At the end of the lesson, Dana decided to broach the idea of him teaching Patty and Lucy the test routes. 'Only if you've got the time, mind you, and they said they're willin' to chip in for the petrol.'

Lenny's eyes twinkled as he gazed at her. 'Will it make you happy if I take them out?'

'If it means they pass and we've a chance of stayin' together, then yes, it would make me very happy,' said Dana.

He rubbed his chin thoughtfully and Dana could hear his fingers scrape against the newly formed stubble. 'Tell you what, if you agree to come out with me this weekend, I'll teach your pals the routes.'

Dana felt the blush begin around the base of her neck, but she could hardly see how she could refuse, especially as Lenny had proved himself to be every bit the gentleman. 'I hope your intentions are honourable, Lenny Ackerman,' she teased.

Placing his hand across his heart he nodded solemnly. 'I'll be the perfect gentleman ...' An impish grin twitched the corner of his mouth. 'So is that a yes?'

Unable to stop herself from smiling, Dana nodded. 'How could I say no?'

As they pulled up outside the gate Lenny placed the car in neutral and pulled the handbrake on. He turned to Dana. 'If you like, I could take one of them now.'

'I'll go and see who wants to go first.' Shutting the passenger door, Dana leaned through the open window.

'And thanks again, Lenny, you've been marvellous, far better than the instructors. Have you ever thought about a change in career?'

He shook his head. 'I prefer bein' under the bonnet!'

A few days later Lenny took Dana into Barmouth. They enjoyed a ride on the steam train, took a walk by the river and bought fish and chips which they ate on a park bench. 'I must say,' said Dana as she held a piece of succulent battered fish to her lips, 'I think I got the better end of this deal.'

Lenny, who could barely keep his eyes from her, swallowed his mouthful before speaking. 'I get to take the most beautiful girl in the station out for the day. From where I'm sittin' I'm definitely comin' out on top.'

'It's lovely here, isn't it?' said Dana, who couldn't help wondering if Lenny would be as keen if he knew she used to live in a wagon. She almost felt as though she was lying to him, which didn't sit too well with her as she had a lot of respect for Lenny, who had treated her and her friends as if they had known each other for years.

He grinned. 'You're not much good at takin' compliments, are you?'

She shook her head shyly.

'Well, I reckon it's somethin' you're goin' to have to get used to, especially if we're goin' to keep in touch.'

A small smile curved Dana's lips. She would very much like to stay in contact with Lenny and was pleased to hear he was just as keen. 'That would be nice – to stay in touch I mean,' she said.

'I promised to be a gentleman, so I won't ask for any more than that,' Lenny assured her, adding with a cheeky grin, 'Not for now anyway.'

Dana slipped another chip into her mouth. She hadn't known Lenny for very long, and most of the time they spent together was taken up with Lenny teaching her how to drive effortlessly, but she very much enjoyed the company of her new friend. He was never judgemental, always encouraging, and he treated her like a lady, something Dana was definitely not used to. Her father never opened doors for her, or paid her compliments, unless it was to tell her how well she was doing at fishing, or riding.

When she returned to their billet later on that day Patty and Lucy were keen to hear her news.

'What did you do? Where did you go?' said Lucy.

'Did he kiss you goodbye?' said Patty, keen to cut to the chase.

Dana chuckled at her friend's forthrightness. 'We went to a little village called Barmouth ...'

'Oh, for goodness' sake!' said Patty impatiently. 'Did he kiss you?'

'No! He was, as he promised to be, the perfect gentleman,' said Dana.

Patty wrinkled her nose in disappointment, but then another thought occurred to her. She grinned hopefully at Dana. 'Did you want him to kiss you?'

Dana laughed. 'You're incorrigible, Patty Blackwood, and before you ask again, no I did not want him to kiss me!' She crossed her fingers behind her back, because this was only partly true. 'I've never so much as held hands with a boy before, I think I'd faint if one tried to kiss me.'

Patty stared in disbelief. 'He didn't even hold your hand?'

Seeing Patty's face, Lucy chuckled. 'Listen to you, Patty, you know as well as me that none of us have been kissed before, you only want Dana to do it so you know what to expect when it's your turn.'

'Too bloody right I do!' said Patty briefly. 'Let's face it, with Dana as competition me and you won't get a look in.'

Lucy roared with laughter. 'Thanks a lot, Patty. I'd like to think I'm in with a bit of a chance.'

Patty chuckled as her words caught up with her. 'I didn't mean it quite like that ...'

'So I'm not bug ugly then?' Lucy giggled in her turn.

'Of course not! I only meant Dana's so beautiful most men will home in on her first,' explained Patty.

'Home in on me?' said Dana, a trifle surprised. 'You make me sound like a target.'

Patty raised her brow. 'Let me see: beautiful long strawberry-blonde locks, wide green eyes, perfect lips ...'

Lucy eyed Dana thoughtfully. 'She's right, you know, you'll have the pick of the crop.'

'And we'll be left with the weeds,' sighed Patty.

'Speak for yourself,' retorted Lucy. 'I may not be as pretty as Dana, but it's different strokes for different folks. I'm sure there's plenty of fellers who are after a short dumpy lass.'

'Well, if you put it that way, let's hope there's a few after a gawky brunette,' said Patty.

'Honestly, you two!' said Dana. 'The way you carry on you'd think it was all about looks, but it's not. As soon as they find out what I am, you watch 'em run for the hills.'

Lucy rolled her eyes. 'Not that old chestnut! I reckon it'd take more than that to put Lenny off.'

'I can't believe you never held hands,' said Patty, who was still feeling disappointed that her friend hadn't been kissed. 'I'm dyin' to know what it's like to have your first kiss.'

Dana laughed. 'Then I suggest you find yourself a boyfriend, 'cos it's goin' to be a while before I kiss anyone. Crikey, me dad'd have me guts for garters if he thought I were kissin' boys!'

In the following days Lenny proved to be every bit as helpful as he had promised, spending most of his free time taking the girls round the routes, telling them where they were going wrong and how to improve their driving, something which Lucy, who was only four foot ten, found very useful when it came to reversing the big lorries.

'Keep the door open with one hand and steer with the other, that way you can see what's behind you and how close you are to anything,' said Lenny as Lucy slowly backed the lorry up to some traffic cones.

'It ain't easy when you've short arms and legs,' said Lucy as she inched towards the cone.

'It's like Dana with the gear changes,' said Lenny, 'the more you practise the better you'll get. Concentrate on one thing at a time, and don't forget, you don't need to lean right out to see behind you, just a little bit will do.'

102

'Done it!' beamed Lucy.

Lenny gave her a small round of applause. 'Keep practisin' and you'll be as good in reverse as you are goin' forward,' he assured her.

The day of their test loomed and Lucy, Patty, Dana and Lenny waited by the cars.

Dana smiled nervously at Lenny. 'I don't think I'd ever have got this far without all your hard work.'

He tried to smile in a nonchalant fashion, but he couldn't keep the widespread grin from forming on his cheeks. 'It's not just down to me, you all put in a lot of time and effort.' Then he spoke directly to Dana: 'I'm goin' to miss our evenin' jaunts.'

The corporal who was conducting the test beckoned the girls over. 'Let's be having you.'

Dana blushed as Lenny gave her a quick peck on the cheek. 'Good luck, and don't forget ...'

She held a hand to her cheek where he had kissed her. 'Double-declutch,' she said shyly. 'Are you goin' to wait for us?'

He winked. 'I ain't leavin' 'til I know how you've fared.'

It was an hour later before the girls returned. Seeing them get out of the lorry Lenny glanced anxiously at each girl in turn. 'Well?'

Dana shrugged. 'We think it went well but we won't know until we pass out.'

Lenny nodded. 'Any trouble with the gears?'

Dana smiled. 'Didn't forget once!'

Smiling back he glanced at Lucy. 'Reversing?'

'Spot on!' said Lucy.

Almost afraid to ask he raised an enquiring eyebrow in Patty's direction. 'Hill starts?'

'Like I were on the flat!' Patty confirmed.

Seeing the relief on Lenny's face, Dana chuckled. 'I don't know who's more anxious, us or you!'

'Nerves can get the better of folk,' said Lenny, 'and I know you were all desperate to pass, which can add to the pressure.'

Dana slipped her arm through his. 'That's where we had the upper hand, Lenny Ackerman, 'cos we had us a secret weapon.'

Lenny looked at her inquisitively. 'You did?'

'Course we did!' said Dana. 'We had you, silly!'

Lenny looked bashful. 'I dunno about that.'

'We do!' said Patty. 'Now let's get a drink, me mouth's gone dry from all the nerves!'

Passing-out day had arrived and the girls were on tenterhooks as they approached the board on which their results had been posted. Patty ran her finger down the list of names. She turned to face Lucy and Dana, whose hopeful smiles soon faded at the sight of her solemn face. 'But we can't have failed!' wailed Lucy. 'Not with all that extra practice …'

Giggling, Patty hushed Lucy by holding her finger up to her lips. 'I were havin' you on. Of course we passed!'

With a whoop of joy Dana and Lucy clutched Patty in a tight embrace. 'You bloomin' rotter, Patty Blackwood, you had us goin' for a minute there,' said Dana.

'But where are we goin' an' are we stayin' together?' said Lucy anxiously.

Patty clapped a hand to her mouth. 'I forgot to look!' She hastily turned back to the board and traced their details with her forefinger; then she turned back and looked into their expectant faces. 'Where's Innsworth?'

'Gloucester,' said Lenny, who had come to see how the girls had got on.

'We're goin' to the same station – isn't it fabulous?' said Dana. She turned to face Lenny. 'Although we would never have got this far without you, Lenny.'

'Too right!' said Lucy. 'C'mon, Lenny, I think you deserve a drink – our treat. Let's go to the NAAFI and see what they've got!'

As they made their way to the NAAFI Lenny pulled Dana to one side; he winked at the others, who had turned to see where their friend had got to. 'You go in, girls, I won't keep her long.'

Giggling, Patty and Lucy disappeared into the NAAFI.

Looking slightly flustered Lenny took his cap from his head and twiddled it around in his hands. He looked up at Dana, who was gazing at him with expectation. He opened his mouth to speak, cleared his throat and tried again. 'I wanted to have a quiet word with you before you head off to your first station.'

Dana smiled. 'You've been a marvel, and a good friend to boot—'

Lenny, who had taken a deep breath, let it out in one go as he butted in. 'I don't want to be your friend.'

Dana's face fell. 'I thought we got on rather well? You even said you wanted to keep in touch—' she began before being interrupted once more.

'We do, but I want more than that.' His cheeks reddened as he tried to find the right words. 'What I'm tryin' to say is I was rather hopin' you might agree to be my girlfriend.' The words finally out, his cheeks glowed hotly.

Dana, too, was blushing. 'We could be stationed at opposite ends of the country.'

Taking her hands in his, he gazed into her eyes. 'I know but I really like you.'

Dana squeezed his fingers in hers. 'Trust me, Lenny, you don't even know me.'

Looking silently affronted Lenny continued: 'I admit we haven't known each other long, but I'd like to think I knew you well enough to know I want to get to know you better.'

Dana looked at him awkwardly as she tried to explain herself. 'You don't know where I come from ...'

He chuckled. 'Yes I do, you're a Liverpool lass. You can't hide an accent like that.'

Dana averted her gaze. Should she tell him what she really meant? She didn't want him to think she didn't like him because nothing could be further from the truth, but what if she told him and he was as repulsed as some of the folk she had come across? Her heart sank. What if he told others? Word could spread like wildfire and then where would she be? She locked eyes with his. 'Lenny, I really like you, but I'm only just starting out as a Waaf, and I think it's a little early for me to get into a relationship.'

Lenny nodded. 'I understand. If I'm honest I knew you were out of my league.'

'You couldn't be more wrong—' Dana began but Lenny shook his head.

'Don't worry, cariad, there's no need for you to explain ...' He hesitated. 'We can still be friends, can't we?'

Blinking back the tears of frustration which threatened to invade her eyes, she nodded quickly. 'Course we can.' Every part of her wanted to tell Lenny how much she liked him, that she thought he was wonderful, but doing so would mean she would have to tell him the truth. Something which she was not prepared to do, not yet at any rate.

He held out the crook of his arm. 'Come on, cariad, let's have us a goodbye drink.'

Later that evening, as he returned to his billet, Lenny was met with an expectant look from Bob, one of the men who held a share in the car. 'You've been a while, I'm taking it things went well?'

Sinking down on to his bed Lenny untied his shoelaces. 'Not exactly. They all passed, but she said she weren't ready for a relationship and that we didn't know each other well enough.'

Bob shook his head. 'In other words, now she's got no more use for you, she doesn't want to know.'

Frowning, Lenny heaved his shoes off and placed them under his bed. 'She's not like that, or at least I don't think she is. I reckon she probably doesn't fancy me, 'cos she did come out with a few excuses.'

'Like what?' said Bob.

'The usual stuff, being stationed too far apart ...' He paused for a minute. 'I didn't get her last excuse though – it didn't make any sense.'

Bob leaned up on one elbow. 'Oh?'

'She said I didn't know where she came from ...'

'With an accent like that?' Bob said with surprise.

'That's what I said, but she just changed the subject.'

Bob placed the tip of his little finger in his ear and waggled it around enthusiastically. 'Sounds a bit rum. D'you reckon she's got summat to hide?'

'I can't think what. I don't care where she comes from!'

'P'raps her folks are Germans ...' Seeing the shocked look on Lenny's face he hastily added, 'They're probably not.'

'It would explain why she didn't want to tell me where she was from ...' mused Lenny.

Bob cast his eyes to the ceiling. 'I was only joking – put it out of your head, for goodness' sake.' Eager to change the subject he added, 'She was probably looking for an excuse 'cos she didn't want to disappoint you.'

Lenny looked up. 'Maybe.'

Lying back down, Bob pulled his hanky out from under his pillow and blew his nose. 'Are you going to keep in touch?'

Lenny hung his clothes on the wooden clothes hanger. 'Yes, she said she'd like to stay friends.'

Bob yawned. 'Maybe you'll find out what's going on in due course then.'

'I hope so, 'cos I really like her,' said Lenny as he pulled back the bedcovers.

There came the sound of muffled laughter from Bob's bed. 'No need to tell me. That's all I've heard since you first saw her – it's Dana this and Dana that.'

Lenny slid beneath his covers. 'I know and it ain't goin' to be easy to get her out of my head.'

'You'll find it easier when she leaves,' Bob said bluntly.

'No I won't, it'll make things ten times harder because I won't know where she is or who she's with!' Lenny said sullenly.

'I wouldn't worry too much. I don't think she's the sort to go from one chap to the next.'

'Me neither,' said Lenny, before adding, 'Goodnight, Bob.'

Lenny heard Bob give a stifled yawn as he replied, 'G'night, mate.'

Lying in the darkness, Lenny thought back to the conversation he had had with Dana. *You don't know where I come from.* Those had been her exact words. The more Lenny thought about it the more he wondered whether Bob was right. How did that saying go? Many a true word was said in jest? It might seem a little far-fetched but it would make sense. He turned on to his side. He would have to do as Bob said and see what happened in due course.

'Why do we have to travel at night?' moaned Lucy. 'You can't see nothin' out of these winders, and I can't get comfy enough to go to sleep.'

There was a general murmur of agreement from the other passengers aboard their carriage, apart from Patty who was already starting to snore.

Lucy nodded in Patty's direction. 'We was all laughin' at her for fallin' asleep on the coach to initial trainin' – well, I ain't laughin' now. I'd love a good kip.'

'I wonder what we'll be doing,' said a small mousy-haired Waaf who had travelled with them from Pwllheli. 'Won't it be exciting if we're driving pilots round and about?'

'It's more of a training camp than an active airfield,' said a Waaf who had boarded the train at a different station from theirs. 'It's where I did my two weeks initial training, so you can forget any ideas of handsome pilots whisking you off into the sunset.'

'Back to square one?' moaned Dana. 'I thought we'd be on a proper station!' She sighed as she peered at the moon, which was partly hidden behind a bank of cloud. 'Still, at least we'll be spendin' our days drivin' and not marchin' round till your feet hurt.'

Lucy thought it would feel rather good to be entering a station as a fully qualified Waaf; even if she was the lowest rank of ACW2, it was still better than being a trainee. She caught the attention of the Waaf who had spoken last. 'If we ain't goin' to be ferryin' handsome pilots around, what are we goin' to be doin'?'

The Waaf grinned. 'Let me see, the main jobs for Waaf drivers were' – she began to tick the list off on her fingers – 'ambulances, coal lorries, cranes and the fire engine.' She clicked her fingers. 'Sorry, almost forgot the ablutions lorry.'

Lucy wrinkled her nose in disgust. 'Bagsy anythin' but the coal and the ablutions lorry.'

Several hours later the girls arrived at their first RAF station. It was much larger than Dana had expected, and the MT huts were very much like the ones they had been allocated in Bridgnorth. Placing her kitbag on the floor beside her bed, Dana yawned as she began the task of laying out the biscuits. They had been to see the orderly on arrival, and he had instructed them to head to the MT section. They had been greeted by the sergeant in charge. He was a jolly fellow with a large bushy moustache, which Lucy later said reminded her of a walrus, and he appeared to find the idea of young women driving large lorries most amusing. He had led the girls to an area where the cars and lorries were parked and after a brief chat, he assigned each girl to a vehicle.

'It'll be up to you to keep the vehicle in good working order,' he had explained. He pointed towards the Hillman Minx. 'Treat it like it was your own,' he said to Dana, who was sighing thankfully. He continued walking along the line of vehicles. Patty and Lucy hesitated.

'Has he forgotten us?' said Lucy, following him past the rest of the cars. Patty was just about to clear her throat to remind him of their presence when he stopped abruptly and pointed at the fire engine. Turning to Lucy, he beckoned her over, much to the amusement of a couple of aircraftmen who were passing by. 'Treat it like it's your own,' he said, before marching off, leaving a wide-eyed, open-mouthed Lucy in his wake.

He stopped at the last lorry, which was covered in coal dust. 'I know, I know,' sighed Patty. 'Treat it as if it were me own.'

The sergeant beamed at her. 'Splendid!' He looked at Dana and Lucy. 'Any questions?'

Dana shook her head, and Lucy just stared up at him, open-mouthed. As he disappeared from view, she turned to the aircraftmen who had wandered over. 'Is he havin' a laugh? How the hell am I meant to get in the damned thing, lerralóne drive it!'

The younger of the two, who was a good deal shorter than his counterpart, winked at Lucy. 'I'm sure you'll have no end of volunteers offerin' you a leg-up.'

Lucy stiffened. 'Ha bloody ha!'

Dana looked from the fire engine to Lucy. 'Why don't you try gettin' in? It might not be as bad as it looks.'

Lucy walked over to the engine and lifted her leg on to the step – no mean feat considering she was trying to keep her knees together in order not to reveal her knickers. Dignity more or less still in place, she climbed into the driver's seat and called back down to her friends. 'It's not that bad. Come an' look.'

Dana and Patty stood on the long step which ran along the side of the vehicle and peered into the cab. Lucy was sitting behind the wheel, a broad grin on her face as she puffed her chest out with pride. 'And to think I thought he was bonkers! I can't wait to go racin' to the rescue . . .' She glanced at the two men who had gone around the vehicle and were peering through the other window. 'Not that I'm wantin' anywhere to go on fire, you understand.'

The younger of the two men shrugged his indifference. 'I wouldn't get your hopes up, it only does fifteen miles an hour . . .'

'Ringing the bell's fun though,' said the other man.

'Aye, there is that,' said his friend.

'Fifteen miles an hour! Is that all?' said a disappointed Lucy.

He chuckled at her response. 'Sounds like we've got a Richard Penn on our hands, Lofty.'

'Who on earth is he?' said Lucy, much to the delight of the aircraftmen who disappeared from view as they fell about laughing.

'Not into racin' cars then?' chuckled the taller of the two.

'No,' said Lucy, rolling her eyes. Deciding to ignore the aircraftmen, she turned to Patty and Dana. 'What d'you think?'

'It looks more excitin' than a coal lorry or a staff car,' said Dana, who was admiring the various knobs and dials. She pointed to the side of Lucy. 'That must be the bell he was on about.'

Gathering themselves together the two men reappeared in the window. 'All jokin' aside, I reckon you'll make a great firefighter,' said the younger one. He pointed towards his friend. 'This is Lofty and I'm—'

'Shorty?' volunteered Lucy, who hadn't appreciated being the butt of someone else's joke.

He nodded. 'Fair do's. I reckon I deserved that.' Leaning through the open window, he held out a hand. 'I'm Taffy.'

Lucy begrudgingly shook his hand. 'I'm Lucy and these are my pals Dana and Patty.'

He nodded at the girls before continuing. 'You like it then? The fire engine I mean.'

Lucy nodded. 'It's not as big as I thought it was. It may be slow but that's probably just as well if I've got firemen standin' on the runners.'

Taffy nodded. 'Fifteen miles an hour may not seem fast, but if you go over a bump too fast the front wheels leave the ground, an' you'll get a right rollickin'.'

Lucy smiled. 'Thanks for the tip.'

'Any time ...' He ran the palm of his hand over the back of his neck. 'Seein' as how you're new to Innsworth, I could show you round if you like?'

With her cheeks turning pink she turned to face Patty and Dana; Patty was wriggling her eyebrows suggestively whilst nudging Dana in the ribs.

Turning back to face Taffy, Lucy shrugged. 'I s'pose it couldn't harm.'

Beaming, Taffy jumped down from his side of the vehicle and held out a hand to Lucy, who shook her head, determined to manage on her own. 'Thanks all the same ...' she began before the back of her heel caught against the step causing her to pitch forward.

Taffy managed to catch Lucy before she fell to the ground. 'You all right?' he said, still holding on to her arm.

Lucy nodded. 'I'll have to watch out for that in future.'

Taffy waved a vague hand at the surrounding buildings. 'Where would you like to start?'

'How about the NAAFI?' said Lucy, straightening her skirt.

'As good a place as any,' said Taffy.

Lucy glanced at Lofty and the girls. 'Are you comin'?'

'Unless you want to be on your own?' teased Dana.

Lucy cast her eyes to the blue skies. 'Don't be silly, Dana, Taffy volunteered to show us all round, not just me.'

Lofty glanced at the watch on his wrist. 'Seeing as I already know where everything is, I think I'll head over to the cinema and see what's on.'

Taffy stuck his thumb in the air. 'Righto, I'll see you later.'

Lucy hoped that Patty and Dana wouldn't leave her alone with Taffy and was grateful when Patty tucked her arm through hers. 'Show us what's what, Taffy!'

It took Taffy a good hour to show the girls around the station. 'This is where me and Lofty are training to become engineers,' he said, indicating the door to the engineering school, 'so if you ever want anything you know where to find us.'

Lucy smiled gratefully. 'Thanks, Taff, you've been really helpful. None of us have been on a station this big before.'

'My pleasure.' He looked shyly at his feet before glancing at Dana and Patty. He stared at them for a few seconds before Dana got the hint.

'Come along, Patty.' Taking her friend by the elbow Dana guided her away from Lucy and Taffy.

With the girls out of earshot Taffy smiled awkwardly at Lucy. 'Just in case I don't bump into you beforehand, would you like to meet up this Saturday after brekker and go into Gloucester for a bit of lunch?' Adding hastily, 'My treat of course.'

Lucy nodded. 'That would be lovely.'

Taffy's smile returned, this time wider than ever; looking to where Dana and Patty stood, he gave them a cheery wave. ''Bye, girls.'

Her face puce, Lucy walked over to join her friends, both of whom were grinning like a couple of Cheshire cats.

'Looks like you said summat to make Taffy happy,' Dana said with a giggle.

'He's takin' me out for lunch on Saturday,' said Lucy, who was trying, unsuccessfully, to swallow her smile.

Patty's eyes grew wide. 'Blimey, you're a fast mover. We've only been here for two minutes and you've already got yourself a boyfriend!'

'He is not my boyfriend!' said Lucy, adding a moment later, 'Is he?'

Dana giggled. 'You mean you don't know?'

Lucy shook her head. 'He never asked me to be his girlfriend, but he did ask me out for lunch. He never said it was a date so perhaps he meant as friends ...'

'Judgin' by the smile on his face he's after a lot more than friendship!' Patty chuckled but seeing the look of despair on her friend's face she added, 'Although I'm sure he wouldn't dream of makin' a move unless you gave him the all clear.'

'Oh heck, why do things have to be so complicated?' moaned Lucy. 'I was happy when I thought I was goin' to get a nice lunch in a new city, but now I'm worried he might be after a kiss, and I've never kissed anyone – not even a peck on the cheek. I dunno what I'd do if he tried to kiss me on the lips!'

Dana smiled sympathetically at her friend. 'Why don't you ask him what's what before you leave? That way you'll both know what to expect.'

Lucy's eyes rounded. 'I can't ask him whether I'm his girlfriend – I'd look like a right twerp especially if he said no!'

Dana mulled this over for a moment or two. 'How about you tell him that you're glad he's your friend, because it's difficult when you go somewhere new; that way he'll know that you only want to be friends ...'

She paused, seeing the wretched look on Lucy's face. 'You do want him as a friend and nothin' else, I take it?'

Lucy shrugged. 'I'm nineteen and never been kissed, I've gorra do it sooner or later, only I want to be prepared.' She was beginning to wish Taffy had never mentioned Gloucester.

'You mean you want to practise poutin'?' said Dana. 'You can do that in the billet.'

Lucy clutched her tummy, which felt as though it had been invaded by butterflies. 'I don't know what I want,' she finished miserably.

Patty, who had been unusually quiet, piped up. 'If he's a nice boy he won't try to kiss you on the first date, and I reckon Taffy's nice, don't you?'

Lucy nodded. 'Are you sure about that though?'

'That's what me mam's allus said.' Mimicking her mother, she wagged a reproving finger as she rattled off her mother's words of advice: 'Just you remember, our Patty, good girls don't kiss on the first date, and nice boys don't ask.'

'That's that then,' said Dana as they made their way towards their billet. 'Taffy looked quite shy to me. I dare say he's not the sort to try and kiss a girl on the first date. In fact, you could be his first kiss too.'

Lucy giggled. 'Oh, great, so neither of us will know what to do!'

'You wanna be grateful some bugger's asked you out,' said Patty with a hint of bitterness. 'No one's so much as looked in my direction, yet you and Dana've both had fellers vyin' for your attention.'

A small smile crossed Lucy's cheeks. 'Golly, that's right, isn't it! A month ago I was worried I'd not get a look in with Dana around, but Taffy come straight for me, didn't he?'

'There you are, so stop whingein' and just you be grateful.'

'Don't worry, Patty, you'll find someone. Trust me: if I can, anyone can.'

The girls had been at Innsworth for several months and Patty stared gloomily at her reflection in Lucy's compact mirror as she got ready to go to the dance in the NAAFI; then, snapping it shut, she placed it on the bed beside Dana. 'Silk purses an' all that.'

Speaking through a mouthful of hairgrips, Dana glanced at Patty. 'Stop bein' so hard on yourself; there's nowt wrong wi' the way you look.' Picking up the mirror, she checked her own reflection. 'I take it you're hopin' to catch the attention of a certain corporal?'

'Any flippin' corporal would do,' said Patty with a heartfelt sigh. 'Although I must admit I wouldn't shy away from that new feller what's startin' the aircraft fitter's course.'

Fluttering her eyelashes Lucy clasped her hands to her chest in a theatrical manner. 'You mean Corporal Ricky Evans?'

Patty aimed a playful swipe at Lucy, who managed to dart to one side. 'It's all right for you with your ...' She imitated Lucy by batting her lashes. '... darlin' Taffy.'

Lucy grinned. 'My darling Taffy,' she repeated. 'Whoever thought all these months later we'd be official?'

118

Dana and Patty exchanged a meaningful glance. 'Everybody bar you?' said Patty.

Lucy entwined her fingers around her tie in a dreamlike fashion. 'Since I came to Innsworth I've had me first boyfriend, me first kiss and me first ...' She looked at Patty, whose eyes had rounded with interest. Lucy straightened her tie. '... me first taste of beer! Honestly, Patty Blackwood, what type of girl do you take me for?'

'Whatever do you mean?' said Patty with a chuckle. She looked at Dana. 'Have you heard from Lenny lately?'

Dana took the last grip from between her lips and pushed it firmly into place. 'Yes, he's still at Pwllheli.' A small frown creased her brow. 'For some odd reason he kept talkin' about how we should be kind to the German ex-pats who were livin' in this country.'

Lucy pouted. 'That's odd, and I'm not sure I totally agree with him.'

Dana looked up from the handheld mirror. 'I haven't the foggiest what he was on about.'

Patty eyed her friend curiously. 'Do you ever regret not tellin' him the truth?'

Dana shook her head. 'Better to have him as a friend than not at all.'

'If he didn't want to be with you because of your heritage, then surely he wouldn't be a true friend?' said Lucy reasonably.

Standing up from her bed, Dana pushed her feet into her shoes. 'Like everyone here, you mean?' She looked at the blank expression on her friends' faces. 'I've lots of friends in Innsworth, but none of them know who I am.'

Patty pulled a face. 'I dare say they wouldn't give two hoots if they knew the truth.'

Dana shrugged. 'Mebbe you're right, but if you're not, why would I want to build a rod for me own back? Life's hard enough as it is.'

Lucy took Dana's tie and placed it around her neck. 'You and Lenny could have had summat special. It seems a shame you won't even try.'

Dana shot her a wry look as Lucy pushed her tie into place. 'That's all very well for you to say, you landed lucky with Taffy.'

Standing back, Lucy looked at Dana's tie and then stepped forward to adjust it slightly. 'I s'pose so, or at least I don't know how he'd have felt about me if he hadn't been an orphan too.'

'There you are then,' said Dana, 'but I don't think Lenny's a traveller, d'you?'

Lucy was about to shake her head when she thought better of it. 'How can you tell? I'd never have known you were, unless you'd told me, so whilst I'll grant you it's unlikely, I wouldn't say it was impossible.'

This was something Dana hadn't considered until now, but she supposed Lucy was right. Dana couldn't possibly be the only traveller in the services, and in uniform everyone looked more or less the same, so ... She shook her head. 'There's coincidences, like you and Taffy, and then there's ...' Her brow furrowed as she tried to think of something bigger than a coincidence. '... a miracle?' she ventured. 'Or at least summat like that.'

'I wish I were in your position,' said Patty to Dana. 'It must be nice to be wanted. No one here's given me a second glance. I bet someone sufferin' with the plague'd have more chance with the fellers than me.'

Lucy stifled a chuckle. 'A little birdie told me that Halitosis Winston had been puttin' the moves on you. What's wrong wi' him?'

Patty shot Lucy a withering look. 'For the little birdie's information, Halitosis Winston was not tryin' it on wi' me, he was merely askin' my advice on the quickest route to his destination.'

Lucy shuddered. 'I hope it was the dentist.'

A giggle slipped Patty's lips. 'You'd be lucky. Poor feller, I don't think he's gorra clue.'

Dana glanced at the clock above the door to their billet. 'Seein' as how the dance started ten minutes ago, I suggest we stop talkin' about Halitosis Winston and make our way to the NAAFI.'

Patty straightened her jacket. 'Do I pass muster?'

Lucy eyed her fondly. 'Yes you do, you allus have, the only person who doesn't believe it is you.'

Patty pouted. 'Then why don't any of the fellers ever ask me out?'

Dana paused. This was a subject which she and Lucy had been discussing earlier that day, whilst Patty was making her deliveries around the station.

'It can't be the way she looks,' Lucy had said as they joined the queue for lunch. 'And she always smells nice.'

'And it's not as if she's shy around them.'

Lucy nodded fervently. 'You're tellin' me! She's allus the first one to volunteer for anythin' and she can do any job the fellers can.'

'Mebbe that's it,' said Dana. 'Mebbe they feel a bit intimidated. I saw her heavin' a sack of coal on to her shoulders the other day when they were fallin' behind wi' the deliveries.'

Lucy grimaced. 'You mean they're after a lady, not one of the lads?'

'Precisely!'

'D'you reckon we should tell her?' Lucy had asked apprehensively. 'I wouldn't want to upset her; she's a heart of gold has Patty.'

Now, as they made their way to the door, Dana said, tentatively, 'You know how you help the fellers when they're runnin' behind?'

Patty nodded. 'What of it?'

'Mebbe they see you as one of them, and that's why they don't ask you out.'

Patty's brow furrowed even further. 'Your dad allus said you were as good as any feller, yet they still ask you out!'

Dana mulled this over. 'True, but Dad meant when it came to ridin', or handlin' the horses.' She pulled an awkward face. 'I didn't carry sacks of feed, or anythin' heavy. I left that to the fellers.'

Patty's lips formed an O as the penny dropped. 'I thought I was bein' helpful ...'

'And you were,' said Lucy. 'Only perhaps a tad too helpful.'

'So don't carry coal?' said Patty a trifle uncertainly.

Lucy nodded. 'A feller wants to be the man in the relationship, the strong one; he don't want to wonder whether his girl can lift more sacks of coal than him.'

Patty giggled. 'When you put it like that ...'

'No more actin' like one of the lads?' said Dana.

'From now on I'm goin' to be every bit the lady!' said Patty.

March 1941

Lucy entered the NAAFI at a brisk trot and scanned the tables with a nervous eye until she found Dana and Patty, both of whom were waving in order to gain her attention. The piece of paper gripped firmly between her fingers, she headed towards them.

Patty pushed the chair opposite her out with her foot and smiled up at Lucy, although her smile soon faded when she saw the look of dismay etched on Lucy's face. 'What's up, chuck?'

Lucy handed the piece of paper over for Dana and Patty to read.

Dana couldn't believe her eyes – their friend was being relocated. 'When did this happen?'

'Just now,' said Lucy. 'I were on my way here when Sarge called me over and handed it to me.'

'Have you told Taffy?' said Patty, a spoonful of rice pudding halfway to her mouth.

Lucy shook her head. 'He won't come off duty until later on this evening.'

'Have they said why you've been posted to Yeovil?'

'No, just that it's where they keep the barrage balloons, and that I'm needed there, although he did say we'd all be leavin' sooner or later.'

Dana read the piece of paper again before handing it back to Lucy. 'I can't believe it. I know it may sound a bit naïve, but I honestly thought we were goin' to stay together throughout the duration of the war.'

'Me too!' Lucy agreed. 'I nearly dropped on the spot when he handed me this. I asked if there was someone else who could go instead of me, and that's when he said it didn't make any difference because we're all goin' to be reposted.'

Patty and Dana exchanged worried looks. 'Did he say when?'

'No ...' A large tear plopped off her cheek on to the paper.

Dana got off her seat and sat next to her friend. 'On the bright side, Taffy's goin' to be passin' out soon, which means he'll be leavin' for pastures new. If you're lucky, you may go to the same station, but if you were to stay here you'd be split up for definite.'

'But I don't sleep with Taffy.' The words were out of Lucy's mouth before she realised how they sounded. For the first time since receiving the news, she giggled. 'I meant I don't share a billet with Taffy, or boot polish, or make-up ...'

'Lucy, sweetheart,' said Dana, 'it's not the end of the world. We'll write all the time, and we can allus come an' visit.' She smiled brightly at Lucy in an attempt to reassure her. 'It'll be like a little holiday.'

Sniffing back the tears, Lucy nodded. 'I know, it's just ...'

'Not how you thought things would pan out,' said Patty.

Lucy nodded miserably. 'I wish you two were comin' with me. I'm not goin' to know anyone there.'

'You'll soon make friends, just like you did with us.' Standing up, Dana jerked her head in the direction of the counter. 'How about a nice cup of tea and a bun?'

'Thanks, Dana.'

Patty scraped the last of the rice pudding from her bowl. 'You've still got a few days before you go, why don't we nip into town and have a bit of a wander? That allus cheers you up.'

'I haven't got any money,' said Lucy, who was not in the mood for cheerful outings.

Patty, however, was determined to lighten her friend's mood. 'The cathedral's allus good for a visit, and it's free of course,' she said brightly.

Dana placed the bun and cup of tea down in front of Lucy. 'There you go. Get that inside you – you'll soon feel better.' Sitting down in the seat next to Lucy, she continued, 'Are you goin' to tell Taffy as soon as he gets off this evenin'?'

Lucy, who had already taken a large bite of the bun, spoke rather thickly. 'Mmm-hhmm. I don't see the point in puttin' it off.' Her shoulders deflated. 'At least I'll get letters now.'

'Heaps of them,' said Patty. 'We'll not give you time to miss us, will we, Dana?'

'Nope. We'll want to know everythin' you do from the moment you get up to the minute you go to sleep, what the station's like ...' She paused uncertainly. 'Did you say you were goin' somewhere where they had barrage balloons?'

'That's right. Why?'

'You'll be the first one amongst us to go to a real RAF station, where things actually take off and land. I bet it'll be way more interestin' than sittin' round here all day.'

'No more darnin' socks whilst waitin' for a call in the fire engine.' Patty shook her head. 'I still reckon they had a bloomin' cheek askin' you to darn their socks. I bet they wouldn't've asked a feller!'

Lucy smiled. 'I didn't mind. It's better than sittin' round twiddlin' your thumbs all day.'

Dana glanced at the clock above the door to the NAAFI. 'I'm afraid I've got to go, but how about we see if there's a dance somewhere this evenin' – off camp that is?'

'Sounds good to me.' Lucy paused for a moment. 'Gosh I'm goin' to miss you two!'

As Dana left the NAAFI her tummy did a somersault. If what Lucy said was true, they would all be leaving the safety of Innsworth and heading out to real stations with working aircraft. Not only that, but it was highly likely they wouldn't be posted together, or anywhere near each other, come to that. It was all very well her telling Lucy that she'd soon make friends and to look on the bright side, but Dana's stomach was doing cartwheels at the very thought of going off on her own. It hadn't come to her attention until now, but landing on Patty's doorstep and making a good friend straight away had made life a lot easier. Had Eccleston House been full that night, she would more than likely have headed back to the safety of her parents and the wagon, no matter what she might have told herself at the time. Life with friends was a lot easier than life without them, especially when you were a minority, but she couldn't tell Lucy that, the poor girl was upset enough as it was. Dana's imagination started to race as she wondered where she would be sent and what it would be like. It would be good if they sent her back to Pwllheli, she mused, then she would be close to Lenny. Dana's lips curved into a smile at the thought of Lenny. She'd never admit it to Patty or Lucy, but Dana had quite a crush on the Welsh corporal; she regarded him as her knight in shining armour, because he had managed to teach her to drive properly when everyone else had failed. If she told her friends, she knew they would only encourage her to accept any future advances Lenny might make, whereas Dana would rather keep things how they were, at least until she knew for sure how he would react to the news that she was a traveller. She felt guilty about turning him down in Pwllheli, but she would rather that than run the risk of seeing the look of disappointment on his face if she were to tell him the truth. Her heart sank as she pictured his face when she turned him down. It had been like scolding a puppy, and she'd taken no pleasure in hurting his feelings, especially when they were reciprocated, but what choice had she had?

When he had said he wanted to stay friends, Dana had thought he was only saying this to save face, and that she would probably never hear from him again. After all, a lot of men would have sulked – but not Lenny; true to his word he wrote at least once a fortnight. His letters were always fun and light-hearted, and he never once mentioned their relationship; he had respected her feelings and as a result she never felt badgered. She heaved a sigh. Any woman would jump at the chance if Lenny were to ask them out, and she had to admit she would not like to hear that Lenny had found himself a girlfriend, even though she had no right to object.

Heading towards her staff car, she tried to shake the thought of Lenny with another woman from her mind. No sense in upsetting yourself, she thought grimly, Lenny's probably too busy to meet anyone. She imagined him taking another Waaf for extra lessons in his car and then scolded herself. She was being silly; if she were to write to Lenny telling him she'd like to meet up, she was pretty sure he'd be here quick as a flash. You're only gettin' upset, Dana thought to herself, because you're worried you might be taken away from your friends. You've come a long way from that girl who got turned away from every house bar one, you've lived a little and it's not done you any harm, nor would it do you harm to spread your wings and fly on your own should the need arise. With this thought she opened the boot of her car, removed the crank handle and headed towards the bonnet.

Pete admired the brevet that adorned the left breast of his jacket. He had worked hard for this, and he had loved every minute. Never had he felt as alive as when he was sitting on the grassy runway, waiting for the order to take off. The only thing that irked him was that his father had been a pilot in the last lot, and when Pete had told him the good news, all he did was make comparisons between the two of them. It wasn't that Pete didn't love his father, because he did, he just didn't like being compared to him. His father was boring – the sort of man who paid people to do all the hard work whilst he reaped the rewards. Whereas Pete was a worker; he loved being in the thick of things and relished the danger that flying brought. To Pete, life was one big adventure. Knowing that his father had once flown against the same enemy, but was now a fat old man who thought himself above everything and everyone, made Pete shudder. He'd rather die than turn out like his father.

He cast his mind back to the telephone call he had made, hoping to speak to his mother.

'Pete?' he heard his mother turn away from the phone to call out to his father. 'It's Pete.'

'Mum?' said Pete urgently, hoping that she would remain on the line, 'I've got some good news—'

'Have you, by God?' came the voice of Archie Robinson, Pete's father. 'I trust you're ringing to say you've got your wings?'

Pete swore in the privacy of his own head. He hadn't wanted to tell his father because he knew he would turn the conversation to himself and his time in the RFC. 'Yes, Dad.'

'You're your father's son all right, passed first time just like your old man, eh?' Turning away from the receiver Pete heard his father relay the news to his mother.

'That's wonderful news, Pete, well done and congratulations!'

His father turned back to the receiver. 'Did you get that?'

'Yes, tell her—' Archie Robinson broke in before he could finish.

'It was a bit different in my day of course, we didn't have half the swanky new equipment you fellers have today, lot more dangerous too ...'

Pete tuned out as his father continued to drone on.

When I have a son, or rather if I have a son, thought Pete, I'll make sure he's the one standing in the limelight. He wondered what other people would think if they knew how he felt about his life. They would probably think that he was an ungrateful little rich boy, who had it all, wanted for nothing, and was too spoilt to see it. How could he explain that he'd willingly give up the money, the horses and the fancy house, just to have his father tell him he'd done well? All he wanted was his father to be proud of him, instead of telling him how he could improve his life. He'll be banging on about me getting myself a nice little Waaf next, thought Pete sullenly.

'You've still a long way to go before you catch up to your father, but it'll take some time to make flight lieutenant – that's if you get there of course.' He paused briefly, and Pete was about to make his excuses and end the call before his father continued, 'You got yourself a girlfriend yet? Now you're a pilot you'll have a much better pick of the crop, but don't get too serious, because as you climb the ladder, the fillies get better!' His father roared with laughter at his own words.

Pete shook his head. 'I've got to go, Dad, give my love to Mum.

'What? Oh, very well. Goodbye, Peter.'

'It's Pete, not Peter,' said Pete as the noise of the receiver being hung up came down the earpiece.

Pete placed his own receiver down and stared at the telephone. Why couldn't his father be happy with him the way he was? Pete could understand if his father wanted Pete to do better for himself, but he didn't. He wanted Pete to do well because he wanted Pete to be just like him. He gave a short mirthless laugh. It made Pete want to do the exact opposite of his father, but he couldn't give up flying: whether he liked it or not, that was one thing he and his father had in common.

Trotting across the wooden floor of their billet, Patty slit the envelope open with her finger. 'Letter from Lucy! I wonder how she's gettin' on.'

Dana shuffled up so that Patty could sit on the bed beside her. 'I hope she's all right. I know she put on a brave face, but you could tell she were nervous about leavin' …'

Both girls fell silent as they began to read the letter.

Dear Dana and Patty,

What a journey. I didn't get to ****** 'That must have said "Yeovil",' said Dana. *until the early hours of the morning, I couldn't see me lift when this feller turns up on a motorbike, grabs me* ****** Patty glanced at Dana. 'I think that was "kitbag" before the censors had their fun!' *and says, 'Are you* **** *Lucy Jones?* 'That'll be "ACW2",' said Patty. *I've come to take you to* ****** '"Yeovil",' Dana supplied. *You could've knocked me down with a feather! I was going to say that I'd never been on a motorbike when I noticed the sidecar. It was a real hoot riding at the side of Ted — that's the name of the* *********** '"Aircraftman", probably,' guessed Dana. *who came to pick me up. I felt like Biggles himself was whisking me off on an adventure!*

131

Things are far more relaxed here and I share a two-bedroom terraced house with four other *****. '"Waafs",' of course,' said Patty. *They're all friendly and they made me feel right at home straight away which was nice.*

It's a lot more fun here than it is in ********* 'That's "Innsworth",' Patty volunteered. *because you get to go off station every day and I'm always meeting new people.*

I can't wait for you both to come and visit, just wait till you see the ******* ******** 'Must be "barrage balloons",' guessed Patty. *they're enormous! The men and women who operate them are incredibly strong, not to mention brave.*

Taffy wrote to say he's at one of the ****** ******** '"Bomber stations"?' surmised Patty. *in *******.* 'Can you make that out? Does it say "Lincoln"?' Dana said, squinting at the page. *He's going to come and see me first bit of ****** 'I think that means "leave",' said Patty. *he gets, so between him and you two I'm hoping I shall never be short of company. How I wish you were here with me!*

Love to both,
Lucy xxx

Dana folded the letter and placed it in her locker. 'I was dreading being moved to a different station, but after reading that, I'm rather looking forward to it.'

'It certainly sounds exciting,' agreed Patty. 'And it must be nice to do the job you've been trained to do. She sounds like she's havin' a ball.'

'Fingers crossed we go somewhere like Lucy's airfield. I can't wait to go an' see her,' said Dana.

Patty nodded. 'But not until we've seen me mam. I can't explain why, but I've had this awful sense of impending doom lately, like summat bad's about to happen.'

Chapter Five

May 1941

As she looked out of the small attic window in Eccleston House, Dana's bottom lip trembled at the scene of devastation below. Lord Street had been reduced to rubble, and from what the taxi driver had told them the previous evening, much of Liverpool was the same.

'I ain't never seen owt like it,' said the driver as he wound his way around the deserted streets. 'There was hundreds of 'em, droppin' their bombs willy nilly. I'm surprised there's anythin' left of the city.' He half turned in his seat to look at the girls. 'In fact I reckern it were a good job they quit when they did else you'd not have a home to go to.'

Despite the blackout, the girls could still see the carnage which had been inflicted on their beautiful city during the first week of May. Dana, tears in her eyes as they passed yet another street bereft of its buildings, turned to Patty. 'If it hadn't been for that sergeant changin' his mind, we'd've been in the thick of it.'

Patty nodded pitifully. 'I was mad as fire when he reneged on our leave, but who knows what would've happened if he hadn't?'

Now, peering out of the window, Dana gazed in disbelief at the city which she no longer recognised.

Patty knocked briefly on the attic door. 'You decent?'

'Come in.'

Patty's face appeared around the corner of the door. 'Mam wants to know if you're ready for brekker.'

Nodding, Dana picked her cap up off the bed and walked towards the door. 'Have you seen outside?'

Patty nodded. 'Sickening, isn't it?'

'Dad did the right thing by leavin', although I may not have thought so at the time,' said Dana as they descended the stairs. 'We'd not have stood a chance in the wagon.'

'That's what me mam said. She reckerns it were fate, of course.' Patty rolled her eyes.

Dana glanced guiltily at Patty. 'Imagine if they'd stayed because of me?' She shuddered. 'I'd never've forgiven meself.'

'When are you goin' to telephone them?'

'Dad asked if I'd let him know how Freddie and the other carters were, so I thought we could go an' see them first, then go for a wander round the city. That way I'll have all the news before I ring them round eleven.'

One of Mrs Blackwood's lodgers stood to one side at the bottom of the stairs in order to allow the girls through. He gave them each a small courteous nod. 'Ladies.'

Dana returned the greeting, before realising who the man was. She waited until she heard him ascend the stairs before hissing to Patty from corner of her mouth. 'I remember him; he were the one who said he'd leave if your mam didn't get rid of me.'

Patty grinned. 'I know.'

'Well he's certainly changed his tune! D'you reckern your mam said summat, mebbe warned him to keep a civil tongue in his head?'

Patty grinned. 'Oh, she said summat all right. She told him he were welcome to leave. That soon shut him up, but that's not why he's bein' polite.' Her grin broadened. 'He didn't recognise you in your uniform.' She started to chuckle. 'He'd be spittin' feathers if he knew he'd been nice to you!'

Dana glanced back up the stairs. 'I've half a mind to go up and remind him who I am, just to see the look on his face!'

'Who knows, it might teach him a lesson.' Patty wagged her finger in an admonitory manner. 'You shouldn't judge a book by its cover.'

Mrs Blackwood peered around the corner of the kitchen door, holding a wooden spoon in one hand. 'I hope you two aren't upsettin' me customers.'

Dana beamed. 'Wouldn't dream of it, Mrs B.' Careful to avoid the porridge-covered spoon, she hugged her friend's mother. 'It's so good to see you again, and it's great to be back, even if I can't tell one street from the other any more.'

Mrs Blackwood ushered them into the kitchen. 'Aye, a lot's changed, that's for certain. You an' Patty're a

136

real sight for sore eyes. It's good to have you back, the pair of you. Now sit yourselves down and have a bit of brekky. If you're intendin' to have a wander around the city, and I dare say you are, you'll need to know what's what 'cos there's a few places what's been cordoned off for everyone's safety – a lot of the buildin's close to the bombin' are on the brink of collapse.'

After a hearty breakfast of tea, toast and porridge, Dana and Patty headed into the city, or what was left of it. 'I know your mam warned us, and I've seen a fair bit from my attic winder, but you can't imagine how bad it is till you get in amongst it.'

'It's hard to imagine this is the same city I grew up in,' said Patty.

The girls made their way to Ashfield Street and Dana was pleased to see a familiar face, even if it did belong to a horse. 'Neanor!' A man's head appeared above Neanor's rump.

'Who's that?'

Dana beamed. 'It's me, Mr McGregor.'

Norman McGregor peered at her suspiciously, before his cheeks broke into a wide grin. 'Blow me down, if it ain't our Dana!' Resting the grooming brush on top of Neanor's rump, he strode round the back of the horse and placed a friendly arm around Dana's shoulders. 'Fancy seein' you here, and lookin' right smart in your uniform. Someone said you'd joined the Waafs – can't think who. How's your mam and dad, have you heard off 'em?'

'I'm goin' to telephone around eleven o'clock. Dad asked me to pop by before I did, so I could tell him how you're all gettin' on. He's heard about the bomb-in's of course.'

Norman jerked a thumb towards Neanor. 'She's lucky to be alive – we all are, come to that.' He leaned against the side of the house. 'The air raid sirens were goin' off like all hell were breakin' loose, but we didn't think much of it 'cos we hadn't had much since Christmas.' He had removed the cap from his head and was feeding the rim through his fingers. 'We couldn't've been more wrong. I seen 'em as soon as I stepped outside, like a cloud of mossies they was, and the 'osses was goin' mad with fear. Freddie, Martha and some of the others went to the shelter in Gaskill Road ...' Looking up from his cap his eyes briefly connected with Dana's before he hastily looked back at his hat. Dana was sure she had seen tears forming in his eyes. 'Me missus wanted to take the kids and go wiv 'em, only I remembered what your dad said about how he hated the shelters 'cos you was like sittin' ducks, so I told me missus and the little 'uns to stay wi' me.' He shook his head. 'She was callin' me fit to burn.'

Dana felt her throat go hollow. 'We've just passed Gaskill Road, there's nothing left ...' She looked at him, but he kept his head down. 'God, no,' she whispered beneath her breath.

Nodding solemnly, Norman continued to stare at his feet. 'It were a direct hit – poor blighters never stood a chance. The bombs rained heavy all night; we didn't get a chance to try and help until the early hours, but we were too late. There was nowt we could do.' He shook his head miserably. 'Did you know they hit the stables on Vauxhall Road?'

Silent tears trickled down Dana's cheeks. 'Dad used to love goin' there, reckoned it reminded him of Ireland when he were a nipper.'

Wiping an errant tear from his cheek, Norman forced his lips into a smile. 'No point cryin' over the past; what's done is done. You can tell your dad I owe him big time. If it weren't for him we'd've been in that shelter with the rest of them poor buggers.'

'I will.' She averted her gaze to Neanor. 'What about Millie?'

Coughing, Norman shook his head. 'We ain't seen her since the bombin'. We don't know whether she run off or whether she's ...' He glanced meaningfully at Dana, who tearfully nodded her understanding. He pushed himself away from the wall and, in what Dana presumed to be an attempt to change the subject, pointed admiringly at Dana and Patty's uniforms. 'Has your mam and dad seen you in your uniform?'

Dana nodded. 'I sent them a photograph. Mam reckons Dad carries it in his toolbox, shows it to anyone who'll stand still long enough.'

He chuckled softly. 'Nowt wrong wi' bein' proud, I'm proud of you and you ain't even mine.'

Patty nudged Dana. 'Sorry to interrupt but we'd better gerra move on if you want to ring your mam and dad on time.' She pointed at the small face of her wristwatch.

Norman placed his cap back on his head. 'It's been good to see you again; the missus'll be sorry she missed you. Make sure you give your folks our best.'

Dana nodded. 'Ta-ra, Norman.'

Norman called after her, 'Make sure you look after yourself, chuck.'

The girls scoured the ruined streets in the hopes of finding a telephone box, so that Dana might ring her parents, but their search was proving fruitless.

'They've all gone!' said Dana. 'I'll never get to speak to them at this rate.'

Patty pulled a face. 'P'raps we could ask at a police station, see if they can give us some advice, or at least point us in the right direction?'

'That's if we can find one,' muttered Dana. 'I haven't a clue where I am – I feel like I'm a stranger in me own home.'

Patty stopped short. 'Am I seein' things or is that ...?'

'A telephone box!' squealed Dana. Crossing her fingers she trotted towards the smart red box, which stood out like a sore thumb amongst the ruined buildings.

'Does it work?' asked Patty with doubtful anticipation. Dana lifted the receiver, dialled zero and nodded to Patty as the sound of the operator's voice came down the line. Dana spoke into the telephone. 'Can you connect me to Clarke's Bar, Fair Street in Drogheda, Ireland, please?'

Patty watched as Dana went through the motions, crossing her fingers. Dana waited anxiously.

Colleen's tinny voice came down the line. 'Hello? Is that you, Dana?'

Beaming, Dana spoke hurriedly into the telephone for fear they might get cut off. 'Yes, Mam, I'm in Liverpool! How are you and Dad?'

Colleen's voice went distant as though she had turned away from the telephone. 'It's our Dana.' Her voice became clear once more. 'It's grand to hear your voice, luvvy. How are you?'

Dana giggled with relief that her mother sounded so well. 'I'm fine, Mam. How are you an' Dad?'

'Oh, we're all right. Not a lot happens here war wise, but we've been keepin' up with the news 'n' the papers an' that.' She paused. 'Is it as bad as it looks?'

Dana twisted her fingers around the telephone cable. 'Worse! There's hardly anythin' left.' The other end had fallen silent. 'Mam?'

Dana's father's voice came down the telephone. 'Sorry about that, love, your mam's havin' a bit of a cry.'

'Dad!' Her voice wobbled as she looked at the scene of devastation around her. 'I'm so sorry! You were right about the city, and how we'd be better off leavin'. I should never've said the things I did—'

Her father interrupted before she could continue. 'Don't be daft. I'm just glad you're safe. Have you seen any of the carters?'

'I saw Norman and Neanor earlier ...' Dana relayed Norman's story about the shelter on Gaskill Road, and when she got to the bit about the Tidswells, she heard her father gasp.

'Didn't I say them bloody shelters were dangerous!' said Shane, and Dana could hear her mother in the background, asking what he was talking about. 'Thank goodness he didn't go in.' Dana heard her father turn away from the receiver and relay the conversation to her mother, who then said earnestly to her husband, her voice nasal from crying:

'Tell her not to go in any shelters.'

Her father passed the message on, adding for his wife's benefit, 'I bet they've proper shelters on the RAF stations.'

In truth, the shelters were no better on the stations than they were in the cities, so Dana sidestepped the answer. 'I bet you don't need shelters in Ireland.'

'We do,' Shane admitted. 'We have to in case we get caught in the crossfire, but we ain't in any real danger, not like you poor buggers over there.'

Dana felt a sudden wave of nostalgia. 'As soon as I get a decent bit of leave I'm goin' to come straight over to Ireland.'

'No!' said Shane sharply.

'Why?' said Dana, who couldn't help feeling a little hurt at her father's abrupt response.

Shane's voice softened. 'Me an' your mam've talked about you comin' over, and we reckern it's too dangerous. Wait until things've calmed down. The seas are treacherous an' we don't want you riskin' your life just to come an' see us.'

Dana wanted to protest, but deep down she knew her father was right.

'Well, as soon as it's safe to do so, I'll be on the first ferry.' She hesitated. 'How's work goin'?'

She could hear the smile in her father's voice as he spoke down the receiver. 'Couldn't be better. Turns out the feller who was seein' to the horses before I come home decided to sign up.' He cleared his throat in a boastful fashion. 'And accordin' to old man

O'Brien, he weren't anywhere near as good as your old dad.'

'Caller ...' the operator's voice cut across before Dana had chance to answer.

'I'll have to go, Dad, but I'll write as soon as I get back to Innsworth.'

'Ta-ra, Dana, take care, luv ... and Dana?'

'Yes?'

'You're doin' us proud, kiddo,' was all Shane managed to say before the line went dead.

Patty slipped her arm through Dana's. 'Happy?'

Dana nodded. 'Very!'

July 1941

Blazing sunshine poured through the window of the Nissen hut directly on to Dana's bed. In an attempt to cool off she had stripped down to her vest and knickers and was currently sitting on the floor, fanning herself with a copy of *Woman's Own*.

The door to the hut burst open and Patty walked towards her flourishing a fistful of envelopes.

'You've one off Lenny, and I've another off me mam, but two of 'em are official. Sarge handed me them – he says it's our new placement.'

Dana placed the magazine down to one side. 'Looks like we're leavin' together.'

Patty grinned. 'Let's hope we're goin' to the same station.' Slitting her envelope open she scanned the contents before looking eagerly at Dana who was reading her own. 'Well? What does it say?'

Dana looked up. 'Somewhere called Harrowbeer, in Devon ...'

Grinning triumphantly, Patty turned her letter round to show Dana. 'Snap!'

Dana smiled. 'We'll have to tell Lucy so she'll know where she can reach us. According to this I've got four days' leave before I have to be there. Are you the same?'

'Oh, I'm not sure, hang on a mo ...' Patty glanced back at the paper before giving a short squeal of excitement. 'Me too! But will it be enough to go and visit Lucy?'

Dana stood up. 'I dunno. Lucy's in Yeovil and I've no idea how far that is from Devon. They could be on opposite sides of the country for all I know.'

One of the Waafs from further down the billet piped up. 'Yeovil's about halfway between here and Devon, four days should give you plenty of time to visit your pal.'

'We'll have to tell everyone where we're movin' to.' She nodded at the letter in Dana's hands. 'What does Lenny say?'

Dana pulled Lenny's letter from its envelope.

Dear Dana,

Good news! I'm coming to Innsworth in a few weeks. I'm hopin' to be there for a few days ...

Dana hurriedly scanned the rest of the letter, searching for a date but could find nothing. She held it out to Patty, who was still reading the letter from her mother.

'Lenny's coming to Innsworth in a few weeks, but he doesn't say when. What if he comes the day we're leaving, or after?'

'You'd better telephone his station and see what his plans are. It'd be a real shame if he came all this way for nothing ...' She hesitated. 'Is he comin' on leave or ...'

'Dunno.' Dana was tying her shoelaces as she spoke. 'Sooner I speak to him sooner we can sort it out. I'll telephone his station now, see if I can get hold of him.'

She crossed the yard and entered the NAAFI. Once inside she made a beeline for the telephone. After a moment or so a man's voice came down the line.

'I want to speak to Lenny Ackerman, is he there?' said Dana.

'Hold on a mo.' The man's voice was muffled as he placed a hand over the receiver and called over his shoulder, 'Lenny, there's a woman on the phone for you.'

A chorus of cheers went up and Dana could hear Lenny informing the room in general that the woman was probably his mother.

'Is that you, Mam?' said Lenny cheerfully.

Hearing his dulcet tones, Dana smiled. 'It's me, Dana.'

'Dana!' said Lenny, sounding surprised. Dana heard the catcalls in the background, which Lenny hastily hushed into silence. 'Did you get my letter?'

'Yes, that's why I'm ringin', you didn't say when you were comin'.'

'Didn't I? Oh well, not to worry. I'll be there on the twenty-fifth ...' He hesitated. 'You're not goin' anywhere, are you?'

Dana smiled with relief. 'Me and Patty are movin' to RAF Harrowbeer in Devon, but we're going to see

145

Lucy a few days before that. We finish here on the thirtieth. It would've been such a shame if we'd left before you arrived.'

'It sure would. Am I to take it you've missed me?' said Lenny, a hint of hopefulness entering his voice.

Grateful that Lenny could not see the blush adorning her cheeks, she spoke shyly into the receiver. 'Course I have. Haven't you missed me?'

'From the minute you left,' said Lenny bluntly.

Dana grinned. 'Are you comin' on leave or work?'

'Work, I'm afraid, but I should get some free time. Have you anything in mind?'

'I thought it might be nice to take a stroll around Gloucester,' said Dana. 'It's not too far from here.'

'Sounds grand. Will it just be the two of us?' asked Lenny, who was keeping his fingers crossed that the answer would be yes.

'I can ask Patty if she'd like to come too, if that's what you'd prefer?' teased Dana.

'No, or rather I don't mind …' said Lenny, although he had no desire to share Dana with anyone else.

'I shouldn't imagine Patty would like to play gooseberry …' Dana began.

'Gooseberry?' said Lenny, the hope returning to his voice, 'As in …'

'As in two's company, three's a crowd, nothin' more.'

She heard him grinning as he spoke. 'There I was gettin' my hopes up just to have you dash 'em.' He chuckled into the receiver and Dana felt a wave of excitement flow through her body. Lenny must still be single; he'd not have made such a remark otherwise.

'Make sure you look me up as soon as you arrive. I'd better be off – I were gettin' ready for me shift when your letter come.'

''Bye, cariad.'

'Ta-ra, Lenny.'

Lenny smiled as he replaced the receiver. The evening before Dana had left Pwllheli she had made it clear there was no hope of a romantic relationship between the two of them, or at least not until they got to know each other better, and he had resigned himself to the fact that they would never become an item. Yet she obviously liked him enough to ensure they could meet up when he went to Innsworth. Perhaps absence had made the heart grow fonder. Dare he hope that Dana had had a change of heart? They hadn't seen each other for many months. He conjured up an image of Dana in his mind's eye. She was in uniform, her long strawberry locks blowing free in the wind; she held a hand out for him to join her. Sighing wistfully, Lenny placed his hands in his pockets and whistled the tune 'It's A Hap-Hap-Happy Day' as he made his way back to his table.

Dana swore as the horn from a passing vehicle caused her to catch her hand on the handle of the lorry she was trying to start. Sucking her knuckles, she turned to give the driver a piece of her mind.

'Lenny!' she said as she rubbed her knuckles better.

Lenny, who had left his vehicle to go over and say hello, looked at her injured hand. 'I hope I didn't cause that?'

Not wishing for him to blame himself Dana shook her head.

Lenny wasn't having any of it. 'What an idiot! I should've realised I might startle you. I did it without thinkin', as soon as I saw your …' He hesitated whilst he rethought his words. 'I recognised you straight away, and it was a gut reaction.'

Dana, realising that it had only been her bottom on display, eyed him shrewdly. 'You recognised me?'

Lenny grinned. 'Be fair. We went out in the car nearly every night in Pwllheli, and starting the car was part of your training!' Holding her hand up, he examined her reddened knuckles. 'No broken skin, but I bet it hurt.' His soft lips kissed her fingers and Dana felt her tummy flutter. 'Sorry about that.'

Forgetting all about the pain, she glanced towards his staff car. 'Have you just got here?'

Lenny followed her gaze. 'About half an hour ago. I thought I'd go for a ride around the station, get myself acquainted and meet the natives.' He looked past her to the vehicle she had been trying to start. 'Have you got time for a cuppa or were you just off somewhere?'

She smiled. 'I've allus time for a cuppa, and as for that' – she gestured at the lorry – 'I'm only takin' it to park up for the night.'

Lenny walked towards the front of the lorry, placed both hands on the crank handle and swung it into life. 'Least I could do,' he said as Dana thanked him.

Climbing into the driver's seat Dana leaned out of the door. 'Follow me.'

She parked the lorry with ease between two others and joined Lenny, who was waiting for her.

'You did that well,' he said, indicating the parked lorry. 'I'm impressed. You've obviously come along in leaps and bounds since you left Pwllheli.'

Dana beamed. 'I've had plenty of practice driving the fire engine. Goodness knows how Lu coped with her little legs.'

Lenny looked surprised. 'They put Lucy on the fire engine?'

Dana nodded. 'That's how she met Taffy, her boyfriend,' she said, adding, 'Thanks,' as Lenny held open the door of the cookhouse.

Lenny ordered and paid for two cups of tea, while Dana found them a table away from the noise of the kitchen. Sitting down in the seat opposite, he handed Dana her tea. 'I see they serve the same gnats' pee here as they do everywhere else.'

She blew the steam off her mug before taking a tentative sip. 'Have you been to many stations then?'

'Being a mechanic means I can get called to all sorts of places. I can be in Inverness one day and London the next.'

'A bit like a driver then,' said Dana. 'Did you learn to be a mechanic here?'

'No, it was my trade before war broke out—'

A voice hailed them from across the room. 'Wotcher!' It was Patty.

Lenny grinned. 'How's tricks?'

'Same old. Still drivin', still single, still on the lookout for Mr Right ...' She pulled out the chair next to

Lenny's and sat on it. 'Scrap that, Mr Anybody would do at the moment. I'm one of those, Lenny, allus the bridesmaid, never the bride, or in my case allus the friend, never the girlfriend.'

'Things'll be different when we get to Harrowbeer,' Dana assured her. 'New station, new start.'

'I hope so,' said Patty with feeling. 'Have you two decided where you're goin'?'

Lenny looked enquiringly at Dana. 'What d'you reckon? I'm here for a few days – the engine I'm supposed to be workin' on is stuck in Newcastle, so I'll be free all day tomorrow.'

Dana rubbed her hands together. 'Perfect! I don't have to be on duty till three, so that gives us plenty of time to visit the city.'

Lenny looked expectantly at Patty, who, much to his relief, shook her head. 'I'm coverin' for Marnie the next two days: she's got a forty-eight, so it looks as though it's goin' to be just the two of you.'

'That's a shame,' said Lenny.

'Is it?' Patty chuckled. ''Cos I could allus try and wangle some time off if you really want me to.'

Dana took a playful swipe at her friend. 'Stop teasin', Patty Blackwood.'

A soft blush invaded Lenny's neckline and he quickly changed the subject in case either of the girls noticed. 'I'd like to see the cathedral. I've heard it's magnificent.'

'It is,' enthused Dana. 'We visit quite often because it's free, although it's a bit spooky in some parts, what with all them tombs.'

Patty grinned. 'You'll be able to hold Lenny's hand this time.' She jumped out of her seat before Dana's outstretched hand could connect. 'I'm only sayin'!' She turned to Lenny. 'She squeezed mine so tight I lost all the feelin' in me fingers.'

Dana laughed. 'It was dark! I couldn't see properly and I'm tellin' you I'm sure I heard summat!'

Lenny's eyes sparkled at the thought that Dana might hold his hand. 'Sounds more tempting by the minute.'

'I shan't be so silly this time,' said Dana, ''cos I know there's nowt to be afraid of.'

Lenny cocked his head to one side. 'Very true. The dead can't hurt you.'

Dana swallowed. 'Don't mention dead people, that's what gives me the heebie-jeebies. One look at them tombs and I start wonderin' who, or rather what's inside ...'

'Tell me about it,' said Patty. She glanced at Lenny. 'She stuck to my side like glue, and she was white as a ghost by the time we left.'

'That's 'cos I get claustrophobic,' said Dana with a satisfied smile. As far as last-minute excuses went, she felt this was a good one.

Patty opened her mouth to ask how Dana could possibly suffer from claustrophobia when the cathedral was a lot bigger than the small wagon Dana used to live in, when she realised she would be giving away her friend's secret.

'Whatever the weather, I'm sure we'll have fun,' said Lenny, who was very much hoping that Dana would cling to him as she had Patty.

'After we've seen the cathedral we can have a wander round the shops; there's some lovely little cafés close by that serve the most delicious teas ...'

'Take him to Betty's,' said Patty, who was licking her lips at the very thought. 'She makes the best sandwiches and as for their scones ...' She sighed. '... heaven!'

Dana drained the tea from her cup. 'Shall we meet at the gate around ten tomorrow?'

Lenny nodded reluctantly. 'You haven't got to go now, have you?'

'Afraid so, a quick cup of tea and then back to it.'

Patty wrinkled the side of her nose. 'Me too ...' She paused. 'Where are you billeted?'

Standing up, Lenny followed the girls out of the NAAFI. 'In a house not far from here,' he said. 'I haven't actually been there yet, I've been driving most of the day and I wanted to come straight here ...' He glanced at Dana. 'But I suppose I really should go and find my billet; it's gettin' late and I've got a busy day sightseein' tomorrow.' As he spoke he leaned into the cab and produced the crank handle, and started the car. Taking his seat behind the wheel, he closed the door and wound down the window. 'See you tomorrow.'

'Ten o'clock, don't be late,' said Dana, waving him a cheery goodbye.

Patty waited until Lenny's car had disappeared from view before slipping her arm through Dana's and squeezing it excitedly. 'He's still keen on you!'

Dana gave a small moan of dismay. 'I know, and I were excited at first, 'cos I thought I'd be able to bite the bullet and tell him the truth, but now I'm not so sure.'

Patty knitted one eyebrow. 'Why not?'

Dana's stomach lurched unpleasantly at the thought. 'As soon as we were face to face, I clammed up!' She eyed Patty nervously. 'What if he runs for the hills?'

Patty wanted to say that Dana was being silly and that she should take the risk, but what if Dana was right? 'I'd like to say that Lenny isn't that shallow, and that he adores you for who you are, but we both know that prejudice can run deep, so I'm afraid you won't know his feelin's until you tell him the truth.' She heaved a sigh. 'It's a toughie: tell him and risk losin' him, or stay shtum and keep things the way they are.'

'Trust me, it's not tough,' said Dana decidedly. 'I'm goin' to hold my tongue and keep him as a friend.'

Lenny waved to Dana from the gate. 'I thought it might be nice to catch the bus into Gloucester.'

'I prefer the bus,' said Dana. 'It makes a nice change from drivin', and it gives you a chance to look at the beautiful scenery.'

Lenny grinned, pleased that Dana had approved of his decision. 'Do you go into the city much?'

'About once a fortnight if we can – they have a lovely dance hall, and the food is better, but it's cheaper to stay on the station, so we tend to stay put most of the time.'

'Same here,' said Lenny, 'although I don't go to many dances. I prefer the cinema. Have you seen ...' He clicked his fingers a few times as he tried to recall the name of the movie. '... *Rebecca*?'

A shiver went down Dana's spine. 'Yes I have, and it's enough to put you off men for life!'

'You do know it wasn't a true story?' Lenny chuckled. 'Besides, it was that Rebecca and Mrs Danvers who were the baddies, not Maxim. If anything, you should feel sorry for him.'

Dana signalled the bus, which had crested the brow of the hill and was slowly making its way towards them. She shrugged. 'My point is you never really know anyone, not really. Take Mrs de Winter: if she'd known her new husband had disposed of his wife's body in a boat and his housekeeper was bonkers, she'd have run a mile!'

Stepping on to the bus, which had pulled up beside them, Lenny took a seat by the window. 'I suppose you've got a point. If you really like someone you have to spend as much time as possible with them.' He grinned. 'But just for the record, I've never been married, and I don't own a mansion, and I've not got some mad old biddy lookin' out for me.'

Dana had started to giggle when the clippie sauntered up from behind. 'Nice to see two smilin' faces,' she cooed. 'You off into the city?'

Lenny nodded. 'Two tickets for Gloucester please.'

Dana opened her bag to get her money out, but Lenny placed his hand over hers. 'It's all right, I'll get these.'

The clippie winked at Dana. 'You've got yourself a gentleman there, love, you wanna hang on to him.' She punched a hole in each ticket and handed them to Lenny.

Lenny grinned. 'You should take the lady's advice.'

Dana arched her eyebrow. 'How do you know I'm not spoken for?'

Lenny's face dropped. 'You're not, are you?'

Dana stared out at the passing scenery, before looking back at Lenny. 'No, nor will I be, or at least not when there's a war on. I don't fancy havin' me heart broken.'

Lenny rubbed his chin thoughtfully. 'But we've no idea how long the war will go on for. What if it's still goin' in ten years? You can't tell me you're goin' to stay single for ever?'

Dana's eyes widened. 'You can't seriously think it'll go on for that long?'

Lenny shrugged. 'I hope not, but then again, I didn't think we'd still be at war nigh on two years after it began.'

Dana gazed out at the cow parsley, dandelions and daisies which covered the grass verge like a carpet. 'I suppose I'll have to cross that bridge when I come to it,' she said simply. Hearing the bus driver grind the gears, a faint smile formed on her lips and her eyes flickered towards Lenny. 'Double-declutch,' she said softly. She cocked her head to one side and gazed steadily at Lenny who, too, was smiling at the memory. 'What made you decide to join up?'

'Duty? Curiosity? Wanting to be part of things?' Lenny shrugged briefly. 'All of the above. There's lots of old-timers that can take my place in the garage, but there's not many that can walk straight into my role in the RAF, or any other service for that matter. I knew they'd need engineers; it seemed like the obvious thing to do. What about you?'

Ridiculous as it seemed, Dana hadn't expected him to ask her the same question, and of course she couldn't tell him the whole truth so ... 'I wanted to help, and so did Patty, so we decided to sign up together.'

'Have you known each other since you were kids then? You and Patty, I mean?'

Dana remembered the rhyme her mother used to say whenever she caught Dana in a fib. 'Oh, what a tangled web we weave ...' She's bloomin' right, thought Dana bitterly, I'm goin' to have to tell another lie to hide the first, only there's no way I can invent a whole childhood. Her mouth had begun to go dry; deciding it was better to skirt around the truth, she licked her lips. 'When Mam and Dad went back to Ireland I needed a place to stay, and Patty's mam owns a lodging house.'

'Gosh, I'd never have guessed your folks were Irish,' said Lenny, who felt an overwhelming sense of relief to hear her parents weren't Germans after all.

Dana had been fiddling with the zip of her black handbag, when to her annoyance the zip pull broke off. 'Damn and blast!' she exclaimed whilst feverishly trying to fix it back in place.

Lenny held out his hands. 'May I?'

Nodding, she pulled the strap of her handbag over the top of her head and handed it to him along with the zip pull. Lenny examined the pull for a moment before easing it back on to the slider. Smiling, he tested his work and then handed it back to Dana. 'There you go, good as new.'

'Thanks,' said Dana, who was almost glad the zip had broken as it had changed the subject. She stood up. 'This is where we get off.'

Lenny looked out of the window. 'I can see the cathedral.'

'Come on,' Dana said, descending from the bus, 'I can't wait to show you the stained-glass windows in the cloister. They allus look their best on a sunny day; the light casts the colours of the glass on to the floor.'

Lenny had to agree with Dana; he had never been to a church or cathedral as beautiful or magnificent as this. From the stained-glass windows to the fan-vaulted ceilings, Lenny was impressed. 'I don't see why you think it's spooky, or claustrophobic, I think it's wonderful.'

'It's those awful tombs. Why on earth they couldn't be buried like everyone else is beyond me, and I dread to think what's inside 'em after all these years.'

'Dust, I should imagine,' said Lenny, 'but certainly nothin' that could harm you. Let's finish the tour and then I'll take you for a spot of lunch in Betty's.' He rubbed his stomach. 'I've not had anythin' since breakfast.'

'Honestly!' said Dana. 'I don't know where you fellers put it all ...'

The tour guide, a stout woman in her late fifties wearing a plain green shirtwaist dress, raised her voice. 'When you're ready ...'

Dana hissed out of the corner of her mouth to Lenny, 'She were givin' one of her tours last time me and Patty come here. Patty sneezed and everyone in the group nigh on jumped out of their skins, and I got a fit of the giggles.' She grinned sheepishly. 'She weren't happy. I reckern she thought Patty'd sneezed on purpose, and to top it off, I screamed because I thought I'd seen a ghost, only it turned out to be me own reflection.'

Lenny rolled his eyes. 'That's what you call lettin' your imagination run wild!'

Dana chuckled softly, but the noise reverberated around the stone walls and she ducked behind Lenny as the woman turned and glared accusingly in their direction.

'You're gettin' me into trouble,' Lenny hissed.

Dana giggled. 'Sorry!' Holding on to Lenny's arm, she peeked around the side of him to make sure the formidable woman had moved on. Dana frowned; instead of heading towards the vestry as she had in the last tour she was standing before a door which Dana had never been through before. The woman waited until she had the group's attention before speaking in clear tones.

'The door behind me leads to the crypt, which has been out of bounds to the public as they have been using it for storage. Unfortunately they have recently discovered a significant amount of damp, so they've opened it up to sort things out. Bad news for them, but good for us as it means we are allowed a rare peek inside the crypt itself.' Several of the people in the group looked at each other with approval. Lenny looked at Dana as if this were good news.

'I say, aren't we lucky?' he exclaimed, adding: 'What's up?' when he saw the look of dismay on Dana's face.

'It's a crypt, Lenny! Why would anyone want to go into one of them?' she said, looking horrified. 'Isn't that where they keep all the dead people?'

Lenny clapped a hand to his mouth to stop himself from laughing. 'Oh, Dana, cariad, you do make me laugh!'

Dana pouted. 'I don't see what's so funny.'

Gazing into her eyes, he brushed a lock of hair back behind her ear. 'When she said they'd been using it as storage she didn't mean they were storing bodies.'

Dana's brow puckered. 'You're sure there aren't goin' to be bodies down there?'

Lenny offered her his hand. 'Trust me.'

Dana slid her hand into his. 'Promise me we'll leave if we see any coffins.'

Lenny placed a hand to his heart. 'Promise! We'll even keep to the back; that way we can be the first to leave should someone see a mummy ...' He snorted a chuckle. 'I'm joking! You only get mummies in Egypt.'

Dana smiled uncertainly. She had no idea what was in the large tombs they had seen inside the cathedral, but she didn't wish to appear ignorant in front of Lenny. She nodded towards the group who were disappearing into the crypt. 'Come on, we don't want to get left behind ... or lost.'

The crypt was as dark and spooky as Dana had expected, although she was thankful to see it was also free of tombs. She did let out a short gasp when the guide told them about the Bone House, so called because of the enormous quantity of bones which had accumulated in the crypt.

Sliding her hand out of Lenny's, she placed it firmly through the crook of his elbow. 'See!' she hissed quietly. 'I *told* you they used to keep dead bodies down here!'

Lenny, who was feeling mischievous, turned his head to one side and gently blew across the nape of Dana's neck from the corner of his mouth.

A short squeal escaped Dana's lips as she covered the back of her neck with the palm of her hand.

Their tour guide spun round, her eyes narrowing on Dana. 'You!' she snapped. 'I might've—'

'Sorry, that was my fault …' Lenny began.

Dana, who was clinging to Lenny for dear life, looked at him with frightened eyes. 'Can we go?'

Lenny nodded. He hadn't meant to get Dana into trouble or frighten her so much, but he was rather enjoying being held so tightly.

'Thank goodness we're out of that awful place,' said Dana as they exited the crypt.

Lenny muttered an apology underneath his breath as he led her out of the cathedral.

Dana looked confused. 'Why are you apologisin'?'

Turning his head again Lenny gently blew across the back of Dana's head.

Releasing her hold on his arm she slapped him across the bicep. 'You pig!' she gasped. 'I nearly had kittens.'

Lenny grinned. 'What's the matter?'

'You blowin' down me neck, that's what.'

'Who did you think it was?' said Lenny innocently.

Dana shot him a long-suffering glance. 'You know full well *what* I thought it was, that's why you done it.' She hesitated. 'How'd you make that growlin' noise?'

Lenny blinked. 'I didn't make a growlin' …' As he spoke his stomach let out a low rumbling sound.

Dana pointed accusingly at it. 'I can't believe you done that on purpose.'

'I did say I was hungry …' Lenny chuckled, adding, 'And I got a nice cuddle out of it.'

Truth was, Dana had also enjoyed getting close to Lenny, even if she had been scared out of her wits, not that she was about to admit it to Lenny. 'What shall we do now?'

Lenny gave her a lopsided grin. 'Lunch?' He nudged her playfully with his arm. 'My treat, seein' as how I gave you a bit of a fright?'

Dana looked up into his eyes, and for a second it felt as though her heart had stopped. She had forgotten how blue and deep-set they were, and how they twinkled when he smiled. Realising she was staring she looked down; her gaze settled on his lips, and her tummy fluttered as she recalled how the same lips had kissed her knuckles so gently the day before. Dana gave herself a mental shake. Stop staring and answer the man! 'That would be lovely, but no more playin' silly beggars, deal?'

Lenny nodded. 'Deal.'

Lenny and Dana headed for the only unoccupied table in Betty's café. 'We're lucky to've got a seat leavin' it as late as we have,' said Dana. She pointed to a large blackboard that graced the back of the counter. 'That's the menu. They change it daily 'cos they never know what they'll have, what with rationin' an' that.'

Stroking his chin, Lenny peered at the board. 'I'll have sausages, chips and beans, with some extra bread and butter. You?'

'I'll have the fishcakes,' said Dana promptly. 'They're allus good.'

Lenny ordered the food as well as a pot of tea from the woman behind the counter and was impressed when it arrived. Stabbing one of his sausages with his fork, he grinned at Dana. 'Proper sausage that! Not like the ones they serve in the RAF.'

Dana nodded. 'Told you it was good here.'

After they had finished their meals, Lenny pointed at the Victoria sponge which was visible beneath the cover of a cake stand. 'Fancy a slice?'

Dana nodded hesitantly. 'I shouldn't because I'm stuffed, but I can't turn down a slice of Betty's sponge, it's too delicious!'

Lenny smiled approvingly. 'I like a girl who likes her grub. I can't be bothered with all this watchin' your weight business,' adding, 'Not that you need to, mind you.'

Dana shrugged. 'Life's too short. Who knows what tomorrer'll bring?'

'We've got more in common than I thought,' said Lenny. He waved a hand in order to gain the waitress's attention. 'Strike whilst the iron's hot, that's what I reckon ...' He called to the waitress who was standing by the counter. 'Two slices of Victoria sponge please.' He opened his mouth to continue talking to Dana, but then looked back at the waitress. 'Make that three.'

Dana chuckled. 'Someone's hungry!'

'Not for me, for Patty. She said this was one of her favourite places to eat; it seems a shame she should miss out.'

Dana stared at him. Could he get any better? Kind, thoughtful, caring, not to mention handsome, albeit in a cheeky sort of way. 'Lenny, that's a lovely thought.'

He shrugged. 'I like Patty, and Lucy ...' His eyes flickered up to meet hers. '... and you of course.'

Dana shook her head. 'It's a shame Lucy's not here. I know she'd like to see you again.'

'I can always come an' see you when you go to Devon,' said Lenny. 'Maybe we could fix it so that Lucy comes too?'

'That would be lovely – just like old times.'

The waitress appeared with three slices of cake, one of which was wrapped in a serviette. Reaching into his pocket, Lenny pulled out a handful of change, which he counted out along with a generous tip. 'Thanks, cariad.' Using his fork to cut a chunk of cake, he smiled at Dana. 'That's good to hear.'

Dana, who thought he was talking about the cake, gazed inquisitively at him. 'Sorry?'

'That you'd like to meet up again. I was hoping you would.'

'Of course I would. We've been through a lot, you and me – heck, if it weren't for you I'd probably still be crunchin' me way through the gears.'

'Oh,' said Lenny. He couldn't help but feel a little disappointed.

Dana spoke thickly as she held a hand over her mouthful of cake. 'Isn't that what you meant?'

'Yes.' Lenny rallied, although in truth he rather hoped that Dana wanted to meet up because she had started to reciprocate his feelings. He placed the forkful of cake into his mouth and let it melt on his tongue; smiling to himself he nodded approvingly. 'Bloomin' lovely.' He leaned closer to Dana. 'Although not as good as me mam's. You'd love her Victoria sponge; she makes her own jam.' He joined the tips of his fingers to his thumb and kissed them. 'Does your mam bake?'

Dana inhaled in surprise; then she started to cough as some of the cake went down the wrong way. Tears pouring down her cheeks, she pointed at her back. Lenny, however, had already got to his feet and was standing behind her; the flat of his hand raised, he slapped her sharply between her shoulder blades.

Dana raised a thumb in the air as she started breathing once more.

'You're meant to eat it, not inhale it,' he joked.

Dana smiled as she wiped the tears from her cheeks. 'Sorry, that was my fault, not concentratin'.'

The waitress came over with a glass of water. 'You all right? Take a sip of that.'

Dana nodded thankfully before taking a few small sips. 'Thanks, that's a lot better.'

'You sure you're OK?' said Lenny, his face full of concern.

Dana nodded. 'Although I think we should save talkin' until we've finished eatin'.' She was grateful when Lenny nodded. Thinking back, she could easily have answered Lenny without giving the game away. Her mother did in fact bake, and not just bread and pies but all kinds of delicious cakes and pastries, and all in a small stove, something which Dana had always marvelled over.

With the cake eaten and Patty's slice placed safely in Dana's handbag, they left the café. 'I had an idea whilst we were eatin',' said Dana. Slipping her arm through Lenny's she set off at a brisk pace.

'What's the hurry?' said Lenny.

'You'll see.'

Rounding a corner, Dana looked up at one of the buildings. 'Good, we're just in time.' She pointed to the top storey. 'That there is the Old Bell and Baker's Clock. There's an Englishman, a Scotsman, a Welsh woman and an Irish lady and that one there is Old Father Time; they strike their bells every quarter of an hour.' She nudged him as the figures began to strike their bells.

Dana watched Lenny, who was clearly enjoying the show. From this angle she could see the strong jawline as he tilted his head to look. You're a handsome devil, Lenny Ackerman, Dana thought to herself, yet you've not gorra big head like some of 'em. I just wish I knew how you felt about travellers. She sighed inwardly. Who in their right mind would hitch their wagon to someone like her? Especially someone like Lenny, who could have any girl he wanted. She thought for a moment whilst she came up with the best way to describe him. Good husband material! That was Lenny from head to toe.

As the figures finished their routine, Lenny met Dana's gaze. 'What next? Although ...' He glanced back at the clock. 'It's a quarter to two now, and didn't you say you had to be back on duty for three?'

Dana nodded. 'We'd best start makin' our way back.' She jerked her head in the direction of the road. 'The bus stop's not far from here.'

As they walked, Dana asked, 'What do you think of Gloucester then? Did you enjoy it?'

He nodded enthusiastically. 'I love visitin' cathedrals and castles, and that clock thing was good too. Thanks for showin' me round 'cos I 'spect it's old hat to you by now.'

'It's more fun goin' with someone who hasn't seen it all before.' Placing her hand on her handbag she remembered the cake. 'Thanks for lunch by the way. It's not often I get treated.'

He smiled. 'My pleasure. If that engine hasn't arrived perhaps we could do it again tomorrow.'

Dana nodded quickly; she might not have found the courage to confess her feelings to Lenny today, but who knew what tomorrow might bring? 'How about a walk down the canal?'

'Sounds grand to me ...' He nodded towards an approaching bus. 'Is this one ours?'

Dana peered up the road. 'Yes.'

They joined the back of the queue just in time to board. Despite Dana's protests, Lenny paid the clippie. 'I understand you're an independent girl, but I'm a firm believer in treatin' a woman like a lady. Besides, I make more money than you.'

'I appreciate you wantin' to treat me like a lady, but I wouldn't want anyone thinkin' I were takin' advantage of you,' adding as point of proof, 'Me dad allus says you shouldn't be beholden to nothin' or no one.' The words had left her lips without her realising. She prayed Lenny wouldn't grasp the thread.

Lenny looked at her, intrigued. 'You shouldn't care what other folk think, and your father's right about not bein' beholden to anyone, but this is different.' Just as Dana thought she had got away with it he added, 'Is that an Irish thing then, encouragin' a girl to be independent?'

Dana's cheeks flushed. Why, oh why had she mentioned her father? If she didn't answer him now, he'd think her rude. She shrugged. 'I'm not sure. I've never lived in Ireland so I couldn't say.' Crossing her fingers, which were hidden beneath her bag, she prayed for the conversation to take a different route.

Lenny gazed out of the window. Dana's cheeks had flushed red as soon as she mentioned her father. She'd done something similar earlier that day when they were in Betty's café … He frowned. Was Dana embarrassed about her parents? And if so, why? They couldn't be that bad – they'd certainly done a good job bringing her up, and she had spoken of her father with fondness. He drew a deep breath. Whatever the reason, he would have to find out with time, when she was ready to tell him. He glanced at Dana as she looked out of the window. He didn't like seeing her uncomfortable, so he decided to chat about their intentions for the next day. 'How about we take a picnic down the canal tomorrow?'

Relieved for the third time that day that the conversation had taken a different route, Dana nodded. 'Sounds like a good idea. When will you know whether you're free?'

'I'll go straight back to my billet from here, and see what's what; if you don't hear anythin' from me, I'll pick you up same time tomorrow?'

The bus slowed down and several Waafs along with Dana got to their feet. She nodded. 'Thanks again, Lenny. See you tomorrer.'

Lenny smiled. ''Bye, cariad.'

Dana hurried off the bus before the driver had a chance to drive off. Standing back, she waved goodbye as the bus pulled away.

As the bus gained speed Lenny thought about his day in Gloucester. Dana had seemed to enjoy his company as much as he had hers; she had even said she wanted to see him the next day, and again when they went to Devon. A line creased his brow. Maybe she had been telling the truth when she had said she didn't want to start a romantic relationship with anyone in wartime? He pulled a face. She definitely liked him, he could see it in her eyes, but was she really determined to keep things on hold until the war was over? Come to that, was he prepared to wait? He pictured Dana, her hair loose around her shoulders, smiling up at him. What was he thinking? He already knew the answer was yes; he would be prepared to wait for Dana, no matter how long it took.

Dana placed the receiver back on to its hook and rejoined Patty, who was sitting at one of the tables nursing a mug of tea.

'What's up? You look like you've found a penny but lost a pound?'

'That was Lenny, he's had a telephone call to say they couldn't waste any more time and that he'd have to go to Newcastle without delay.'

'Poor Lenny, he must be dreadfully disappointed. I know you said he was lookin' forward to the two of you goin' to the canal tomorrer.'

'So was I, although I must admit I'm a tiny bit relieved in case I said summat else stupid.' She rolled her eyes. 'Honestly, Patty, I put me foot in it that many times today, I'm sure he must've thought summat was up, only he was too polite to say. I'll never get the courage to tell him the truth, not at this rate.'

Patty thrummed her fingers against her chin. 'You don't think he suspected anythin'?'

Dana shook her head. 'I reckon I got away wi' it, but that won't last for ever. I feel so at ease with him, an' I don't think before I speak.' She paused. 'Perhaps Lenny goin' to Newcastle is a good thing. I can't put my foot in it if I'm not with him.'

Patty frowned. 'You can't avoid him for ever!'

Dana shrugged. 'If that's what it takes.'

'You're bonkers,' said Patty. 'In fact I'll go one further: if you're goin' to risk never seein' him again in case he finds out the truth then what've you got to lose?'

'Everything!' said Dana with feeling. 'Not only would I have lost the man I ...' She heaved an exasperated sigh. '... I think a lot of, but I'd also have lost a good friend, and everything I ever thought he was.' Blinking back the tears, she shook her head. 'It'd break my heart.'

Patty placed her arms around Dana's shoulders. 'I wish I could tell you what to do or find some way of makin' everythin' all right. As it is, all I can do is be here for you.'

Sniffing back the tears, Dana nodded. 'I know you are. In fact I don't know what I'd do wi'out you.' She caught a tear before it fell. She had put Lenny on a pedestal, the ideal man, loyal, caring and non-judgemental, but even Dana knew that this image wasn't true, because Lenny wasn't in possession of all of the facts. If he were she might see a very different side to him, especially if he didn't like travellers. And if that was the case then her image of Lenny would be destroyed, along with everything she had ever believed him to be.

Chapter Six

August 1941

Patty and Dana placed their kitbags on the floor before embracing Lucy, who was beaming. 'I've missed you two! I'm so glad you found the time to visit on your way to Devon. I've managed to get some leave so it really will be like a little holiday.'

'It's good to see you too!' said Dana, leaning back from their embrace as she admired her friend. 'You're lookin' well. Did you manage to speak to someone about takin' us to see the barrage balloons?'

Lucy nodded eagerly. 'I had a word with Sergeant Hastings. He was made up someone wanted to see the balloons; he said most folk are only interested in seein' fighters and bombers, so he's given me special permission to take you to see 'em up close.'

'Oh Lucy, that's wonderful! I've only ever seen 'em from far away, but everyone reckerns they're enormous up close!'

'They are, but you'll see for yourself soon enough, I've arranged for us to meet Toby – he's a driver same as us – in town.' She glanced at her wristwatch.

'Bloomin' heck, we'd better get a move on, I said we'd meet him in the square at six, which gives us fifteen minutes.'

Patty hefted her kitbag over her shoulder. 'Is it far? This thing weighs a ton!'

Lucy shook her head. 'Nah, we'll make it in time.' She turned to Dana, who had fallen into step alongside her. 'What happened with Lenny? Are you two an item?'

'I haven't the guts to tell him the truth, Lu. I wish I did, but ...' She shook her head. ' ... I don't.'

'Oh dear,' said Lucy. 'It seems such a shame when I know how well the two of you get on.' She looked up at Patty. 'And what about you? Have you found yourself a feller yet?'

'No I bloomin' well haven't. I don't understand it. I stopped bein' one of the lads, like you and Dana advised, but it ain't made the blindest bit of difference. I reckon I must have "steer clear" written on me forehead.'

'Mebbe you're too eager,' said Lucy thoughtfully. 'Fellers don't like a girl what's too keen. How about you try forgettin' about fellers for a bit, see if that works?'

'May as well,' said Patty morosely. 'I'll give anythin' a go if it works.'

Lucy pointed to a monument which stood in the town square. 'We're meetin' Toby by the—' She was interrupted by a large army lorry pulling into the square. 'Talk of the devil ...'

Toby jumped down from his cab and let down the tailgate of the lorry. He stood to one side as the servicemen and women piled out; then, seeing Lucy waving to get his attention, he approached the girls. 'You made it!' He turned to Dana and Patty. 'I hear one of you lovely ladies wants to see the balloons?'

Dana held up an eager hand. 'Yes please!'

Toby's glance travelled approvingly up and down Dana's form as he extended a hand. 'I'm Toby.'

Dana took his hand in hers. 'Pleased to meet you, Toby. I'm Dana and this is my pal Patty.'

Still holding Dana's hand he glanced briefly at Patty. 'Hello Patty,' he said before turning his attention back to Dana. 'Make me a happy man and tell me you're comin' to stay with us?'

'Afraid not, we're passin' through on our way to RAF Harrowbeer in Yelverton.'

'Harrowbeer? Have they got their own brewery?'

'No, silly!' said Lucy.

'Oh well, you can't win 'em all.' He slapped the back of the truck with the palm of his hand. 'All aboard!'

The girls took their places on the wooden benches which flanked the sides of the lorry. 'I noticed he didn't ask me whether I were stayin',' said a disgruntled Patty. 'And I were tryin' me best not to look desperate.'

'Our Dana only has to show up an' the men start fallin' at her feet.' Lucy chuckled. 'But never fear, Patty, you'll get your own Prince Charmin' one of these days.'

'Hold on!' instructed Toby as the lorry jerked into action.

Lucy nodded her head in the direction of the cab. 'Toby's only here for a few weeks, he's fillin' in for one of the Waafs who broke her leg.'

'How on earth did she break her leg drivin' a lorry?' said Dana, who was keen not to make the same mistake.

'She wasn't drivin' a lorry, she was operatin' the winch on the balloons when she got tangled in one of the ropes.'

'Crikey, I didn't realise it was so dangerous,' said Patty. 'We won't be goin' near the winch, will we?'

'Golly no!' said Lucy. 'You can only get that close if you've been properly trained. They've had to have a good old shuffle round to get someone to replace her, and that's why Toby's here – it's all a bit complicated. He'll be goin' back to Liverpool when her leg's mended.'

'Lucky sod!' said Patty. 'I wish we'd been sent to Liverpool: we could've stayed at home with me mam when we weren't on duty.'

'As if the RAF would send us where we wanted to go!' Dana commented. Although in truth Dana didn't like seeing her beloved city in ruins; it just reinforced the fact that her father had been right when he made the decision to leave, which made Dana feel guilty about her behaviour that evening.

The lorry came to a brief halt before setting off once more. Looking out of the back, Dana saw a gate close behind them; the guard gave her a cheery wave, which she returned. They continued to drive until they reached a huge field and Dana could see a massive balloon tethered to the ground. She stared, open-mouthed, from the back of the lorry, which had come to a stop.

'Impressed?' Toby laughed as he released the tailgate.

She nodded. 'Very.' She took his hand in hers as she deftly jumped down from the lorry. 'Ta,' she

174

murmured, marvelling at the balloon, which was tethered a few feet above the ground.

Toby turned to Lucy. 'If you want a lift back into town I'll be leavin' here around ten to ten.'

Lucy patted his arm in a friendly fashion. 'Thanks for the offer, but we've only come for a quick peek. Sarge said he'd give us a lift back when we've finished.'

'Fair enough.' He indicated Dana, who was already walking towards the balloon. 'Your pal's a bit of a looker – you don't get many like her in the WAAF.'

'Thanks!' laughed Lucy. She looked over at Dana and Patty, who were getting closer to the balloon. 'I'd best catch up wi' those two before they get too close. Ta-ra, Toby.'

Toby nodded. 'Ta-ra, chuck.'

Lucy trotted over to join her friends. 'Well?'

'It's magnificent,' breathed Dana. 'I never dreamt they were this big.' She dragged her gaze away from the balloon. 'They look like they weigh a ton. How on earth do they ever get off the ground?'

'Gettin' 'em off the ground's the easy part; it's stoppin' the bloomin' things takin' off what's hard,' said Lucy, as though speaking from experience.

'I never understood why they use them as a deterrent; it seemed silly to put balloons up because they haven't any guns. I didn't understand why the Luftwaffe didn't fly straight through them, but after seeing this one, I see it's not as simple as that, especially when there's lots of them.' Dana shot Lucy an envious glance. 'You're ever so lucky workin' on a station like this, we don't have anythin' this excitin' on ours.' Then she

175

turned to Patty. 'If Harrowbeer is half as good as it is here, we'll've well and truly landed on our feet. This is what I'd call a proper station.'

Lucy beamed proudly. 'I know what you mean, but we need trainin' camps like Innsworth to prepare us for stations like this. I would've found it a lot harder had I come straight here from Bridgnorth,' she said. 'Innsworth was good preparation for the real thing, as it were.' She eyed Dana and Patty cautiously. 'Have you ever spoken to any of the Waafs what've served on a fighter station?'

Dana shook her head. 'No, why d'you ask?'

'I've met a few of them, and they reckon Yeovil is child's play compared to a fighter station. Some of them were rather rude, callin' balloon command the "spare force", like we were a bunch of kids playin' war games.'

Patty stared up at the balloon. 'I don't call that playin' war games, I call it bloody dangerous. Who on earth do these women think they are?'

Lucy nibbled the end of her thumbnail. 'I know what you're sayin', and I don't believe they meant to be rude, but from what they told me, life is very different on a fighter station, 'cos of the high ...' She hesitated. 'Because you lose a lot of pals.'

'But that goes wi'out sayin',' said Patty, who couldn't understand why Lucy was paying any attention to a bunch of women who had clearly not seen the balloons up close like she and Dana had. 'It doesn't mean balloon command do any less of a job.'

A small appreciative smile flickered across Lucy's lips. 'Like I say, I don't think they said it to be rude; if anythin' I think they were a bit envious – it can't be easy watchin' your pals take off, wonderin' whether you'll ever see 'em again.'

'That's not the fault of them runnin' the balloon sites,' said Dana, still annoyed. 'I joined the WAAF because I wanted to do anythin' I could to defend my country, whether it be servin' meals in the canteen or drivin' pilots to their planes. We've all got to pull together, which is why I couldn't understand why Dad wanted to go back to Ireland; it kind of felt like he was desertin' his country.'

'It's not his country though, is it?' said Lucy plainly. 'He's from Ireland.' She held up a hand as Dana tried to butt in. 'I know he lived here, but it wasn't where he was born, and you have to admit, he wasn't entirely welcome in Liverpool.'

'The carters liked us,' said Dana defensively.

'I'm sure they did – from what you've said your father saved them a lot of money. But that's a small group of people. Why should your father have risked his family for them what looked down their noses at you?'

Dana pictured the girl from the air raid shelter who had been so rude to her, and the lodgers in Eccleston House who had demanded she should leave. Lucy was right but it didn't matter; as far as Dana was concerned, Liverpool was her home, whether they wanted her there or not, and she said as much to Lucy.

'You haven't lived your life through the same prejudice as your mam and dad. You never saw any of that until you left them behind, so has it changed your mind? Has it made you think you'd be better off in Ireland?'

'Gosh no! As far as I'm concerned nothin' changed; you're goin' to get good and bad in all walks of life. There's no way I could leave you, Patty and Lenny to fight this thing on your own, just because of some silly old men back home.'

Lucy grinned. 'You're right, we all have to pull together, and the only reason I brought up that business about the fighter stations was because I didn't want you to compare this place to Harrowbeer, thinkin' it were goin' to be plain sailin'. It's a completely different kettle of fish, and far more dangerous.'

'I know, and I won't,' Dana promised. She looked at Patty and then Lucy. 'It's such a shame we're goin' to be separated again,' she said, 'cos if anyone can help me through the bad times it's you two.'

Lucy smiled thoughtfully. 'The only real family I've ever had has been me pals back in the orphanage, but I've not seen any of them in years. I s'pose when all's said and done you two are the closest thing I've got to family.'

'I feel the same,' said Patty. 'I know I've got me mam an' dad, but I ain't got no sisters or brothers.'

Lucy blinked. 'I never thought you saw us as family 'cos you've gorra mam and dad, and so does Dana come to that ...'

'It's not the same as havin' someone your own age to talk to,' said Dana.

'D'you reckon this is what it'd be like to have a sister then?' said Lucy.

178

'I'd've thought so,' said Patty. 'Someone you can share your biggest secrets with, and a shoulder to cry on when things go wrong. Bit like a mam but younger, I s'pose.'

'All I've ever wanted is a family of me own.' Lucy sniffed. 'Someone to love me, look out for me, worry how I am. S'pose that sounds silly to you two.'

'Not at all! Everyone wants to be loved Lu,' agreed Dana, 'and whilst I've a mam and dad, I daren't tell mine half the things I've seen durin' the war, 'cos I know they'd only fret, but you two know what it's like. It's easier to share stuff with you, an' I know you'll allus be there for me, same as I will for you, an' if that ain't like havin' a sister I don't know what is.'

Patty raised an expectant eyebrow. 'Sisters?' She placed her hand forward palm side down.

Dana put her hand over Patty's, and Lucy placed hers on top of Dana's.

Looking at each other they grinned. 'Sisters.'

Lucy caught hold of Dana and Patty in a firm hug. 'Golly, it's good to know you feel the same way as me. Who'd've thought I'd find me family in the services!'

Dana leaned back and wiped the tears from Lucy's cheeks, then she fished a hanky from out of her pocket and dabbed her own eyes. 'We really do have summat special, don't we? If I'd had a sister growin' up I'd've had someone me own age to play with. Not bein' allowed to go to school meant I never had any friends.' Tears still shimmering in her eyes, she continued: 'I've allus wanted a sister; now I've got two!'

'Heavens to Betsy, stop it, you two!' Patty exclaimed. 'Some reunion this is, all blubbin' away.'

Lucy chuckled. 'Good tears though.'

'The best,' agreed Dana.

A man's voice hailed them from a distance. 'Are you ready to go back into town?'

Lucy hurriedly wiped her cheeks with the backs of her hands. 'That's Sergeant Hastings. You'll like him.' She turned to face the man and waved a hand. 'Be with you in two ticks.' Turning back, she pulled a camera from out of her bag. 'Stay where you are and show us them pearly whites.'

'A camera!' breathed Dana.

'Where'd you get that from?' said Patty, who was trying to smile and talk at the same time.

'One of the Waafs in my billet loaned it to me because I've started a scrapbook of my time in the WAAF.'

'What a marvellous idea!' said Dana.

Lucy took the photograph. 'It'll be a good memory, and I can send you a copy of the photograph.' She turned and waved to the sergeant. 'Coming!'

Standing on the platform Dana, Lucy and Patty watched the train come to a squealing halt.

'Take care of yourselves. Don't forget you're in the real air force now!' teased Lucy as the girls scanned the line of carriages, looking for the emptiest one.

Patty pointed out one of the carriages to Dana, who nodded. 'You too, and tell Taffy he's to write more often than once every three weeks!' They hugged Lucy briefly before picking up their kitbags and boarding the train.

Lucy grinned at the girls who had opened the window of their carriage. 'Is that all he does? Cheeky monkey! Don't worry, I'll tell him.'

'I'm guessin' he writes a lot more often than that to you,' said Patty with a wink.

'I should say so. He'd soon know about it if he didn't.' Lucy chuckled, adding, 'Blimey, he's not keen to hang about, is he?' as the guard started slamming the carriage doors shut.

'At least we remembered to bring sandwiches with us this time!' said Dana, waving a greaseproof package at Lucy.

'Don't forget, Patty, if any of the fellers give you any trouble in Harrowbeer, tell 'em your big sister Lucy'll come and box their chops for 'em.'

'I will!' said Patty.

Blowing his whistle, the guard gave the signal for the train to depart.

Lucy jumped as the train's whistle pierced the air. 'Ta-ra, girls! Take care of yourselves, and don't forget to let me know how you're gettin' on!'

Patty and Dana waved until Lucy was lost from view. Sinking down into the seat, Dana scanned the platform to see if she could still see her.

'Wishin' she were comin' with us?'

Dana nodded. 'We're like a set of summat, we belong together, it's not the same when one of us is left behind.'

'I can't imagine how hard it is for Lucy,' said Patty, 'Although she did put on a brave face over brekker.'

'It's the small things I'll miss the most,' said Dana. 'Like goin' out for a fish supper, or sittin' down to breakfast together.' She stifled a yawn with the back of her hand

Patty pulled back her cuff and looked at her watch. 'I don't know about you, but I'm goin' to try and catch forty winks; we've a few hours yet before we need to change trains.'

'Good idea,' agreed Dana, 'although I'll probably snooze more than sleep.'

Patty placed her jacket between her head and the window and snuggled up against it. 'Me too.'

Dana lifted her own kitbag up to cushion her head against the window, then smiled as the familiar sound of Patty's gentle snores filled the carriage. It never ceased to amaze her how quickly her friend could go from wide awake to fast asleep. Settling herself against the bag, she pulled her cap down to cover half her face as she listened to the sound of the wheels racing along the track. Clickety clack, clickety clack.

It seemed as though Dana had barely closed her eyes when someone slid back the door to their carriage. She peered at the newcomer from underneath the peak of her cap. It was two RAF aircrew, one of whom wore a pilot's brevet on his left breast. She wondered whether they too were bound for Harrowbeer. She tried to ignore them as they stowed their belongings and frowned as one of them cracked his knuckles.

'I wish you wouldn't do that!' said his companion. Dana cocked an ear as she heard the familiar tones of a Liverpudlian accent.

'And I wish I was sitting down to a nice plate of Chicken Provençal ...' said the other.

'Chicken Proven-what?' said the first man, who had chosen the seat next to Patty.

Dana peeked cautiously from underneath her cap again, and saw that the man sitting next to Patty was an RAF engineer, like Lenny.

'Chicken stew to you,' chuckled the pilot.

'What's wrong wi' egg and chips?' said his friend huffily.

The pilot wagged a reproving finger. 'Nothing, and neither is there anything wrong with Chicken Provençal.'

'Why d'they call it Provençal if it's stew?'

'Because it's French.'

'Bloomin' Froggies. Why can't they just say stew like the rest of us?' muttered the engineer.

'Because it's a French dish, and they're our allies – in case you'd forgotten,' said the pilot.

'Only 'cos they need us,' said the engineer, adding as a point of proof, 'You do know they eat horses?'

Startled, Dana shifted in her seat, only to hear the pilot hiss, 'Yes I do. Now keep your voice down; these girls are trying to get some sleep.'

The carriage fell into silence and Dana fervently wished she had not overheard their conversation. In an attempt to take her mind off Crystal being served up as a stew, she listened to the sound of the wheels against the track; with no further conversation coming from the two men, she drifted off to sleep.

'Dana, wake up! It's our stop!' Patty was shaking her by the shoulder. 'Come on!'

Sitting up with a start, Dana looked bleary-eyed around the carriage. 'What happened to the airmen?'

Patty frowned. 'What airmen?'

'The two …' She shook her head. 'Never mind.' Getting to her feet, she heaved her kitbag on to one shoulder. For all she knew she might have dreamt the whole thing, which was just as well, because she would find it hard to be allies with a nation of people who served a horse up as a main course.

Descending on to the platform, Patty pointed at a sign that read *Ladies*. 'Come on, we've got a few minutes before our connection.'

Trotting behind Patty, Dana turned her thoughts back to the airmen. They'd seemed so real she could have sworn she had smelt their aftershave, or at least the one who was sitting next to her.

Seeing the door flip from *Engaged* to *Vacant* Dana stood back to allow Patty to leave the cubicle. 'What a relief, any longer and I might not've made it!' said Patty as she washed her hands at the sink. 'What were you sayin' about them fellers in our carriage?'

Dana's muffled voice came from the other side of the cubicle door. 'Doesn't matter – I reckon I must have been dreamin'.'

'Were they good-lookin'?' said Patty as she dried her hands on the rough towel.

The toilet flushed and Dana joined Patty by the sink. 'Dunno. I couldn't really see them, and I didn't want to appear nosy. If I'd known it were a dream I'd've taken a proper look.'

Patty gave a short mirthless laugh. 'I can't believe I've got so desperate I'm askin' about men what don't even exist.'

Dana frowned. 'They were talkin' about eatin' horses.'

Patty screwed her nose up in disgust. 'And you couldn't figure out whether you were dreamin'? I should think that's your answer right there, only I'd call that more of a nightmare.'

'Not them eatin' them, the French,' said Dana.

Patty grimaced. 'I'm not sure that's much better, but whether it were a dream or not we'd better get a wriggle on else we'll miss our connection.' As she spoke she craned her neck for any sign of the next train. Dana scanned the waiting passengers to see if she could spot a pilot and an engineer travelling together; she knew it was silly, but for some reason she felt there was something awfully familiar about them.

'Here it is,' said Patty. 'Let's see if we can get us another window seat; it's nice to have summat to look at.'

Dana glanced at the crowded platform. 'If all this lot are waitin' for the same train as us, we'll be lucky to get a seat at all, window or otherwise.'

To her dismay the crowd surged forward, all eager to board the train. 'Good job it's gorra corridor,' said Patty as they passed carriage after carriage already crammed with people.

Stopping in her tracks, Dana took a step backwards. 'This 'un's got two empty seats. Quick, Patty.'

'I know it has,' said Patty, 'but it's also gorra snotty kid sittin' next to one of 'em. Quite frankly I'd rather stand all the way to Yelverton than sit next to him.'

The train lurched forward, causing Dana to cannon into the back of Patty. 'Sorry.' She looked at the grubby child, who was blowing bubbles with one nostril. Sliding the carriage door open she glanced sideways at

185

Patty. 'Don't worry, I'll sit next to him. You never know your luck, he might get off at the next stop.'

Sitting in the seat next to his, Dana tried to make as much room as possible between herself and the small boy. She watched as he proceeded to wipe his nose along the length of his sleeve, before smiling brightly at her. Smiling back, Dana looked pleadingly at Patty, who slowly shook her head with a smile. Dana couldn't figure out which was worse: dreaming of airmen who ate horses, or a snotty boy within touching distance.

It was just her luck that the small child was still aboard the train as it pulled into Yelverton. 'I don't want kids,' said Dana flatly as she descended on to the platform beside Patty. 'Not ever.'

Patty chuckled quietly. 'You can't fool me,' she teased. 'You couldn't keep your eyes off him the whole way here.'

''Cos I were waitin' to see what disgustin' thing he were goin' to do next,' said Dana sullenly. 'His mam really needs to teach him what a hanky's for. Did you see him wipin' the contents of his nose on the arm of the chair?'

Patty grimaced. 'I'm afraid I did, but I wouldn't let him put you off ...' She fell silent. Dana was pointing at two men in air force uniform.

'It's them. They were the ones in my dream,' she said, nudging Patty with her elbow.

'If that's the case they weren't a dream,' said Patty as she hefted her kitbag over her shoulder. 'Not only that, but they'll probably be goin' to Harrowbeer.'

Dana stared after them. 'I hope they do. I dunno what it is, but there's summat awfully familiar about 'em. If I could just see their faces I'm sure it'd all fall into place.'

Patty's brow puckered. 'It's not like you to go chasin' after fellers. What's so special about these two?'

Dana gazed blankly at Patty. 'I don't know; it's the oddest feeling.'

Shrugging, Patty walked towards a corporal who was looking at them expectantly. 'Names?' he said as he cast an eye over his list.

The girls recited their names and he instructed them to climb on board the waiting lorry.

'I wonder what our new station will be like,' mused Patty.

Dana, who had been very impressed with the small house Lucy shared with four other women, eyed her friend hopefully. 'Do you think we could be in a billet like Lucy's?'

'Gosh, I hope so. Four of you to one bathroom!' Patty sighed. 'Sounds like heaven!'

'Certainly better than twelve of you racin' to be first to the loo!' Dana added enviously.

The aircraftman who was driving the truck slammed the cab door and placed the truck into gear. The girls instinctively gripped the edge of the bench as the vehicle moved forward. 'You never know your luck,' said Patty. 'And it would make a nice change from rushin' round like a blue-arsed fly every mornin'.'

'So much for a cosy billet like our Lucy's,' said Patty as she thumped her kitbag down on to the top bunk. 'We never have any luck!'

187

Dana spoke over her shoulder as she unpacked everything into her locker. 'Do you fancy goin' for a look around before we go to the Ops Room? I'm starvin'. I know we had them sarnies, but that was ages ago.'

Patty opened her own locker and grimaced. 'For cryin' out loud! Look at the state of this locker! Whoever used this last didn't bother to clean it out. It's full of dust – I won't be able to put my stuff away until I've given it a thorough wipe-down.'

Dana craned her neck round the side of Patty's locker and wrinkled her nose. 'Filthy beast. Fancy leavin' your mess behind for someone else to clear up.'

The girl in the bottom bunk next to Dana's leaned up on one elbow. 'Doesn't surprise me. The girl who had it before you was always moaning and whining about cleaning. She reckoned that she was an MT driver, not a cleaner, and that we had enough to do and the army should hire someone to clean.' She chuckled at Dana and Patty's disbelieving faces. 'We nicknamed her Moaning Minnie, after the air raid siren, 'cos she made you want to stick your fingers in your ears as soon as she opened her gob.'

Dana and Patty burst into giggles. 'She sounds delightful,' said Dana.

The girl put down the magazine she had been reading, got to her feet and extended a hand over Patty's mattress. 'I'm Melanie Carter, but everyone calls me Mel.'

Patty shook Mel's hand. 'I'm Patty Blackwood and this is Dana Quinn.'

Mel shook Dana's hand. 'Nice to meet you. And I must say it's a bit of a relief. I was worried that Moaning Minnie might end up whingeing her way back in. You see, our sarge is a bit of a canny lass, and she was as fed up with Moaning Minnie as the rest of us, so when they asked for volunteers to go to a new satellite station just up the road, she volunteered Moaning Minnie.'

'Good idea,' said Patty.

'Seeing as how she was always complaining about having to share a hut with twenty other women, we thought she'd jump at the chance, but she even moaned about that, saying it wasn't fair.'

'At least you don't have to listen to her whingein' any more,' said Patty positively.

Mel rolled her eyes in an exaggerated fashion. 'You're joking, aren't you? According to her the house she's been billeted to is practically derelict, stinks of mould, and the lavvy's crawling with all sorts.'

'Probably is if she's the one doin' the cleanin'.' Dana chuckled.

Patty blew her cheeks out in relief. 'If that's the case I'm glad they put us here!' She smiled at Mel from across the top of her mattress. 'So what's Harrowbeer like? We've only been on a trainin' camp, so we've not seen any action yet.'

'You'll see far more action here than you'd want to,' said Mel gravely, 'and if you take my advice you won't give your heart to any of the pilots. There's plenty of women on this station who've fallen in love with a pilot only to be left devastated when he doesn't return from an op.'

'No worries there then,' said Dana. 'I ain't interested in gettin' into a relationship and Patty's sworn off men.'

'Sure have,' said Patty plainly. 'I can hardly see a pilot askin' me out when the feller what drives the bin lorry doesn't think I'm worth a second glance.'

'Keep it that way,' said Mel grimly. 'You'll thank me when you're not the one nursing a broken heart.'

Patty closed the door to her locker. 'That's me done. Are you ready for a wander?'

Dana nodded. 'You fancy showin' us round, Mel?'

Mel shook her head. 'I'm on duty in twenty minutes, but it's pretty much like every other station as far as what's where, so you'll soon get your bearings.' She jerked her head in the direction of the door to their billet. 'There's a dance in the NAAFI tomorrow night if you fancy it.'

'We're allus up for a dance,' said Patty. 'It's a good way to meet everyone. Workin' on a trainin' station there were allus new people arrivin'.'

Mel wiped a tiny piece of fluff from Patty's blankets. 'It's like that here, but not for the same reason.' Looking up, she smiled brightly at the girls. 'The NAAFI's just to the right when you go out the door.'

Dana stopped leaning against Patty's bunk and stood up straight. 'Come on, my tummy's rumblin'.'

The billet door swung shut behind them. 'Blimey, she were a bit doom and gloom, weren't she?' said Dana.

Patty nodded. 'Lucy said the girls who serve on fighter stations were sombre; I can see what she meant.'

Dana pointed at the large building that Mel had said was the NAAFI. 'Come on, let's see what they've got to offer.'

Over the following weeks Dana and Patty began to realise what Mel had meant when she said there was plenty of action at Harrowbeer. Barely a moment had gone by when they weren't either taking pilots to their planes or picking them up on their return – if they returned, that was.

'I try not to make eye contact,' Patty had told Dana one evening as they settled down to a late supper. 'That way I won't know if they were one of the ones who never made it back. It's the only way I can cope.'

Dana, who had never been superstitious, found she had adopted a ritual which she repeated with every pilot. 'Wish 'em luck twice before they get out the car and don't look 'em in the eye.' She knew it sounded silly, but ever since her first pilot, she had gone through the same routine, and so far, she hadn't had one who didn't make it back.

Now, with no more operations scheduled until later that afternoon, the girls were relaxing on a couple of chairs outside the NAAFI when an aircraftman who had been strolling by paused for a moment. 'Blimey, you two look like you're on your hols!'

'Wish we were,' said Patty conversationally. She watched him go before addressing Dana. 'Remember when we were on our way here and you thought you saw that pilot in our carriage?'

Dana nodded. 'What of it?'

'Have you seen him here? You did say you thought you'd reckernise him should you come across him again, and we've been here for nearly a month now, so …'

'I try not to look at the pilots I take to the aircraft, but even so I'm sure I'd know if he got in the back of my car.'

'Bit like déjà vu?'

'S'pose so. Why?'

'Dunno really; I haven't thought about it in a while, mainly 'cos we've not had time to think, but …'

The air raid siren rang loud and clear across the station seconds before a Messerschmitt flew overhead, firing bullets indiscriminately. Dana and Patty as well as a number of other Waafs raced towards their cars, which were lined up ready in case of an emergency. Adrenalin pumping, Dana started her engine in a couple of turns and got into the driver's seat. She heard the car door open behind her, and she drove off as the pilot slammed it shut. Her heart thumped in her chest as she sped towards the parked planes. Overhead, they heard the Messerschmitt go into a steep dive, his tracer bullets ripping into the side of the control tower; Dana ducked instinctively as the enemy craft started to go into a steep climb.

She was so focused on getting the pilot to his plane she was surprised when she heard a cracking noise coming from the rear of her car. Without thinking, she instinctively looked into the rear-view mirror; he was cracking his knuckles, just as the pilot in their carriage had done. As soon as she realised she had broken her own rules she tried to look away, but his eyes locked with hers.

'You!' said the pilot and Dana gave an audible gasp before stepping on the brakes more heavily than she had intended.

'Sorry, I – I ...' stammered Dana.

Grinning, he leaned forward and kissed her cheek. 'Fancy seeing you here.' He flung the door open and ran towards the Spitfire before Dana could catch her breath. The driver behind blasted her horn in order to get Dana to move.

In her panic, she crunched the gears to the car, muttering under her breath. 'Double-declutch, Dana, double-declutch!'

As she made her way back, she glanced in her rear-view mirror again to see the pilot get into the cockpit of his Spitfire. It was Pete, the man she had seen in the Grafton all that time ago. To think it was he who had travelled part of the way to Harrowbeer with herself and Patty. What were the chances? Dana cringed as she heard more tracer bullets; this time they pierced some of the Spitfires.

She pulled up alongside Patty's car. 'I've seen him! The pilot from the train, and it was Pete, Patty, the one we saw in the Grafton, so he wasn't lyin'.'

Patty stared open-mouthed at Dana, before frantically pointing over Dana's shoulder. 'Move!'

Looking over her shoulder, Dana saw the Messerschmitt coming towards them. Without waiting to see what would happen, she ducked under the car, only to hear bullets piercing the body. Panting, she looked at Patty, who was lying flat on the ground next to her.

'C'mon, we can't stay here, if they hit the tanks they'll go up like a bomb!' They half ran, half crouched their way to the air raid shelter, but Dana was reluctant to go inside.

'What're you doin'?' yelled Patty.

Dana was scanning the sky. 'I didn't wish him luck, Patty. I practically called him a liar when we first met him, and I've not wished him luck. If anythin' happens to him ...'

Taking Dana by the wrist, Patty pulled her into the shelter, which was not much more than a trench in the ground with a heap of sandbags for cover. 'Standin' there ain't goin' to help him,' she said with certainty. 'And before you start pointin' the finger of blame, just you remember, all that stuff is mumbo jumbo,' adding, 'no matter what me mam thinks.' She hesitated. 'Are you sure it was him? Did he reckernise you?'

Dana nodded. 'Straight away. He kissed me on the cheek and was gone, just like that.' Two large tears trickled down her cheeks.

'Why are you cryin'?' said Patty.

Dana sniffed. 'I know you say it's mumbo jumbo, but what if it's not?'

'Dana, sweetheart, just because you didn't wish him luck doesn't mean to say owt bad's goin' to happen to him, and it's not as if you did it on purpose; he caught you by surprise. Let's face it, none of us was thinkin' straight wi' that swine tryin' to shoot holes in us, and very nearly succeedin', but you'd be no use to him stood out there like a human target,' she said reprovingly.

Dana grimaced. 'I know, and I'm sorry.' She glanced up at her friend. 'He's got to come back, Patty. I'd never forgive meself if owt happened.' She held up a hand to quell Patty, who was about to protest once more. 'I know what you're goin' to say but I can't help the way I feel.'

Patty rubbed Dana's shoulder in a comforting fashion. 'I know, chuck, I know.'

The air raid siren sounded the all clear and Dana and Patty made their way back to their cars. Dana let out a groan. 'He shot the bloomin' radiator. Look at the water.'

Patty's brow rose towards her hairline. 'It could've been a lot worse, Dana Quinn, he could've shot you!' She pointed to a bullet hole which had pierced the driver's side of the window. Shielding her eyes with one hand she pointed skywards. 'Look! They're comin' back.'

With her own car out of action, Dana had to be content with standing by, hoping to catch a glimpse of Pete. Car after car went by and there was no sign of him. When Patty returned, Dana asked if she had seen him, but her friend shook her head. 'Just 'cos I haven't seen him don't mean one of the others hasn't. We'll ask Mel and the rest of 'em when we get back.'

'Of course!' said Dana, relieved. 'Why didn't I think of that?'

''Cos you're in a right old flap! It's hard to think straight when you're gerrin' shot at. C'mon, you can ride with me,' said Patty.

Pete stood beside his aeroplane, Lady Luck. He had very much hoped to bump into Dana again so that he could carry on where he left off, and was eagerly scanning the cars as they pulled up, to see if any of them was being driven by Dana, but it seemed he was out of luck. 'Damn and blast,' he muttered softly.

'I can't believe she's slipped through my fingers again.'

A car pulled up beside him and Pete sank into the back seat. Glancing towards the driver, he wondered whether she might know who Dana was and how he could find her, maybe even pass a message on that he was looking for her. Leaning forward he smiled pleasantly at the Waaf. His smile faded as she turned to face him. It wasn't that he disliked the woman known as Moaning Minnie, but every time he'd seen her she had made it plain that she was keen on him.

As their eyes met her face lit up. 'Hello, Pete.'

'Hello. I wonder if you might do me a favour?'

Her eyes sparkled as she looked at his reflection in the mirror. 'Of course I can.'

'Do you know a Waaf in the MT called Dana, she's a driver like you?'

Her smile vanished in an instant. When Pete had asked her to do him a favour, she had not expected it to involve another woman. She shrugged disinterestedly. 'Can't say I do, should I?'

'I was hoping you might because you're both drivers. Although I've not seen her round here before, so I think she's probably new to the station.'

Putting the car into gear, the Waaf began the short journey back to the debriefing room. Every now and then Pete caught a glimpse of her eyes in the rear-view mirror. In hindsight, asking Moaning Minnie might not have been a good idea. His pal Eddie had warned Pete that women like her didn't take kindly to being turned down. 'Hell hath no fury an' all that,' Eddie had said. 'Some gels need lettin' down gently and some need avoidin' like the plague – an' take it from me, this one's the latter.'

Pete's attention was brought back to the present as Moaning Minnie began to talk. 'In case you didn't know, I've been billeted to a satellite station just up the road, so I don't get to see much of the other girls,' adding, 'Thank God,' under her breath.

Nodding, he tried to hide the smirk behind the palm of his hand. From what he remembered, there had been quite the celebration the day she had left.

'Do you want me to pass a message on if I see her?' Her voice radiated innocence, but Pete caught the malicious glint in her eye and knew it would be a mistake to ask her to say anything to Dana.

He pretended not to hear. 'Is there still a dance on in the NAAFI this Tuesday?'

The Waaf nodded eagerly; she was eyeing him with interest for the first time since he had mentioned Dana's name. 'Are you goin'?'

Pete rubbed his fingers along the side of his bristly cheek. 'From what I remember she likes dancing.'

The Waaf pulled the car to a rather abrupt halt outside the debriefing room. If the handsome pilot intended to ask another girl to the dance, she was no longer interested in anything else he had to say.

Pete checked his wristwatch as he sat down on one of the chairs in the debriefing room. He hoped the squadron intelligence officer wouldn't take too long – he was eager to tell Eddie all about his brief encounter with the beautiful Dana. He brightened. If he had bumped into Dana by accident, there was every chance that Eddie might also have seen her, maybe even spoken to her. He smiled. One way or another he'd find her, only next time he'd make sure he didn't let her slip away so easily.

Dana and Patty headed towards their billet at a brisk trot. The station was alive with talk of the Messerschmitt, which had been shot down somewhere over the English Channel, or so rumour had it.

They entered the Nissen hut, hoping to find anyone who may have seen Pete arrive back safely. 'Where is everyone?' said Dana, disappointed to see it was deserted except for Mel.

Mel looked up as they walked towards her. 'Wotcher!' Taking a closer look, she added, 'What's up?'

'I'm worried about one of the pilots,' said Dana.

'Oh? Is it someone you know?'

Dana began to nod, before changing her mind. 'I wouldn't say I know him exactly, I only met him once – we were in the Grafton in Liverpool – but that was nigh on a year ago and I've not seen him until today when I took him to his Spitfire. I don't know whether he's safe or not.' She cast an eye around the empty beds. 'I was rather hopin' one of the girls might've seen him.'

Mel rubbed a small amount of polish on to her shoes. 'Do you know his name?'

'Pete, only I can't remember his last name,' Dana explained. 'He told us he was a pilot, but we thought he were tellin' porkies, 'cos he wasn't in uniform—'

'And he said his dad owned a racing stud—' Patty interrupted before being interrupted in her turn by Mel, who grinned.

'You're talking about Pete Robinson.'

Dana, who had been trying to remove her stockings without snagging them, looked up sharply. 'That's him!' She looked hopefully at the other woman. 'I don't suppose you've seen him since the attack?'

Mel nodded reassuringly. 'Not personally, but Moaning Minnie's telling everyone how he waited until her car was free before going to the debriefing room, even said he'd asked her to the dance on Tuesday but she'd turned him down 'cos she was on duty.' She rolled her eyes in a disbelieving fashion. 'There's no way Pete'd ask her out on a date, 'cos everyone knows how clingy she is when she gets herself a feller, and that's not Pete's style; he likes to keep things low key.'

'Oh?' said Dana; curiosity getting the better of her she added, 'Does he see a lot of women then?'

Mel began vigorously brushing the polish off her shoes. 'Good Lord, yes, he doesn't make a secret of it, he reckons wartime's not the place for commitment.' She waved the toe of her shoe at the girls. 'And as you know, I agree with him, but that doesn't stop some of 'em from trying to win his heart, each as unsuccessful as the last.' She hesitated as she picked up her next shoe. 'Why didn't you believe him when he told you he was a pilot?'

Dana nodded guiltily. 'It was all a big mix-up from beginnin' to end ...' Dana told Mel about her brief encounter with the handsome pilot.

'Cor!' Mel chuckled. 'I reckon that's the first time a woman's turned him down!' She eyed Dana with admiration. 'Won't have done him no harm, mind you. I think fellers like Pete need taking down a peg or two

199

every now and then just to remind 'em they're not God's gift.'

An image of Pete appeared in Dana's mind. 'He's not used to hearin' the word "no" then?'

'Golly no! He only has to look at women and they go weak at the knees!' Mel shook her head. 'They all reckon they'll be the one to change him from Casanova to consort.'

'Consort?' Patty giggled. 'I know he's got it all, but I didn't think he were royalty!'

'Oh, I don't know, he reminds me of a Prince Charming,' said Mel with a wry smile. 'Although I blame the women for throwing themselves at him.'

Dana glanced awkwardly at Mel. 'Casanova aside, I really should apologise for makin' him out to be a liar.'

Mel picked up her handbag. 'I wouldn't worry about it; he's not the sort to hold a grudge. If anything he probably thought it funny. He's got a good sense of humour has Pete, doesn't take life too seriously.'

Patty handed Dana her wash bag. 'There you are! No harm done, and you know he's back safe and sound.' She cocked an eyebrow. 'And it looks like turnin' him down was the right move, 'cos it doesn't sound as though Pete's the loyal type.'

Mel coughed on a chuckle. 'You can say that again. He never asks anyone out, not officially, so he can't be accused of being unfaithful.' She paused whilst they mulled this over. 'Maybe that's why he does it, maybe it hasn't got anything to do wi' the war, it's just a good excuse to have his cake and eat it.' She glanced at the rows of bunks flanking the hut. 'And there's an awful lot of cake to get through!'

Colleen held her ear next to the earpiece alongside Shane's. They had heard about the attack by the Messerschmitt and were keen to know that Dana was all right.

'Honest to God, I promise you I'm fine,' came Dana's voice down the receiver. 'Me car's mended and everything's back to the way it was. Please try not to worry.'

Colleen pulled the mouthpiece towards her lips. 'We're your parents, Dana, worryin's what we do!'

Shane ran his fingers along the length of the wire. 'How on earth did the blighter get so close wi'out bein' picked up, that's what I'd like to know!'

Colleen heard her daughter heave a sigh. 'It's not like it happens every day, Dad.'

'Well, just you keep your wits about you!' advised her father.

The operator's nasal tone announced that their time was up.

'I will! Speak soon,' said Dana.

'Love you,' said Colleen, just as the line went dead. She waited until they were out of earshot of passers-by before talking to her husband. 'I know we said we'd wait until things have calmed down, but surely you must see that if we don't act soon you may never get a chance to tell her the truth and I know you said you wanted to be the one to tell her ...'

Shane shrugged. 'If that's the case then what would it matter?'

'Shane!' snapped Colleen. 'How could you say such a thing?'

''Cos it's true?' he said simply.

Colleen shook her head despairingly. She knew her husband would much rather leave sleeping dogs lie, but the older Dana got the more Colleen worried that her daughter might stumble across the truth by accident, and then where would they be? She shot Shane a sidelong glance. It wasn't the only matter he had chosen to sweep under the carpet. 'Have you made an appointment to see Dr Daniel?'

Shane thrust his hands into his trouser pockets. 'No, I ruddy well haven't, nor am I goin' to for that matter!' He shook his head chidingly. 'I dare say the doctor's got a lot more important things on his mind than my hay fever. I know I ruddy well have.'

Colleen wanted to reprimand him, to insist he go, but she knew she would be wasting her time, same as with trying to persuade him to tell Dana what she had every right to know. Trouble with Shane was he didn't like talking things through; he'd far rather ignore them until it was too late. She slipped her arm through the crook of her husband's. He was infuriating, obnoxious and stubborn, but she loved him with all her heart.

It was the Tuesday after the attack on Harrowbeer and Dana and Patty were heading towards the NAAFI.

Dana had thought long and hard about what Mel had had to say, and had come to the conclusion that there was no excuse for bad manners. She would apologise to Pete first chance she got. She had kept an eye out for him but it seemed that Pete was as elusive as ever, not surprising, considering she had been on the station for a whole month and only bumped into him once. They entered the NAAFI and Dana scanned the room, only to be disappointed when she found he was nowhere in sight. She turned to Patty. 'I feel like such a fool. All week I've been determined to seek him out so that I can apologise, and it seems that he couldn't give two hoots.'

Patty shrugged. 'You heard what Mel said. As far as Pete's concerned it's easy come, easy go; he probably got over it before he'd left the Grafton. Who cares what Pete Robinson thinks? Besides, he could be on operations.'

Dana frowned. 'No he's not! He flies Spitfires, and they don't fly at night. Besides, they went out this mornin'.' She shot Patty a worried glance. 'I hope he got back all right.'

Patty sighed heavily. 'If he didn't, it won't be because you didn't wish him luck because you didn't see him this mornin', so for goodness' sake stop your frettin'.' She indicated the dance floor, which was awash with pilots and aircrew. 'And there's plenty more fish in the sea.'

'Patty!' said Dana. 'I'm not interested in them,' hastily adding, 'And I'm not interested in Pete either, I just wanted a chance to apologise for callin' him a fibber and—' She gave a short sharp squeak and pointed towards the door. 'It's him!'

'Not that you're interested.' Patty chuckled, nudging Dana in the ribs with her elbow. 'Aye up, he's lookin' for someone. I wonder who that could be?'

'From what Mel says, anyone in a skirt,' said Dana, her tone heavy with sarcasm.

'Blimey, what happened to "I hope he got back all right"?'

Dana wrinkled her nose. 'That's when I thought he might be dead. Now I know he's not I'm not so bothered.'

Patty got to her feet. 'Well, I don't know about you, but I didn't come here just to sit on me backside.' She held her hand out to Dana. 'Come on, let's show 'em how it's done ...' She broke off as a young man in an engineer's uniform tapped her on the shoulder.

'Excuse me, miss, would you like to dance?'

Dana suppressed a giggle as Patty swapped her hand from Dana's into his without so much as batting an eye, and led him towards the dance floor. Dana watched with amusement as the two fought to take the lead, before Patty succumbed.

The chair to the side of Dana scraped back and she automatically placed her hand on the seat. 'Sorry, this one's taken ...' she began before realising it was Pete.

He glanced at Patty, who was smiling fit to burst. 'I don't think she needs it for a minute or two. I know Eddie likes to dance.'

'His luck's in tonight then.' Looking at the grin on Patty's face she added, 'I can't see her lettin' Eddie go anytime soon.'

'Now that your pal's dancing does that mean you'll do me the honour? Or were you just using your pals as an excuse in the Grafton?' He ran his hand down the buttons on his jacket and then fingered the insignia on his left breast. 'From what I recall you thought me to be a bit of a rogue.'

Dana folded her arms. While she was willing to acknowledge she had been wrong about him telling fibs, she didn't feel she was entirely to blame. She arched an eyebrow. 'It did seem a bit far-fetched.'

He furrowed his brow. 'Was that an apology?'

Dana cursed inwardly. Why was she being so defensive? She had unfairly accused him of being untruthful, yet here she was acting as though it was all his fault! She shook her head impatiently. 'I don't know what got into me.' She smiled up at him. 'Sorry.'

He smiled back and Dana scolded herself for feeling instantly drawn to him. Don't add yourself to his list, she warned herself, you've already been told that he's the love 'em and leave 'em sort, so pack it in and stop lookin' into those deep brown eyes.

Placing his arm on the back of her chair, he leaned forward. 'Does that mean you'll dance with me?' He gazed into her eyes. 'Call it my way of accepting your apology for calling me a liar.'

Dana's brow wrinkled. 'I didn't call you a liar exactly ...'

He raised his brow but said nothing.

'Oh, all right,' said Dana wretchedly. 'Just the one though.'

Taking her by the hand, he led her on to the floor and slid his arm around her waist, pulling her close. Feeling the warmth of his cheek next to hers, Dana felt as though she could melt into his arms, and cursed herself inwardly: don't go fallin' for him like all the others. She wished the dance would hurry up and be over. She glanced up at his chiselled jawline, his defined cheekbones and the deep-set eyes which looked at her as though she were the only woman in the world ... She bit her lip; he was looking at her the same way Lenny had. Only it felt different when Pete did it, more authoritative, more confident. She huffed to herself; of course he was more confident. Unlike Lenny, Pete wooed lots of women. She glanced at the other dancers, a lot of whom grinned at her, whilst others looked peeved. Patty swirled past and Dana looked at the man she was dancing with. Pete had said the man's name was Eddie, hadn't he? She looked up into Pete's downturned face, and for a foolish second she felt her heart skip a beat. He's a charmer, Dana reminded herself, don't fall for his tricks. 'The man who asked Patty to dance, did you say his name was Eddie?'

Smiling, Pete nodded. 'Why?'

'What made him ask Patty to dance? Bit of a coincidence, don't you think?' She narrowed her eyes. 'Some might say it was convenient, 'cos it left me all on me tod.' Just where you wanted me, she added in the privacy of her own mind.

Dana could have sworn she saw a flicker of guilt cross his face, but if she had, it was soon replaced with a look of innocence. Shrugging, he smiled down at her, his soft lips parting to reveal white teeth which glinted in the light. 'I'm sure I don't know what you mean ...'

Dana, who was annoyed at herself for noticing his kissable mouth, regarded him with mistrust. 'Really? There's lots of Waafs in this room – why do you think he chose Patty?'

Pete's brow wrinkled and Dana was annoyed to see it did nothing to interfere with his handsome looks.

'Are you suggesting he only asked your pal to dance so that I could be alone with you?'

'Yes!' said Dana triumphantly; she was certain Pete was playing games and she was determined to get to the truth.

'Why?' said Pete, who was eyeing Patty cautiously. 'Is there something wrong with her?'

'What? No! That's not what I said ...' said Dana, who felt as though he had pulled the rug from under her.

But Pete was chuckling softly. 'Calm down, I was pulling your leg.'

'That wasn't funny!' said Dana. She tried to push him away but his arm tightened around her waist.

'I didn't mean ...'

But Dana wasn't in the mood to listen. 'Patty was really pleased that someone had asked her to dance, but it was all a set-up so you could be alone with me. I don't mind you playin' your silly games with me, because I'm big enough to take it, but I won't have you doin' the same to Patty!'

Pete released his grip from her waist. 'I don't understand ...'

'You wouldn't, would you? Accordin' to rumour you allus get what you want, but not this time, Peter Robinson!' Turning on her heel she stormed over to Patty, who was smiling happily at Eddie. 'C'mon, we're leavin'.'

'But—' began Patty before Dana interrupted.

'You can stay here if you want, but in my opinion he's as bad as his pal,' said Dana stiffly; she was glaring at Eddie, who looked bewildered.

'I don't know what Pete's done,' said Eddie, 'but it's got nowt to do wi' me.'

Pulling Eddie to one side by his elbow, she hissed in his ear: 'Try askin' someone to dance because you want to, not because your pal told you to.'

He looked blankly at Patty and then Dana. 'Nobody told me to ask Patty to dance, I asked her because I wanted to.'

Dana's jaw dropped as she stared at him. Judging by the look of innocence radiating from his face, the man was telling the truth. She opened her mouth to apologise but before she could get a word out Pete appeared by her side.

He was eyeing her with disapproval. 'You really don't believe a word I say, do you?'

Dana looked at Patty and Eddie, her face hot with humiliation. 'I'm so sorry,' she gabbled, 'I hope I haven't ruined anything.'

Eddie, who had been looking annoyed, relaxed. 'No harm done.'

Patty stared at Dana, who could see the disappointment in her eyes. 'Is that why you think he asked me to dance?'

Dana shook her head miserably. 'Of course not, I were jumpin' to the wrong conclusion,' she shook her head chidingly, adding, 'again.'

Seeing the discomfort her friend was in, Patty held a hand out to Dana. 'We can go if you like?'

Dana looked mortified. 'No! I'm not goin' to ruin your night just 'cos I got the wrong end of the stick and let my insecurities get the better of me.'

'You sure?' said Patty.

Dana nodded fervently. 'Positive. Now get back on that dance floor and please forget I ever opened my stupid mouth.' She turned to Pete. 'I'm so sorry, I'm ashamed to admit I listened to rumours and that was wrong of me.'

Pete looked deep into her eyes as if working out whether to forgive her or not. He took her in his arms. 'If these rumours are about my having a bit of a reputation when it comes to the ladies, then I can't say I blame you. Whatever you've heard probably isn't too far from the truth.'

Too embarrassed to look him in the eye, Dana hid her face in his chest. 'They said you were a bit of a ladies' man, flittin' from one to the next. They said you don't get involved 'cos of the war, but they reckon it's because you wanna have your cake and eat it, and I thought you wanted me to be your next slice.'

Pete laughed heartily, and Dana felt his chest muscles tighten beneath his jacket. 'My next slice, eh? Well, whoever told you I don't get involved because of the war was telling the truth. The way I see it is any of us could buy it at any time, living on a fighter station.' He squeezed her gently in his arms. 'It's got nothing to do with me wanting to play the field; I just don't want to see some poor Waaf broken-hearted because I'd bought it.' She felt his chest rise and fall as he breathed out a sigh. 'This war's caused too much pain as it is.'

Dana hadn't thought she couldn't feel any lower until he voiced what Mel had already told her. Pete wasn't some sort of gigolo. Far from it.

By the end of the evening, Dana had apologised so many times Pete had forbidden her to keep doing so.

'You thought you were protecting your friend, which is admirable; I'd have done the same for a pal of mine. You've nothing to apologise for.'

Dana smiled gratefully. 'Thanks for being so understandin', I can't believe I got you so wrong.'

'Don't go blaming your pals for giving you the heads up,' said Pete pleasantly. 'They were looking out for you the same as you were for Patty.'

Dana still felt ashamed. How could she have jumped to conclusions without giving him a chance? She of all people knew what it was like to be judged unfairly.

Eddie and Patty left the NAAFI ahead of Dana and Pete, and Dana was pleased to see they were holding hands.

'I've had a wonderful time, Eddie,' said Patty, who hadn't stopped smiling all evening.

'I'm so pleased to see I didn't make a complete pig's ear out of the night,' said Dana, glancing at their hands.

Across the way from where they stood, a car horn sounded. The four of them turned to see who was trying to get their attention, but the Waaf who had accidentally pressed the horn was doing her best to duck down out of sight.

Releasing Patty's hand, Eddie spoke directly to Pete. 'I think it's time we were off.'

Pete, who had craned his neck in order to get a better view of the Waaf, nodded. 'Too right. That's Moaning Minnie in that car. She asked me if I was going to the dance tonight; it wouldn't surprise me if she'd come down here to spy on me.'

Eddie shook his head with a chuckle. 'Blimey, if your head gets any bigger you won't be able to close the cockpit!'

'Oh ha, ha,' said Pete. 'If you must know, it was the day of the Messerschmitt attack. I asked her if she knew who Dana was; she knew I was coming to the dance and I reckon she thought she'd come and have a quick shufti.'

'We've never met her,' said Patty, 'but she doesn't sound like a very nice person.'

Dana tried to catch a glimpse of the infamous Moaning Minnie, who ducked back down after peeking over the steering wheel.

'Why on earth does she keeps duckin' down like she's pretendin' no one's in the car?' said Patty. 'It's obvious we know she's there!' She twirled her forefinger beside her temple. 'I don't need anyone to tell me she's cuckoo, I can see it wi' me own eyes!'

Dana had to agree; the other girl's behaviour seemed odd. 'Well, I'm not standin' round here so she can get a good eyeful.' She looked at Patty. 'You ready for the off?'

Patty nodded but before they could leave Pete broke back into the conversation. 'All in all, tonight's not been the best night. How about we meet up again, start from scratch as it were?'

This sounded like a good idea to Dana. 'I'm goin' to be doin' a week of nights startin' tomorrer, but I'll be free the Saturday after that. How about we all go to Plymouth for the day, providin' you're free of course?'

Eddie shook his head. 'Sorry, no can do, but I could go the week after?'

Pete shrugged. 'I'm free, but if we try and find a day when we're all off at the same time we'll never get there.'

Patty shrugged. 'I'll be workin' too, so I'm afraid that counts me out.'

'Looks like it's just me and you,' said Pete to Dana, 'providing you're still up for it of course?' He winked before she had time to answer. 'I wouldn't want you to think I was taking advantage.'

Dana punched him playfully on the arm. 'No more teasin'!'

He held his hands up in a gesture of mock submission. 'OK, OK, I surrender.'

'I don't see why these two should have all the fun,' Eddie said to Patty. 'I'm free tomorrer night. I wouldn't have time to go into Plymouth but we could go to the station cinema, see what's on?'

Patty beamed. 'Sounds good to me. We can do Plymouth another time.'

'That's settled then,' said Pete. 'How about I meet you outside the gate, say around nine, on Saturday week?'

Dana nodded. 'As long as you let me pay for lunch. It'll be my way of apologisin' for everythin'—'

To Dana's surprise Eddie cut in. 'Don't be daft, I'm sure Pete's had enough of the whole business, haven't you, Pete?' He stared at Pete as though daring him to say otherwise.

'What?' said Pete. 'Oh yes, wouldn't hear of it.' He looked across to where Moaning Minnie was still hiding. 'Shall we put her out of her misery and go our separate ways?'

Giggling, Dana nodded. 'Ta-ra, Pete, Eddie.'

'Ta-ra, Dana,' said Eddie, adding, 'See you tomorrer, Patty.'

She grinned. 'Ta-ra, chuck.'

As Dana and Patty strode off in the direction of their hut, Patty tried to catch a glimpse of Moaning Minnie, but the woman kept her head lowered as they passed by. Patty slipped her arm through Dana's. 'Isn't Eddie lovely?'

Dana nodded. 'Is it my imagination or did you sense a little tension between him and Pete just now?'

'You've apologised more times than necessary; he probably thought it best forgotten.'

Dana thought about this for a minute. 'I reckern you're right. It were silly of me really.' She nudged Patty with her elbow. 'You and Eddie seem to've hit it off.'

Patty beamed. 'He's wonderful, Dana. I can't believe he asked me to dance, but I'm glad he did.' She glanced sidelong at her friend. 'You and Pete seemed to get on well an' all.'

Dana nodded distractedly. 'I can't help thinkin' he's hidin' summat.' She glanced at Patty. 'I know he's proven himself to be truthful, but I can't help it, I just don't trust him. Is that an awful thing to say?'

Patty shook her head. 'Not if it's the truth. And you've not known him long; you'd be daft to trust someone you hardly know.'

'Do you trust Eddie?'

'I think so, he's very open, and he likes a good natter, bit like me. He told me he met Pete when he went to work for Pete's dad as a groom, and they've been good pals ever since; apart from that he didn't mention him.' Patty thought for a moment before continuing. 'Are you interested in him?'

Dana shook her head. 'No.'

'Then does it really matter whether you can trust him or not?'

Dana would be lying if she said it didn't matter, because for some reason it very much did. Trouble was, she didn't know *why* it mattered. She had no intentions of starting up a relationship with someone who had already admitted to wanting nothing serious. She rested her head on Patty's shoulder as they walked on. 'Don't say anything to Mel or the others, will you? I don't want them to know I made a complete idiot out of myself tonight, nor that I've agreed to go out with a man I swore blind I wasn't interested in, because they'll think I'm lyin'.'

Patty smiled reassuringly. 'Don't worry, I won't even mention Eddie, just in case she puts two and two together.'

Dana, who knew Patty had always said she would shout it from the rooftops should a boy ever ask her to the cinema, appreciated her friend's loyalty. 'Thanks, Patty, I knew I could rely on you.'

Eddie waited until the girls had disappeared from view before turning angrily to Pete. 'Don't ever ask me to do your dirty work again.'

Pete leaned back, as though surprised by his friend's outburst. 'What's got into you?'

'You know full well,' said Eddie. 'I had to lie to someone I really liked tonight and that's your fault.'

'Pfft,' said Pete. 'How can you really like her? You hardly know her.'

'She's a nice girl, Pete, and she don't deserve to be lied to, and nor does Dana.' He shook his head in exasperation. 'Why didn't you tell her the truth?'

Pete eyed Eddie sharply. 'You'd have preferred that, would you? That the only reason you'd asked her pal to dance was because I'd asked you to?'

Eddie shook his head. 'Of course not, but it's better than lyin'.'

Pete pointed a finger in the direction of Dana and Patty's hut. 'Feel free! Go and tell her it was all a lie. I'm sure that'll make her feel much better.'

Grumbling, Eddie stuffed his hands into his pockets. 'It's too late now. I'm just sayin' I won't do it again.'

'Then stop taking it out on me!' said Pete. 'How was I to know she'd twig? Or that her pal was so hard up she'd—' He got no further.

'She's not hard up!' snapped Eddie. 'She's just quiet. I'd rather that than some of the mouthy mares you've had in the past.'

Pete raised a warning eyebrow. 'Be careful what you say, Eddie. I'm sorry if I trod on your toes, or made you do something you now regret, but let's not get personal.' In an attempt to lighten the mood, he added, 'Besides, they're passionate, not mouthy. I like a girl with a bit of fire in her belly.'

Eddie took several deep breaths in a bid to calm himself. 'You shouldn't've spoken badly about Patty.' He brushed Pete off as he attempted to place a friendly arm around his shoulders.

'Come on, Eddie, there's no need to be like that. If it's any consolation, you're right, I started it, and it's my fault things went pear-shaped.' He gave his friend a sidelong glance. 'I'm sorry I got you involved. I won't do it again.'

Eddie relented. 'Well, don't ask me to help in any more of your hare-brained schemes, 'cos the answer'll be no.'

Pete relaxed. He hated it when he and Eddie fell out, because Eddie was the only person who truly understood him. Everyone else viewed him as a spoilt little rich boy, whereas Eddie had worked for Pete's dad and knew the truth. With the disagreement behind them, Pete decided that now would be a good time to point out the positives. 'Just think, if I hadn't asked you to dance with Patty, you two might never have got together.'

Eddie mulled this over for a moment or so. 'True,' he said reluctantly.

'So, if anything, I've done you a favour. If it weren't for me—' Pete began.

'Don't push your luck,' Eddie interrupted, but then he chuckled.

'You really like her then?' said Pete, grateful they had cleared the air.

Eddie nodded. 'She's not like the rest of 'em; she's not interested in how many wings I've got on me chest, or how many exams I've passed ...'

'You're quids in then.'

'Sod off,' said Eddie, pushing Pete in a playful manner. 'As I was sayin' before I was so rudely interrupted, she's after a nice, honest man, so that's you well and truly out the picture.'

'Oh-ho! Like that, is it?' said Pete. He went to kick Eddie's feet out from under him, but his friend, who knew Pete's tricks all too well, had dodged out of the way in the nick of time, causing Pete to stumble over his own feet.

'Gettin' slow in your old age!' said Eddie, keeping a wary eye on his friend for any reprisals.

'I must be if you're getting the better of me.' Pete cocked his head to one side. 'Although I did fly all the way over to France this mornin', shot down some Jerries and got back just in time for lunch, so that's probably slowed me down a tad.' Huffing his nails he pretended to polish them on his jacket.

'Ruddy big head!'

Pete placed his arm around Eddie's shoulders and was pleased to see that Eddie no longer tried to shrug him off. 'Joking aside, I'm glad for you, I hope it works out. Dana seems pleasant enough so I'm sure she has nice friends.'

'You're not goin' to string that Dana along just to go and dump her, are you?' said Eddie anxiously. 'Only I don't want Patty to take it out on me if you do. She might think we're the same.'

Pete shook his head. 'Be fair, I never string any of them along, they always know the truth from the start. I even told Dana tonight I don't want a serious relationship with any woman, not in wartime.'

'Not in any time, that's the bit you don't tell 'em,' said Eddie.

'That's not strictly true. I'd make an exception should the right girl come along,' said Pete plainly.

'You don't think Dana's the right one then?'

Pete shook his head. 'Dana's different, interesting, but that's where it ends.'

Eddie rubbed a hand round the back of his neck. 'That's the Pete we know and love. See you in the mornin'.'

Pete nodded. 'Goodnight, Eddie.'

Walking back to his billet Eddie reflected on Pete's words. It didn't matter whether Pete encouraged Dana or not, if she was the same as the rest of them she'd want to try and win him over. Eddie kicked a stone ahead of him. He didn't like women like that, and God only knew there were plenty of them in the WAAF. But then he smiled as he thought of Patty. Normally, when Eddie danced with women, they spent most of the time looking in Pete's direction, or asking questions about him. Patty had been different; she hadn't mentioned Pete once, and had only been interested in Eddie, a rarity indeed.

With the coast clear, Moaning Minnie sat up in her seat. Bloody car horn, she thought bitterly, nearly give me a soddin' heart attack, as well as blowin' me cover! She had planned to attend the dance so that she could see with her own eyes just who this Dana woman was. She had already been running late when the sergeant in charge of the satellite station sprang a surprise inspection on her billet.

The sergeant had run a slender white-gloved finger along the mantelpiece in the aircraftwoman's room. 'You were sent here to help set up the new satellite station, but from what I can see, you're doing the opposite. This place is like a pigsty!' She showed the tip of her finger, covered in a thick layer of dust, to the Waaf, a look of disgust on her face.

'It's hard keepin' everythin' clean 'cos we haven't got the same facilities here as they have over at the main station, and this place was a right hovel before we moved in. It's not fair that I should have to clear up everyone else's mess!' Quickly adding, 'Ma'am.'

The sergeant stared icily at her. 'You've got two hours to get this place shipshape.'

The Waaf's eyes rounded. 'But the dance ...'

Ignoring her pleas, the sergeant walked towards the door. 'If you want to go to the dance I suggest you get a move on!'

By the time the sergeant came back, the billet was sparkling. The Waaf, however, looked as though she was in need of a good bath. Frowning her disapproval, the sergeant began her inspection.

The Waaf held her breath, praying that the other woman didn't find anything, and was relieved when, with a nod, her sergeant announced that she might drive her back to the main station.

The last thing she wanted to do was drive the sergeant anywhere. The other woman had ruined her evening, but she knew better than to refuse. So, still covered in muck, she dropped the sergeant off, and was about to head back to her billet for a bath when she saw Pete and Eddie leave the NAAFI, together with two women. Presumably one of them was this Dana person. It was at this point that she had accidentally leaned against the car horn in order to get a better look. Afraid she would be discovered she'd ducked down out of sight until the coast was clear and she could start the car without being seen.

She was about to drive off when a banging on the passenger door window startled her out of her wits. Holding a hand to her chest, she scowled at the Waaf who was grinning broadly at her.

It was her roommate Maisie. 'Any chance of a lift?' She settled into the passenger seat without waiting for an answer.

'What on earth do you think you're playin' at?' she snapped. 'You damn near gave me a heart attack!'

'Sorry, I did wave but you were in a world of your own.'

'I've had to spend the entire evenin' scrubbin' our billet with no help from anyone' – she slipped the car into gear – ''cos that stupid cow of a sergeant did a surprise inspection.'

'When you say our billet, do you mean your half of our room?'

She ignored the question. 'I ain't doin' all that on me own again.' She held a hand up for examination. 'Look at me nails, they used to be lovely, but they're all chipped and grubby now.' She shot a sullen glance at the NAAFI as they drove past. 'And I missed the dance.'

Maisie grinned. 'I managed to pop in for ten minutes. You were right about Pete; he was with the same girl all night – not that I'm surprised; she's a real stunner. Gorgeous hair.'

'Oh?' She turned to face the other girl. 'Did you reck-ernise her?'

Maisie shook her head. 'Never seen her before in my life, nor her pal; they must be new.'

She nodded as the guard opened the gate and waved her through. 'I saw her briefly when they came out-side. It was hard to get a proper look but she didn't look owt special to me.'

'Well, whoever she is and wherever she's from don't make no odds to us,' said Maisie. 'Judgin' by the way Pete were lookin' at her, I dare say it won't be long before he's officially off the market.'

She swerved the car around a pothole, causing Mai-sie to clasp to her chest the bag of mints she had just removed from her pocket. 'Steady on, I nearly lost the lot there,' Maisie said, peering into the bag.

'Bugger your mints,' she snapped. 'And I don't believe Pete's the type to go weak at the knees for some tart.'

'Oooh, someone's gettin' their knickers in a twist!' Maisie chuckled but, seeing the furious scowl forming on the other woman's face, she quickly wiped the smirk from her lips.

'I'm not gettin' my knickers in a twist as you so crudely put it, I was simply statin' that any girl who throws herself at Pete must be a tart. Nice girls get to know a man first.'

'Like you, d'you mean?' said Maisie.

'Yes I do. I've liked Pete for ever such a long time but you don't see me throwin' meself at him.'

This was such an enormous lie Maisie couldn't look the other woman in the eye; instead she turned her attention to the dark hedgerows as they sped by. Maisie had been there the first day Pete arrived at Harrowbeer and could recall her roommate's words all too well.

'See him?' she had said, pointing at Pete.

Maisie had nodded.

'He's mine. Anyone goes near him and they'll have me to deal with.'

Maisie had arched an eyebrow. 'You can't say that! There's plenty of women on this station – how are you intendin' to stop them?'

'I've got more to offer than any of this lot. Once he's met me and found out who I am, it'll be game over for the rest of you.'

The comment had annoyed Maisie, but she couldn't be bothered arguing so had watched with interest as the other girl trotted over to introduce herself.

When she returned she gave Maisie a smug smile. 'Give it a week, ten days tops, and we'll be an item!'

Maisie eyed her levelly. 'Really? What makes you so sure?'

'Because I know a feller with breedin' when I see one, and—'

'Opposites attract?' said Maisie. She knew she shouldn't deliberately try to vex her roommate but if she had to share a billet with the other girl, she was determined to have a little bit of fun.

'More like birds of a feather,' she snapped. 'Honestly, Maisie, you have a very strange sense of humour at times.'

A fortnight had passed before Maisie asked whether she and Pete had become an item without her knowledge.

'No,' had been the icy reply. 'What's more, I don't know whether I'm that interested. He seems to have a very high opinion of himself, like he thinks he's better than everyone else.'

Maisie couldn't believe there was another person alive who had a higher opinion of themselves than the infamous woman known as Moaning Minnie.

Now, as she continued to gaze out of the car window, she wondered what would happen if the mystery woman formed a romantic relationship with Pete. She cast her eyes heavenward as she envisaged living with a woman scorned. Maisie would just have to hope the other girl got moved to a different station, or that her roommate found a new love interest, but knowing how the other girl's reputation for a sharp tongue preceded her, she imagined there wasn't a man within a fifty-mile radius who would consider asking Moaning Minnie out on a date. Hearing the other girl stifling a yawn with the back of her hand she prayed the conversation would not continue when they got back to their billet. She was relieved when Moaning Minnie disappeared to their room, ordering Maisie to tell the others how she'd cleared up their mess.

Maisie shook her head in disbelief. Why couldn't she see she was her own worst enemy?

Chapter Seven

It was the morning of Dana's trip to Plymouth and she had woken well before reveille sounded in order to get a head start in the ablutions. She had stripped down to her vest and knickers and was running a flannel over her arms. Patty, who had decided to get up at the same time, spoke to her from one of the cubicles.

'Do you realise this is the only place on the whole station where you can have a private conversation?'

Dana placed a small amount of toothpaste on her brush. 'We've had some of our best chats in the loos. If everyone does the same as us, these walls could tell a tale or two!'

There came a flushing sound from Patty's cubicle and Patty joined Dana at the next sink. 'As long as they don't tell people how me and Eddie shared our first kiss last night ...'

Dana, who had been vigorously brushing her teeth, stopped to stare at her friend's reflection. She removed the brush from her mouth and spat into the sink. 'Did you just say ...?'

Patty grinned. 'Yup! Properly too, not the pecks like your mam gives you, but real smoochin', although not tongues like they reckern them Frenchies do. That's disgustin', if you ask me.'

Dana eyed her friend with awe. 'What was it like?'

Patty considered this carefully before answering. 'I'd like to say the earth moved, or summat romantic like that, but in truth it were a bit awkward. I don't think Eddie had kissed a girl before, so it were all a bit clumsy. It were much better second time round.'

Dana slapped Patty with the corner of her flannel. 'Second time! Blimey, I haven't had me first yet!'

Patty giggled. 'Who'd've thought I'd be kissed before you?'

'Was there a third time?'

Patty shook her head. 'Only twice, but I'm hopin' for more next time.'

Giggling, Dana finished brushing her teeth before turning her attention to the back of her neck – there was nothing worse than a clean shirt with a rim round the collar, and Pete was tall enough to see!

Patty watched Dana in the reflection of her mirror. 'Do you think you and Pete might—'

'No,' said Dana firmly before Patty could finish the sentence. 'Nor do I intend to, not with Pete or any other man for that matter.'

Patty rolled her eyes. 'You may as well become a nun ...'

'Suits me!' said Dana, who had moved on to her legs.

Patty took her toothbrush out. 'If you aren't keen on him, why are you havin' such a thorough wash?'

Dana stopped momentarily in order to look up at Patty. 'Because I don't wish to be dirty or smelly, not because I want to make myself more attractive for Pete Robinson!'

'Fair dos,' said Patty, who proceeded to brush her teeth.

Dana kept her head lowered until the blush had faded from her cheeks. It was true that she didn't wish to be dirty or smelly, but untrue that she had not been taking extra care in order to impress Pete. She knew it was silly, because she really didn't have any intentions of pursuing a relationship. Instead of subsiding the blush deepened. It's because he's dazzlingly hand-some, and he sends you weak at the knees whenever he looks at you, that's why, Dana's inner voice said frankly. You want him to find you as attractive as you find him; you want to impress him.

Patty's voice cut across her thoughts. 'Are you all right?'

Standing straight Dana nodded. 'Why, shouldn't I be?'

'You've been washin' your legs for so long all the blood's rushed to your face,' said Patty innocently.

'Nothin' wrong wi' bein' thorough.'

Patty flinched as the cold water hit her flannel. 'I reckon it'd be a lot easier to stay clean if they gave us hot water ... even tepid'd do.'

'You'll be askin' for warm towels next.' Dana chuck-led. 'If the RAF wanted to make life pleasant, they wouldn't give you biscuits made of straw and itchy blankets.' Wrapping her greatcoat around her shoulders she headed back to the billet, calling over her shoulder as she went: 'I'm off to get dressed.'

Even though there were patches of blue sky, it was still raining heavily and the walkway between the ablutions and the hut looked more like a gully. Jumping gingerly from one relatively dry patch to another, Dana entered the hut just as reveille sounded.

'It's rainin' cats and dogs out there!' she said to the room in general.

'Someone's early,' Mel said suspiciously.

Dana shrugged as she ran a stocking up one arm. 'Day off, so I thought I'd nip into Plymouth.'

'It's all right for some,' yawned Mel. 'Is Patty goin' with you?'

Dana pulled the stocking over her toes. 'Can't, she's on duty.'

Knuckling her eyes Mel grinned sleepily. 'She was in quite late last night. I reckon she must've found something interesting to do.'

Dana eyed her sharply as she pushed her arm into the sleeve of her blouse. Did Mel know?

Mel thrust her arms into the air and stretched. 'She was with that Eddie, wasn't she? Kelly was out with that lad who flies the Wimpys ...' She scratched the top of her head. 'What was his name now ...'

'Blow his name,' said Dana, hastily buttoning her blouse. 'What did Kelly say?'

'That she saw Patty with Eddie, nothing else. I take it they're an item?'

Dana didn't know what to do for the best. She didn't want to lie to Mel's face, but she didn't think it her place to tell the truth; she was wrestling with this thought when someone slammed the door to their hut wide open, shouting angrily, 'Which one of you is Dana Quinn?'

Dana pulled a face at Mel, who was rolling her eyes at the newcomer's presence. Turning, Dana said, 'I am ...' As soon as she clapped eyes on the newcomer her heart sank into her boots. It was that dreadful girl from the air raid shelter in Liverpool. Worried the other girl might recognise her, she quickly turned back and lowered her head.

The girl stalked across the room to Dana's bed. 'This ain't mine, it's yours. I want mine back!' As she spoke she flung the blouse at Dana.

Dana looked at the label, which had her name written on in black ink. Of all the rotten luck, she thought as she hastily unbuttoned the blouse she had already put on. Without turning to face the girl, she held the blouse out over her shoulder, muttering, 'Sorry,' as she did so.

'Thievin' little tart.'

'Oi, there's no need for that!' said Mel. 'It was an honest mistake. Dana could just as well accuse you of nicking hers.'

'I weren't on about the blouse,' the girl said, much to their confusion. 'I were talkin' about—' She stopped speaking as Patty entered the room. Pointing an accusing finger in Patty's direction, she spoke through gritted teeth. 'What the hell are you doin' here?'

Patty's look of surprise turned to one of amusement. 'Well, well, if it isn't Lexi, or should I say, Alexa Stewart. I'd bet a pound to a penny you're the one they call Moanin' Minnie, am I right?' A ripple of stifled giggles ran around the otherwise silent room. Without waiting for a

228

reply she continued, 'Still bangin' on about how great you are compared to us ne'er-do-wells? I might've guessed that even the RAF wouldn't be good enough for you.' Unaware of Dana's predicament Patty swung her coat from around her shoulders as she walked over to her bunk. 'Please don't tell me you're movin' back in.'

Alexa stared steely-eyed from Patty to Dana. 'I wouldn't move back in here if you paid me, and I can't say I'm surprised you're sharin' a bed with someone who nicks other women's blouses.'

Patty blinked. 'Dana wouldn't nick anyone else's blouse.' She glanced at Alexa from head to toe, adding, 'Especially not one that was too big.'

Wishing for the quarrel to be over, Dana flourished the blouse above her head. 'For goodness' sake, just take it.'

Alexa marched round the end of the bunk and snatched the blouse from Dana's fingers. 'Next time—' She stopped speaking. Bending down, she studied Dana's downturned face. 'I knew it,' she said softly, before continuing in a louder voice, 'I bloody knew it! You're the girl I seen down the air raid shelters back in Liverpool.' Standing up she spoke loudly enough for everyone to hear. 'Your lot'd nick anythin'.' She glanced at the girls who had gathered round. 'You wanna be careful. I'd check me stuff every night before I went to bed and again when I wake up in the mornin' if I were you.' Her eyes glinted as she smiled spitefully at Patty. 'Well, well, well, the Traveller and the Tart ...'

'Tart!' echoed Patty. 'That's rich comin' from you.'

Alexa's eyes rounded like saucers. 'Me? I'm not the one livin' in a knockin' shop ...'

229

'Are you referrin' to my mam's lodgin' house, the same one your dad stayed in when he first came to Liverpool?' Patty's eyes narrowed. 'I'd think very carefully before answerin' if I were you.'

Alexa turned an accusing finger on Dana. 'That don't take away from the fact that she used to live in a wagon.' Holding the blouse to her face with her chubby fingers, she wrinkled her nose in disgust. 'Even smells like one.' Casting a disapproving eye round the hut she added, 'You lot are bonkers if you let her stay here. If I were you I'd tell Sarge, 'cos I bet she don't know.'

Taking a step forward, Patty stood toe to toe with Alexa, whose spiteful little eyes suddenly looked uncertain. 'What right have you to say that one person is worth more than another just because of where they live? It's idiots like you that start wars.'

'Little Hitler!' snapped Mel. 'That's what you are.'

Her face the colour of beetroot, Alexa sidestepped Patty. Clutching her blouse to her chest she looked at the other girls for support, but they were all staring at her with disapproval. With no one on her side Alexa half walked, half trotted out of the room, slamming the door loudly behind her.

Patty glanced round the room, then looked down at Dana who had buried her head in her hands. She opened her mouth to speak, but Mel got in first.

'Don't worry about Moaning Minnie, nobody listens to a word she says ...'

Looking up, Dana spoke thickly. 'It's true, I did use to live in a wagon.' She looked around the sea of faces which were eyeing her with uncertainty. 'But I'm not a thief, I wouldn't nick anythin' from anyone.'

One of the girls who had appeared unsure of Alexa's accusations nodded slowly. 'I believe you.'

Dana looked past her to a girl called Joan, who was trying not to make eye contact.

Following Dana's line of sight Patty raised an eyebrow. 'Joan?'

Joan looked at Patty and then Dana. 'I'm sorry, Dana, I believe you're not a thief, but we had a lot of trouble with travellers when they come to our village ...'

Snorting her discontent Patty had opened her mouth to object when Dana waved her into silence.

'She's right, Patty, some people have terrible trouble with travellers. I know because me mam told me, but it's like she said, there's good and bad in all folk.' She gave Joan a small smile. 'Don't worry, Joan, you aren't the first, and you certainly won't be the last, especially now that Gob Almighty knows.'

'Gob Almighty.' Mel giggled. 'How many nicknames can one girl get?'

One of the girls from further down the hut came forward. 'It doesn't bother me what you are, you're here with the rest of us and I think you're jolly brave 'cos I don't suppose you had to be here?'

'She didn't,' said Patty, relieved that things were taking an upward turn. 'She could've gone to Ireland with her mam and dad, but she said she wanted to stay and fight for her country.' She beamed at the smiles of admiration.

'Says a lot for you does that, Dana. Most folk would've run for the hills,' said the girl who slept in the bunk above Mel's. She jerked her head towards the door. 'I reckon we wouldn't't've seen Moaning Minnie for dust.' She shot Joan a look of disapproval. 'I know who I'd rather share a hut with.'

'I'm not saying I'd rather have Moaning Minnie in here than Dana,' said Joan miserably, 'I just need time to adjust to the idea, that's all.'

'Well, I don't reckon it changes a thing,' said another girl. 'Dana's Dana, simple as.'

There was a murmur of agreement. Another Waaf came over and sat on the bed next to Dana's. 'I have to admit, if I hadn't met you first and someone told me you lived in a wagon I probably would've been a bit cautious – to say the least – and I'd be lying if I said I hadn't heard the rumours about travellers, like Joan over there.' She glanced around the assembled girls, some of whom nodded. 'But I know you wouldn't nick stuff, because that's not who you are ...' She hesitated momentarily. 'Does that make sense?'

Dana nodded. 'Thanks.'

A smaller Waaf called Valerie squeezed her way to the front. 'Can you tell fortunes?'

Shaking her head Dana started to giggle. 'And before you ask I haven't got any clothes pegs, nor lucky heather neither.' She continued to laugh and several of the girls joined in.

'One of the traveller boys tried to sell my brother a lucky rabbit's foot ...' Joan volunteered, eager to ease the tension.

Dana screwed up her face in disgust. 'Dear me, although that might be a boy thing ...'

Joan nodded with a chuckle. 'I reckon you're right, 'cos my brother brought it home!' She waited for the disgusted groans to subside before continuing. 'My mother made him bury it in the back garden.'

There was another ripple of laughter before one of the Waafs realised the time. 'We'd better get a move on, reveille was ten minutes ago!'

They started to head for the ablutions, leaving Dana and Patty on their own. Dana clapped a hand to her mouth. 'I've just remembered, I'm meant to be meetin' Pete but I can't possibly see him now.'

'Why not?' said Patty. 'He's goin' to find out sooner or later – not from any of us, I hasten to add, but I should think Alexa will positively thrive on tellin' the whole station.'

Mel, who had overheard the conversation, stopped at the door of the hut. 'It won't make any odds to Pete.'

Dana stared at Mel. 'How can you be sure?'

Mel shrugged. 'Pete doesn't care where people are from. We know that because Alexa tried to impress him with stories of her father's sweet shop empire ...' Seeing the look of disbelief on Patty's face, she added, 'We know it's not true, but it didn't make any difference to Pete – he's not impressed by that kind of thing.' She winked at Dana. 'You're a bit of a dark horse! You never told me you had a date with Pete!'

Dana blushed. 'It's not a date, we're just friends.'

'In that case what does it matter what he thinks?'

Dana was trying not to grin. 'It doesn't. Oh and thanks, Mel, and can you tell the other girls I said thank you too?' she said.

Mel nodded. 'Course I will, and try not to worry, not everyone's like Alexa,' adding, 'thank goodness.'

Dana's bottom lip trembled as she tried to hold back her tears. Her worst nightmare had finally come true, but instead of being met with looks of hatred and disgust, the girls had surprised her by taking the news in their stride. Even Joan had appeared to come round in the end. Buttoning up her blouse, she turned to Patty. 'Thanks, Patty. You allus said you'd look out for me, and you have. I don't know how I'd have got through any of this without you.'

'That's what friends are for!' said Patty. Standing up, she adjusted her skirt before making her way towards the door. 'If you see Eddie, and he's seen Alexa, tell him I'm not a tart!'

Dana started to giggle herself. 'Will do!'

Darting back across the hut, Patty kissed Dana on the cheek. 'Good luck, luv, and don't forget I'll want to know everythin' when you come back!'

Maisie, who had seen the furious look on Alexa's face as she left the hut, quickly speeded up in the hope of getting into the cookhouse before the other girl spotted her. She cringed as she heard Alexa shout out behind her. 'Hang on, I'll come with you!'

Cursing inwardly for not being quicker off the mark, Maisie stood still. She knew that Alexa had been intending to return her blouse to this Dana girl, and knew too that it was the same girl that Pete Robinson had been showing a keen interest in, so she had no desire to eat her breakfast listening to Alexa tearing Dana to shreds.

'Didn't you see me?'

Maisie decided to sidestep the question. 'I take it you saw Dana?'

Alexa nodded angrily. 'She's a traveller!'

Maisie pushed the door to the cookhouse open. 'That's not a very nice thing to say about someone you've only just met ...'

Alexa shook her head. 'I mean she lives in a wagon. I met her years ago down an air raid shelter in Liverpool.'

Much to Alexa's disappointment Maisie shrugged her indifference. 'What does it matter where she's from? It doesn't make any odds to me ...' Seeing the look of delight on Alexa's face, Maisie groaned inwardly. 'You're goin' to tell him, aren't you?'

'Can you blame me?' pouted Alexa, who thought her roommate would show a bit more support. 'Besides, he's a right to know.'

'But it's not up to you to tell him, and what's more I doubt he'll thank you for it.'

A crease furrowed Alexa's brow. 'Why not? I'd be doin' him a favour. Imagine how embarrassed he'd be if he found out he'd dated one of her kind!'

Maisie shook her head. 'Haven't you heard of shooting the messenger?'

Alexa picked up a tray. 'Course I have. I'm not stupid, but there's always an exception to the rule, and I reckon this is it. Besides, you know what stations are like when it comes to gossip, and I reckon he's better off hearin' it from someone who cares.'

Pointing to the lid of a pan, Maisie addressed the cook behind the counter. 'What's in that?'

'Porridge,' said the girl, who was poised, ready to ladle the dish of their choosing on to the plate. 'Did I hear something about gossip?'

Maisie looked sharply at the server. 'No you didn't—'

Seizing her opportunity Alexa butted in. 'Yes she did. It's about one of the Waafs ...'

Maisie shook her head. 'I thought you wanted Pete to hear it from you?'

Alexa paused. Maisie was right; if she told the fat cook, she was bound to tell everyone else and Pete would find out before she'd finished eating her breakfast. 'You're right, Maisie, it's not nice to gossip.'

'I still say he should hear it from the horse's mouth,' said Maisie.

'She'll lie,' spluttered Alexa. 'Her sort are well known for it ...'

Maisie stared pointedly at the cook, who was leaning forward eagerly.

Alexa held her plate out. 'Don't be tight with the porridge, and keep your nose out!'

Scowling, the girl slapped a ladle of porridge on to Alexa's plate with such force little bits splashed on to her uniform. 'Idiot!' snapped Alexa, 'No wonder you're only a cook.'

Not wishing to end up wearing her breakfast by association, Maisie shook her head. 'Just toast for me please.'

They took a seat far away from the kitchen, to make sure they were out of the cook's earshot. Maisie took a large bite of her toast, and chewed it thoughtfully before speaking. 'If you know what's good for you,

you'll let someone else tell Pete.' She held a warning finger up to stop Alexa from protesting. 'If you tell him, he'll think you're jealous' – because you are, she said in the privacy of her own mind – 'and even though you'll be proven right, the damage will already have been done, so why not let someone else do the dirty work for you?'

Alexa eyed Maisie hopefully. 'You?'

Maisie's brow shot towards her hairline. 'Good God no, I'm not gettin' involved in things like that. And I'd appreciate it if you didn't – I don't want to be tarred with the same brush just because we share a room.'

'But you're my friend,' said Alexa reproachfully.

Maisie sighed. She didn't really consider Alexa to be a friend as such, but nor did anyone else, which is why she made time for her. If anything, she felt sorry for the other girl. 'That's why I'm lookin' out for you. These things have a nasty habit of blowin' up in people's faces.'

Alexa sulkily wiped the bit of porridge off her sleeve with her forefinger. 'All right, I promise to keep shtum.' Seeing the pleased look on Maisie's face she added, 'For now.'

Maisie's smile broadened. 'That's all I'm askin'.'

Making her way towards the gate, Dana decided she would tell Pete before Alexa's spiteful tongue had a chance to do its vicious work. If he didn't want to see her again, then that was up to him, but it wouldn't matter because she had a lot of friends who would support her no matter what. Smiling apprehensively,

Dana waved at Pete, who was already waiting for her. Holding her hat firmly on to her head she trotted towards him. 'Morning! Have you been waitin' long?'

Pete shook his head. 'Got here a few seconds before you. Are you ready?'

'Yes, although I'd like to have a word before we set off.'

'Nothing wrong, I hope?' said Pete.

Dana drew a deep breath. 'I'm a traveller,' she said frankly. 'I wanted you to know before we spent the day together.' She looked up shyly at him from under her lashes. 'I understand if you want to change your mind.'

Pete blinked. 'Is that it?'

Dana nodded. 'I hadn't said anything before because I was worried people might not like me because of it, but, well, that Moanin' Minnie let the cat out of the bag ...'

Pete tutted loudly. 'Let the cat out of the bag, or deliberately told everyone in order to be spiteful?'

'The latter,' confirmed Dana. 'Not that it matters.'

'That girl's never happy unless she's making someone else miserable,' said Pete, shaking his head. 'What business is it of hers who you are?'

Dana shrugged. 'I've only met her once before, and it wasn't an experience I'd care to repeat. I was a bit naïve at the time, and saw nothin' wrong with telling her I lived in a wagon.' She tutted under her breath. 'I soon found out how people's opinions could change once they learned I were a traveller.' She glanced in the direction of the Nissen hut she shared with Patty.

'Poor old Patty went to the same school as her.' Hearing Patty's words in her head, she grinned. 'She wants you to let Eddie know she's not a tart, as Alexa suggests.'

Pete chuckled. 'He will be disappointed.'

Dana dug him playfully in the ribs with her elbow. 'No he won't, he's a nice feller.' She glanced towards the bus stand. 'Do you still want to go to Plymouth?'

He held out his arm in answer, which Dana accepted. 'It doesn't bother me if you live in a wagon or a castle.' Leading her towards the stand, he paused briefly. 'I remember you saying you used to work with horses. At the time I didn't know what you meant, but if you lived in a wagon I presume you had a horse to pull it?'

'Yes ...' Dana went on to explain all about Crystal, her parents, and her father's connection with horses. By the time she had finished, Pete knew all about Dana, her history and the lead-up to her joining the WAAF. It was lovely for Dana to be able to talk openly about her past to a member of the opposite sex without fear of retribution; she wished fervently that she had been able to talk to Lenny this way.

He eyed her admiringly. 'Sounds like you're a bit of a rebel when it comes to your father. I'm like that with mine. He wants me to be just like him, boring and unadventurous, whereas I want to go out there and explore what the world has to offer.'

A line creased Dana's forehead. She didn't purposely rebel against her father's wishes; under normal circumstances she always did what her father asked. 'I suppose I was a little bit rebellious at the time, only that's not the way I saw it; it was more like an urge to do the right thing. Dad's allus said I was headstrong.'

A broad grin creased his cheeks. 'Passionate.'

Dana nodded. 'When it comes down to it, then yes, I suppose I am.'

'I've seen the odd glimpse.' Pete chuckled.

Dana hailed the bus, which drew to a stop beside them. They paid the clippie and took their seats. 'I'll fight like a lioness when it comes to my friends and family,' agreed Dana. 'Same for my country.'

He eyed her curiously. 'You say you were a bit naïve when it came to Alexa, but if she was the only one who reacted in such a foul manner, why assume others might do the same?'

'She wasn't the only one, some of the fellers recognised me in Eccleston House, that's how I came to tell Patty.' She shrugged dismissively. 'They demanded her mam threw me out.' She glanced up at him. 'She didn't, of course.'

'That's because Patty and her mother are nice people who wouldn't see a young girl out on the streets because of what some silly old bigot demands.' He gazed out of the window. 'I can't stand people like that.'

Dana looked surprised. 'Don't tell me people look down their noses at you!'

Pete turned to face her. 'Only one person. My father.'

'Oh Pete, that's dreadful,' said Dana, coming from such a close family she could not imagine what it was like to have your own sit in judgement over you.

He nodded. 'You'd think he'd support his only child; instead he looks down on me because I'm not as good as him, or at least that's what he thinks.'

'What about your mam?'

Pete's expression softened. 'She loves me for who I am, no expectations; she's happy no matter what I do,' he said, adding, 'Although she'd prefer it if I wasn't such a risk-taker.'

After getting off the bus, which had stopped in the city centre, Pete and Dana stood on the pavement whilst they decided where to go. 'Do you want to go for a walk round the outside of the Royal Citadel?'

Pete nodded. 'I bet they never thought it'd still be in military use some three hundred years after they first built it.'

They walked arm in arm and Dana risked a few side-long glances at Pete to see if she could see any trace of disquiet regarding her recent revelation, but she saw nothing but quiet content. She wondered what Lenny's reaction would have been if she'd told him the truth. The very thought caused her stomach to lurch unpleasantly. Looking at the paving beneath her feet she wondered why this was the case, especially when she had found it relatively easy to tell Pete. Perhaps it was because she knew she had little choice: it was either her or Alexa. Or maybe it was the boost of confidence the girls in her hut had given her when they first heard the news. A frown furrowed her brow. If that was the case surely it should be easier to tell Lenny because he didn't live on the same station? She envisaged him standing before her as the words 'I'm a traveller' left her lips. Her heart sank as she saw the disappointment on his face. I'll never tell Lenny, Dana thought to herself, I'd rather live a lie than risk losing him altogether.

She glanced from Pete's clean-shaven chin to his smiling cheekbones. He was quite possibly the most handsome man she had ever laid eyes on. An image of Lenny formed in her mind. He wasn't as handsome as Pete, or as high ranking; when you compared the two on paper Pete should win hands down, so why didn't he? She sighed heavily.

Pete's voice cut across her thoughts. 'Someone sounds like they've got the weight of the world on their shoulders.'

Embarrassed that she had been caught thinking of another man, Dana searched for something to say. 'I – I ...'

Pete slipped his arm from hers and placed it around her shoulders, giving them a reassuring squeeze. 'Don't tell me you're still worried about other people's opinions?'

'Sort of,' said Dana guiltily.

'If you're worried about what they think, then they're not the kind of people you should concern yourself with,' he said, adding, 'Take Alexa for example. I bet you wouldn't want her as a friend.'

Dana shook her head fervently. 'Golly no, and not just 'cos of what she thinks of me. I've heard how mean she was to Patty in school.' She paused for a moment before adding, 'Like me dad used to say, with friends like that who needs enemies?'

'Exactly!' said Pete.

Dana nodded reluctantly. She agreed with Pete as far as Alexa was concerned, but not when it came to Lenny. Pete began talking about the history of the Citadel but Dana was only half listening. If Lenny was bothered about her heritage, it meant he didn't like her for who she was, and if that was the case, it meant Lenny wasn't the man she thought he was. Perhaps this was what really irked her. It would mean she had befriended, maybe even fallen for, the wrong man. An embarrassed blush invaded her cheeks; she wished it away before Pete noticed. Hitchin' your star to the wrong wagon, thought Dana gravely, that's what you thought you'd be doin' with Pete, yet you couldn't have been more wrong. True, he was popular with the ladies, but that was hardly his fault. He'd made it plain that he wasn't after a serious relationship whilst the war was on. With this being the case, she could stop surmising whom she liked best because it really didn't matter. Pete wasn't the man for her, and for all she knew, neither was Lenny.

It was late evening when they returned to Harrowbeer. Pete had proved to be delightful company as well as the perfect gentleman, and she had thoroughly enjoyed her carefree time with the handsome pilot. As he bade her goodnight, Dana wondered what conversation he would have with Eddie when he saw him next. She was sure rumour would have reached Eddie's ears by now. She cast an eye around the station. There were a lot of people heading off about their business, one or two of whom caught her eye. Did they know anything? If they did, they certainly didn't let it show on their faces. Dana smiled. All that worry for nothing! She would tell Patty about her time in Plymouth, and how she and Pete were good friends.

Pete opened the door to his billet and was surprised to find Eddie waiting for his return.

'I take it she told you?' were the first words out of Eddie's mouth.

Pete hung his jacket up before answering. 'About being a traveller?'

Eddie nodded.

'Bit like you, it was the first thing she mentioned,' said Pete.

'Does it bother you?' asked Eddie, although he was pretty sure by his friend's stance the answer would be a no.

'Bother me?' Pete chuckled as he slid his tie from around his neck. 'I told you she had a fire in her belly, and that explains why!' He sighed wistfully as an image of Dana appeared in his mind. Her long strawberry-blonde locks were blowing in the wind whilst she sat bareback astride a black stallion. 'She's everything I've ever wanted in a woman.' He began ticking the list off on his fingers: 'Fiery, strong, independent, beautiful, rebellious and with a thirst for life ...'

'Crikey,' said Eddie, who was also envisaging Dana, but as he saw her: hair pinned back beneath her hat, standing to attention as a sergeant walked past. He eyed Pete curiously. 'What did she say exactly?'

Pete gave Eddie a lop-sided smile. 'It wasn't so much what she said, it's who she is.'

A frown creased Eddie's brow. 'I don't understand ...'

'She's a traveller, Eddie my boy, and we all know what that means!'

'We do?' said Eddie.

Hanging his trousers on to the clothes hanger, Pete slapped Eddie on the shoulder. 'That she's fiery by nature. All traveller women are the same.'

Eddie, who could not shake the mental picture of Dana obeying orders out of his mind, stared uncertainly at Pete. 'They are?'

Pete nodded with a chuckle. 'You bet they are. Dana's the woman I've been searching for!'

Shrugging, Eddie, who had only come over to hear what his friend's thoughts were on the matter, walked towards the door. 'Your father won't be impressed when he finds out.'

Pete grinned. 'You're right there: he'll be bloody furious. I'll get him to sit down before I break the good news.'

Eddie paused, his hand on the door handle. 'I know he can be a pain, but why does it give you so much pleasure to irk your father?'

'Because he wants me to be just like him,' said Pete irritably, 'and I'd rather be anything but. He never has a good word to say about me, yet he has plenty to say about how I should be living my life.'

Eddie stayed quiet. He had seen first-hand how dismissive Pete's father could be, from chastising his son for acting in a reckless manner when he rode the stallions, to criticising him for not being man enough if Pete took his mother's side in an argument.

'What's more,' added Pete, 'I want a woman who dares to speak out, to stand up to me when she thinks I'm wrong.' He tutted under his breath. 'I love my mother, but I wish she'd have the guts to tell him to shut up once in a while.'

'You sure you're not wantin' to be with Dana just to annoy your father?'

'No,' he said simply. 'That's a bonus, but not the reason why I want to be with her. I meant what I said earlier; I want a woman who can match my spirit, my sense of adventure, and I believe that woman is Dana.'

Eddie knew Dana was high-spirited and adventurous, but so were a lot of women. He wanted to believe Pete when he gave his reasons for liking Dana, but as far as Eddie could see the biggest difference between Dana and the others was that she was a traveller, something which would infuriate Pete's father should he discover the truth.

Back in the Waafs' ablutions Dana was filling Patty in on their trip round Plymouth. 'He wasn't at all bothered about who I am,' said Dana, hastily splashing her face with cold water whilst Patty sat half on, half off the sink next to hers. 'If anythin' he was impressed ...' She gasped as the cold water hit her neck. 'Did Eddie say owt?'

Patty shrugged. 'Don't think it bothered him in the slightest. He did say he'd be surprised if Pete held it against you.'

Dana rubbed her face with the rough hand towel. 'We talked a lot about horses. His father buys them, but that's where it ends; he pays the grooms to do all the hard work.'

Patty nodded. 'Eddie said he and Pete used to break them in ready for the jockeys to race; he said it can be quite dangerous at times, and that's what Pete finds thrillin'.'

Dana slid her arm through the sleeve of her great-coat. 'He certainly seems to find danger exciting. That's probably what makes him such a good Spitfire pilot.'

Patty pulled a face. 'Can't see the attraction meself. I'd rather have both feet firmly on the ground!'

Dana held the door of the ablutions open for Patty. 'Me too. I can't think of owt more stomach-wrenching than goin' up in one of them things, with or without Germans tryin' their best to shoot you down!'

Patty shuddered. 'Don't! I'm glad my Eddie's an engineer.'

Dana's brow rose. '*My* Eddie?'

Tutting, Patty grinned. 'It's just a figure of speech, nothin' more.'

'I'm only teasin'.' Dana chuckled. 'I think it's rather sweet.'

Tiptoeing into the hut so as not to wake the other girls, Patty spoke softly. 'Do you think you'll be sayin' "My Pete" before too long?'

Dana stopped so abruptly Patty stubbed her toe on the foot of her bunk and swore, causing several of the girls to stir in their sleep. 'No I don't!' said Dana. 'He's a lovely feller and all that, but he's not for me; nor is anyone else for that matter.'

Patty rubbed the offended toe. 'Righto, keep your hair on,' she said. 'I were only askin'. I thought it might be nice if we could go on double dates.'

Dana sat down on the bottom bunk. She would very much enjoy going out on double dates with Patty and Eddie, but would rather it were with Lenny than Pete. She rolled her eyes at her own stupidity. She was acting as though she had the pick of the crop, whereas she had nothing, or rather she could have something if only she could find the nerve to tell Lenny the truth. She sighed breathily. She'd have no one to blame but herself if she ended up a lonely spinster.

Lenny read his latest letter from Dana. She seemed happy at RAF Harrowbeer despite being shot at by a Messerschmitt. Lenny had asked his sergeant whether it would be possible to take a few days' leave, so that he could go and see his friends in Yelverton.

The sergeant had chuckled. 'You do know where Yelverton is?'

Lenny nodded. 'Of course I do.'

'Then you'll know you'll need more than a few days' leave. Hell, you'd get there and have to turn straight back. Sorry, lad, but a few days is all you're owed, and it isn't enough.'

Lenny stared at Dana's letter. If only he'd had a few more days in Innsworth … He was sure Dana was keen on him; he'd seen the affection in her eyes. If he could just talk to her, persuade her … He remembered his mother's words of wisdom when it came to the fairer sex.

'You treat a woman like a flower, our Lenny. You'd not try to force the petals of a flower open, because you

248

know you'd only damage it, so why treat a woman any differently?'

He sighed. If his mother was right, and she usually was, then he would have to wait until Dana was ready for a relationship if he didn't wish to risk losing her altogether.

December 1941

'It's all over the news – the Japs've attacked Pearl Harbor,' gushed a Waaf as she entered the NAAFI.

Pete, who had been standing behind Dana in the queue, nudged her in the ribs. 'Shan't be a mo.'

Dana glanced at Patty, who shrugged. 'Don't ask me, I've never even heard of Pearl Harbor. Perhaps it's not far from here?'

Eddie chuckled as he slid his arm around Patty's waist. 'It's in Hawaii and if it's true, it means the Japs have made a mistake that Hitler won't thank them for, 'cos Pearl Harbor's an American base.'

Dana stared as the gravity of this sank in. 'So they've attacked America?'

Pete came back into the NAAFI. Cupping his hands around his mouth, he ordered everyone to quieten down. 'I've spoken to Squadron Leader Linken and he's confirmed the Japs have sunk a fleet of American warships. It looks like America will finally join the war.' He punched the air with his fist. 'As our allies!'

The NAAFI erupted with people cheering and whooping for joy.

Grinning, Pete strode towards Dana, swept her off her feet and swung her round.

'Oi!' protested Dana, but she was laughing.

Pete allowed her to slide back down to the floor but his arms remained encircled around her waist; he looked down at her, his expression grave. 'The attack happened at ten to eight, their time.' He slid his hands up to her shoulders. 'A lot of them would've still been in bed. It must've been like shooting fish in a barrel.'

Dana hid her face beneath her hands. 'Don't, Pete, I can't bear it.'

He shrugged. 'They've made a big mistake.' Taking her hands in his he kissed her knuckles. 'This will change the whole war. We're finally going to show the Jerries where they can shove their Swash Sticker.'

'I hope you're right, and I know it's good that they're goin' to join the war, but it seems wrong to be celebratin' over someone else's tragedy.'

Pete drew a deep breath. 'That's the cost of war. You can't afford to dwell on things; you have to get on with life. Talking of which, are you going to the dance this evening?'

'I will if it's just me and Patty, but not if Eddie's goin'. I don't fancy sittin' on me tod all evenin'.'

Pete raised a brow. 'You could go with me?'

'I wouldn't want to cramp your style. There's a lot of women hopin' to have a turn around the floor with the handsome Pete Robinson!'

He shrugged. 'Maybe it's time I stuck to one woman.'

'I don't believe you,' laughed Dana. 'Not Pete Robinson!'

Eddie cocked an ear. 'What about Pete Robinson?'

'He reckerns he wants to stick to one woman.'

Eddie half chuckled, half coughed. 'Call the doctor! The man's ill!'

'Oh ha blooming ha,' said Pete. 'I don't see what's so unbelievable!'

Dana rubbed his arm in an affectionate manner. 'We're only pullin' your leg. Besides, everyone deserves a night off, even you!'

Folding his arms across his chest, Pete eyed Dana curiously. 'Name the last woman you saw me with.'

Dana thought about this; then she thought about it some more. She looked up. 'I don't think I've seen you with any women, ever!'

'Does that not tell you anything?'

Eddie nodded. 'I'll vouch for him on that one. The only woman he's bothered with since you guys met up is you, Dana.'

Dana blushed.

'So let's start again, shall we?' said Pete. 'Will you go to the dance with me?'

Dana smiled apologetically. 'Of course I will.'

'Good! Now how about going as my girlfriend?'

The NAAFI went so quiet, you could've heard a pin drop.

'No, no, no, no, no, no, no!' A woman's voice broke the silence; it was Alexa. Staring fixedly at Pete, she stormed across the NAAFI. 'I've kept me mouth shut because Maisie said I should, but I can't stand by and watch you ask' – she shot Dana a withering glance – '*that* to be your girlfriend!'

'I beg your pardon?' said Pete.

Dana could see a small muscle twitching in his jawline.

Alexa pointed an accusing finger at Dana. 'She's a traveller, Pete. I'm sorry to be the bearer of bad news an' all that ...'

Pete wrinkled his brow. 'I don't know about bad news. Old news, yes, but not bad.'

'I don't think you heard me correctly ...' she said uncertainly.

Pete nodded solemnly. 'Yes I did. You said Dana was a traveller, and I said I already knew.' He glanced up at the ceiling as he worked through the figures. 'I've known for a long time now. Months, in fact.'

Alexa's eyes darted around the crowded room. If Pete hadn't been standing in front of her, she would never have believed it. How could someone like him, a rich, successful man of means, ask someone like that to be his girlfriend? It didn't make sense! What had Dana got to offer that Alexa didn't? She glared disapprovingly at Dana. She knew that Maisie believed the other woman was beautiful, but that's where it ended; as far as Alexa knew the girl didn't have two pennies to rub together. Pete wasn't short on offers when it came to women, all of whom lived in houses, or at least they did as far as Alexa was aware, so what made Dana so desirable? She looked from one to the other when a thought occurred to her. Dana must be willing to put out. Her mouth tightened as she imagined Dana giving in to Pete's manly needs.

Alexa's chest was heaving in anger when she pointed an accusing finger at Dana; she was trembling. 'Slut!'

Pete had managed to keep his temper under control until that word left her lips. He pointed towards the door to the NAAFI. 'Out!' he bellowed

Dana was surprised to see that Alexa was shocked at his outburst; surely she must have realised she had embarrassed Pete in front of a room full of people?

'I – I never meant you,' stammered Alexa.

Pete shook his head. 'If you're insinuating what I think you're insinuating then what does that make me?'

Alexa ran a nervous tongue around her lips. The last thing she had meant to do was to accuse Pete of ungentlemanly behaviour; it was Dana she was trying to have a go at. Why couldn't he see that? She wanted to explain herself properly, to say that she thought Dana's intention was to get pregnant so that Pete would have to marry her, but she realised that if she were to say so now, Pete would be even angrier with her than he already was. She looked around her for moral support but as her eyes met others', they either shook their heads chidingly or averted their gaze. Alexa walked out of the NAAFI before the tears of humiliation came. As the door swung shut behind her, she allowed them to fall.

Inside the NAAFI, the deadly silence was broken by the sound of people continuing their conversations, although Dana felt sure that half of those conversations had changed to discuss Alexa's outburst.

Pete turned to the woman behind the counter. 'Two iced buns and two teas please.' He looked at Dana. 'Do you want to get a table?' He hesitated before continuing, 'Somewhere out of the way, I think. I've had enough of people discussing my private life in public for one day.'

'Are you sure you don't want to forget about it?' said Dana.

Pete nodded. 'It'll be yesterday's news this time tomorrow, and that's fine by me.'

'Come on, chuck,' said Patty, 'I'll come wi' you.'

They chose a table as far away from the counter as possible, denying the women serving a chance to gossip. 'Are you all right?' Patty asked Dana. 'I've never seen Pete that angry before.'

'Me neither, although I can't say I blame him.' She looked pointedly over Patty's shoulder. 'Pete's comin'. Change the subject!'

Pete placed the contents of the tray down on to the table. 'You might want to give Eddie a hand, Patty, he's gone and spilt your drink all over the floor!'

Getting to her feet, Patty shook her head reprovingly at Eddie, who was picking up the broken pieces. 'Honestly, he's a clumsy bugger ...' She let out a groan of dismay as Eddie, who had been searching out the various bits of broken mug, stood up beneath a table, causing the contents to scatter across the floor. 'Back in a bit,' said Patty with a resigned sigh.

Pete looked expectantly at Dana.

'What?'

'Don't make out like you've forgotten, Dana Quinn. I'd just asked you whether you'd go to the dance as my girlfriend.'

What with one thing and another the question had completely slipped Dana's mind. Alexa's words, however, hadn't. She pulled a piece off her bun. 'You've told me your father is always wantin' you to do better. I don't think he meant for you to court someone like me …'

Pete laughed mirthlessly. 'I couldn't give a monkey's what he wants. It's my life; I'll see who I want.'

'I dare say you don't, but I don't want to cause a rift in your family.'

He shook his head. 'You can't cause what's already there. Me and my dad don't get on, haven't done for years; that's got nothing to do with you.'

Dana leaned on the table surface. Whoever married Pete Robinson was going to be a very lucky woman, she thought to herself.

Pete went on, 'As long as we're happy, I couldn't give two hoots about my father and his precious stables. Who wants to end up like him anyway?'

Dana swallowed the piece of bun she had been chewing. 'My parents wouldn't dream of tellin' me who I should or should not court.'

Pete considered this. 'Wouldn't they want you to court another traveller?'

Dana choked on a chuckle. 'Good God no. My dad doesn't have anything to do with travellers – he even fell out with his own family. I should imagine he'd rather I married anyone but.'

Pete lifted his cup of tea to his lips, paused for a moment before taking a swig and placing the cup back on its saucer. 'Do you think he'd approve of someone like me?'

Dana nodded with conviction. 'Oh yes, Dad loves his horses, same as you.' Tilting her head to one side, she gazed speculatively at Pete. 'You've quite a lot in common when I think about it.'

Pete was intrigued. 'Really? How so?'

'You're both thrill seekers; you're loyal and honest, and you fight for what you believe in, no matter the cost.' She heaved a sigh. 'I miss him terribly. I can't believe I haven't seen him since I joined the WAAF. I know he says it's too dangerous for me to cross the Irish Sea, and he's right, but that doesn't stop me wishin' I could see him, and Mam of course.'

Pete grinned. 'Your father sounds like a splendid chap!'

'He is ...' mused Dana, and so are you, she thought in the privacy of her own head. Her inner thoughts threw an image of Lenny into her mind's eye but she dismissed it. Lenny isn't here, she told herself, and the last letter he wrote was hardly filled with passion. She scoffed inwardly at the thought of her hanging on to see what Lenny had to say about her heritage only to have him turn her down. Not only that, but it didn't bode well for their relationship if she was too scared to tell him the truth. Pete fell silent and Dana realised he must have asked her a question. 'Sorry, what?'

'I said, so what do you reckon, are you going to give me a chance?'

'Yes!' The word had left Dana's lips before she had chance to change her mind.

Taking his cap from his head Pete held it up to hide his face as he leaned across the table; gesturing Dana to lean towards him, he kissed her gently. So lost was she in her own world Dana was surprised to hear several of the male occupants of the NAAFI drum their hands against the tables in solidarity for a fellow who had claimed his girl.

As their lips parted Dana eyed Pete shyly. 'I've never kissed anyone properly before. Was it all right?'

In answer Pete leaned forward, cupped her chin in his hand and kissed her again, only this time his eyes gazed into hers. Dana needed no further sign of approval; she felt as though she was going to melt through her chair and on to the floor. Pete Robinson, the man who had never asked a girl to be his girlfriend, was kissing her with soft lips.

'Slow down, Alexa, what's the rush?' said Maisie as she raced across the parade ground.

Alexa grabbed her hat from her head and twisted it between her fingers. 'That bitch!' she said, wiping the tears from her cheeks. 'She just tried to humiliate me in front of everyone!'

'Who did?' said Maisie. Alexa's enemies were plentiful.

'Isn't it obvious?' Looking at the blank expression on Maisie's face, she continued, 'For goodness' sake, Maisie, you are slow sometimes. I'm talkin' about Dana! Pete asked her to be his girlfriend in front of the whole NAAFI. I warned him not to, but it was no use.'

Maisie wore an innocent frown. 'I don't understand – how did she humiliate you? Surely you did that all by yourself?'

'That's not the point.' Alexa sounded awkward.

'Oh? Then what is?' said Maisie mildly.

'He doesn't care that she's a traveller, that's the point. Not only that but he looked at me as though I were the one in the wrong! Me!' she scoffed. 'I come from a good, hard-workin' family, who stay on the right side of the law.'

'Don't her family work?' said Maisie.

Alexa rammed her cap back on to her head. 'If you could call it that.' She glared sidelong at Maisie. 'Whose side are you on anyway?'

'No one's,' said Maisie. She gave Alexa a warning look before she could object. 'I told you not to go blabbin' to Pete, but you ignored me; that's down to you, no one else.'

'I can't believe he's takin' her side over mine,' whined Alexa, 'when it's clear that I'm the one in the right.' A small frown etched her brow as she looked in the direction of two Waafs walking excitedly towards them. 'Why are you two lookin' so pleased wi' yourselves?' she snapped.

The taller girl nudged her pal. 'Go on, tell her.'

'Pete just asked Dana to be his girlfriend, although you already know that bit ...' The two of them sniggered behind their fingers. 'She said yes, and then they kissed.' Narrowing her eyes, she grinned maliciously at Alexa. 'We reckon they make a lovely couple.'

Alexa blushed hotly. 'Who cares?'

'You!' snorted the tall girl. She slid her arm through her friend's. ''Bout time someone knocked you off your high horse, you're always making out like you're better'n the rest of us!'

'Well, I am better than you, Mildred Hopkirk!' yelled Alexa as the two girls walked away. 'You had nits when you first come here – I seen 'em wi' me own eyes!'

Mildred Hopkirk gestured to Alexa from over her shoulder.

'And the same to you too!' screamed Alexa.

Maisie shook her head. 'I think you'd best go back to the billet, give you a chance to calm down before you say or do summat you'll regret.'

Alexa looked at Maisie; her eyes were spitting fire. 'I'm goin' to teach Pete and Dana a lesson. They'll rue the day they crossed me. By the time I've finished, everyone on this station will see them for who they are!'

Maisie shook her head gravely. 'I don't want to know, but if you take my advice – although I'm sure you won't – you'll forget about Pete and Dana, and leave them be.' She wagged a warning finger. 'You try and take revenge and it'll be you what'll end up worse off. Haven't you learned anything?' she added incredulously.

'Yes I have!' snapped Alexa. 'Look after yourself and hang the rest, that's what I've learned, and if you don't want owt to do with it, then that's fine by me, you're no good to me anyhow.'

'You're acting like a spoiled brat!' said Maisie hotly. 'When are you going to realise you can't have everything you want?'

'Who says I can't have everythin' I want?' said Alexa with a malicious smile.

Maisie stared at her wide-eyed. 'You can't seriously believe Pete will choose you, not after this?'

Alexa's eyes flashed. 'Yes I do, and what's more it'll be him that comes to me, beggin' my forgiveness, and tellin' me I were right about Dana all along!'

Maisie breathed out slowly. She remembered how she had wondered what it would be like to live with Alexa should he and Dana ever get together; she had known it would be no picnic but even she hadn't imagined it would be this bad. Alexa's face was still puce with anger. There's no sense in trying to reason with her, not whilst she's in such a bad temper, thought Maisie. I'll wait until she's calmed down and see if I can't persuade her to leave well alone.

Chapter Eight

July 1942

With winter behind them, Dana, Pete, Patty and Eddie were sitting on the tailgate of one of the lorries enjoying the warmth of the summer sunshine. RAF Harrowbeer, along with many airfields across the United Kingdom, was playing host to the Americans, many of whom took pleasure in treating the Waafs to luxuries such as stockings and candy.

Eddie squinted at one of the Mustangs coming in to land. 'That's the feller what give Patty them chocolates ...'

'You mean Antonio?'

Eddie looked sullenly at Patty. 'That's the one. Who does he think he is, buyin' another feller's girlfriend presents?' He took a mint humbug from the bag Patty was offering round and placed it into his mouth. 'I reckon he's after summat!'

'Is he indeed?' said Patty with mild amusement. 'I wonder what that could be?'

Eddie muttered something inaudible under his breath which Patty suspected was a jibe at their American allies.

'You may not like them but they've saved our bacon,' said Pete.

'You'd be singin' a different tune if he started givin' Dana gifts,' said Eddie as he watched the American airman climb down from the cockpit. 'Comin' over here, all white teeth and tanned.'

Patty burst out laughing. 'That's not a tan, you twit!'

'How was I to know?' sniffed Eddie. 'He don't look like a darkie!'

Patty clapped a hand to her forehead. 'That's 'cos he's a Mexican!'

'Bloomin' show-off.'

Chuckling, Pete glanced at his wristwatch, the smile instantly vanishing from his lips. 'I'd best be off, Dad's train'll be here in half an hour.' Placing his hands on Dana's knees he gave her a quick peck on the lips. 'Are you sure you don't want to come?'

Dana pulled a face. From what Pete and Eddie had told her Mr Robinson was a formidable man who wasn't shy of giving his opinion. 'Probably better you see him on your own for now.' She screwed her lips to one side. 'Have you told him about me?'

Pete nodded. 'Not that he was interested, mind you. As soon as I said you were a driver he started telling me about his pal's daughter, who's landed a job working for Churchill.'

Dana felt a hot blush invade her neckline. This friend of Pete's father sounded very important. 'I'm surprised he didn't try an' introduce the two of you.'

'He did, only I told him I wasn't interested,' said Pete frankly. 'He reckoned I should give her a chance, but as I said, I already have a girlfriend.'

'I'd love to be a fly on the wall when you tell your father you're datin' a traveller,' chuckled Eddie, quickly adding, 'No offence.'

Dana shrugged. 'None taken.'

Leaning forward Pete kissed her gently on the lips before clapping his hands together. 'I'll see you lot later!'

Dana waited until Pete was out of view before turning anxiously to Eddie. 'I'm dreadin' meetin' his father.'

Eddie waved a nonchalant hand. 'He's a surly sod, but he's like that with everyone, so I wouldn't worry too much about it.'

'I wouldn't want him makin' Pete's life difficult just because he was seein' me.'

Eddie shrugged. 'He'll think you're another one of Pete's fads – I doubt he'll take it seriously. It's not as if you're engaged to be married or owt like that.' He chuckled darkly. 'Now that really would annoy him …'

Dana looked at him sharply. 'What do you mean, another one of his fads?'

Eddie shrugged. 'Pete used to be passionate about horses, until he were old enough to ride a motorcycle; after that it was cars; now it's aeroplanes.'

Dana mulled this over. If Eddie was right about Pete's infatuations, then it might only be a matter of time before he got fed up with her too, and she said as much to Eddie. Eddie quickly shook his head. 'Don't go puttin' words in my mouth. I said that's what his father would put it down to, not Pete!'

Dana relaxed a little. 'Sorry, I thought … Never mind.'

Patty nudged Eddie in the ribs. 'Why'd you have to go and open your big gob?'

'Don't blame Eddie,' said Dana hastily. 'I've been dreadin' meetin' his father ever since he told me he were comin'.'

Eddie slid off the tailgate. 'The way I see it is this: Pete's as bloody-minded as his father, not that he'd admit it, and he'll do what he wants to do, regardless of his father's wishes. Besides, he can't keep runnin' round like a big kid for ever.'

Dana gave a short mirthless chuckle. 'Just like Peter Pan.'

'Nail on the head,' said Eddie.

Dana watched another Mustang as it came in to land. She was very fond of Pete, but could she really imagine spending the rest of her life with him? It was something she would have to give serious consideration to before Pete told his father the truth about her heritage.

Maisie walked into the billet to find Alexa packing her kitbag.

'You off somewhere?' she asked hopefully.

Alexa nodded. 'I'm goin' home for a week's leave startin' tomorrer.'

'When was all this arranged? I don't remember you mentioning anything.'

'I asked ages ago, after all that trouble with Pete and Dana.' She placed a couple of vests into the bag as she spoke. 'They said they couldn't spare me till August, but when one of the girls cancelled her leave, Sarge said I could go instead of her.'

Maisie sat down on the bed opposite Alexa's and began to untie her shoelaces. 'Well, I think it's a good idea; it'll do you the world of good to get away for a bit. I know it wasn't nice for you to hear that Pete and Dana were an item, but you handled it really well, and this break is the perfect opportunity for you to lick your wounds.' She smiled brightly up at Alexa. 'I'm proud of you.'

Alexa stopped packing her bag and stared at Maisie. 'What are you on about? It's not me who has wounds to heal – I was over that two seconds after it happened. I can't speak for Dana and Pete, of course; I expect it'll be a lot harder for them, but that's none of my concern.' Her lips curved into a small, brittle smile. 'They shouldn't have set out to humiliate me.' She shot Maisie a warning glance as the other girl opened her mouth to object. 'You can keep your thoughts to yourself. If it weren't for you I'd've said summat long ago, and if I had I dare say Pete would've seen sense and things wouldn't have gotten this far.'

'You're seriously blamin' me?' said Maisie, her brow rising in disbelief. 'If you'd kept your mouth shut, you'd not be in this mess full stop, but as usual Alexa knows best.'

Alexa grinned knowingly at Maisie. 'You're right there, I do know best, and from now on I'm goin' to do things my way.'

Tying her hair up into a bun, Maisie grabbed her wash bag from her locker. 'For goodness' sake leave well alone. Anything you say or do now will look like a case of sour grapes. You're just goin' to end up with even more egg on your face!'

Alexa smiled smugly to herself. 'It won't backfire, because I ain't goin' to say anythin' to either of 'em. That's where I went wrong in the first place, but I've had time to think since then: that's why I thought it best to go straight to the organ grinder, instead of the monkey!'

Maisie's brow wrinkled as she thought this through. Alexa obviously wasn't talking about Dana or Pete's superiors because they wouldn't be interested in idle gossip. If she was referring to Dana's parents, then Maisie doubted they would care; besides, she knew they lived in Ireland. She looked sharply at Alexa. 'Please tell me you ain't goin' to see Pete's dad?'

'All right, I won't tell you I'm goin' to see Pete's dad.' She smirked sarcastically at Maisie. 'That better?'

Maisie stared at the other girl as though she thought she had lost her mind. 'I've heard of a woman scorned but you're bein' ludicrous.'

'Scorned!' hissed Alexa through gritted teeth. 'I couldn't give a rat's behind for those two. I'm doin' this to show Dana that her kind don't belong wi' the rest of us.'

'It'll end in tears,' warned Maisie, and they'll likely be yours, she added silently. She went through to the bathroom and closed the door behind her. She turned on the taps and watched the water fill the sink; taking her flannel she dipped it into the cold water and gently wiped the heat of the day from her face. She wondered exactly what it was that Alexa planned to do. Should she warn Dana and Pete, or should she keep her fingers crossed that Alexa was full of hot air? If she did tell Dana and Pete, and Alexa didn't go through with it,

Maisie would have caused all that trouble for nothing. Maisie ran the flannel beneath her arms before rinsing it through. She called out to Alexa from the bathroom. 'What time are you off in the morning?'

'Seven o'clock train. Why?' Alexa looked in the direction of the bathroom with suspicion. She wouldn't put it past Maisie to warn Dana or Pete of her intentions, either that or try to talk Alexa out of it.

'Nothing. Just wondered.'

Folding a blouse across her arm Alexa placed it into her bag. 'I'm quite lookin' forward to havin' some time off – it'll be good to see Mam and Dad again. And I've not been on a train in ages. Last time was on the way here; there were some dishy servicemen in my carriage; I hope I have the same luck this time. That'd show Pete Robinson.'

Maisie smiled. This was a new tack, and a welcome one at that. If Alexa was prepared to forget about Pete, then surely that meant she wouldn't waste her time going to see his father? All she needed now was a boyfriend to take her mind off it altogether. 'You're right. Don't bother with Pete's father – best form of revenge is to find yourself a new feller!'

Alexa, who had only heard the last part of what Maisie said, nodded. 'You're right there.'

Maisie breathed a sigh of relief. She would have to keep her fingers crossed that Alexa bumped into a man who would take her mind off Pete and Dana.

Pete stood outside the door to the Who'd Have Thought It public house. Clasping Dana's hand tightly in his, he glanced down at her. 'Ready?'

Dana nodded. 'As I'll ever be ...'

Pete led Dana into the beamed bar room and nodded at a stern-looking man who sat next to a large open fireplace. 'Evening, Dad.'

Eddie had said that Pete's father looked like Reginald Owen, the actor who had played Ebenezer Scrooge in the film of *A Christmas Carol*. Dana had thought he was making it up to unnerve her, but seeing him sitting in the chair, she realised he had hit the nail on the head. The only wrinkles on Shane Quinn's face were the laughter lines that flanked his eyes; Pete's dad didn't have any laughter lines. What he did have was a deep crease that ran between his bushy eyebrows, giving the impression he was permanently scowling.

He stood up as Dana approached and held out his hand. Dana took it expecting to feel rough calluses, like Pete and her father had, but his hands were smooth. Dana was surprised when he returned her smile.

Hating awkward silences, Dana spoke first. 'Hello, Mr Robinson. I'm Dana Quinn.'

He sank back down into the captain's chair. 'I know who you are. Pete said he'd ...' He paused. '... got a friend in the MT.'

Dana noticed how he had deliberately left the word 'girl' out. Taking a deep breath, she decided it would be better if they talked about a subject they all had an interest in. 'I believe you own a racing stud? I know a thing or two about horses.'

'Really?' said Mr Robinson, clearly not interested. 'Isn't that nice.'

Dana stared at Pete's father. He was staring at the whisky glass he was currently rotating in his fingers.

The man was being deliberately rude and arrogant, and that was before he knew the truth. It wouldn't matter if I were the Queen of Sheba, Dana thought bitterly, he doesn't like me, because I'm Pete's choice not his.

'Pete said you were a pilot in the last lot,' she said in a desperate attempt to make conversation.

He looked up from his glass and peered at her over the top of his half-moon spectacles. 'Peter tells me you're a driver.'

Dana nodded.

'Do you have any ambition or are you happy at the bottom?'

Dana stiffened. He was deliberately trying to belittle her. 'I do whatever it takes to get the job done. I didn't join the WAAF as a career choice, I joined because I wanted to do my part.'

Mr Robinson rubbed his grey moustache whiskers with one hand. 'What does your father think of you being a driver?'

Pete went to interject but Dana placed the palm of her hand against his arm. 'It's all right, Pete, I can answer for myself.' She stared Mr Robinson square in the eye. 'My father, Mr Robinson, is very proud of me no matter what I do, as long as I try my best.'

He held her gaze for a few seconds before glancing in the general direction of the bar. He clicked his fingers at the barman. 'Two whiskies and a G and T for the little lady.'

Dana's jaw flinched. 'Make that three whiskies.' She glanced levelly at her host. 'I don't like G and T.'

His mouth twitched as if he were about to smile. 'And bring the menu.'

Dana glanced at the clock that hung above the bar. Half past six? Is that all it was? She glanced hopefully at the watch on Pete's wrist, but it confirmed the time written on the clock behind the bar. If she had her way she would stand up, tell the rotten old sod to shove his drink and leave, but she knew that this was exactly what he wanted her to do, and she would be damned if she would give in to the old git.

Pete looked at the glass of whisky the barman had just placed in front of Dana. The last time he had offered her a taste of whisky she had coughed and spluttered so much they had to get her a glass of water. He knew of course that Dana had only ordered the drink out of protest, but what would she do now? In answer to his thoughts, Dana picked up the drink and downed it in one. Pete's eyes rounded in surprised admiration. He got ready to move out of the way should Dana bring the whole lot back up. He frowned. She hadn't reacted at all! A slow smile began to curve his lips – a small tear was trickling from the corner of her eye.

Dana casually wiped the tear away as she took the menu from the barman. She glanced at it hoping to find something that wouldn't take long so that she wouldn't have to spend a minute more in the old man's company than necessary, but there were only two choices, both of which were hot meals.

'I'll have sausage and mash please,' said Dana.

Pete's father chucked his menu down on the table. 'Bloody rubbish. You'd think they'd serve something better than this!'

Dana picked up her glass as the menu skidded across the table and landed at the waitress's feet. Dana bit her lip to stop herself from giving Pete's father a mouthful. The waitress bent down to pick up the menu; judging by the look on her face, Mr Robinson had been as rude to her as he was being to Dana.

Mr Robinson shrugged like a petulant child. 'I'll have the same as that one,' he said, jerking his head towards Dana.

The waitress cast Pete and Dana a sympathetic glance. 'And for the gentleman?'

Pete, who hadn't taken his eyes off his father, glanced up at the waitress. 'Stew, please.'

Mr Robinson muttered, 'Miserable-faced so-'n'-so,' as the waitress turned to leave.

Dana's jaw twitched. 'I don't expect she's normally bad-tempered, she's probably havin' a bad day.' She locked eyes with the intolerable man; she could see the fire burn within them as he willed her to say or do the wrong thing. He's fishing for an argument, thought Dana, don't bite.

When their food arrived, they ate in silence. Pete's father pushed his sausages around the plate, slopping the gravy and mashed potato on to the table. Dana ate hers slowly. She knew the old man wanted her to get up and cause a scene, but there was no way she was going to give him the satisfaction.

When the meal was over, Pete, who had hardly said a word all night, got to his feet.

Mr Robinson grumbled his displeasure. 'It's still early!'

Pete nodded. 'Early to bed an' all that.'

Dana bade Mr Robinson a brief goodbye and was halfway through the door when he called out from behind, 'You know, I don't recall you saying what your father did.'

'I didn't,' said Dana, and left the pub without another word.

Once outside, Pete tried to place an arm around her waist but she pulled away. 'Why didn't you say summat? He made me feel about this big.' She indicated the gap between her forefinger and thumb. 'I came so close to telling him I was a traveller, and that I was expecting your baby, just to see the look on his face.'

Pete gave a small chuckle. 'You trying to kill him?'

Dana shrugged. 'I felt like it.'

He put his arm around her shoulders. 'I think he rather liked you, especially when you reordered your drink.'

Dana rolled her eyes, and then giggled. 'I don't know how I held it down! Talk about pride comin' before a fall.' She frowned. 'If he likes me then why was he so horrid?'

'Because I like you, and you're my choice not his,' said Pete plainly. 'You could be Churchill's daughter and he still wouldn't approve.'

Dana rubbed her forehead with her fingers. 'I'm sorry, Pete, but I don't want to see him again, do you mind?'

Pete shook his head. 'Neither do I, but I'll have to. He's here for a few days yet.'

Dana rested her head against his shoulder. How could a father and son be so different?

Maisie woke just in time to see Alexa heading towards the door of their bedroom, her kitbag slung over one shoulder. 'What time is it?' she asked sleepily.

Alexa, who had believed Maisie to be fast asleep, jumped six inches. 'I'm runnin' late. I'll see you when I get back!'

Maisie stifled a yawn. 'Have a nice time, and Alexa?'

Alexa's face appeared round the side of the door. 'Yes?'

'I'm glad you decided not to tell Pete's dad. You know it makes sense in the long run.'

A frown creased Alexa's brow. 'Who on earth said I'd changed my mind?'

Maisie's heart sank. 'You did, last night. You said ...'

Alexa shook her head. 'I was talkin' about Pete not bein' the only fish in the sea. I didn't say nowt about not tellin' his father ...' A car horn sounded from outside. 'Gorra dash!'

'Wait!' yelled Maisie, swinging her legs out of bed before running to the front door just in time to see the back of the car disappearing up the road. 'Damn and blast! Why on earth did I assume she meant she'd changed her mind?' Rushing back to the bedroom she hastily began to dress.

Amanda, one of the other girls who shared their billet, peeped round the door and looked at Maisie through a sleep-encrusted eye. 'Whassup?'

'Got to get to the train station before Alexa makes the biggest mistake of her life ...' She carefully placed the toe of her stockings over her foot. Amanda was watching her with interest. 'Amanda, be a pal and drive me to the railway station? I'm not on duty today so my car's back at Harrowbeer.'

'What's the silly mare done this time?'

'Nothing yet, but she will if I don't stop her.' Maisie hastily tied her shoelaces. 'Ready?'

A minute later Amanda had flung her greatcoat over her nightdress and slid her feet into her slippers. 'I hope to God we don't break down!'

Rushing on to the platform station, her kitbag bouncing against her back, Alexa scanned the platform for the train, but there was no sign. Worrying she'd missed it, she approached the railway guard. 'Don't tell me the train's gone?'

He shook his head with a chuckle. 'Oh aye! Like anythin' ever leaves on time any more! It's not even here yet.'

Sagging with relief, Alexa looked around for somewhere she could grab a bite to eat; a few rounds of toast would go down a treat. Her eyes settled on a small sign above an open doorway which read *The Steam Room Café* and she walked in. An elderly woman wearing a sour expression glared at Alexa behind the counter. 'Yes?'

'Cup of tea and two rounds of toast please,' said Alexa as she fished around in her handbag for the correct money.

The woman held out a weathered hand. 'I'll bring it over when it's ready.'

Taking a seat by the window, Alexa glanced around her. A man peered icily at her from over the top of his newspaper, before disappearing behind the pages, shaking his head in a reproving fashion. Miserable bunch of so-'n'-sos, thought Alexa.

The old woman placed a cup of extremely weak tea and two barely browned pieces of toast, dabbed with the smallest amount of butter, in front of Alexa. She turned sharply as someone burst through the café door. Seeing that the ash from the old woman's cigarette was about to fall on to her toast, Alexa snatched the plate off the table in the nick of time.

'Thank goodness you've not gone,' panted Maisie, sitting down heavily in the seat opposite Alexa's. She looked at the toast; then, waving a hand, she glanced at the waitress. 'Can I have the same please, only can I have my toast cooked?'

The old woman glared at Maisie, before holding out a hand. 'That'll be sixpence.' Maisie handed the money over. Alexa waited until the waitress had left before speaking.

'If you've come to talk me out of it then you're wastin' your breath,' she hissed.

Maisie glanced around to make sure no one was listening. 'You're making a big mistake. How would you feel if someone went and saw your dad behind your back?'

'If they were warnin' him that I was makin' a mistake I'd be grateful,' Alexa said defensively.

'I very much doubt you would, because you know full well it's not up to anyone else to decide what's right or wrong, only Pete and Dana can make that decision, and they won't thank you for poking your nose in. Neither will his father, come to that.'

'I think he will.' Alexa sniffed loftily. 'It's not just his livelihood what's at stake, it's his good family name. Pete's family've owned that racin' yard for generations. I shouldn't imagine his ancestors would be too chuffed if they knew it were goin' to be taken over by a bunch of travellers.'

Maisie shrank in her seat as she saw the reflection of the man peer over his newspaper whilst the woman, who was busily making another pot of tea, stopped pouring the water from the kettle into the urn. 'Keep your voice down,' she hissed. 'You're talkin' nonsense. Dana's family've got a business of their own – why would they want to move into a house? They're travellers, for goodness' sake, they don't want to live the way we do.'

'What do you expect me to do, wait till she's pregnant and then say summat? 'Cos it'll be too late by then. It'll be a shotgun wedding and she'll have her feet well and truly under the table, and there won't be a damned thing Mr Robinson can do about it.'

'Don't be ridiculous!' squeaked Maisie. 'Dana's not that sort of girl, and I doubt Pete would be silly enough to get caught out if she were.' Aware that the others in the café could hear their conversation, she leaned further towards Alexa. 'I know you're smartin' 'cos he asked Dana to be his girlfriend, but it doesn't mean to say they'll last.'

'That's why I need to strike now whilst the iron's hot!' reasoned Alexa. 'If I wait too long, she'll be preggers before you can say knife!'

'Say you do tell Mr Robinson? What next?'

Alexa leaned back whilst the old woman placed Maisie's tea and toast on to the melamine tabletop. The woman began to wipe the table they were using, obviously hoping to hear more, but Alexa was having none of it. She waved a dismissive hand. 'Don't let us keep you.'

Glaring at Alexa the woman moved away.

'If he's any sense he'll telephone Harrowbeer and forbid him from seein' Dana.' She pulled a face as she bit into the undercooked toast. 'Why, what do you think will happen?'

'I reckon all hell will break loose and you'll get caught in the crossfire. What's more, if Pete really is besotted with Dana, as you seem to think he is, it won't make one iota of difference to their relationship, but everyone'll know it was you who told his father, and that won't go down well. Pete's ever so popular in Harrowbeer; so is Dana, come to that.'

'I don't care what any of them say,' said Alexa. 'You're the only one who bothers to spend time with me anyway, so long as you …' She hesitated. Maisie was shaking her head slowly.

'Not if you do this. You're taking things too far, and there's no need. Let people sort their own lives out.'

Alexa stared wide-eyed at Maisie. 'What is it about that woman and why am I the only one who can see her for what she is?'

'I could say the same to you,' said Maisie levelly. 'Why don't you like her? As far as I know she's done nothin' to you, yet you decided you didn't like her from the start. Why?'

'She's not one of us!' snapped Alexa. 'Do I need another reason?'

'Yes, you do; you can't dislike someone just because they used to live in a wagon—' Maisie began.

'I can, and you don't know what you're talkin' about. Their kind are all the same; they don't mix wi' us 'cos they reckern they're better than the rest of us; they don't wash and they don't work neither …'

277

Maisie closed her eyes as she tried to hold on to her temper. 'Dana is clean, which is more than I can say for you; you let that room of ours turn into a pigsty ...' She held up a finger as Alexa tried to interrupt. 'And she's not the one who thinks she's better than anyone else, that's why she shares a billet with twenty other women; you were the one who got moved to a satellite station because you thought you were too good to be in the hut. Also, from what I hear, Dana and her father have an excellent reputation with the carters, as good as any vet, so they work too!'

Alexa's bottom lip trembled. 'I'm better than her, but you're tryin' to make out like she's better than me!'

Maisie shook her head. 'You're no better than each other, and that's my point. My God, Alexa, the whole world's at war and what do you want to do? Pick on your own kind!'

Alexa's jaw dropped. 'My own kind?'

Maisie nodded firmly. 'She's British through and through, no different to me or you.' Arching an eyebrow she continued, 'Imagine what it would be like if we all started arguin' with each other because we weren't the same. Where would it end?' She paused before finishing sarcastically, 'Oh, that's right, it'd end up in a world at war!'

A train whistle blew loudly, catching Alexa and Maisie by surprise. 'I've got to go!' said Alexa.

Maisie got to her feet and held the door open as Alexa and the old man walked out. 'Promise me you'll reconsider?'

Alexa nodded miserably. She knew she couldn't afford to lose Maisie as a friend. 'He's too good for her.'

Maisie smiled kindly. 'Maybe he is, but it's his choice. Besides, you don't even like horses.' She glanced along the length of the platform. 'Looks like your luck's in, there's hardly anyone here.'

Alexa leaned back as the guard slammed the carriage door shut. 'Thanks, Maisie. I'll never like Dana, but I s'pose you're right, it would've been a bad idea. I promise to keep it zipped!' The guard blew his whistle and Alexa gripped the window of the carriage door as the train lurched into action.

'Glad to hear it!' Maisie called.

With Maisie no longer in view, Alexa began making her way down the corridor. She was disappointed to see that all the carriages were full bar one; slipping inside she stowed her kitbag beneath her seat and removed her jacket before sitting down next to the window. The train entered the countryside and Alexa closed her eyes, listening to the rhythm of the wheels; she imagined a handsome ... No, she thought, she didn't want an airman; they didn't seem to be her sort. A sailor, that was better ... she imagined a handsome sailor coming into her carriage and chatting as they made their way back to Liverpool. With this thought in mind she was just beginning to nod off when the door to her carriage opened. She supposed it must be a railway guard because everyone else had already taken their seats. Hearing the door slide shut she was startled to hear someone taking the seat opposite. She opened her eye just enough to see the newcomer. It was the old man from the café. Just my rotten luck, she thought bitterly, why couldn't it have been a hand-some sailor? She sighed. She had been looking forward to a peaceful journey in her own company. Still, he hadn't tried talking to her in the platform café, so he was hardly likely to now. She watched him watching her, and wondered whether he could see her peeking at him from between her lashes; he picked up his paper and opened up the pages. Happy that the other passenger did not intend to strike up a conversation, she settled down for a quiet snooze.

'What happened? Nothin' serious, I hope?' said Eddie as Pete slumped down on to the chair next to his.

Pete shrugged. 'From what I could gather one of the fillies has fallen lame, and they need Dad to make a decision as to what to do for the best.'

'Dana'll be relieved.'

Pete rested his ankle on his knee. 'That makes two of us. I wasn't lookin' forward to another lecture about my life and how I was getting it all wrong!'

Eddie grinned. 'What did they say at the pub, apart from hooray?'

'Just that he had a telephone call yesterday evenin' not long after we left.'

'You'd think he'd've rung to say he was off,' said Eddie. 'Save you the bother of goin' there this mornin'.'

Pete gave a short, sarcastic laugh. 'It wouldn't enter his head unless it affected him directly.'

'Good job you didn't tell him about Dana. She'd've been convinced he'd left because of her.'

Pete shook his head irritably. 'You should've seen him, Eddie. I could've turned up with Princess Elizabeth on my arm and he'd still have disapproved.'

'She's a bit young for you, isn't she?' Eddie chuckled.

'You know what I mean. I don't know what his problem is, but he seems to think me incapable of making my own decisions.'

Eddie, who had been writing a letter, twiddled the pen back and forth between his fingers. 'He's got a bit of a point though.'

Pete stared at Eddie in disbelief. 'What?'

'I'm still not convinced you're with Dana for the right reasons. You weren't that bothered until you knew she used to live in a wagon, and I don't think it's a coincidence you know it'll royally rile your father when he finds out the truth.'

Pete pulled a face. 'I asked Dana to be my girlfriend because I like her; I never said it was going to be for ever.' He held up a hand as Eddie shot him a warning glance. 'How can I? None of us know what the future holds.'

'But if she wasn't a traveller,' said Eddie, 'if she were just plain Dana, what then?'

'She's not though, is she?' said Pete matter-of-factly.

Eddie shook his head reprovingly. 'Don't go upsettin' the apple cart just to spite your father. It's not fair on anyone, especially Dana.'

'Who's to say Dana and I won't last?'

Eddie half smiled. 'I know you, Pete Robinson. You love the single life, but when Dana came along it gave you the perfect opportunity to put the wind up your father.' He paused. 'Put it this way, if you really like Dana, and I mean *really* like her, why haven't you told your father?'

Pete shrugged petulantly. 'Dunno.'

Eddie eyed Pete thoughtfully. 'Supposin' you tell your father about Dana? What then?'

Pete folded his arms across his chest. 'What do you mean?'

'Well, your father would be livid, say you were makin' a big mistake, and likely as not give you an ultimatum.'

Pete pulled a face. 'What ultimatum?'

Eddie rubbed his chin between his fingers. 'He could say that you were to cut all ties with Dana or lose your inheritance.' He locked eyes with Pete. 'If he did, what would you do? Would you tell him to shove his inheritance and continue dating Dana?'

'Be fair! I know he wouldn't be happy, but he wouldn't go that far!' said Pete, although his voice was tinged with uncertainty.

'Humour me, and let's say he does and you choose Dana,' Eddie continued. 'Where would you live after the war? In a wagon?' He shook his head with a smile. 'We both know you'd never agree to that, so what would you do? Insist she lived with you, and if so where? There's no way your father would allow a woman like Dana to live under his roof! So you'd have to find somewhere else, and a new job, and even if you stayed in the RAF you'd climb the ranks – just like your father – and how do you think those at the top would react when they found out your wife used to live in a wagon?'

Pete heaved a sigh. Placing his elbows on his knees he stared thoughtfully at Eddie over steepled fingers. 'I don't know. I hadn't thought that far ahead.'

Eddie took pity on his friend. 'Dana's a lovely girl and she's good for you, but don't lead her on if there's no end in sight.'

'I wouldn't do that to Dana, not intentionally,' said Pete. 'It's taken a lot for her to trust me.'

Eddie ruffled the back of his hair with his hand. 'I'm sure you wouldn't, but promise me you'll think before you tell your father?'

Pete nodded. 'Thanks, Eddie, you've certainly given me food for thought.' Adding in the privacy of his own head: And a wake-up call to boot!

Running towards the waiting lorry, Patty apologised to the driver, who helped her over the tailgate. She sat beside Dana on the end of the bench. 'Sorry, folks, took longer than I expected!'

'Anything?' said Dana hopefully.

Patty opened the zip on her handbag and pulled out a clutch of letters, two of which she handed to Dana. 'One's off Lucy, the other's off your mam and dad.'

'Who're yours off?' said Dana.

Patty held up the remaining envelopes. 'One off Mam, one off Dad, one off Lenny and one from Lucy.'

Dana peered at the envelopes in Patty's hands. 'Why didn't I get one off Lenny?'

Patty slit open the envelope of Lucy's letter. 'Perhaps yours has been held up in the mail.' She quickly scanned the letter. 'Lucy's lost her scrapbook, the one she keeps photos in. That's a shame.' She read in silence for a second or two before adding, 'She's got some leave comin' up and wants to know if she can come over for a visit.'

Dana glanced up from reading her mother's letter. 'Does she say when?'

'The seventh of August.' Patty's lips moved silently. 'So that's two and a bit weeks from today.' She glanced at the pages in Dana's hands. 'Does your mam say much?'

'Only that everythin's OK, but Dad's had a sore throat and a cough. That's nowt new; he suffers with hay fever quite a bit during the summer: runny eyes, nose, sore throat, you know the sort of thing.' She glanced from her letter to Lenny's unopened one. 'Are you goin' to open it?'

Patty stared at her for a second or two before slitting it open. She pulled a face as she read the content. 'He doesn't say anythin' much; he's still gettin' moved around a fair bit ...' She glanced at Dana. 'That's probably why your letter hasn't arrived yet.' Then she continued to read, '... and he'll ring when he gets the chance.' She folded the first two letters and placed them back into her bag. 'When was the last time you heard from him?'

'A few weeks ago. He didn't say much – I'm wonderin' if he's gorra girlfriend.'

Patty raised her brow. 'Would you be bothered if he had?'

Dana glanced around the rest of the occupants of the lorry before speaking in a lowered voice. 'I know I'm with Pete, but ...'

Patty nodded encouragingly. 'But?'

'It's his dad.'

'Him!' huffed Patty. 'Well, just remember what I said: it's not him you've gorra kiss, it's Pete.' She hesitated. 'Or are you keepin' your options open with Lenny?'

A line creased Dana's brow. 'No!' Then she hesitated. 'Sort of.'

Patty wagged a reproving finger. 'You mustn't be greedy, Dana.'

'I'm not!' said Dana quickly. 'I – oh, I don't know what I want.'

'More like who,' said Patty. 'You can say what you like, I know you still carry a torch for Lenny ...'

Dana hushed Patty into silence as a flush crept up her neckline. 'Not here – too many ears.'

Patty peered past Dana. 'We'll talk more once we're in Plymouth.' She opened the letter from her mother.

The lorry eventually came to a halt and Dana and Patty jumped down. 'Where to?' said Patty.

'Let's go for a walk around the shops. I know we've got no money but we can still look.'

Setting off in the direction of the city centre, Dana hoped her friend would forget the conversation on the lorry.

Patty turned to Dana. 'Is Pete goin' to tell his dad?'

'No, I told him not to.'

'Why'd you do that?' said Patty.

Dana slipped her arm through Patty's. 'I think it's silly. We've not been courtin' long and who knows where we're headed, so why risk causin' upset for summat which might not last?'

Patty stopped walking and turned to face Dana. 'Did you actually say that to Pete?'

Dana shook her head hurriedly. 'God no, I just said there weren't no sense in rockin' the boat.'

Nodding, Patty broke back into step. 'I understand your reservations, but you're bein' awfully pessimistic. After all, who's to say you won't be married a year from today?'

Far from looking delighted, Dana looked stunned. 'Me! I don't want to get married, not for a long time.'

'What if Lenny were to ask?'

Dana groaned as she continued to walk. 'I thought you'd forgotten about that.'

'Not a chance. I saw the look on your face: you're worried he might have a girlfriend, aren't you?'

Dana nodded wretchedly. 'Although I don't understand why. Pete's a wonderful man, and I know I'm the envy of many women, but no matter how hard I try I just can't get Lenny out of my head!'

'If you want my opinion it's because you never told Lenny the truth and you can't move on until you know his thoughts,' said Patty simply.

Dana looked fearful. 'I can't tell him. I don't know what I'd do if he walked away from me for ever. I know it shouldn't bother me, 'cos he's not worth knowin' if he doesn't like me for who I am, but I can't help it.' She gave Patty a wobbly smile. 'The thought of losin' Lenny hurts so much I'm beginnin' to think I might be in love with him.'

'I knew it!' said Patty with a triumphant air. Then she hesitated. 'Hang on, do you love him, or are you in love with him?'

Dana breathed out. 'I'm not sure. What's the difference?'

Patty shrugged. 'Damned if I know.'

Gazing at the shops ahead of them Dana conjured up a picture of Lenny in her mind: twinkling blue eyes, blond curly hair and white teeth, the front two of which were slightly uneven. An image of Pete appeared beside Lenny; he had sparkling brown eyes and short-cropped dark hair, but his teeth were even, and he had a cleft chin on a square jaw. 'If I'm honest I think I might be in love with both of them.' She looked at Patty. 'I'm so confused.'

'I'm not surprised!' said Patty. 'If I were you I'd cut my losses and tell Lenny, then maybe you'll know how you really feel.'

Dana drew a deep breath. 'I'll tell Lenny if he comes to Harrowbeer.' She pointed up at a billboard. '*The Road To Zanzibar*. Why don't we go and see that? Bob Hope allus manages to cheer me up.'

'Good idea. After that we can have us some lunch at the chippie.' Patty pulled her purse out of her handbag. 'Whilst we're on about good ideas, I think you're doin' the right thing by tellin' Lenny, but why wait until he comes to Harrowbeer? You have to bite the bullet sooner or later so mebbe give him a telephone call when we get back?'

Dana shook her head. 'If I'm goin' to tell Lenny I'd rather do it face to face.'

Alexa looked at the old man from the Steam Room Café; each time she changed trains, or stopped at a station, she'd expected him to leave, but so far they had wound up in the same carriage. She eyed him suspiciously; was it her imagination or was he following her? True, the trains were full to bursting and she supposed he had had very little choice as to which carriage he got a seat in, much the same as her, but why then, on one leg of their journey, when neither of them was lucky enough to get a seat, did he still choose the same carriage? Hearing the squeal of the train's wheels, she looked out of the window to see which station they were pulling into. She smiled to herself: not long before she would be back in Liverpool. She wondered whether she should wake Grouch – the nickname she had chosen for her unwanted companion – and tell him where they were in case this was his stop. She had been gazing at him thoughtfully when his eyes snapped open. Blushing, Alexa quickly looked out of the window.

The old man spoke for the first time. 'Where are we?'

'Chester,' said Alexa, adding hopefully, 'Is this your stop?'

He shook his head. 'Liverpool, you?'

'Same.'

'You were the young Waaf in the Steam Room, in Yelverton.'

Alexa nodded. 'That's right.'

'Are you stationed at Harrowbeer?'

She nodded.

Leaning forward, he cleared his throat. 'I hope you don't mind my saying but I couldn't help overhearing your conversation with your pal ...'

'That's eavesdroppin',' snapped Alexa irritably.

He raised a doubtful brow. 'I don't know whether it is; you were shouting.'

Alexa blushed. 'Still no excuse,' she muttered.

He nodded. 'You're right, and I know I shouldn't have, only I was sure I heard you say they're letting travellers into the WAAF?'

Nodding, Alexa's blush deepened.

He shook his head. 'I must say I agree with you about that.'

A crease wrinkled her brow. 'Agree with me about what, exactly?'

'That they don't belong in the services.'

Alexa was beginning to lose patience. 'I never said that!'

He held his hands up in an apologetic manner. 'Sorry, my mistake. I knew you were objecting to them for some reason, but I obviously got it wrong.'

'Yes, you did,' said Alexa hotly.

He rubbed his whiskery chin. 'That's right! I remember now – you wanted to warn some chap about this Lana woman, let him know who she was, am I right?'

'No, because her name's Dana, and anyway I was wrong, it's nowt to do wi' me!' Alexa said sulkily, adding, 'Nor you.'

They sat in silence for the remainder of the journey, Alexa glaring out of the window whilst the old man returned to the book he had been reading.

She felt an overwhelming sense of relief as the train pulled into Lime Street Station. Thank God for that, thought Alexa, who wished the old man hadn't bothered talking to her. She waited for the train to come to a stop before risking picking up her kitbag. Looking out of the window she saw her parents waving to her from the platform. The old man was the first down off the train; turning, he held his hand up to help Alexa down with her kitbag.

Glancing swiftly at him from under her lashes, she muttered her thanks.

'Not at all, my dear, and I'm sorry if I offended you ...' He knitted his brows. 'Sorry, what was your name again?'

'Alexa,' she said.

He smiled briefly. 'Thank you, Alexa, and I hope you enjoy your leave.'

'What do you mean?' she started, but it was too late, he was already walking briskly towards a man who appeared to be waiting for him.

'Good trip, sir?'

'No, it bloody well wasn't,' he growled. 'Although if it hadn't been cut short, I'd've been oblivious to my son's idiotic behaviour.'

The driver opened the rear door of the Daimler. 'I'm afraid it's not lookin' good back home either, sir.'

'Don't tell me they've shot the bloody thing?'

Taking his place behind the wheel, the chauffeur shook his head. 'No, but, well, you'll see for yourself.' He glanced nervously in the rear-view mirror. 'I hope you found your son in good health?'

'Physically, yes, but not mentally. Mentally he's lost his bloody mind!' snapped the older man. 'Enough with your questions, just get me home.'

'Yes, Mr Robinson.' The driver of the Daimler knew his employer's son took delight in antagonising his father, and wondered what he had done to incur the old man's wrath this time.

Chapter Nine

'Lucy!' yelled Dana and Patty together.

Lucy glanced down at the stripes on her arms 'That's Corporal Lucy to you!' She pulled some change out of her purse and handed it to the driver.

Rushing over, the girls admired Lucy's stripes. 'When?' said Dana, running her finger around the insignia.

'About a week ago. I wanted to keep it as a surprise,' said Lucy, adding, 'Taffy's right proud of me.'

'As are we!' said Patty. 'Are you goin' to go for sergeant?'

Lucy shrugged; then she nodded. 'I'd like to, and they reckon I've got a good chance, so …'

Picking up Lucy's kitbag, Dana slung it over one shoulder and then threaded her other arm through one of Lucy's whilst Patty took the other. 'Golly, I think I'd be too thick to go for summat like that,' mused Dana. 'And I reckon Alexa would pass out if she thought I were a rank above her.'

'She still givin' you earache?' said Lucy.

Patty glanced at Dana. 'Actually she's been awfully quiet since she come back from Liverpool, don't you think?'

Dana nodded. 'I ain't askin' why though. Dad allus said you shouldn't poke a sleepin' bear.'

'Sound advice.' Lucy chuckled. 'Do you think she might've found a boyfriend?'

'Don't know, don't care, as long as she leaves me and Pete alone.'

'Talkin' of Pete, is he here?' Before either of them could answer she added, 'And Eddie, of course. I can't believe I've not met him yet.'

Patty nodded proudly. 'I can't believe my luck. He's wonderful, Lucy, you'll get on like a house on fire. I know you will.'

Lucy heaved a sigh. 'I envy you two; it must be such fun to go out in a foursome. I haven't seen Taff for ages.'

'How long are you here for?' said Dana.

'A whole week, not includin' travellin'. I've been savin' me leave and of course I haven't got any family …'

'… apart from us,' said Patty firmly.

Lucy smiled. 'Apart from you! So I thought I'd spend some time with the two of you.'

'Why not Taffy?' said Patty. 'Not that I don't want you to spend your time with us.'

Lucy grinned. 'When I leave here I'm bein' posted to Lincoln, not far away from Taff, so we should be able to see each other more often.'

'What luck!' said Patty.

'Isn't it?' breathed Lucy. 'I reckon I deserve some; when it comes to pals, I'm the only one of us who's on her own.'

'And Lenny,' said Dana.

Lucy glanced at Dana and then Patty. 'Haven't you heard?'

The colour drained from Dana's cheeks; whatever it was it sounded bad. 'No, what?'

'He wrote to me a couple of days ago, said he was being posted to Harrowbeer ...' She looked at the blank expressions on their faces. 'Oh dear, I hope I haven't spoilt the surprise.'

Dana beamed with relief. 'There was a delay with the mail this mornin'. We haven't had it yet.' She squeezed Lucy's arm in hers. 'This is the best news I've had in a long time! When's he comin'?'

Lucy pouted. 'A fortnight's time so I'm afraid I won't get to see him.'

Grabbing Dana's elbow, Patty let out a small gasp. 'You said you'd tell Lenny if ...'

Dana clapped a hand to her forehead. '... he came to Harrowbeer.'

'Tell Lenny what?' said Lucy.

'Dana's decided she's goin' to bite the bullet and tell Lenny she's a traveller,' said Patty. She glanced at Dana. 'Are you goin' to go through with it?'

Dana nodded decidedly. 'I've got a fortnight to make me mind up how I'm goin' to tell him.' She rested her cheek against Lucy's shoulder. 'I wish you were bein' posted here too.'

Lucy patted her hand reassuringly. 'Don't worry – you'll be fine. Besides, I don't reckon Lenny'll bat an eye.'

'Looks like we're soon goin' to find out,' said Patty pragmatically.

293

Dana let out a small groan as she clutched her hand to her stomach. 'Don't. I'm not lookin' forward to this, even if you are, Patty Blackwood.'

'I wouldn't say I was lookin' forward to you tellin' Lenny, but I am lookin' forward to knowin' whether your feelin's will change when he knows the truth.'

Dana's brow wrinkled. 'Why?'

'Because I reckon you an' Lenny are better suited than you an' Pete. Lenny's more reliable, more grown-up,' she said simply.

Lucy looked reprovingly at Patty. 'That may be, but don't forget about Pete. I know I don't know him, but I don't like the idea of him gettin' hurt.'

Dana eyed Patty thoughtfully. 'Supposin' you're right, and it turns out I have stronger feelin's for Lenny than I do for Pete, it doesn't mean to say they'll be reciprocated.'

Lucy and Patty burst out laughing. 'Yes they will,' said Lucy with conviction. 'I remember how he used to look at you in Pwllheli.'

'Me too,' agreed Patty. She turned to Lucy. 'I don't want to see Pete gerrin' hurt any more than you, but if Lenny and Dana do have a connection, it would be wrong of Dana to stay with Pete.'

'Oh dear,' said Lucy. 'Looks like someone's goin' to get hurt, either way.'

'Neither of you'll say anythin' to Pete about Lenny, will you?' said Dana.

'Course not!' said Patty.

'Thanks. I need some time to think, and I don't want Pete jumpin' to conclusions, especially if they're the wrong ones.'

Lucy turned to Patty. 'All this chat about Pete and Eddie: when am I goin' to get to see them?'

'We thought it might be nice if we all went out for lunch tomorrer,' said Patty. 'Dana said you were stayin' at the Who'd Have Thought It?'

Lucy nodded. 'It's about the closest to you; besides, I can't afford to stay in the Moorland.'

Dana chuckled. 'Pete took me there for a meal the day his father went back to Liverpool. It was lovely, but the prices!'

'Keepin' the riff raff out,' said Patty. 'Eddie said he'd take me if he were on a pilot's wages.'

Dana pulled a face. 'I prefer the Who'd Have Thought It, or the Rock: good honest pub grub. These posh places are all well and good, but they're not my cup of tea.'

'H'I wouldn't know,' said Patty in mock tones, 'we peasants can't afford to h'eat there.'

Lucy giggled. 'Golly, how I've missed you two!'

Pete stared at the letter in his hands.

Eddie, who was sitting across the table from his friend, looked up from his plate of sausage and chips. 'Everythin' all right?'

Pete looked grave. 'Have you said anything to my dad about Dana?'

Eddie shook his head in an annoyed fashion. 'No I have not. What would make you ask such a thing?'

Pete handed the letter over to Eddie, who wiped his hand on his trousers before taking it. Pete bit the end of his thumbnail as he waited for his friend to finish the epistle. Eddie grimaced as he handed the letter back. 'Don't look at me, I've not said owt.'

Pete scanned the letter again. 'Well, someone has, and they've done a bloody good job of it. I knew he wouldn't like the idea of Dana, of course I did, but I never thought he'd go this far!'

Eddie raised a fleeting brow. 'Do you mean by cuttin' you out of the will or disownin' you entirely?'

'Either, and it's not a joking matter. If I was going to tell my father I wanted him to hear it from me, but I still hadn't made up my mind what I was going to do. Well, this is going to force me into a decision. Because he says that he doesn't want to hear her name, never mind see her again, and if he hears I'm still seeing her' – he pulled his forefinger across his throat – 'that's the end of me and him.'

Eddie raised his eyebrows. 'I don't like to say I told you so but ...'

'I know, I know,' said Pete irritably.

'What're you goin' to do?'

Pete scowled as he folded the letter and placed it into the pocket of his flying jacket. 'Find out who's been telling tales, and what they've said, then go from there.'

Eddie screwed his face up in thought. 'Don't you think it's obvious?'

Pete shrugged. 'If you're referring to Alexa, then yes, but how? She doesn't know my dad, that's why I thought you might've said something by accident, and Dad was acting irrationally, 'cos if that was the case, I could try and reason with him.'

'Sorry, pal, whoever's pulled the trigger's done more than mention Dana's heritage.' His eyes rounded. 'A lot more.'

Pete rested his chin against his hands. 'I suppose if he's mentioned her back home, one of the old stable hands might know of her and her family. They're well known amongst the Liverpool carters, so it's quite possible someone might have recognised the name.'

Eddie pulled a doubtful face. 'Dana's a fairly common name.'

Pete's eyes narrowed. 'You think it's Alexa, don't you?'

Eddie nodded. 'She's the only one with cause to say summat, she never wanted you and Dana to get together in the first place and, from what I hear, she's not long got back from Liverpool.'

'Surely you can't think she went to the yard to see my father? I know she wasn't happy ...'

'Wasn't happy?' echoed Eddie. 'From what I heard she was spittin' feathers!'

Pete's brow furrowed. 'Even so, I can't see she'd go to those lengths.' He shrugged dismissively. 'Cause trouble between me and Dana, yes, but involve my family?'

Eddie tilted his head to one side. 'I reckon a woman like Alexa would go to the ends of the earth if it meant she broke the two of you up.' He paused momentarily. 'They say hell hath no fury ...' He arched a single eyebrow. 'Why don't you ask her?'

Pete's lips parted as he stared at Eddie. 'All that happened a long time ago. I'll look a fool if you're wrong ...'

'Perhaps she believes revenge is a dish best served cold,' said Eddie. 'Anyway, what if I'm right?'

Shaking his head, Pete ran his fingers through his hair. 'If you're right, then I can find out what she said, and make her tell my father it was all lies, or exaggerated anyway.'

'Then go ask her. You might even get the truth if you catch her on the hop.'

Pete snatched his hat from off the table. 'You coming?'

Eddie nodded. 'Just to make sure you keep your gentlemanly composure.'

Pete drew a deep breath. 'No promises!'

A small frown etched Maisie's forehead as she glanced out of the parlour window. 'What time did you say your lift to the station was getting here at?'

Alexa glanced at the alarm clock. 'Not for another fifteen minutes, why?'

Maisie nodded in the direction of a car which had pulled up outside. 'Someone's here.' Hesitating, she turned sharply to look at Alexa. 'What've you done?'

Alexa scowled indignantly. 'Nothin'. Why, who is it?'

'Pete Robinson and his mate Eddie and—'

Alexa rushed over to the parlour window. 'D'you reckon he's come to ask me not to leave? Or to find out where I'm goin'? Perhaps him and Dana've split up and he's realised—'

This time Maisie cut Alexa off. 'He doesn't look very happy. Are you *sure* you haven't done anythin'?'

'I've not done a soddin' thing!' snapped Alexa. 'Why don't you make yourself useful an' let him in?'

Maisie was half inclined to tell Alexa she could jolly well let him in herself, when she remembered that Alexa was being posted to London, and she would therefore not have to suffer the other girl's bossy attitude for much longer.

Maisie opened the back door just as Pete's knuckles connected with the wood. 'Hello, Pete, Eddie, what brings you here?'

'Is she in?' said Pete, trying to keep his voice level.

Heaving a sigh, Maisie nodded. 'You've just caught her; another quarter of an hour and she'd've been bound for London.' She looked at Alexa, who was straightening her skirt with one hand and patting her hair into place with the other. 'You've got visitors.'

Alexa smiled brightly at Pete and Eddie. 'Have you come to say goodbye? I must say it's awfully nice of you, especially ...'

Pete's jaw twitched as his eyes met hers. 'Have you been to see my father?'

Alexa blinked; then she shook her head. 'No, why would you think I had?'

'Because somebody has told him about Dana.'

Maisie placed one hand on her hip, the other to her forehead. 'You promised you wouldn't.'

Pete glared at Maisie. 'What do you mean, she promised?'

Maisie's eyes were fixed on Alexa, who looked genuinely shocked. 'I didn't, I swear ...'

'Maisie?' said Pete. Careful to keep his voice even, he added, 'I'm not angry with you.'

Maisie's eyes flickered towards Alexa, who had folded her arms across her chest in a forbidding fashion. 'She was goin' to tell your father that Dana was a traveller, but I managed to talk her out of it.' She stared at Alexa in disappointment. 'Why'd you do it? After all we said?'

Alexa's arms flew above her head before flapping down by her sides. 'I didn't!' She looked at Pete in appeal. 'I admit I was goin' to, but when Maisie come to the train station we talked things through and I promised her I wouldn't.' She glanced at Maisie, her gaze beseeching, 'I swear I didn't do it.'

Pete shook his head. 'Well, someone did, and you're the only one with motive. Hellfire, Alexa, you've even admitted you intended to, so why not tell the truth?'

Alexa gave a short burst of mirthless laughter. Turning to her kitbag, she pulled the top closed. 'Do you know what? I wish I had gone to see him now, seein' as I'm gettin' the blame for it anyway. Although it just goes to show I'm obviously not the only one who thought you were doin' the wrong thing.' Swinging the bag on to her shoulder she turned to face the three of them; blinking back the tears that were forming in her eyes, she continued, 'I reckern they've done you a favour, and you can't blame your father for being concerned about the future of his stud with someone like Dana tryin' to take over. It only takes one mistake to make a baby ...'

Pete's mouth dropped open. 'It was you! That's exactly what my father said, more or less word for word.'

Maisie, who had been watching Alexa very carefully, turned to Pete. 'Only I don't think it was. I know Alexa and she'd have admitted it by now if it was her, especially with so much evidence against her.' Her brows knitted, deep in thought. 'Did he say someone had been to see him?'

Pete shook his head. 'Not as such, just that he knew all about Dana, and her plan for a shotgun wedding.'

Alexa and Maisie both went crimson. Maisie looked at Alexa; her voice was hollow when she spoke. 'That's what you said, when we were in the Steam Room Café.'

Alexa grinned triumphantly at Pete. 'See? It wasn't me who told your dad. Someone must've overheard me in the café. That's hardly my fault.'

Pete's breathing quickened. 'When was this exactly?'

'The day I went back to Liverpool, why?'

Pete shook his head angrily. 'Was there a bad-tempered old chap in the Steam Room, same height as me, whiskery grey beard ...' He stopped talking; he could tell by the look on their faces that he was right.

Alexa's grin disappeared in an instant. 'He was on the same train as me too; in fact he follered me the whole way home. I thought it were odd that we kept endin' up in the same carriage, and when he said he'd overheard me and Maisie talkin' about ...' She hung her head for a moment, but then looked up at Pete. 'I didn't mean to tell him, but I reckern it's probably best that I did. Your father has a right to know.'

Pete stared at her in disbelief. 'Know what, Alexa? That Dana was planning on getting pregnant? I understand you can only speak for yourself, but Dana's not like that.' He turned to Maisie. 'Thanks for trying to stop her. You couldn't have known it was my father in the café.'

Alexa glared angrily at Pete. 'Neither could I!'

301

'Makes no difference, she only came to the station to stop you from telling him, because that was your intent, wasn't it?'

A car horn sounded outside the house and Alexa strode towards the back door. 'You'll thank me one day!'

Pete turned on his heel to reply, but Eddie laid an arm across his chest. 'Don't, mate, she's not worth it.'

Within a few seconds Alexa had gone. Maisie twisted her fingers around each other in an awkward fashion. 'I'm so sorry, I should've warned you.'

Pete shook his head. 'Wouldn't have made the slightest difference; in fact it might've only provoked her to do worse.' He drew a deep breath. 'Can you do me a favour, Maisie, and not mention this to anyone?'

Maisie rolled her eyes. 'Don't worry. I don't want anyone thinkin' I had anythin' to do with it. They may not all be as understandin' as you.'

Pete smiled. 'Good girl.'

Eddie nudged Pete with his elbow. 'We're goin' to be late for our lunch with the girls.'

Bidding Maisie a hasty goodbye, the boys piled into the car. As they sped down the high-hedged lane Eddie turned to Pete. 'What are you goin' to say to Dana?'

'Not a dickie bird, or at least not until I've had a chance to speak to my father, and I'm not goin' to phone him until I know what I'm goin' to say. Besides, it'll do him good to stew for a bit.'

Lucy, Dana and Patty sat outside the Who'd Have Thought It, enjoying a cool glass of refreshing lemonade, awaiting the boys' arrival.

'Last time I was here it was to meet Pete's dad,' said Dana, placing her glass on the wooden table and glancing in the direction of the bar. 'I felt so sorry for the staff; he behaved like an arrogant pig. I was worried they might think we were related.'

Patty tipped her head to one side. 'You will be if you and Pete ever get married.'

Dana laughed. 'I can't see that happenin', can you?'

'You never know. Besides, you'd be marryin' Pete, not his father,' said Patty. 'You'd probably only see him on the day of the weddin', and the christenin's, of course. I've allus thought Pete'd be the sort to move abroad after the war.'

Dana coughed on a mouthful of lemonade. 'Abroad? What makes you say that?'

'He just seems the sort.' She glanced enquiringly at Dana. 'Wouldn't you want to get as far away as possible from that awful pig of a man if he was your father?'

Dana nodded fervently. 'I'm not sure I'd leave the country though.'

'So, what do you see for yourself, when the time comes to marry and settle down?' said Lucy plainly. 'A small stone cottage deep in the country with a white picket fence, two children and a dog called Snowy?'

Dana aimed a playful punch at Lucy, who dodged out of the way. 'Nothin' wrong wi' that.'

Patty tried to envisage Pete in an idyllic family setting. 'Do you think that's what Pete sees when he thinks of his future?'

'No, I don't think Pete's plannin' on growin' up, not for a long time yet,' said Dana. 'He's havin' too much fun flyin' his kite.'

303

'*Fun*?' echoed Lucy. 'How can that be fun? Sounds downright dangerous to me.'

'Me too,' agreed Dana, 'but it's the danger that Pete finds so excitin'; he says the feelin' he gets in his tummy when he's in a dog fight makes him feel alive.' She took another sip of her lemonade. 'That's why I think he'll get bored of me, 'cos once this dreadful business is all over and I'm demobbed, I want to start me own business, mebbe a tea shop or summat like that.'

'I know they say opposites attract,' said Patty, 'but you two are poles apart.'

'I agree with Patty,' said Lucy. 'You'd be leadin' separate lives. I know it works for some, but is that what you really want?'

Dana nodded in the direction of a car that had pulled up outside the pub. 'Here they come.'

Pete and Eddie hopped out of the car. 'Sorry we're late,' said Pete. 'You know how it is.'

Pete and Eddie exchanged guilty glances as all three girls nodded. 'Has anyone seen the menu?'

Dana pointed at a blackboard outside the door to the pub. 'We were waitin' for you to arrive.'

Pete rubbed his tummy enthusiastically. 'Let's see what they've got. I'm famished!'

It was a few days into Lucy's leave when Dana got a call to go into the office. The sergeant gestured for her to sit down; he looked grave.

'Have I done somethin' wrong?' ventured Dana timidly.

The sergeant indicated for the corporal to close the door. 'We've had a phone call from your mother.'

The colour drained from Dana's cheeks. 'What's wrong?'

He eyed her sympathetically. 'Your father is very ill, and your mother has asked that you be sent for.'

Frowning, Dana looked from the corporal, who gave a small sympathetic grimace, to the sergeant. 'I don't understand. I spoke to Mam not long ago, she said he had a bit of a sore throat but he's had that for ages. Has he had an accident?'

The sergeant leaned forward. 'He's got throat cancer.'

Dana stared at the sergeant, she felt herself go numb as silent tears trickled down her cheeks. She watched the sergeant's mouth move up and down as he spoke but she didn't hear a word he said. An image of her father, strong and proud, formed in her mind. How could he have cancer? Surely there must have been some mistake? Were the doctors that poor in Ireland that they didn't know the difference between hay fever and cancer? The corporal's voice penetrated her thoughts.

'We've arranged for a car to take you to the station; it'll be here in an hour. In the meantime, we'll arrange for travel passes, et cetera.'

Dana nodded slowly. Placing her hands on the arms of the chair she looked directly at the sergeant. 'Do they think he's goin' to die? Is that why they've sent for me?'

The sergeant swallowed uneasily. 'I don't know; they just said it's imperative you see him.'

Dana gave a small nod before leaving the room. Patty stood outside the office. 'Well?' Seeing Dana's tear-stained cheeks, she immediately embraced her friend. 'What happened?'

Dana's face crumpled. 'It's Dad, he's – he's ...' She burrowed her face into Patty's shoulder.

Patty stroked her friend's back. 'Take a deep breath, chuck.'

'He's got throat cancer.' Leaning back, Dana drew a tissue from her handbag and blew her nose. 'Do you think they might've made a mistake? Mam said he had hay fever ...'

Patty felt certain that any doctor would know the difference between hay fever and throat cancer, but she had no desire to rob her friend of the only sliver of hope she possessed. 'You won't know until you get there ...' She hesitated. 'How *are* you gettin' there?'

'They're sendin' a driver for me in an hour, and they'll arranges passes and the like.' She dried her eyes and glanced up at Patty. 'Can you telephone the pub and let Lucy know?'

Patty nodded. 'It's really serious, isn't it?'

Dana gave a small nod. 'He allus said he didn't want me to cross the Irish Sea until things had calmed down, but they haven't calmed down, have they?'

Patty shook her head.

'It must be bad because they've said it's imperative that I see him.' Her eyes shimmered with tears again.

Pete hailed them from across the way. 'What's happened? Eddie came and said you'd been called into the office?'

Dana opened her mouth to reply, but emotion overwhelmed her. Taking Dana in his arms, Pete looked expectantly at Patty.

'She's been told she has to go to see her father in Ireland. He's got cancer.'

Pete swore softly under his breath. 'When are you going?'

Dana glanced at the watch on his wrist. 'I've got just under an hour, but it won't take me that long to pack me things. Patty's goin' to let Lucy know.'

The hour seemed like an eternity. Lucy had come as soon as she heard. Dana glanced at her friend's kitbag. 'You leavin' early?'

Lucy nodded. 'You could say that. I'm comin' with you.'

Dana gaped. 'How? You've gorra go to Lincoln – you'll never make it to Ireland and back in time!'

'As soon as I put the telephone down to Patty I rang the station and spoke to Sergeant Hastings. He's the one you met when you came to visit.'

Patty nodded. 'I remember, he was a nice chap.'

Lucy smiled. 'When I told him about Dana, he said I could take extended leave.'

Dana shook her head. 'You're meant to be on your hols.'

'And now I'm goin' to be spendin' them in Ireland,' said Lucy plainly.

Dana gave Lucy a rather wobbly smile. 'Thanks, chuck.' Looking down at her travel passes, she handed some to Lucy. 'I thought he'd made a mistake, given me too many, but I'm guessin' these must be yours?'

Lucy took them from her. 'Sarge must've telephoned Harrowbeer and asked them if they could arrange some for me too.'

A car pulled up beside the gate. 'Looks like you're off,' said Pete.

Swallowing hard, Dana nodded. 'Thanks for stayin' with me.'

'Not goin' to leave you on your own, are we!' said Patty. 'Not after news like that.'

Dana hugged Pete and Patty goodbye before getting into the back seat of the car. She wound down the window. 'I'll let you know what happens.'

Patty slid her arm through Pete's. 'Good luck and take care, and give our love to your folks!'

Lucy and Dana waved goodbye. Glancing over her shoulder, Dana saw Patty burrow her face against Pete's arm. Bottom lip trembling, Dana turned to Lucy. 'I reckern I must be the luckiest girl in the world to have pals like you.'

Lucy dabbed her eyes with her handkerchief. 'We're the lucky ones.' Placing her hand in Dana's, she looked at the cowslips that bowed their heads as the car drove past; the fields behind the hedgerows were laden with golden corn that stood bright in the sunshine. Squeezing Dana's hand in hers, she wondered how something so awful could be happening on such a beautiful day.

Twenty-four hours after first hearing the dreadful news, Dana and Lucy arrived in Ireland.

'It's beautiful,' said Lucy as the taxi drove through the city of Dublin. 'It's just like Liverpool used to be before the bombin'.'

'You're lucky, you know,' Dana informed the taxi driver, 'not to be involved.'

The taxi driver shrugged. 'It's got nuttin' to do wi' us.' His eyes met hers in the rear-view mirror. 'Do you have family in Drogheda?'

Dana nodded. 'Me mam and dad …' The last word came out in a whisper.

He nodded. 'Lovely part of Ireland is Drogheda – you'll like it there.'

Pete sat in the cockpit of his Spitfire, Lady Luck. The operation was a simple one, which was just as well, because right now all he could think about was Dana's father and how he wished he could have gone to Ireland to support her. He knew you were only granted compassionate leave if things were really bad. He feared that her father had very little time left and he had said as much to Eddie the previous evening.

'I'm worried she's going to lose him, Eddie, and she idolises that man; she's been beating herself up because she's not seen him since she joined the WAAF.'

Eddie had frowned. 'It was her father's wish that she not undertake the journey – hardly Dana's fault.' He had come out from under the vehicle he was working on. 'Talkin' of fathers, have you worked out what you're goin' to say to yours?'

'I'm too upset to deal with him at the moment. I'll only end up giving him a right earful. Besides, I'm more worried about Dana at the minute.'

Now, as Lady Luck joined the other Spitfires on the runway, Pete pushed the lever forward and smiled as the plane gathered speed. Once he was in the air he would forget all his worries and concentrate on the task in hand. He'd try telephoning Dana on his return, but for now he would enjoy the peace and quiet as they crossed the Channel.

Dana looked up at the sign above the ward. 'This is the one, St Enda's.' She looked anxiously at Lucy. 'I'm scared, Lu. Mickey Davies, one of the carters, had cancer and he went from a huge beast of a man to a skinny weakling, too tired to do anythin' for himself.' Her bottom lip quivered. 'I don't think I could bear to see me dad like that.'

Lucy stroked Dana's shoulder. 'Don't worry, chuck, I'll be with you every step of the way. Stiff upper lip an' all that.'

Nodding, Dana banished the tears that were threatening to form. She placed the palm of her hand against the door and pushed. A nurse paused mid-step as Dana and Lucy entered the ward. '*An féidir liom cabhrú leat?*'

Dana and Lucy exchanged blank glances. 'I'm here to see my father, Shane Quinn?' Dana ventured.

The nurse smiled warmly at Dana. 'You must be Dana.' She held out a hand. 'He's been talkin' about you all mornin'; the thought of you comin' has really cheered him up. I'll take you to him.'

Dana followed the nurse into the ward. Her father waved to her from one of the middle beds. 'Dana, darlin', you are a sight for sore eyes.'

Dana stared. The man who had hailed her from the bed was a shadow of his former self. Lucy nudged her in the small of her back and Dana strode over to his bed. 'Dad?'

He smiled weakly. 'Come an' give your dad a kiss.'

Tears flowed down her cheeks as she bent to kiss him. He turned his face to meet hers and Dana felt his lips brush against her cheek as he attempted to kiss her back. Forcing a smile she sat down on the bed beside him. 'I'm so sorry.'

'Whatever for? This ain't your fault ...' he said hoarsely.

'I should've come with you. If I had, things might've been different.'

He shook his head weakly. 'I didn't get cancer because you stayed in Liverpool.' He looked past Dana to Lucy.

Dana gestured Lucy to come closer. 'This is Lucy, she's one of me bezzies.' She glanced around her. 'Where's Mam?'

Shane smiled up at Lucy. 'Hello, Lucy, it's nice to know our Dana has good friends.'

Hearing the sound of approaching footsteps, Shane went on, 'Here's your mam.'

Standing up, Dana stared at her mother; a frown of incomprehension wrinkled her brow. She lowered her voice so that only her mother could hear. 'You told me he had hay fever.' She glanced at her father from over her shoulder before fixing her mother with an accusing stare. 'Does he look like he's got hay fever to you?' She continued before her mother could answer: 'He's skin an' bone, for God's sake!'

Silent tears fell down her mother's impassive face. 'We really did think it was hay fever at first, but your father went downhill really fast, only he refused to go to the doctor's, and by the time he did it was too late. I wanted to tell you, but he didn't want you to worry, and he was too ill for me to upset him by goin' against his wishes.' She hung her head guiltily. 'I'm so sorry, love.'

Dana softened. She knew what her father could be like when he got an idea in his head. 'I should be the one apologisin'. I should've realised you'd know it were more than hay fever, and I know how headstrong Dad can be. I don't blame you, not really.'

She sat back down. 'When are they goin' to operate?'

Her father glanced up at his wife, who looked at Dana. 'Who said he was havin' an operation?'

Dana glanced around the ward. 'He's in hospital.' She looked at the two of them. 'If they're not goin' to operate, then what's the point in bein' here?'

The colour drained from Colleen's cheeks, and she gazed at Dana through soulless eyes. 'This isn't the sort of hospital where they make you better, love ...'

Dana frowned, but Lucy gestured to the other patients, all of whom looked as though they were at death's door.

Realisation dawned. Dana shook her head. 'No, Dad needs to go to a proper hospital, gerra second opinion.' She looked at her father earnestly. 'You don't belong here.'

Shane smiled sympathetically. 'They can't fix me, love, that's why they called for you.'

Dana felt Lucy lay a hand on her shoulder. Turning, she tried to smile, but all pretence was gone. If she was honest, she'd known there was no hope the second she laid eyes on her father. 'How long?'

Shane tried to shrug. 'Dunno, luvvy, but not too long, I hope.'

The tears trickled down her cheeks. 'Are you in much pain?'

He tried to nod, winced and smiled.

'Oh, Daddy.' Dana sank to her knees and placed her face next to his. 'This bloody war! I should've come over the first bit of leave I got. I shouldn't've left it so long.'

He stroked her hair back from her face. 'You're here with me now, an' that's all that matters.' He gently kissed the top of her head. 'You've made me the proudest father in the world, and I wouldn't change a single thing.'

Sniffing back the tears she glanced up. 'What d'you mean?'

He looked at Colleen. 'It's time, luv.'

Colleen glanced at Lucy. 'Would you mind?'

Lucy stepped back. 'I'll be outside.'

Dana's mother pulled the curtains around the bed and knelt down beside Dana. 'There's summat we've been meanin' to tell you for ever such a long time. We'd planned on tellin' you when you turned eighteen, but war broke out and ...' She shrugged. 'Everything changed.'

'Tell me what?' She hesitated as a thought crossed her mind. 'Has this got summat to do wi' Dad's side of the family?'

Colleen nodded. 'It's better if I start at the beginning. Me an' your dad wanted a baby, but after tryin' for over a year the doctors did some tests, an' that's when they told us I couldn't conceive. As you can imagine we was devastated by the news. We wanted a child more than anythin', but there was nothin' we could do about it.

313

The doctor suggested we might go down the adoption route, but we dismissed the idea; after all, who'd want to give their child to travellers?' She slipped her hand into Dana's. 'To cut a long story short, the doctor come to see us in the wagon one night, he said there was a woman due to give birth, an' she had to give her baby up.' Tears brimmed in Colleen's eyes as she recalled the memory. 'He said we would have to make up our minds there and then.' She glanced lovingly at Shane, who nodded. 'We already knew the answer.'

Shane smoothed Dana's cheek with the back of his fingers. 'You were tiny, just over five pounds.'

Dana stared at them in disbelief as the penny dropped. 'I'm adopted?' As the words left her lips she felt the blood drain from her face and she began to feel light-headed. 'I – I can't be!'

Shane nodded, his face full of concern. 'Are you angry with us?'

Dana shook her head fervently, which made her feel dizzy, so she took a deep breath before continuing. 'Why would I be angry with you?' She glanced reassuringly at her mother. 'Either of you? And what had any of this to do with the rest of the family?'

'When we took you back to the wagon, we explained what had happened to the rest of the family ...' Colleen looked dumbfounded as she recalled the memory. 'Your uncle were furious. He said it were better to go wi'out a child than bring an outsider into the family.'

'I was a baby!' said Dana quietly.

'They didn't care,' said Shane bitterly. 'They told us we had to make a decision, you or them.' Raising

Dana's hand, he kissed the back of her fingers. 'We left right there an' then.'

When Dana next spoke the words came out in a whisper. 'Thank you.'

Shane's brow furrowed. 'What for?'

'For takin' me in when me own mother didn't want me, for givin' me a home, for choosin' me over your own family. Why on earth do you think I'd be angry?'

''Cos if we hadn't been so selfish and said yes, someone else might've,' explained Colleen. 'And you could've had a normal life, gone to school, played in the streets ...' She stopped speaking as Shane raised a withered hand.

'You'd not have been an outcast, Dana,' he said simply.

Dana kissed her father's forehead. 'Thanks to you I never felt like an outcast.' She gently placed the palm of her hand against his hollow cheek. 'You've no need to worry. You gave me a brilliant life; I've been ever so happy. If it weren't for you, God only knows where I'd've ended up.'

The worry lines etched on her father's face relaxed.

Colleen looked lovingly at her husband. 'You've made me and your father very happy, Dana.'

Seeing his daughter's cheeks wet with tears, he tilted his head to one side. 'Do you remember what I used to do when you got upset as a child?'

Dana nodded. 'You used to give me a butterfly kiss because it tickled, and I'd stop cryin'.'

He beckoned her to lean forward. Dana could just about feel his lashes flutter against her cheek. 'Don't cry, luv, and look after your mam for me.'

Turning her head, Dana kissed his cheek. 'Course I will. Now stop your worryin' and get some rest. I love you, Daddy.'

A faint smile crossed his lips. 'I love you too, my darlin' Dana.' As he sank back into his pillows, Dana saw the sparkle in his eyes fade.

Pete scoured the skies for a sign of the Focke-Wulf that one of the Yanks claimed to have seen. Seeing phantom aeroplanes was not uncommon when flying through a cloud-studded sky, and it had been a few seconds since the sighting, so Pete began to think the other pilot had been mistaken and he started to relax. It was a routine operation, something which Pete had done many times before. He looked down at the choppy waters of the English Channel and wondered what his father had been like as a pilot. He couldn't imagine he ever got nervous, or that he allowed his imagination to get the better of him. Arrogant sod, Pete thought bitterly, he probably thought the Krauts wouldn't attack him because of who he is! He glanced at a plane to the left of him just visible through the patches of cloud; for a second he thought it was the Focke-Wulf, until he saw the familiar roundel of the RAF. Annoyed, he chastised himself for allowing his mind to wander. He bet his father had never allowed his thoughts to wander when he'd been in the RFC. Hearing the sound of gunfire Pete looked wildy around him. Was it friendly fire by another pilot who thought he'd seen the Focke-Wulf? Seeing a plane come out through the clouds, his eyes rounded in horror as he realised it was the Focke-Wulf and it was heading straight for him, emptying its guns as it went. Pete watched helplessly as the tracer bullets hit the side of his plane, from engine to tail. There was no time to manoeuvre, no time to retaliate; Lady Luck had been hit and black smoke was billowing from her engine. Looking at the floor of the cockpit, Pete saw flames licking his flying boots. He slackened the straps and tried to open the canopy, but it was stuck fast. He pounded his fists against the catch, but in vain – it wouldn't budge – and he had just resigned himself to the inevitable when he heard a click followed by the sound of rushing air. Relieved to be free, Pete pushed himself out, only to find that he had forgotten to jettison the canopy, and he was wedged on the lip which protruded over his backrest. Flailing wildly, Pete's foot caught the stick and the aircraft bunted; Pete felt the rush of air as he left Lady Luck. There was a sharp jerk as he pulled the cord to his parachute and it snapped open. Within seconds, his feet hit the sea. Pete saw his dinghy, which had opened automatically, floating away from him. He tried to swim towards it, but it seemed that with every stroke the dinghy drifted further away. Exhausted from the effort of trying to free himself from the burning Spitfire, darkness swam in front of Pete's vision. He saw Dana, reaching out to him, his father looking down on him with disapproval, and then, closing his eyes, Pete sank into a world of darkness.

Lenny pulled up beside the guard's gate to RAF Harrowbeer. He looked expectantly round him, hoping that he might see Dana or Patty, and was miffed that neither of the girls had bothered to show up. True, he hadn't had much time to tell them of the change of plan, but he had left a message with one of the Waafs in the NAAFI who claimed to know them. He wrinkled his brow; what was her name again? Melanie! She'd said something about Dana visiting her parents, and was unsure as to when she would be back, but he knew Patty was here.

'You can park by the Ops Room, second building on the right,' said the guard. He looked at Lenny and then cleared his throat to get his attention.

'Sorry, what was that?' said Lenny.

Shaking his head, the guard pointed to the Ops Room. 'Park over there.'

Nodding, Lenny put the car into gear, musing that Patty was probably on duty and she would catch up with him later. Getting out of his car, he decided the best place to go, after he'd signed in of course, was the NAAFI; if you wanted to know what's what on any station, the NAAFI was always your best bet, and someone was bound to know of Patty and Dana's whereabouts.

After being told where he would be sleeping, and what his duties for the following day would be, Lenny entered the NAAFI. He scanned the tables to see if he could see either of the girls. He knitted his eyebrows. Unlike most of the other stations he'd visited, Harrowbeer didn't seem too friendly; everyone was walking around with miserable expressions on their faces. He approached the Waaf behind the counter. 'Cup of tea and ...' He leaned back to see if he could guess what was in the sandwiches lined up behind the counter. '... a corned beef and tomato sarnie?'

Nodding, she fished the sandwich out and placed it on to a plate. 'Anything else?'

He grinned encouragingly at her. 'A smile?'

Glancing up, she stared at him without smiling. 'You're new.'

Lenny puffed his cheeks out. 'What gave it away: the happy face?'

Pushing the tea towards him, she held out her hand for the money which he placed in the palm of her hand. 'You've come at a bad time.'

He glanced around the rest of the NAAFI. 'Thank God for that, I'd hate to think this was normal.' Chuckling, he turned back to face the Waaf, but one look at her face told him this was not your normal bad day. 'I don't suppose you know Patty Blackwood, or Dana Quinn?'

She nodded. 'Dana's still on leave. Patty's in the tower.'

'Thanks. I'll nip along and see her after I've finished these,' he said, holding up the sandwich plate and the mug of tea.

'How do you know Patty and Dana?'

'We met when they were doin' their trainin' in Pwllheli,' said Lenny. 'I gave them some extra tuition to help get them through the exam and we've been firm friends ever since.'

She cocked her head to one side. 'Do you know Pete?' Seeing the blank look on Lenny's face, she added, 'Pete Robinson, Dana's boyfriend.'

Lenny stared at the Waaf. He felt as though he had been punched in the stomach. Dana had spoken of a pilot named Pete in her letters, but Lenny had assumed he was a friend. Aware that she was waiting for a response, he shook his head. 'Not personally; Dana's mentioned him in her letters though.' He looked at her quizzically. People didn't usually ask him so many questions when he arrived on a new station. 'Has something happened?'

She pointed to a table near the counter. 'Take a seat. There's something you should know before you speak to Patty.'

The funeral had been a quiet affair with few in attendance. Shane had been buried in the church where he and Colleen had been married. Dana had plaited a lock of her own hair with her mother's and Crystal's and placed it in her father's hands. Crystal had pulled the funeral hearse and they had sung hymns.

Dana had asked her mother what she intended to do without her father and Colleen's answer had been a simple one. 'Carry on. That's all I can do. Mrs O'Brien said she's got some sewin' work to keep me goin' and I've still got the wagon, so I've a roof over me head.'

'What will you do with Crystal?'

Colleen frowned. 'What d'you mean, what'll I do with him? Keep him of course.'

Dana opened her mouth only to be hushed into silence. 'I know what you're goin' to say, Dana, and I know he's more work, and I know I could get a pretty penny should I sell him, but he was your father's pride and joy. He's not for sale.'

'As soon as I'm demobbed I shall come straight back to Ireland,' said Dana with determination.

Colleen's brow shot towards her hairline. 'You'll do no such thing! I'm not havin' you put the rest of your life on hold just to keep me company ...'

'But Mam!' said Dana.

'No buts about it, young lady. I shall be movin' the wagon into one of the O'Briens' fields, so I'll not be short of company.'

'Promise me you'll let me know should you ever change your mind ...'

Colleen smiled. 'I will, but I won't be changin' me mind, so don't go puttin' any plans on hold.' She glanced at Lucy. 'From what you've said, our Dana's got a couple of eligible bachelors vyin' for her affections?'

Lucy nodded. 'She sure has.'

Colleen nodded approvingly. 'Good, 'cos I shall want grandchildren at some stage.'

'Mam!'

The taxi pulled up behind them and honked its horn. 'Goodbye, sweetheart; phone me when you get back.'

Nodding, Dana kissed her mother goodbye.

As the taxi wound its way towards the train station, Lucy looked out of her window at the people milling round the pavements, going about their business without a care in the world. 'It's goin' to be strange goin' back home, isn't it? I'd almost forgotten we were at war.'

'That's not the only thing that's goin' to be strange,' said Dana thoughtfully. 'I came to Ireland knowin' who I was, but I'll be leavin' as ...' She shrugged. 'I don't know what I am.'

Lucy leaned her elbow against the car door. 'Do you think you'll try and find your real mam?'

'Birth mam,' Dana corrected. 'And why would I want to waste my time lookin' for someone who happily gave her child away to strangers?' Hastily adding, 'Luckily for her my parents are good people, but she didn't know that.'

'I must admit I hadn't thought of it like that, but you're right, 'cos that's exactly what she did.'

Dana looked at Lucy. 'How could anyone give their baby away to strangers? Me mam and dad were desperate for a child, they'd not dream of handin' me over, so what does that say about me birth mam?'

'That she were desperate, probably like my mam.'

Dana clapped a hand to her mouth. 'Oh, Lucy, I didn't mean …' She took a deep breath. 'Your mam made sure you were safe by givin' you to the orphanage; my mam could've handed me over to murderers for all she knew.'

'What I'm tryin' to say is, lots of people find themselves in a position where they can't look after their children for lots of different reasons. Look at it this way: accordin' to your dad, you were a newborn, which means your birth mam probably wasn't thinkin' straight; she must've been under an awful lot of stress at the time.' She took Dana's hands in hers. 'I know you say me mam made sure I were safe, but I'm a foundling, dumped like a sack of rubbish on the doorstep of the orphanage – and I'm not the only one, it happens more than you think.'

Dana blinked slowly. 'I s'pose it must do.' She gave Lucy an apologetic smile. 'Sorry, Lu, I didn't mean to upset you.'

'Don't mention it – you've had a heck of a shock. You've lost your father and your identity in less than a few days; you're bound to be out of sorts. In a way I'm lucky, 'cos I've allus known I come from nowhere, so bein' an orphan is normal to me.'

'I'm angry, Lu, not with my parents but with me birth mam. I should be grievin' the loss of my father, but instead I'm wonderin' who my birth father was, 'cos he obviously didn't want me either.' A few drops of rain hit the window as she gazed at the rolling green hills spread as far as the eye could see.

Lucy's voice cut across her thoughts. 'I know you've spoken to Patty, but have you told her?'

'Only about me dad. I'll tell her the rest when we're face to face; same with Pete. I suppose I'm still tryin' to come to terms with it all.' Dana's mind's eye projected an image of her and Pete standing side by side in their uniforms; then another image of herself in a long skirt, a shawl round her shoulders and her hair blowing loose about her face, the curls entangling themselves with each other. 'Huh!' she murmured under her breath.

Lucy leaned towards her. 'What was that?'

'I've had suspicions for a long time now that Pete's only keen on me because I used to live in a wagon.'

Lucy raised her brows in surprise. 'I wonder what he'll say when he finds out the truth?' She smiled. 'You do know you're goin' to ruin Alexa's day when she finds out, 'cos she won't be able to make any more snide remarks.'

Another thought occurred to Dana. 'Thank goodness Pete never told his father! He'd look a real fool havin' to tell him he'd got it wrong.'

'From what you've told me he was rather looking forward to telling his father the truth, just to vex him.'

'That's what I mean,' said Dana thoughtfully. 'My past was a bonus to Pete; his father wanted him to wed someone prim and proper, someone who toes the line, keeps her mouth shut and does as she's told – bit like his mam by all accounts.'

Lucy let out a small squeal. 'Lenny!'

'What? Where?' said Dana, looking wildly around her.

'I mean, you've been worried about tellin' Lenny you're a traveller in case he doesn't want to know, but you don't have to worry about that any more because you're not!'

Dana's face was clouded with doubt. 'Not technically, but it's who I was, all I've ever known before I joined the WAAF.'

Lucy deflated a little. 'I suppose you're right, you've still got to tell him.' She shook her head. 'Poor Dana. If you're right about Pete you'll lose him because you aren't a traveller and if you tell Lenny you might lose him too! I can't say I envy you.'

'As if losin' my father wasn't bad enough!' Dana sniffed and blew her nose into her hanky. 'I don't think I could bear it if I lost both Pete *and* Lenny.'

Chapter Ten

Eddie held Patty's hand from across the table. 'When's Dana back?'

Patty's eyes flickered towards the clock above the door of the cookhouse. 'Her train arrived half an hour ago, or at least it should have if it was on time.'

'When's Lucy goin' to Lincoln?'

'In a couple of days.' She shook her head resignedly. 'Poor Lu, she'll never want to come and see us again, not after this.'

He smiled grimly. 'Yes she will, that's what pals are for, to help each other out in bad times. Has Dana spoken to anyone on the station since she's been away?'

Patty shook her head. 'No, there was only me and Pete who knew the number to the hospital.'

'Are you goin' to wait in here for her?'

Patty cast an eye around the almost empty cookhouse. 'I think so, she'll want a bit of privacy, and even though the other girls are keen to comfort her, it might be a bit overwhelmin'.'

Pushing his chair back, Eddie got to his feet. 'Sorry, chuck, but I've gorra get back.' He kissed her lightly on the cheek. 'You know where I am if you need me.'

Patty watched Eddie walk out of the door to the cookhouse before allowing the tears to fall. She opened her handbag and drew out a handkerchief. She couldn't stand the tension of waiting for Dana to return; she wanted her home now.

Each time the door to the cookhouse opened, Patty looked up in the hope of seeing Dana, only to find it was someone else. So when the door swung open and Dana walked towards her, Patty's heart skipped a beat.

'Bob said I could find you in here.'

Patty's face crumpled.

'Patty darlin', what's happened?'

'Oh Dana, it's been awful.'

Dana placed a comforting arm around her friend's shoulder. 'Is Eddie all right?'

Patty nodded.

'Your mam?' As Patty nodded again, Dana remembered Patty's father was serving in France. Her heart sank. 'Not your dad an' all?'

Patty gripped Dana's hands in hers, her eyes shining with tears, her lips trembling as she spoke. 'It's Pete. They all went on a sortie the day after you left ...' Closing her eyes, she allowed the tears to seep down her cheeks. 'We didn't realise anythin' were wrong at first, until someone overheard one of the girls sayin' Pete had been shot down over the Channel.' Her lips wobbled as she tried to maintain her composure. 'Two of the Americans saw him go down ...' She looked up at Dana, her face wet with tears. 'They didn't see him bail

326

out.' She began to gulp back her sobs. 'I'm so – so sorry.'

Dana stared blankly at Patty before slowly shaking her head. 'You're wrong, you must be.'

Patty wiped her nose with her hanky. 'I wish I were.'

'Why didn't anyone tell me?' said Dana, her voice hollow.

'You'd just lost your father; we thought it better to wait until you got home, or at least that's what I told meself. I reckern I were hopin' there was goin' to be some kind of miracle and Pete would come strollin' through the door.'

Dana scoffed disbelievingly. 'Pete can't be gone – he's the luckiest so-'n'-so out there. It must've been someone else.'

Patty dried her puffy eyes. 'Eddie said the same, but the lads in the Mustangs saw the trail of smoke comin' from Lady Luck as she went seaward; they were in different positions but they both gave the same story.'

Numb from losing her father, Dana's face remained impassive as tears flowed down her cheeks.

Patty clasped Dana's hands from across the table. 'I'm so sorry ...' She looked at the NAAFI door. 'Where's Lucy?'

'She'd already had her leave extended and she didn't want to push her luck so she went straight to Lincoln.'

Patty shook her head. 'How's your mam copin'?'

Dana spoke through downturned lips. 'Dad didn't just want me to go back so he could say his final goodbye, he wanted to tell me that I were adopted.'

Patty's jaw dropped. 'You can't be!'

'I am.' Dana leaned the side of her face against the palm of her hand. 'I wanted to wait 'til we were face to face before sayin' owt, 'cos I knew it were a lot to take in and I wanted your advice on what I should say to Pete.' She began to gulp back the tears. 'Because I thought the news might change things between us ...' Her voice trailed off.

'Darling Dana, you don't deserve this,' said Patty quietly.

'Me 'n' Lucy were talkin' about how people would react when they heard the news.' Dana told Patty about the conversation with Lucy in the back of the taxi on their way to the bus station, and how she feared she might end up losing Pete and Lenny as well as her father.

'Oh Dana, luvvy, it's not fair, is it? First your dad, now this. I bet you don't know whether you're comin' or goin'!'

'You're right there.' She glanced towards the door as an airman walked in. 'I'm just glad Pete never told his father about me.' She looked at Patty who had turned pale. 'What now?'

Patty grimaced. 'Pete had received a letter from his father, sayin' about you bein' ... well, you know.'

Dana's eyes rounded. 'No! How on earth did he find out?'

Patty looked awkward. 'It were Alexa. Pete and Eddie paid her a visit a few days before you left for Ireland. Eddie said she denied it at first but after a while she admitted talkin' about you in the Steam Room Café in Yelverton Station.' She shrugged helplessly, 'Alexa couldn't have known it at the time, but

Pete's father was in the same café and he overheard every nasty word that come from her lips.'

'I knew she were a cow, but I never thought she'd go that far!' snapped Dana. 'You wait 'til I see her!'

'She's gone,' said Patty. 'Posted to somewhere in London.'

'Just as well,' said Dana, adding, 'What did his father say? Did he think she was lyin', or did he do what he should have done and told her to hold her vile tongue and mind her own business?'

Patty thinned her lips. 'I'm afraid he believed every word, and the letter he wrote to Pete was horrid, tellin' him to finish things with you or lose his family and his inheritance.'

Dana's jaw dropped, but something Patty said earlier came back to her. 'You said Pete confronted Alexa before I'd left for Ireland, which means Pete knew about the letter but he never mentioned anythin'. I wonder why not?'

Patty nodded. 'That's what I said to Eddie. He reckoned Pete wanted to speak to his father before sayin' owt to you.'

Dana rested her chin against her knuckles whilst she thought this through. 'He knew how his father felt, knew what Alexa had done, so why not just say? It was obvious I'd find out sooner or later and his father's a stubborn mule, he'd not change his mind.' Her eyes flicked towards Patty. 'Do you reckern there were another reason why Pete kept shtum?'

Patty gave a small shrug. 'Perhaps he needed to think what he would say if his father stuck to his guns, like whether he should see you in secret, or tell his father to go take a runnin' jump, or ...'

'Or finish things with me?' Dana slid her head down so that her forehead was resting against her knuckles. She spoke thickly through her arms. 'All this because of me!' When she looked back up her eyes were filled with tears. 'I wish he'd never met me.' She pointed towards the ceiling of the cookhouse, drawing the attention of several diners. "Cos his father would never have sent him that rotten letter and he'd have been doin' what he should've been doin' up there, concentratin' on the job in hand.' Patty began to shake her head but Dana continued, 'Think about it, Patty, all these years he's been flyin' and not one bullet, not one! Yet a few days after he receives this letter ...' Unable to say the words, she splayed her hands out imitating an explosion. 'And that's all down to me.'

Patty wagged a reproving finger. 'I'll have none of that! None of this is your fault, you weren't the one tattle-talin', or makin' threats and ultimatums.'

Dana sat up; stony-faced, she spoke through pursed lips. 'You're right! It's his fault, his big fat stupid stuck-up arrogant beast of a father. I hope he knows what he's done.' Before Patty could intervene she added, 'Because if he doesn't he soon will.' She scraped her chair back as she went to get up, only to have Patty lay her hands on top of hers.

'No! You can't. Don't you think he's lost enough? His father's in bits, Dana. Not only has he lost his son, but the last correspondence he had with Pete was that letter.' She shook her head chidingly. 'Accordin' to Eddie, Pete never responded, so his father never got the chance to take back the words. That's summat he's got to live with for the rest of his life! Hate him or not, he's got one hell of a cross to bear, and he don't need anyone tellin' him what he already suspects.'

Dana slumped back into her chair. 'It's not fair, Patty, it wasn't meant to be like this. Pete's a wonderful, wonderful man; he was so full of life and adventure.' Dana gazed at Patty; her tears turned from anger to remorse. 'He had his whole life ahead of him, and I know he would've done wonderful things with it, far more than I'll do with mine, and he was a brilliant pilot, never missed his mark, allus came ...' Her voice faded as emotion took over.

Patty stroked the back of Dana's outstretched hands. 'I know, I know,' she said soothingly, 'and I'm sure Pete knows his father only had good intentions, same as any other parent.' She hesitated. 'What?'

Dana, who had been shaking her head, looked at Patty through narrowed eyes. 'Not every parent. Take my so-called birth mam – she didn't care, did she? Else she'd never have given me to strangers. If she'd've kept me I'd never have met Pete and he'd still be alive.'

'I can understand you're angry, but you can't blame someone you've never met – you've not gorra clue what was goin' on in her life. For all you know losin' you could've broken her heart.'

Dana shook her head. 'My mam 'n' dad would've fought tooth an' nail to keep me with them no matter what, that's the reason why Dad's family cast him out, because of me – they didn't agree wi' him takin' in a child what weren't of traveller descent, and my dad told 'em to go to hell.' Having got it off her chest, she sighed heavily. 'I know Lucy said there's lots of reasons why people get into a pickle, but I can only speak as I find.'

'I didn't realise ...'

'Neither did I,' said Dana. 'They allus told me that it were complicated, but they never said how exactly because they couldn't – if they did I'd know I were adopted, and they were worried I might hold it against them!' She shook her head in disbelief. 'How could I resent them for savin' me from someone who couldn't give two hoots about me?'

'Darling Dana, I wish I could turn back the hands of time. If I could I'd've stopped Pete from flyin' that day – I don't know how but I'd've found a way – and I'd've—' She stopped short, having been interrupted by Dana.

'Do you know what I'd've done? I'd've gone back and told me mam to keep her legs shut, just for that night, do whatever she wanted after, but not that night, 'cos that way I'd never have been born.' She threw her hands up in frustration as hot tears wet her cheeks. ''Cos I'm tellin' you now, Patty, I ain't never experienced pain like this in my whole life. I've lost me dad, me boyfriend and me heritage all in the matter of a few days!'

Patty's eyes rounded in horror. 'You can't mean that. You've had a fantastic life, with amazing parents! Your real mam may not have been able to take care of you, but at least she gave you to someone who could. There's folk out there who get rid of their babies before they're born, but your mam didn't.' She looked at Dana imploringly. 'Don't you dare say you wish she had!'

332

Dana shook her head. 'No ... I just want the pain to go away. I want to feel like I did a month ago.' She glanced at the ceiling. 'I just want me dad an' Pete back. I wish none of this had ever happened.'

'But it has, chuck, an' you're just goin' to have to get on with things, but I'll be right by your side.' She got to her feet. 'I've gorra go spend a penny, are you comin'?'

Nodding, Dana stood up and the two set off in the direction of the ablutions. 'I know it's silly because he couldn't do owt, but I don't half wish Lenny were here.'

Patty stopped abruptly. 'With everythin' else goin' on I forgot to tell you: he arrived early.' She grimaced. 'Same day Pete went down.'

Dana's eyes shone in the darkness. 'He's here?'

Patty nodded. 'He's been brilliant, Dana, a real god-send. He's done all he can to try and find out what happened to Pete, askin' whereabouts the plane went down, how far they were from land, whether Pete could've bailed out before he got hit, even questioned whether he did get hit or whether summat had gone wrong wi' the engine, which is summat we hadn't thought about.'

'He wouldn't have crashed into the sea on purpose,' said Dana, frowning.

'No, but if summat had gone wrong with his engine, he might've had prior warnin' that he were goin' to crash and decided to bail out.' She pulled a face. 'I don't know whether it was because Lenny wasn't a pal of Pete's or whether he's just smarter than the rest of us, but he was thinkin' of all sorts of scenarios which could mean Pete was still alive.'

333

'Good old Lenny. I think it's the mechanic in him; he's allus wantin' to fix things.' She glanced up at Patty. 'I don't suppose any of his ideas were plausible?'

Patty continued to head for the ablutions. 'They were at first, but not now, too much time's passed; they've not had any messages from France to say he made it there, and he's not returned to Blighty so ...'

Dana nodded sadly. 'Worth a try though.'

Patty squeezed Dana's arm in hers. 'Gosh yes, anythin's worth a try, and we were hopeful at first. Lenny was like a ray of sunshine on a dark and stormy day; he gave us hope, which we hadn't had before, but like I say, too much time's elapsed.'

'I'll make sure to go and see him in the morning, thank him for tryin' to find Pete,' said Dana decidedly.

'He's keen to see you.'

'I feel guilty, Patty,' said Dana.

'Not this again!' said Patty, but Dana was shaking her head.

'Because I have feelin's for Lenny the same as I do for Pete.'

'You can't help how you feel!' Patty pushed each cubicle door in turn to make sure they were empty.

'I know, but if me and Lenny had been together, I'd never have gone out with Pete, and things might've turned out differently.'

'You can't stew on what should've been 'cos no one can tell the future.' She sighed heavily. 'Eddie misses Pete dreadfully, and even though I've told him it's unfair to blame Pete's father, I'm afraid Eddie hasn't been so easily convinced.'

'I'm not surprised, he and Pete have been pals for ever such a long time, and he often said Pete's dad was too overbearing.'

'That may be so, but it doesn't do any good to lay blame, or stew in hate – it certainly won't bring Pete back.' Patty nipped into one of the cubicles and shut the door behind her; there was a moment's pause before she continued, 'I was hopin' you might have a word with him, make him see sense?'

Dana stared at the reflection of the door. 'I never said I'd forgiven Mr Robinson, I just agreed not to say owt; there's a big difference.'

There was a flushing sound and the door to Patty's cubicle opened; she was still fidgeting with the waistband on her skirt. 'Mebbe I put that badly. What I meant was you're not altogether blamin' him for what happened to Pete.'

Dana nodded. 'Only because Lenny said it might've been an engine failure. What does Eddie think?'

Smoothing her jacket over her skirt, Patty rolled her eyes dramatically. 'The man who serviced Lady Luck?'

Dana's cheeks flushed red. 'I didn't mean ...'

Patty smiled kindly at Dana's reflection. 'I know you didn't, and any mechanic worth his salt'll tell you engines go wrong, nobody's fault, these things happen, especially when they're bein' pushed to extremes in dog fights. I don't think Eddie'd see it like that though and I don't want him blamin' himself.'

'Poor Eddie.' Dana leaned away from the sink and patted her fingertips against her lips whilst she thought things through. 'I know how he feels, but Pete would say you're in charge of your own destiny. He loved flyin' 'cos it cleared his mind of everything else, and if that's the case, his father really isn't to blame either.'

Patty smiled at Dana. 'He did, didn't he? I'd forgotten all about that. I'd wager Eddie has too – please tell him; it's doin' him no good to dwell in hate.'

Dana nodded thoughtfully. 'Are you sure he won't blame himself if we take Pete's dad out of the equation?'

'Do you think that's why he's so focused on blamin' Pete's dad, so he doesn't have to look at himself?'

Dana shrugged one shoulder. 'Could be.'

'Well, if he tries to blame himself I'll get the others to have a chat with him, especially Lenny – he's good with stuff like this.'

Dana stifled a yawn. 'It's been a long day. I don't feel like I've slept at all this past week.'

The door to the ablutions opened and Mel rushed in. 'Hi, Dana, need the loo.'

Dana smiled as the door to the cubicle banged shut. 'Hello, Mel.'

Silence radiated from the cubicle before Mel's voice came slowly through the door. 'Has … has, er …'

'Yes, I know about Pete,' said Dana.

The toilet flushed and Mel appeared from behind the door. 'You OK?'

Dana shrugged. 'I'll have to be, won't I? Besides, I don't think I've got any tears left; I feel like I've been through an emotional wringer!'

Mel rinsed her hands under the tap. 'Sorry to hear about your dad, by the way.' She jerked her head in the direction of the billet. 'You two kipping in here tonight or are you coming in there with the rest of us?'

'Definitely bed,' said Dana. 'Although I can't imagine I'm goin' to get much sleep.' She tapped her finger against the side of her head. 'Too much goin' on up here.'

Mel placed a comforting arm around Dana's shoulders. 'Don't worry, if you can't sleep give me a nudge, I'll come and chat with you for a bit.'

As Dana changed for bed she cast her mind back to the last time she had seen Pete: young, fit and healthy, with that ever-cheeky grin. She shook her head sadly. How could someone so full of life have gone so soon? They all knew the life expectancy of pilots was short, but no one thought anything would ever happen to Pete. Climbing between the sheets, she pulled them up around her ears before closing her eyes. She ran through what Patty had told her. She couldn't help wondering if the pilots of the Mustangs had got it wrong. If so, Pete could still be out there, waiting for someone to come and rescue him. A picture of Pete clinging on to the broken wing of Lady Luck appeared in her mind. Large tears seeped their way through her closed lids. She couldn't bear to think of him all alone, scanning the skies in hope of rescue.

She wondered whether she should give Mel a nudge and ask what she knew about that dreadful day. Had they done enough to find him or had they taken the pilots' word for it? She fished out her handkerchief from underneath her pillow and blew her nose as quietly as she could. Patty had already told her they had tried everything they could to find him; Mel would only say the same thing. Pushing her hanky back under the pillow, Dana turned her mind to Eddie. According to Patty, he had also refused to believe Pete was gone, so he must have voiced his concerns to those in charge, but even if he had he couldn't force them to send out a search party, especially if they thought Pete's plane had crashed into the sea. An image of Lenny appeared in her mind and a small smile fleetingly curved Dana's lips. Good old Lenny, he hadn't known Pete from the next man, but it hadn't stopped him trying to help. Bringing her legs up towards her chest she snuggled into a tight ball. She would see them both tomorrow as soon as her shift was over. She felt sure they would be able to give her the answers she was searching for. Stifling a yawn behind the back of her hand, Dana drifted into a sleep riddled with nightmares.

She was sitting at a card table, much like the one that Pete and his pals used to play poker on. Her heart sank as she glanced down at the set of cards in her hand. She didn't know how to play poker! What was she thinking of? She looked at the players who sat round the table; a chill filled her body as she looked at their featureless faces. She was about to push her chair back and run away when a hand descended on to her shoulder.

'Where d'you think you're going?' Dana glanced up at Pete's downturned face; he was grinning broadly at her. 'You've got a winning hand there, but don't let them see.'

Dana swallowed hard as she glanced back at the faceless players; she tried to stand up but Pete's hand pushed her firmly but gently back into her seat. She looked at him pleadingly. 'Their faces, Pete, look at their faces.'

Pete glanced at the faceless players. 'That's what you call a poker face. You can't tell whether they've got a good hand or not, which is a sign of a good player. That's what I used to be like, which is why I always won of course.'

Tears welled in her eyes. 'They've got no faces at all, Pete, can't you see?'

A line creased his brow as he looked down at her, his eyes full of concern. 'You're frightened! But there's no need: I've already told you, you've a winning hand.'

Dana stared incredulously at him, but he appeared oblivious to her concerns. She hit the underside of the table with such force it flew into the air. Glancing around, she noticed the players had vanished along with the table. Pete wagged a reproving finger, but he was grinning as he did so. 'Now, now, no one likes a sore loser!'

'I want to go home!' said Dana. Looking around she saw nothing but darkness. 'Where are we?'

'This, my dear Dana, is the English Channel.' He winked before continuing. 'Worked out pretty well for you, hasn't it?'

Dana's brow furrowed. 'Whatever do you mean?'

'My dying of course!' He chuckled softly. 'I'm not saying you wanted me dead, but it's better than having to explain you were in love with another chap, I suppose, especially after all the trouble you caused between me and my father.' He looked at her thoughtfully for a moment before adding, 'You could say it was almost convenient.'

Dana shook her head. The tears that had welled in her eyes were slowly trickling down her cheeks. 'You don't mean that.'

He shrugged nonchalantly. 'I suppose it's something to do with me being dead, I just don't see the point in dressing stuff up any more.' He clicked his fingers. 'Did Eddie tell you about the letter my father sent me?'

Dana nodded.

'Bet the old bugger feels guilty now!' Pete chuckled.

Dana shook her head. 'I don't know who or what you are, but you're not my Pete – he'd never have been so heartless.'

The laughter disappeared from Pete's face and was replaced with a look of contempt. 'Of course I'm heartless, I'm dead, and whilst we're about it, I'm not *your* Pete.'

Dana turned to leave, but could see no way out. 'I want to go home.' As she said the words a breeze stirred the air around her.

He spread his arms wide. 'Go! I'm not stopping you!'

'But I don't know how to get out,' said Dana quietly.

He laughed scornfully. 'Truth hurts, doesn't it?'

Tears of misery dripped off Dana's chin and the breeze was gathering momentum. 'Please don't. I never wanted anything bad to happen to you.'

He mellowed a little. 'I suppose you didn't, but it doesn't take away from the fact that I'm no longer alive, and if I hadn't had that horrible letter from my father ...'

'That's not my fault!' said Dana. 'I didn't tell him to write it.'

'No, but he wrote it because of you.' He gave a haughty sniff. 'If I'd known you were attracted to boring, cowardly men like Lenny ...'

'Lenny's not a coward!' Dana had to yell above the wind that was whipping her hair about her face. 'Stop sayin' such horrid things, it's not like you, you're not the same man I fell in love with!'

'Love!' scoffed Pete. 'You don't know the meaning of the word. If you did, you'd've realised you were in love with two of us. If you ask me, you're just plain greedy!'

Tears coursed down Dana's cheeks and she tried to reach out to him. 'Pete! Please don't . . .'

'Open your eyes, Dana!' Pete said firmly. Dana ceased crying almost immediately – there was something wrong with his voice; she cocked an ear desperate to hear him again, but he had fallen silent. Dana looked around her but there was no sign of him.

'Pete?' she ventured. She clutched at thin air as something began to push her back and forth.

Dana woke with a start. Patty and Mel were looking down at her with sympathetic faces. 'You were havin' a nightmare,' explained Patty.

Dana eyed her suspiciously. 'I am awake, aren't I? You're not goin' to start tellin' me how horrible I am?'

'Of course not. Whatever makes you think we would?' said Patty.

Dana glanced at the slumbering occupants of the beds around her. 'In my nightmare Pete started blamin' me for the letter his father wrote – amongst other things,' she added guiltily.

'That blooming letter!' snapped Mel. 'His father should be ashamed of himself, and he ought to've known better than to send something like that to a chap in the RAF!' She pulled Dana's hair away from her face. 'Pete never blamed you for that letter – ask Eddie; it's your imagination getting the better of you.'

Dana nodded gloomily. She couldn't possibly tell Mel about Lenny; however, looking at Patty's face, she could tell her friend had guessed what Dana was thinking. 'Pete wouldn't blame you for anythin',' said Patty pointedly. 'He thought the world of you!'

Dana nodded. 'Thanks, Patty. You too, Mel.'

Mel smiled kindly at her. 'Try and get some rest. You'll feel better after you've spoken to Eddie.'

Nodding, Dana pulled the sheets up around her ears. 'Will do.' Hearing Patty and Mel get back into their own beds, Dana opened her eyes and stared into the darkness. It wouldn't matter what Eddie said, he'd never rid her of her guilty conscience. I must be the only woman alive to feel guilty about something I haven't done, thought Dana miserably. I've not so much as kissed Lenny yet I feel as though I've been having an affair behind Pete's back. Sitting up, she pummelled her pillow with her fists; then she turned it over so that she could lay her face against the cooler side. No matter what her feelings were for Lenny, she couldn't possibly pursue them now. She hadn't entered the services in the hope of finding love, yet she had ended up falling in love with two men, neither of whom she could have. I should've gone with me mam and dad, thought Dana, I'd've dragged him to that doctor and got him help before it was too late, and I'd never have met Lenny or Pete, and Pete wouldn't have fallen out with his family, and he might still be alive today. I joined up to save me beloved Liverpool yet it still lies in ruins. I've made a real pig's ear out of things;

everythin' I touch goes wrong, so from now on I'm goin' to keep meself to meself! At least that way no one else will get hurt ... And with this thought she slowly drifted into a dreamless sleep.

Dana handed the list over the counter to the corporal who ran a pencil down the items. He looked back over his shoulder and examined the boxed parts which Dana had taken out of the back of her lorry; he raised an enquiring brow. 'Oddie studs?'

Dana blinked. 'Aren't they there?'

He glanced over his shoulder again. 'Nope. Perhaps they're still in the back of the lorry?'

'I'll check.' Leaving the storage hut, Dana groaned as she laid eyes on a box that must have fallen from the pile she'd been carrying. Bending down, she began to put the small studs back into the box.

A man spoke from behind. 'More haste less speed!'

Turning to see who had spoken, Dana left the studs on the floor and stood up to embrace Eddie. 'I was goin' to come and see you,' said Eddie softly.

Fighting back the tears, Dana nodded. 'I was waitin' to sign this lot off before seekin' you out.' Relieved that she had stopped the tears before they fell, she leaned back and looked into Eddie's grey face. Cupping his cheek in her hand, she gave him a wobbly smile. 'I'm so sorry, Eddie, I don't know what else to say.'

He shrugged, and then, holding his hand over the top of hers, he smiled reassuringly. 'Not a lot you can say. If words could bring him back you wouldn't be able to shut me up.'

'I expect you're worn out goin' through the whys and wherefores. I've only known since last night, but I can't stop myself from wonderin' whether they'd mistaken another plane for Pete's, or whether he'd bailed out without anyone seein'.'

Eddie nodded wearily. 'Only all the other Spitfires came back.' He held up a hand as Dana made to intervene. 'They've found a piece of her wreckage, Dana. It washed up in Dover ...' He caught Dana before she fell.

'Oh my God.' She was breathing rapidly. 'He's really gone, isn't he?'

Holding her tightly in his arms, Eddie walked her over to the tailgate of the lorry and sat her down. 'Yes, luv, I'm afraid he has.'

Unable to come to terms with the dreadful news, she tried another tack. 'He still might've bailed out,' she said hopefully.

Eddie smiled again, kindly. 'True, but there've been no reports of a devilishly handsome Spitfire pilot wooing the local mademoiselles ...'

Dana tried to smile but it was no use; she turned to Eddie, her eyes brimming with tears. 'I really did love him, you know.'

Eddie opened his mouth to speak, cleared his throat, and tried again. 'Me and you both, queen.'

Taking a tissue from her pocket she blew her nose quietly. 'I've spoken to Patty and she told me about the letter ...'

Eddie's lips formed a thin line. 'What do you think?'

'I blamed him at first, but then I remembered how Pete said he used to clear his mind of all his worries

344

whenever he went out on an operation.' She pursed her lips into a grim smile. 'Blaming others won't change anything, it'll just eat you up inside.'

Eddie nodded reluctantly. 'I know but it's hard not to sometimes ...' He jerked his head in the direction of an airman who was making his way towards them. 'Your pal was good, did all he could to help.'

Dana looked in the direction that Eddie had indicated and saw Lenny walking towards them; the very image of him caused her heart to palpitate. She wanted to run up, throw her arms around him and pour her heart out, but she couldn't, not with Eddie so close. Instead she smiled a weak greeting as he approached. 'Hello, Lenny, long time no see.'

He nodded. 'I heard you were back, and of course I know about Pete. I'm sorry, that was rotten news to come back to, especially after your father an' all.'

Dana nodded. 'He's allus been so healthy, I can't believe he's gone, and Pete of course.' She broke off as a Waaf whom she'd never seen before approached her shyly.

'I just wanted to pass on my condolences about Pete. It must be awful for you.'

'Thanks,' was all Dana could find to say. As the girl wandered off, Dana glanced at Eddie. 'I know they mean well and Pete had to be the most popular feller on the station, but I don't want to keep hearin' how sorry everyone is, 'cos it doesn't make a blind bit of difference. It certainly doesn't make me feel any better; if anything it makes me want to run a hundred miles in the opposite direction.' Bending down to scoop the studs back into the box, she added, 'I wish I still had some leave so that I could get away for a bit. What with one thing and another I've had more than my fair share of bad news lately.'

Lenny rubbed his chin thoughtfully. 'One of the Flying Officers has asked me to look over a non-runner some feller's got for sale; if I think it can be mended cheaply enough he wants me to buy it on his behalf. I was goin' to ask one of the fellers if they could sit in it whilst I tow it back to the station, but if you're really lookin' for some time out, you're more than welcome to come along; we'll be away the whole day.'

Dana's shoulders sagged with relief. 'That'd be wonderful, Lenny, and it'll give us a good chance to catch up.'

'He said I could go any time, so let me know when you're available and we'll go from there.'

'I could do Saturday if that's any good?' Dana said hopefully.

Lenny smiled. 'Saturday it is.'

She smiled gratefully. 'Thanks Lenny, it'll be good to get away from everyone, no matter how good their intentions, it'll give me a chance to let everything sink in, because I don't think it has yet.' She hesitated as a thought occurred to her. 'Would you like to come too, Eddie? I bet you could do with gerrin' away for a bit.'

Eddie shook his head. 'Thanks for the offer, but me and Patty are goin' into Plymouth. We were goin' to ask if you'd like to come with us, but you'd probably bump into a lot of people who knew Pete, so you're probably best goin' wi' Lenny here.'

Dana heaved a heartfelt sigh. 'You're right there, he wasn't just popular on the station but off it as well. I reckern there isn't a landlord in the whole of Plymouth who wasn't on first-name terms with Pete.'

A car pulled up beside them and the driver called out to Eddie. 'You comin'?'

Nodding, Eddie bade the two of them goodbye, adding, 'If you need to talk you know where to find me.'

Dana smiled. 'Thanks, Eddie.'

Lenny watched Eddie drive away. 'I know I never met Pete, but it seems like he was a really popular feller.'

Dana nodded 'All the fellers wanted to be him and all the girls wanted to date him.'

'You must've been the envy of the station,' said Lenny.

'I suppose I was.' She stooped to pick up the last remaining studs and began to count them out. 'That's all of them. I'd better get them in and signed off before I drop them again!' Turning on her heel she was about to enter the storage hut when she half turned to face Lenny. 'Shall we say ten o'clock on Saturday?'

He nodded. 'I'll meet you by the gate.' Lenny watched as the door swung shut behind her before continuing towards his billet. He could only imagine how broken Dana must be and he was glad he was in a position to take her away from it all, if only just for a little while. He knew it was ridiculous to be jealous of a dead man, but he couldn't help himself; he had held a torch for Dana since their first encounter in the hotel, and hearing she had let another man into her heart had not been easy, even if that man was no longer around. All Lenny had heard since he got to Harrowbeer was how handsome Pete was and how everyone loved him.

By all accounts he was fun to be around and he flew Lady Luck like she was a part of him. Lenny sighed. He would not describe himself as handsome, or daring, so if those were the qualities that had attracted Dana it was no wonder he had never managed to win her heart. Women like Dana belonged with men like Pete, it was as simple as that; fellers like Lenny didn't stand a chance.

Chapter Eleven

Dana smiled as Lenny leaned across the passenger side of the car and pushed the door open. 'Beautiful day for it.'

Dana climbed into the passenger seat. 'Wasn't the rain awful last night? I normally enjoy fallin' asleep whilst listenin' to the sound of the rain as it hits the roof, it reminds me of when I were a kid, but last night it sounded like it were tryin' to come through!'

'I slept like a log. I got quite the shock when I opened the door this mornin' an' seen everywhere soakin' wet.' Lenny's nostrils flared. 'I've always liked the smell of rain after the sun's had a chance to soak some of it up. I hope the farmyard's cobbled, I don't fancy gettin' this covered in muck.' He tapped the steering wheel of the car.

Dana spun round in her seat. 'You never said it were a farmer what had the car. Do you reckern he'll have horses?'

Lenny gave a half-shrug. 'I s'pose so.'

'Do you know where the farm is?' She was rolling down the car window as she spoke. 'I reckern the sun's goin' to make up for all that rain, it's already gerrin' hot.' She nodded to where steam was drifting up from the road ahead.

At the junction Lenny pulled a piece of paper from out of his pocket and handed it to Dana. 'I've got a rough idea, but Waddy gave me this; you can be navigator.'

Dana quickly scanned the directions written on the piece of paper. 'Turn right at the first junction, then stay on that road till you get to the Durham Heifer.'

'Righty-ho!'

She pulled a face. 'Perhaps I should've mentioned I've never been in charge of a car on tow before. Is there anythin' I should know?'

Lenny turned to face her and Dana saw the familiar twinkle in his blue eyes. 'It's pretty simple: keep your eye out for when I brake, and steer the car round the corners. I've brought a length of rope with us, and I've made a towin' sign to stick on the back.'

'Steer round the corners' – Dana chuckled – 'I think that goes without sayin'.'

He raised his brows. 'You'd be surprised. Last time I towed someone they thought my car would pull them wherever I went. Needless to say first corner we came to we had to pull him out of a ditch.'

'Blimey! Who did you say wanted to buy it?'

'One of the Flying Officers – everyone calls him Waddy, short for Waddington. He's a bit of a character. Eddie says he's always buyin' something or other when he's down the pub.'

'I couldn't afford to buy a car tyre never mind a car,' said Dana.

Lenny laughed. 'Me neither, but we're not officers, are we?'

Dana grimaced. 'Nor would I want to be, all that responsibility, shoutin' orders, and makin' important decisions. No thank you.'

'I suppose it's all right for the folk who want to make a career in the RAF, but as for the rest of us ...'

Dana turned her attention from the high green hedgerows to Lenny. 'So, you're not intendin' to stay on when it's over?'

He shook his head. 'Nope, my uncle's got a small garage in Llandudno.' He smiled at her blank expression. 'It's in North Wales, not far from my home in Conwy.' He sighed wistfully as he stared into the distance. 'You'd love it there, Dana, you'll have to come with me one day on leave ...' Realising what he'd just said he sat up straight. '... as a pal of course, and you'd be more than welcome to bring Patty. Lucy too if she could make it.'

Dana's lips curved into a small smile. 'I know you wouldn't suggest anythin' indecent, Lenny, you're far too nice for that, and I'd love to see where you live. Is it in the countryside like this?' She glanced round at the meadows which stretched as far as the eye could see.

He nodded. 'And it's right by the sea too, and there's a huge castle, and you should see the guest houses on the front in Llandudno.' He glanced in her direction and Dana could see the passion in his eyes. 'Not to mention the Great Orme.'

'What on earth's a Great Orme?'

'It's like a small mountain!'

'It sounds wonderful. I'm guessing you get a lot of people goin' there on their holidays?'

He nodded eagerly. 'My uncle's got the only garage for miles, so he gets a lot of business, or at least he did before the war. It's where I learned to be a mechanic – I used to go to the garage every night after school and my uncle would let me help out.'

'Your dad's not a mechanic then?' said Dana.

Lenny shook his head. 'Don't know who he is so I couldn't tell you.' He chuckled at the look of embarrassment crossing Dana's pink face. 'My mam wasn't a wrong 'un, just a bit gullible. She believed any line the fellers spun her and made a few wrong decisions, one of which turned out to be me.'

'Oh,' said Dana, clearly lost for words.

Lenny shrugged dismissively. 'I didn't suffer because of it; Mam did the best she could and my uncle helped by keepin' me out of mischief down at the garage!' He nodded at the stone public house which loomed before them. 'That's the Durham Heifer. Where now?'

Dana studied the piece of paper in her hands. 'Left.'

Nodding, Lenny checked both ways before continuing. 'What will you do when it's all over?'

'Go back to Liverpool and see if I can start my own business, a tea room, summat like that; then, when I'm settled, I'll bring me mam over,' said Dana simply, adding, 'If I can persuade her that is.'

Lenny looked surprised. 'Wouldn't she want to come back?'

'She doesn't want to be a burden, she's worried I won't have a life of me own, but I'm more worried

352

about her; I know she says she'll have Mrs O'Brien for company, but how long will that last? Besides, she can't live in the wagon forever.'

Lenny glanced at Dana from the corner of his eye. 'Wagon?'

Dana's heart was in her mouth. She had been so busy coming to terms with losing her father and Pete she hadn't given a second thought to telling Lenny the truth. She eyed him nervously. 'I forgot you didn't know. You're probably the only person in Harrowbeer who doesn't,' she mumbled.

A small line furrowed Lenny's brow. 'Know what?'

Dana's cheeks grew hot. She had been dreading this moment for such a long time she didn't know what to say. How could she explain who she was when she didn't even know herself? Lenny could see her discomfort; he slowed the car down, pulled off the road and turned to face Dana. 'Whatever it is, spit it out. You may as well, especially if everyone else knows.'

Still fearful of his reaction, Dana focused on her knees. 'I used to be a traveller,' she said softly.

Lenny stared disbelievingly at Dana. 'Is that it?' He put the car into gear, checked the road behind him and pulled back on to the road. 'Bloody hell, Dana, I thought you were goin' to say you were a German spy or some-thing ...' He frowned a little. '... although I suppose if you were, you wouldn't be a very good one, not if every-one knows.'

Overwhelmed with relief that Lenny hadn't been bothered by her revelation, Dana started to chuckle. 'You didn't really think that?'

He grinned. 'Not really, but every time I asked you something about where you came from and who your folks were you went all tight-lipped on me, apart from the time you let slip they were from Ireland. I could see you regretted the words as soon as they left your lips.'

Dana nodded thoughtfully. 'We were on the bus and you had to go the next day because that stupid engine had got stuck.'

Lenny shrugged. 'I remember you sayin' you didn't want to get romantically involved with anyone until after the war. Did you say that because you didn't fancy me?'

Dana's eyes rounded. 'That's not it at all!'

Turning to face her, he winked. 'So you did fancy me then?'

Dana opened her mouth to reply; then she closed it as she folded her arms across her chest. 'Don't you go puttin' words into my mouth, Lenny Ackerman!'

'Oh dear,' sighed Lenny. 'It always spells trouble if a woman uses your full name.' He eyed her sharply. 'Hang on a mo, what do you mean by you "used" to be a traveller ... you either are or you aren't.'

Dana shrugged. 'When I went to see me mam and dad in Ireland, they told me how I'd been adopted, which means I'm not theirs, and I suppose that means I'm not a traveller.'

Coming to a junction, Lenny nodded his head at a pub that stood just off the road. 'I don't know about you but I could do with a drink.'

Dana nodded. 'It is rather hot, isn't it?'

354

Pulling the car over to the kerb, he saw the writing on the front of the pub: *The Weary Friar*.

Entering the pub, Dana admired the low-beamed ceilings whilst Lenny got them both a drink. Placing Dana's glass on to the round table, he took a long swig of his own before putting it down. 'So, you learn that you're adopted, lose your father, then you come back to Harrowbeer to find Pete's ...' He shook his head instead of finishing the sentence.

'That's about the size of it.' She glanced up at Lenny, the glass of squash halfway to her lips. 'I've not told anyone about the adoption apart from Patty and Lucy, although I expect Patty's told Eddie. It's not that I'm ashamed of what me birth mam did, but what with Pete and everythin' I figure one thing at a time.'

'What did your birth mam do?'

Dana paused before answering. 'She gave me away to strangers. Not exactly the act of a lovin' mother, is it? I mean, what sort of woman gives her baby away to travellers?'

Lenny pulled a face. 'A desperate one?'

'Well, yes, obviously a desperate one, but there must've been other alternatives, she didn't know me mam and dad from Adam ...'

Lenny frowned; he was worried he was about to get himself into trouble, but he had to be honest. 'So ...' he began slowly, 'she didn't know they were travellers then?' Before Dana could reply he held his hands up with the air of someone who was trying to be reasonable. 'Only she couldn't have, could she? Not if she didn't know them from Adam.'

Dana knitted her brows. 'If you put it that way, then no, I don't suppose she did know who they were.'

'So for all your mother knew she was giving her baby away to a loving couple with a cottage by the sea?'

Dana took a long drink of her lemonade, placed the glass on the table, folded her arms on the surface and locked eyes with Lenny. 'The hospital knew; they were the ones who handed me over.' Bringing her hands up, she rested her chin on the top of them. 'I'm assumin' they told her.'

'That's one hell of an assumption to make. Are you goin' to look for her?'

Dana sank back into her seat. 'I wasn't, but if you're right, and they never told her ...' She looked curiously at him from across the table. 'What would you do if you were me?'

'Your mam deserves to know the truth, so do you. If it were me I'd at least try and look for her.'

'Did you try and look for your father?' said Dana.

Lenny laughed. 'Nah. It was a holiday romance – Mam hadn't a clue where he lived save he was from down south!' He paused for a moment. 'I'm assumin' you've never seen your birth certificate?'

'Me mam's got it, why?'

'Because it'll have the name of your birth parents on there, and where you were born. It would make tracing your mam a lot easier.'

Dana looked awkward. 'If I ask me mam for it, I'd have to explain why I wanted it, and I don't want to upset her by admittin' I wanted to look for me birth mam.'

'Do you think it would bother her?' said Lenny.

'Not sure, but I wouldn't want her to think that I wasn't grateful for everythin' they've done for me.'

Lenny rubbed his chin thoughtfully. 'I don't know your mam but she sounds like a pretty decent person to me. I'm sure she'd understand.'

Dana smiled at him from across the table. 'You've not said how you feel about me?'

He shrugged. 'You're Dana; nothing's changed as far as I'm concerned.' He chuckled. 'It's not like you've grown another head or anythin'.'

Dana stared at him in disbelief. 'All that time I worried about what folk would say if they knew the truth, and apart from the odd one, most of them couldn't have cared less!'

'I suppose it's the war; it makes everything different. Puts things into perspective as it were.' He drained his glass and indicated for Dana to do the same, 'Drink up, cariad, we'd best get a wriggle on.' As they made their way to the car, Lenny looked sidelong at Dana. 'Why couldn't you tell me who you were? You told the folk in Harrowbeer.'

Taking hold of Lenny's elbow, Dana pulled him to a halt. 'That's not the case at all. I never told a soul – apart from Patty and Lucy of course. It was a Waaf called Alexa Stewart that told everyone. I met her briefly before the war, and when she saw me in Harrowbeer she wasted no time in tellin' everyone.'

'Oh,' said Lenny, feeling slightly relieved, 'why did she do that?'

Dana shrugged. 'Because she doesn't like travellers.'

Once they had climbed into the car, Lenny checked over his shoulder before pulling on to the road. 'What did Pete make of it all?'

Dana chuckled. 'It didn't bother him in the slightest. Pete's father on the other hand ...'

Lenny arched an eyebrow. 'Not keen on the idea?'

Dana turned her attention to the golden fields of corn. 'He sent Pete a horrible letter sayin' he'd disown him if he continued seein' me.' She shook her head sadly. 'All the fault of that bloody Alexa again.'

Lenny glanced at her incredulously. 'What did Pete say?'

A tear trickled down Dana's cheek. 'I don't know; he died before I had a chance to speak to him. I didn't even know the letter existed till I got back.'

'Dana, I'm so sorry. I knew you'd been havin' a bad time of it lately,' his brow creased with concern, 'but I had no idea it was this bad.'

She turned and gave him a wobbly smile. 'I think it's safe to say I've had my fair share of it this year.'

Lenny nodded. 'That Alexa sounds vile. Why go to such lengths?' He huffed under his breath. 'Daft question: she was clearly jealous.'

She nodded. 'She wanted Pete for herself.'

'Well, I can see why he chose you!' said Lenny firmly. 'Beautiful, kind, caring ...'

'I wonder if she knows,' pondered Dana.

'She's not in Harrowbeer any more?'

Dana shook her head. 'She left a few days before I went to see my folks in Ireland.'

'Good job too,' said Lenny. 'I'd certainly have liked to have a word or two with her.'

'She's not worth it,' said Dana. 'She thinks I'm scum and Pete's mad for havin' anythin' to do wi' me. I know because she told me.'

'Well, I'm here now,' said Lenny assuredly. 'And I want you to promise me you'll tell me if anyone says anythin' like that to you.'

Dana smiled. 'I promise.' She drew the piece of paper from her pocket and studied the directions before glancing around her and pointing at a triangle of green grass that separated the roads. 'We're here; turn left and the farm is the first on the right.'

He smiled approvingly. 'Well done, Aircraftwoman Quinn!'

Dana grimaced as the car dipped, jolted and splashed its way down the bumpy track that led to the farm. 'I'm not surprised his car's not runnin', not if he took it down here every day.'

Lenny nodded to a rather squat old man who was opening the gate that separated the farmyard from the track. Dana wound down her window. 'We're here about the car.'

Nodding, he pointed to the far side of the yard. 'Take her over to the muckheap. I'll be with you in a minute.'

Lenny grimaced as he reached the muckheap. 'I hope he doesn't want me to drive through that lot. It'd take me a week to get her clean.'

Dana had opened the passenger door when she saw a gaggle of geese waddling their way towards her. 'Oh Lenny,' she exclaimed, 'aren't they beautiful? Just look at those elegant white feathers.'

Lenny eyed the geese warily. 'I'd wait a minute before gettin' out if I were you – geese can be nasty blighters.'

Tutting at Lenny, Dana exited the car, closed the door behind her and leaned through the window. 'Don't be silly, they're only birds ...' From behind she could hear a strange hissing, and looking over her shoulder she saw the geese were standing to attention, their wings spread wide. Dana was about to turn back to Lenny to ask if he knew what they were doing when the geese rushed towards her honking aggressively. Throwing the car door open Dana climbed in and slammed it closed whilst desperately winding the window up.

Lenny chuckled. 'Don't be silly, they're only birds ...'

'Why on earth would anyone want to keep them?' said Dana, her face flustered.

Lenny shrugged. 'I expect they taste good, and I know they lay huge eggs – and as you've just found out, they make wonderful guard dogs!'

Waving his stick at the geese the old man herded them into a small orchard and closed the gate behind them before gesturing Dana and Lenny to join him.

He grinned toothily at Dana. 'Thems don't like strangers.'

'So I see,' said Dana through pursed lips.

'Oi take it you want to see the car?'

Lenny nodded. 'That was the general idea, yes.'

Pointing his stick, he indicated the far side of the muckheap. 'She's under cover in the Dutch barn. She's not been moved in a while, so holler if you need a hand. I'll be in the house.'

They watched him slowly make his way towards the large stone farmhouse. It had deep-set windows and a low thatched roof; a climbing rose covered one side.

'You know what I said about wantin' to live in Liverpool after the war?' said Dana dreamily.

'Yup.'

'I've changed my mind. I want to live in a farmhouse just like that one.' Glaring at the geese which were pecking the grass in the orchard, she added, 'But without geese!'

Lenny followed her gaze. 'There're a lot of houses like that where we live only not as big.' He glanced at the muckheap. 'I'm not drivin' over that lot until I know whether we're takin' the car back or not.' He held out a hand to Dana. 'Come with me: we'll have to pick our way around the edges.'

Dana took hold of Lenny's hand and the two of them delicately circumnavigated the muckheap. Dana wrinkled her nose. 'I won't have a muckheap in the middle of the yard neither.' They entered the barn and looked around for the car. 'Are you sure this is the right barn?' she asked doubtfully.

Lenny nodded. 'He said it was under cover, so perhaps it's well hidden.'

Dana shrugged. 'I can't see anything apart from the bales of hay stacked in the corner, and I doubt he's hidden it under that lot, they're from floor to ceiling!' She peered at a loose pile of hay next to the stack and frowned. 'Oh no ...' Stepping forward, she pulled a few handfuls of hay away from the pile before bursting into laughter. 'I know he said it was under cover, but I thought he meant a tarpaulin, or a sheet, not under a load of loose hay!'

'For cryin' out loud,' said Lenny. He helped Dana clear the car of its covering of hay. 'Someone's goin' to have to have a word with Waddy about buyin' stuff down pubs. No wonder the lads were laughin' when I told 'em where I were goin'; they probably realised it'd be something like this.'

Dana grinned. 'Do you call him Waddy to his face?'

Lenny looked shocked. 'God no! He's better'n most and he prefers straight talkin' even if he don't agree with you, but he's still an officer.'

When the car was free from hay, Lenny took a look under the bonnet. 'The fan belt's gone, and there's a fair bit of rust ...' He closed the bonnet. 'All the expensive parts look OK, so no major damage that I can see, although I'd prefer to take a look once she's outside. Do you think you could give me a hand to push her out into the open?'

Dana nodded. 'Course I can, just don't ask me to push her through the muckheap.'

They began to push the car only to find it wouldn't budge. Lenny double-checked the handbrake was off and that the car was out of gear before trying again; then he shook his head and called for Dana to stop. 'It's no use, I reckon the brakes have seized. We're going to have to drag her out. You wait here while I fetch Mr Preswick.'

'No need,' said Dana. 'He's comin' over.'

Lenny glanced at the old man, who was leading a huge horse towards them. 'Thought I'd bring Delilah over, give you young 'uns a hand.'

'What for?' said Lenny.

'Pull you out!' said Mr Preswick. 'What did you think I'd brought her over for? She i'n't goin' to drive it if that's what you were thinkin'.' He laughed throatily.

Lenny looked at Delilah doubtfully. 'She'll never manage to pull that, the brakes are stuck fast.' He cast a hopeful eye around the farmyard. 'Haven't you got a tractor?'

Much to Lenny's alarm, Mr Preswick slapped Delilah on the rump. 'No need, not wi' Delilah; she's better'n any tractor.'

Dana, who was not in the least bit afraid of the huge Clydesdale, hurried over to give her a pat. 'She's a beauty, Mr Preswick. How old is she?'

Mr Preswick beamed with pride. 'Nine, and I bred her meself.'

'The size of her feet!' said Lenny. 'They're like dinner plates!' He hastened to put as much space as he could between himself and Delilah.

Dana laughed. 'What's up, Lenny? Don't you like horses?'

'In a field or stable, yes,' said Lenny, 'but not so much up close where they can stand on you by accident.' He was keeping a keen eye on Delilah as though he expected her to leap over the car and land on him at any moment.

Dana and Mr Preswick were busy hooking the traces on Delilah's tack to the towing eye of the car.

'Tell you what,' said Lenny as they got Delilah into position, 'I'll push from my end, that way we should have her out in no time.'

Mr Preswick shook his head with a chuckle. 'Strappin' lad like you afraid of my Delilah!'

'Not afraid,' corrected Lenny, 'just makes more sense for me to stay round this end!' As he spoke, Delilah took the strain, and Lenny was about to say it was no use and they should consider another method when the car slowly slid forward; the wheels which were locked scraped along the floor until the force jerked them free.

Mr Preswick slapped Delilah heartily on the neck. 'Good gel, knew you'd do it.' He beckoned Lenny over. 'C'mon, lad, come and take a look and see what you think.'

Lenny tried to think of a reason why he couldn't join Mr Preswick and Dana, but he knew that any excuse he gave would be met with cynicism, so he joined them, albeit begrudgingly.

'Mr Preswick's goin' to put Delilah back now the car's free. Do you want to say thank you before she goes?'

Lenny grinned. 'Thanks, Mr Preswick.'

Dana eyed him shrewdly. 'You know what I meant! Come and say thank you to Delilah.' Seeing the look of uncertainty on Lenny's face she added, 'I'm not askin' you to kiss her, just a quick stroke of her neck or muzzle'll do.'

Lenny heaved a sigh. 'I don't expect you're goin' to stop badgerin' me till I do?'

'You suppose right!' Dana chuckled.

Lenny walked stiltedly towards Delilah's neck, keeping a close eye on her feet as he did so. Standing so that Dana was between himself and the large mare, he reached forward and gingerly patted her neck.

'There you are!' said Dana. 'Wasn't that bad, was it?'

Lenny was about to say it wasn't when Delilah struck her belly with her hoof. Lenny leapt to one side. 'What's she doin'?'

364

Mr Preswick laughed so much he began to wheeze. 'Blimey, lad, she's only gettin' a fly off her belly.'

Beads of sweat appeared on Lenny's brow. 'She can't half move fast for a big horse!'

Mr Preswick stroked Delilah's cheek. 'C'mon, girl, let's get you back.'

Lenny strolled round the car, every now and then bending down to inspect underneath. Once he'd gone full circle, he lifted the bonnet and started poking around inside the engine; when he had finished he closed the bonnet again. 'The main brake cylinder's gone, and there's a fair bit of rust, but nothin' that can't be mended; she'll need an oil and filter change and a new fan belt as well as four new tyres, but all in all she doesn't look too bad.' He grinned at Dana. 'Looks like keepin' her under a pile of hay wasn't such a daft idea after all!'

'Are you goin' to buy it then?' said Dana.

Lenny nodded. 'Waddy said he trusted my decision, and in my opinion it won't take much to get her runnin', and she'll spruce up nicely with a bit of a polish.' He looked in the direction of the stone farmhouse. 'Come on, we'll go and tell Mr Preswick the good news.'

They were making their way across the yard when Mr Preswick hailed them. 'Over here!' He was standing outside a row of stables, and Dana noticed Delilah was holding up one of her hooves.

'Is she OK?'

He shook his head. 'I reckon she's got something in it, only I can't get down there, not with my back, but if one of you could hold her hoof, I can take a look.'

Dana deftly took the hoof from the old man's hands and peered at the sole. 'She's got a nail wedged in the middle of her frog. I'll need a knife and a pair of pincers or pliers.'

Without hesitation Mr Preswick disappeared into one of his sheds, reappearing a few seconds later with the tools Dana had asked for.

'Thanks.' Taking the knife, Dana gently slid the tip underneath the nail and lifted the head free. Delilah rocked back slightly, but soon settled under Dana's reassuring tone. 'I know it hurts, but we'll soon have it out.'

Lenny looked on anxiously. 'I thought horses were used to havin' nails in their hooves. Isn't that how you keep the shoes in place?'

Nodding, Dana gripped the head of the nail with the pincers. 'Only they go into the hoof wall where there's no feeling, not the frog.' Looking up, she smiled at Lenny. 'You know how you use scissors to trim your nails?'

Lenny nodded.

'Ever gone down too far and caught the skin by accident?'

'I see,' said Lenny slowly. 'Poor old girl, but are you sure that's a good ...'

Dana tugged the nail out in one swift movement. 'Gotcha!'

Mr Preswick, who had been watching in fascination, shook his head. 'Where'd you learn to do that?'

'It was my old job before I joined the WAAF,' said Dana. 'My dad taught me everythin' I know about horses.' She quickly banished the tears which were forming at the memory of her father; it felt as though all she had done for the past few days was cry, and she had promised herself that today was going to be different, and she was determined to keep it that way. She cleared her throat before continuing. 'I could shoe and trim a horse before I were ten.' As she spoke she wiped her hand around the underneath of Delilah's hoof. 'If you could fetch me some salt in warm water, I can clean the puncture wound out, just to make sure no rust's gone in.'

Mr Preswick had already started off in the direction of the house. Dana put Delilah's hoof down and wiped her hands on some hay she had taken from the manger.

'I've never seen anyone do anythin' like that before,' said Lenny with admiration. 'If it were me, I'd've been worried I might hurt her by accident, but you didn't doubt yourself, not even for a second.'

Dana shrugged. 'Water off a duck's back. I s'pose I'm as happy doin' horses as you are mendin' engines.'

'Only a car won't kick me if I get it wrong.' Lenny broke off mid-chuckle to call out to Mr Preswick, who was trying to carry a bowl of water in one hand, whilst holding his walking stick in the other. 'You're going to lose half of that if you go much further! Wait there and I'll come and get it off you.' Lenny jogged over to retrieve the bowl of water along with a small glass syringe, both of which he held whilst Dana flushed the puncture wound out. Happy with her efforts she turned Delilah back into the empty stable.

'It won't take long to close over; she'll be fine after that.' She grinned at Lenny who was stroking Delilah's face over the stable door. 'You soon came round.'

Lenny switched his gaze from Delilah to Dana. 'If I'd had summat like that in my foot the whole world would know about it, but Delilah didn't bat an eye.'

'So not so scary after all?' ventured Dana.

'Appearances can be deceptive,' mused Lenny. 'She may be a giant, but she's a gentle one.' He ran the back of his fingers over her velvety muzzle. 'Soft too.'

'That's why I love them,' said Dana. 'They're more powerful than any man, yet they do his bidding without complaint.'

Lenny looked at the Morris Six that Delilah had pulled free. 'I used to wonder why any farmer would have a horse when they could use a tractor, but I'm beginning to understand.'

Mr Preswick gave Delilah half an apple which she gently snuffled off the palm of his hand. 'That's why my wife, Maud, wanted me to sell the Morris. She reckoned the war could go on for a long time yet and she don't see the point in keepin' summat we can't afford to run.'

Lenny raised a fleeting brow. 'I hope your wife's wrong about the war, but either way it's pointless hangin' on to a car which is only goin' to rust ...' He handed Mr Preswick a small brown envelope. 'Flying Officer Waddington asked me to give you this.'

Mr Preswick peered inside the envelope. 'That'll do nicely.' He grinned at Dana. 'Thanks for all you done with Delilah.' He nodded towards Lenny. 'Your boyfriend could easy've brought one of the lads, and they might've been as bad as this 'un when it comes to horses.' He jerked his stick at Lenny.

Dana blushed hotly. 'Oh no, we're just good pals.'

Seeing Dana's embarrassment, Lenny shook his head sadly. 'She wouldn't have me, Mr Preswick.'

'That's not true!' said Dana; the words had left her mouth before she had a chance to think.

'Looks like your luck's in, lad.' Mr Preswick chuckled. 'I'd not say no, if I were younger o' course.'

Lenny winked at Dana. 'Looks like I'd best get you back before Mr Preswick tries wooin' you out from under me.'

'Mr Preswick wins, 'cos he's got Delilah!' said Dana, grateful that Lenny had made it light-hearted.

'Ditched for a horse! Just my luck.' He jerked his head in the direction of the station car. 'I'd love to stand here discussin' how you find a horse more attractive than me, but I'm fair starvin'. Why don't we call in at that pub on the way home?'

'If you're talkin' about the Weary Friar, they do a smashin' pie and mash,' said Mr Preswick, adding, 'An' if you've still the room, you ought to try their apple crumble.' He smacked his lips together at the very thought. 'Luvverly!'

By the time they reached the Weary Friar, Dana was feeling more at ease with being towed and was looking forward to a spot of lunch. 'I wasn't hungry till Mr Preswick mentioned the pie and mash,' she said as they left the cars.

Lenny held the pub door aside so that Dana might enter before him. 'Funny how the suggestion of food can get your stomach rumblin'. What I'd really like is a nice bit of steak and kidney puddin', although I very much doubt they'll have that on the menu.'

369

Dana looked at the blackboard that hung on the wall above the fireplace. 'Mr Preswick was right about the pie and mash, although they don't say what pie it is ...'

'Meat and veg,' said a man from behind the bar. 'And the fish is trout.'

Dana wrinkled her nose. 'I've allus thought trout tastes a bit earthy – not that I've eaten much mud in my time,' she quipped before Lenny had the chance.

'Too many bones for me,' mused Lenny. 'I only like it battered with plenty of salt and vinegar ...'

Dana looked at him wistfully. 'Oh yes please! Me dad used to take me and me mam to the chippy down by the Albert Dock every Friday; they'd have great big fat cod smothered in thick crunchy batter; they'd gi' you a generous helpin' of salt and vinegar and wrap 'em up in the previous day's *Echo*.' She turned to face the barman. 'Pie and mash and half a bitter please.'

'Make that two, only I'll have a pint instead of the half, please.'

The barman nodded as he placed Dana's half beneath the pump. 'You folks stationed nearby?'

'Harrowbeer, so not too far away,' said Dana as she took the glass from the barman.

'Who does the Morris belong to?' said the barman conversationally as he began pulling Lenny's pint.

'One of the officers on our station has bought it from Mr Preswick. They met down the pub,' said Lenny.

The barman chuckled as he handed Lenny his drink. 'Thought as much. I take it we are talkin' about Bobby Preswick, the old feller from Mumbledown Farm?'

Lenny placed the glass on the counter and wiped the froth from his lip. 'Always doin' deals down the pub, is he?'

The barman glanced at the thick black ceiling beams. 'You could sell him anythin' once he's had a drink; that's how he ended up with the car in the first place.'

Dana looked alarmed. 'Is there summat wrong wi' it?'

'Nah, but he can't drive.' He thought about this for a moment. 'That is to say, he can drive, he's just very bad at it, which is why he's gone through four cars and one tractor in as many years. We all told him he should stick with Delilah.'

'If he can't drive, why on earth did he buy another car?' said Lenny.

'He said it was a bargain, too good a deal to miss, and he was right, it was in great condition when he bought it, but Bobby doesn't know bugger all about cars; he reckons they don't need toppin' up with oil or water. I'm surprised he puts petrol in.'

'How long's he had it?' said Lenny.

'A couple of years,' said the barman after some consideration.

'A couple of years and he didn't think to check the oil or water?' Lenny shook his head. 'No wonder he goes through cars.'

'Good job you didn't try and start it; the engine would probably've seized,' said Dana.

Lenny nodded. 'Or blown up.' He paid the barman and then turned to Dana. 'Where would you like to sit?'

Dana nodded towards a window table.

'I'll bring your food over as soon as it's ready.'

Settling into her seat, Dana smiled at Lenny. 'Thanks for today. It's really helped take me mind off things.'

He smiled. 'I'm glad you feel better. I don't like the thought of you bein' upset.'

'When I were on me way back from Ireland,' said Dana, 'I couldn't take me mind off the death of me father or stop meself from wondering who me real parents were, and why they saw fit to hand me over to strangers. The last thing I was expectin' to hear was that Pete had gone missin'.' She looked up at Lenny's puzzled expression. 'I know they say it's not good for me to pretend there's any hope of him comin' back, but until they find him we can never be certain, not really.'

Lenny eyed her thoughtfully. 'Have you mentioned this to Patty?'

'I did, but she said they'd tied themselves in knots thinkin' of scenarios where Pete could come out of it alive, an' that the sooner I accepted the truth the better.' She saw that he still looked doubtful. 'I know they've found a piece of a plane, but who's to say it was his? There's hundreds of 'em up there, all from different stations, all nearby: I'd be very surprised if they knew for certain that it was a bit of Lady Luck that'd washed up. All Spitfires look pretty much the same to me.'

Lenny nodded. 'I know what you mean, but I don't think they'd say unless they were certain. Besides, these planes have serial numbers, and I'm sure they'd have cross-checked with other stations to see whether another one had gone missin'.'

Dana nodded slowly. 'I just find it so hard to believe he's gone. It's easier to pretend he might come back.'

Lenny fiddled with the bottom of his beer glass. 'Was it love at first sight?' He looked up briefly before turning his attention back to the glass.

Laughing, Dana shook her head. 'Not at all, I thought he were lyin' when I first met him …' She pushed her bottom lip out. 'I s'pose that never really went away, even when I knew him to be tellin' the truth. Don't know why, 'cos he never lied to me, or not as far as I know anyway.'

'Maybe something in his demeanour?' ventured Lenny.

'Our friendship started off on the wrong foot, with me not believin' a word he said. I know that's not his fault, but it kind of made me keep me guard up. I was certain he was with me for the wrong reasons, and if I'm honest I don't think our relationship would've run its course once the war was over because our lives are too different. No matter what Pete might think, him and his father've got more in common than he realised, and I reckern that's why he never told me about the letter.

Dana glanced up as the waitress placed her lunch on the table. 'Thank you.' She waited until Lenny's plate was in front of him before continuing. 'I wouldn't've expected Pete to give everythin' up for me, that would've been a ridiculous thing to do, especially when we'd only been together a relatively short while.' She took a forkful of pie and blew on it gently before placing it in her mouth and chewing thoughtfully. 'I think his father's letter hit a raw nerve, that it was time to stop messin' around and grow up.'

Lenny pulled a face. 'He sounds like a bit of a rebel.'

373

Dana stared open-mouthed. 'You're right! Those were his exact words. He thought I was the same, because I'd gone against my father's wishes and stayed in Liverpool, but of course that was nowt to do with rebellion, but more about loyalty. Pete always did everythin' to the extreme, and courtin' a traveller was a good way of tellin' his dad he'd do things his way, only of course his father found out first.'

Lenny swallowed his mouthful. 'That's why I don't play games, tell it like it is; that way everyone knows the score.'

Dana eyed Lenny wistfully. 'I wish I'd told you the truth. I was just so scared that you might change your opinion of me. I wouldn't've been able to bear it if you had.'

Lenny gazed at her lovingly. 'You could've come from Mars for all I care, I'd still—' He stopped short, glanced at his half-empty plate briefly, and then looked back up. 'Anyway, I'm glad you told me.'

'Me too.'

He pointed at the plate of food before her. 'Does it pass muster?'

She nodded happily. 'Very much so!'

By the time they got back to Harrowbeer, a small crowd had gathered outside the Officers' Mess. Flying Officer Waddington wanted to chat to Lenny about the car, so Dana left to seek out Patty.

'You're back!' said Patty. 'How'd it go?'

'Good,' said Dana truthfully. 'Bit dauntin' at first because it's hard to judge whether the car in front is brakin' hard or soft, but I soon got the hang of it.'

Patty slid her hand into the crook of Dana's elbow. 'Did it help take your mind off things?'

'Kind of, although we did spend some time talkin' about me mam an' dad, and Pete an' his father.' She shot Patty a sidelong glance. 'I told Lenny the truth.' She smiled slowly. 'He said he wouldn't care if I came from Mars.'

Patty nodded. 'That's 'cos he loves you.'

Dana glanced guiltily at Patty from under thick lashes. 'It felt so good to be with him, Patty, like no time had passed since we saw each other last.'

Patty gave a half shoulder shrug. 'You know I allus thought you 'n' Lenny were made for each other.'

'He really helped me talk things through and sort myself out. I feel like a huge weight's been lifted off my shoulders.'

'Have you had any more thoughts about your birth mam?'

Dana smiled. 'I'm goin' to look for her once the war's over.'

Patty gave Dana's arm a loving squeeze. 'I think that's a marvellous idea, and you know me and Lu will help any way we can.'

She stopped walking and turned to face Dana. 'You said you've told Lenny and he couldn't have cared less – how do you feel about that?'

'Like I've been an idiot! But there's nowt I can do to change it.'

Patty cleared her throat. 'If Pete's taught you anythin' it should be that life's short. You've kept Lenny at arms' length for ever such a long time now. I'd hate to see you make another mistake.' Adding hastily, 'I'm not suggestin' you rush into anythin', not so soon, but mebbe consider it for the future?'

'Who knows how I'll feel given time? For now I'm happy on me tod,' said Dana. As they continued to walk, she looked at the guard's gate where Lenny had picked her up earlier that morning. I wish he'd carried on drivin', thought Dana, because I really enjoyed my time with him today, just like we were back in Pwllheli, and had I had the strength to tell him the truth from the get go, and he'd still asked me to be his girlfriend, the answer would've been yes, yes and yes again. She sighed wistfully. If only she could turn back the hands of time.

Chapter Twelve

November 1942

Several months had passed since Pete's disappearance, and the servicemen and women of Harrowbeer were enjoying the benefits of an Indian summer. A Canadian pilot had been sleeping in Pete's old bed, and things were beginning to return to normal.

Dana had accepted that she would never see Pete or her father again, and despite her earlier fears, her mother had grasped life by the horns and was getting on with things over in Ireland. Even so, Dana had asked for a week's leave so that she could make sure Colleen was all right.

'What people say can be ever so different from reality, and I won't rest until I see it with me own eyes,' she had explained to Patty. 'Besides, I've all sorts of questions about the day they adopted me. I don't want to ask her over the phone because I want her to know that I'm not tryin' to replace her; I'd never do that, I'm just curious, that's all.'

This conversation had taken place at one of the dances being held in the scout hut in the nearby village of Horrabridge. 'It's a shame they didn't tell you sooner, although I understand their reasonin'.' Patty scanned the room for an empty table.

'It's a pity you and Eddie can't come with us,' said Dana.

Patty tried to look sympathetic, but deep down she was beaming inside. 'Sorry, chuck, but I couldn't say no when Eddie asked me to meet his parents. Just a shame it coincided with your trip.'

Dana chuckled. 'You're looking forward to meetin' them then?'

'Gosh yes, it's the next step before a proposal, don't you think?'

Dana nodded. 'I reckern so. He's introducin' them to their future daughter-in-law.'

Patty gave a suppressed squeal of delight. 'That's what all the other girls reckern. I just hope his mam likes me, 'cos I know he values her opinion.'

Now, Dana and Lenny were waiting for the train that would take them to Drogheda.

Lenny sat down on the small wooden bench on the platform and placed his kitbag between his knees. 'Are you sure your mam's all right with the idea of you bringin' a male friend along?'

Dana, who was anxiously awaiting the train's arrival, nodded distractedly. 'She thinks it's safer for me to travel with a man.' She patted him on the shoulder. 'C'mon, this is our train.'

Getting to his feet, Lenny hefted his own kitbag over his shoulder, then bent down to pick up Dana's, despite her protests. 'I wouldn't consider myself much of a gent if I allowed you to carry this honkin' great thing. Blimey, I thought mine was heavy but yours weighs a ton!'

They were pleased to see that the carriage was empty save for a couple of strangers. It meant they could take seats next to each other, placing their kitbags on the seats opposite.

'I hope Mam doesn't get upset when I start askin' questions about me adoption.'

'I reckon your mam's probably expectin' it – it's human nature to want to know more. Once you re-assure her that you've no intention of replacin' her, I'm sure she'll be happy to tell you all she knows – although from what you've told me I wouldn't get your hopes up. It doesn't sound like she knows any more than they've already told you.'

'I'm goin' to include her with every step of the search so that she doesn't feel left out.'

Lenny smiled at her fondly. 'God love you, Dana Quinn, here's you wantin' the answers that you've every right to know, yet you're more bothered about your mam. Now why doesn't that surprise me?'

It was the evening of their last night in Ireland and Lenny was in the wagon playing a game of solitaire whilst Dana and her mother prepared the filling for a Woolton pie on the small stove outside the wagon.

'I'm glad to see you've settled down after losin' Dad,' said Dana. 'I know you said you were never short on company livin' so close to the O'Briens, but, well, I'm glad things are working out.'

Colleen emptied the water into the pot and placed it on the stove to boil before standing straight and eyeing her daughter with interest. 'Did you only come to make sure I were all right or was there another reason for your visit?'

Dana glanced back to where she could see Lenny sitting beside the table, the cards laid out in front of him. She had wanted him to join her when she asked her mother about the circumstances surrounding her birth, but Lenny had said it should be sorted out between mother and daughter, so Dana had been waiting for the right time – although of course the right time never comes along. However, now, with her mother asking such a forthright question, Dana seized the opportunity. 'The main reason I came was to make sure you were all right, but I also wanted to know a little bit more about the day I was born.'

Colleen nodded soberly. 'I thought you might.'

Dana's heart dropped. 'I'm just curious, that's all. As far as I'm concerned you and Dad are my real parents; it was you who took me in, looked after me, brought me up as your own, but I'd be lyin' if I didn't want to know more about me birth mam.' Dana's eyes, which usually sparkled with love and affection, now sparkled with tears. 'I want to know why she did what she did. Once I know that I can put it behind me and move on. As it is I feel like I'm in limbo.' She blinked and two tears trickled down her cheeks. 'What with Dad losin' his family, then dyin', and Pete's dad disownin' him and Pete dyin', I've started to wonder whether she might've sensed I were bad news and that's why she got rid of me.'

Colleen's face fell and she took Dana in her arms. 'Don't you ever blame yourself for any of those things! You're the reason your father got up in the mornin's; he were a shell of a man before you come along. And as for Pete's father, well, least said about him the better.' She wiped Dana's cheeks with the hem of her apron. 'You're a fine figure of a woman, Dana Quinn. I don't know why your mam gave you up, but it were nowt to do wi' you! Her loss was our gain; you may not be our blood, but you're a Quinn through an' through.' She jerked her head at Lenny, who was busy studying the cards on the table before him. 'If you want to see the measure of a woman, look at the friends that surround her. That boy used his leave so he could escort you to a different country, as did Lucy, and that says a lot about you.'

Dana had followed her mother's line of sight and was looking at Lenny. 'Says a lot about them too.'

'I just wish I could tell you more about your mam.'

Sniffing, Dana picked up the small knife and began peeling the potatoes. 'What about my adoption papers?'

Colleen stared at the water, which was beginning to steam. 'There weren't none.'

Dana stopped halfway through a potato. 'There must've been.'

Colleen shook her head. 'You were the one who said you were adopted, and I didn't correct you because I couldn't think of a better way to put it, but when it comes down to it, no one ever asked us for any information, or identification, and we were never given any in return.' She glanced guiltily at her daughter. 'I know we should've asked more questions but I were worried they'd say we couldn't have you, so I kept quiet and encouraged your father to do the same.'

Dana's mouth hung open. 'So there's no record of my birth, what does it say on my birth certificate?'

Colleen swallowed. 'I don't know about a record of your birth, an' as for your birth certificate, I'm afraid that won't be of any use to you because me an' your dad are down as your parents. You'd have to ask the hospital in Glasgow; they might know summat.'

'Was I an awkward baby?' She shook her head before her mother had a chance to answer. 'That's not what I meant. I should've said: do you think I knew I'd been taken away from me birth mam?'

Colleen shook her head. 'It were too quick. I very much doubt she were even given the chance to hold you; and as for bein' an awkward baby then no, you were allus smilin', there weren't a person who clapped eyes on you that didn't remark on what a pleasant baby you were.'

'Why on earth was my birth mother so desperate to get rid of me?'

Colleen frowned. 'I dunno, luvvy, but we were told about you before you'd been born, so I s'pose it must've been personal circumstances. I don't think it's a good idea to speculate.'

Dana leaned her cheek against her mother's shoulder. 'Thank you.'

A small crease furrowed Colleen's brow. 'What for?'

Dana's features remained impassive as tears trickled down her cheeks. 'For wantin' me.'

382

Colleen, who had fought to keep her emotions from getting the better of her, lost the war. Tears streaming down her cheeks, she gently cupped the side of Dana's face in one hand and kissed the top of her head. 'I can't explain why your mam gave you up, but I'm guessin' she must've been in dire straits to do so, because you were a beautiful baby, allus full of smiles, anyone in their right mind would've wanted you.'

'I'm so lucky you were there that night,' said Dana. 'Goodness knows where I'd've ended up otherwise.'

'Fate,' said Colleen simply.

'When the Quinns told you to give me up or be cast out from the family ...'

'Your father told me to take you into the wagon whilst he hitched Crystal up to the shafts. His brother Donald thought your dad were goin' to take you back to the hospital, 'cos he said your dad were doin' the right thing.' She chuckled softly. 'Your dad marched up to him and told him straight that he were doin' the right thing, and the Quinns would never see any of us again unless they were prepared to accept you.

'Donald went that red I thought he were goin' to explode, but he never said a word, just turned on his heel and shouted at the others to get back into their wagons and not to come out 'til we'd gone.'

'That was one hell of a price to pay though,' said Dana.

Colleen looked at her sharply. 'You're worth a million of them, and had I known they'd react the way they did before we got you, it wouldn't have made the blindest bit of difference. Don't ever think we've lost out because of you, Dana, because you couldn't be further from the truth.' She took the potatoes, leeks and carrots that Dana had prepared and added them to the water. 'I know you're still smartin' after losin' Pete, but fellers like Lenny are few and far between. Don't rest on your laurels, luv; take it from one who knows: you have to grab every opportunity you're given. I only have to see the way Lenny looks at you to know he's in love, 'cos it's the same way your father used to look at me, and I know you feel the same. It's crazy that two people so obviously in love aren't gerrin' together because of "what ifs". Don't deny yourself the chance to be happy in a world what's full of misery.'

'I know I've not done owt wrong, and I know Pete's not comin' back, but I feel like I'm bein' callous. People say it's different in wartime but I don't see why.'

Colleen heaved a sigh. 'Because in wartime people love and lose more frequently than in times of peace.' She paused. 'Did you give your heart to Pete?'

Dana barely shook her head. 'I loved him, but I didn't give him my heart because I wasn't in love with him, I realise that now, we were just too different.'

'If courtin' Lenny would make you happy then I reckern you should go for it. You deserve to be happy.' A small smile curved the corners of Colleen's lips. 'I know it would've made your father happy. He'd've approved of Lenny.'

Dana smiled. 'He would, wouldn't he? I take it you like him?'

Colleen prodded the potatoes with the tip of her knife. 'He's a good lad, and he obviously thinks the world of you ...'

Dana glanced shyly in the direction of the wagon again. 'I know he likes me, of course I do …' She gently nibbled the corner of her lip. 'What should I do?'

Colleen laid the palm of her hand on Dana's chest. 'Whatever your heart tells you to do.' She watched as a slow smile spread across her daughter's cheeks.

Lenny descended the steps to the wagon. 'Somethin' smells good!'

It was the morning of their final day and Colleen had accompanied Dana and Lenny to the station. 'Don't forget to eat the sarnies I made for you, and watch out for pickpockets.'

Dana rolled her eyes. 'We will, Mam. Honestly, we're not kids, you know.'

'That's as may be! Now don't forget to write, and let me know if you go to Scotland; it'll be interestin' to see what you find out. Most of all good luck an' take care!'

Lenny grinned. 'Thanks, Mrs Quinn, and I promise I'll take good care of her.'

Dana kissed her goodbye and was surprised when her mother slipped a note into her hand. Holding a finger to her lips, Colleen turned to Lenny and hugged him goodbye. 'Don't forget your sarnies.' She winked at him before standing back from the train.

Lenny looked puzzled. Why had she reminded them twice to eat the sandwiches? And why had she winked at him the second time? He started as the guard blew his whistle.

Dana handed Lenny her kitbag. 'Come on, Lenny, we don't want to get left behind.' The guard was walking the length of the train slamming the doors shut as he went. Dana tried in vain to pull the window down but it was stuck fast until Lenny forced it down with a hefty shove. Leaning out, Dana waved goodbye. 'I'll phone Mrs O'Brien as soon as we get home!'

Lenny called out from over her shoulder, "Bye, Colleen, and thanks for everythin'.'

The guard blew his final whistle, waved his flag and stepped back away from the train.

Dana and Lenny waved until Colleen was lost from view. Fishing a handkerchief from her pocket Dana blew her nose gently. 'I don't know when I'll get to see her again – I'm not due any more leave for ever such a long time.'

Lenny pushed their kitbags underneath the seats in the empty carriage. 'How'd it go with your mam last night?'

Dana plonked herself down in one of the window seats, and smiled when Lenny sat down next to her. 'It turns out Mam and Dad didn't so much adopt me as take me in as their own, so there's no paperwork, or documentation of who me birth mam is, so I've no hope of findin' her, unless I go to the hospital where I was born, and I doubt they'll be forthcomin' with information, 'cos the whole thing sounds pretty dodgy to me.'

A frown creased Lenny's brow. 'There's got to be somethin', even if only for their own records.'

Dana shrugged. 'From what me mam said, they were told they could take me and go, no questions asked, no forms to be signed. Mam agreed because she were desperate for a child and thought this could be her only chance.'

Lenny eyed her cautiously. 'How do you feel?'

'Numb!' said Dana. 'I don't know whether to blame me birth mam or the hospital, but someone didn't want me findin' out the truth, that's for sure.'

Lenny gently stroked her cheek with the back of his fingers. 'You know I'll do everythin' I can to help.'

'Thanks, Lenny, you've been a rock as always. Mam really liked you; she reckerned Dad would've too.'

'That reminds me of somethin',' said Lenny as he rummaged in the sandwiches.

'Blimey, don't tell me you're still hungry, not after that fry-up me mam done us?'

Smiling, Lenny held out a piece of paper that had been hidden in the sandwiches. It read: *Faint heart never won fair lady*. Chuckling quietly as she read the note, Dana pushed her hand into her own pocket and pulled out the piece of paper which her mother had handed her, read it and then held it out to Lenny.

He grinned as he read the note. 'You deserve to be happy!' He rubbed his chin in pretended thought. 'Do you reckon your mam's tryin' to tell us somethin'?'

'I reckern so.' Dana chuckled. 'Parents, eh?'

He nodded. 'Always think they know best. Mind you, in your mam's case I reckon she's right, because I'd like to think I'm quite the catch!'

She slapped his arm in a playful manner. 'Talk about tootin' your own horn!'

'Toot, toot!' Lenny laughed.

She gazed up at him adoringly. 'I don't know what it is about you, Lenny Ackerman, but no matter how bad things get, you allus make me feel better, like sunshine on a rainy day. You're the only one who seems to have that effect on me.'

His mouth twitched with amusement. 'I don't think I have that effect on anyone else, so what does that tell you?'

She eyed him levelly. 'You tell me.'

Never taking his eyes off hers, he took her hand in his. 'That your mam's right, you do deserve to be happy, and if I make you happy then ...'

Looking at Lenny, Dana saw his gaze drop down to her mouth and her heart skipped a beat. Her breathing quickened as she wondered whether he would to try to kiss her and what she should do if he did. A lock of her hair slipped from her cap and hung down the side of her cheek. Lenny glanced at the escaped curl and smiled as he pushed it back behind her ear. The touch of his fingers against her skin caused her body to tingle and her cheeks flushed pink. For goodness' sake, Dana, say something, she urged herself, but she couldn't find the words. Instead, she found herself concentrating on his mouth, his strong, firm lips surrounded by a hint of stubble. She opened her mouth to break the silence but before she could utter a word Lenny had removed his cap and was leaning in to kiss her. Having been kissed by Pete she thought she knew what was coming, but when Lenny kissed her it was a whole new experience. He cupped the side of her face in the palm of his hand, and his soft lips brushed gently over hers before taking control; she gazed into his eyes and felt a rush of blood sweep through her body. Breaking away, he brushed his lips over hers murmuring, 'Will you let me make you happy?'

Dana shivered with pleasure as his hand travelled around the nape of her neck; tilting her head to one side she mumbled, 'You bet I will.'

The carriage fell silent as the train went into a tunnel.

Chapter Thirteen

March 1943

Reveille sounded and Dana swung her legs out of bed. Reaching up, she tickled Patty's feet, which were hanging over the edge of her bunk.

Patty squealed as she jerked her feet away from Dana's fingers. 'Someone's full of the joys of spring!' said Patty. Her feet appeared briefly before being followed closely by the rest of her as she jumped off her bunk and sat down beside Dana. 'Not that I can blame you, I wish Eddie were takin' me for a romantic day out.'

Dana smiled. 'I promise to tell you all about it when I get back.'

Stowing her wash kit under her arm, Patty hooked her coat over her shoulders and headed for the ablutions. 'Back in a mo.'

Dana checked her stocking for ladders as she reflected on the past few months. When they'd returned from Ireland, they'd thought it best to break the news of their romance before someone else did.

'If Alexa taught me anythin' it was that "loose lips sink ships" is bang on the money,' Dana told Lenny.

'And even though we haven't told anyone yet, I'll bet you a pound to a penny someone will've seen us cuddlin' on the train, and you know what it's like in Harrowbeer, so we need to get in there first before anyone else has the chance.'

Lenny agreed, and they had made it their priority to find Patty and Eddie before they did anything else.

Dana had half expected Eddie to take the news badly, and was pleasantly surprised when he appeared to take it in his stride.

'Pete would've wanted you to be happy. He hated it when people sat around feelin' sorry for themselves; he reckerned life were for livin'.' He shook Lenny's hand. 'Good luck to you both.'

'Eddie's right,' said Patty. 'Pete lived life for the moment. He allus said you shouldn't dwell on things, but get on with it.'

Dana had breathed a happy sigh of relief. 'I hope everyone else takes it as well as you two!'

Eddie shrugged his indifference. 'Can't see as it's anyone else's business bar yours, but even so I think people are more understandin' than you think.'

Eddie had been right. It seemed as if there wasn't a single person on Harrowbeer who wasn't happy to hear the news.

Dana, Lenny, Patty and Eddie often went out together as a foursome, and Dana was pleased to see that Lenny and Eddie got on like a house on fire.

She carefully pulled her stocking over her toes and ran it up her leg as Patty appeared beside her. 'Whatever is goin' on out there? Has Waddy been down the pub again?'

Chuckling, Dana craned her neck to follow Patty's gaze out of the window. 'Dunno, all I can see is people's backs ...' She paused. 'D'you reckern they're doin' a sweep or summat?'

Patty thought about this for a moment before shaking her head. 'Can't think of anythin', but I've got a spare penny or two so if they are' – she pulled her handbag out from her locker and tipped the contents of her purse out on to her bed – 'do you want me to stick summat on for you?'

Dana shook her head. 'I never have any luck on those things, I'm better off keepin' me money in me purse, but I'll come with you for a look-see.'

The girls left the hut and walked over to the small crowd that had gathered outside the NAAFI. One of the Waafs turned round as they approached, and pointed at Dana. 'Dana!'

Dana frowned as the heads of everyone present all turned to face her. Patty hissed out of the side of her mouth, 'What've you done?'

'Nothin'!' said Dana. 'Or at least nowt I know of ...' She fell silent as the crowd parted.

'Pete!' Feeling her knees begin to buckle, she clasped hold of Patty for support. 'I – I don't understand ...'

Pete walked towards her, took her in his arms and kissed her. 'I realise this must be a bit of a shock ...'

Dana nodded slowly. 'You can say that again.' She looked at Patty with wide eyes. 'Am I dreamin'?'

Patty looked equally shocked. 'No, you're not.' She turned to the people clustering round. 'Come on, folks, I think these two could do wi' a bit of privacy ...'

There was a general reluctant murmur of agreement, and the crowd slowly dispersed along with Patty, despite Dana asking her to stay.

'Sorry, luvvy, but you two need to chat, without me or anyone else around.' She glanced at Pete. 'It's good to see you back. I don't know how you did it, but you can fill me in on all that later.'

Pete gave Dana a smile riddled with guilt. 'I'm so sorry. If I could've got word to you I would, but after I landed in France ...'

'France?' said Dana, who was still reeling from the shock. 'You didn't land in France; the Americans saw you go down over the Channel.'

He nodded. 'I did.' He sighed. 'It's a long story.'

Dana indicated the wall beside the NAAFI. 'You'd better start at the beginnin'.'

Pete sat down on the wall and told her of his exciting escape from the fuselage.

'I thought that was it, my time was up, but luckily for me I got rescued by Estelle.'

Dana arched an inquisitive eyebrow. 'Estelle?'

He nodded. 'She's with the Resistance, she and her sister Marguerite.' He sighed. 'Perhaps it's better that I start from the moment I came to ...' Holding Dana's hand in his he gazed into her eyes as he recalled the memory.

When Pete had first regained consciousness, he had found himself looking into the face of a brunette with brown doe eyes surrounded by a fringe of thick lashes. 'Am I in heaven?'

The woman had smiled pleasantly. '*Non*, you are in Bayeux.'

'Like the tapestry?' Pete had said with a faint smile.

The woman had knitted her beautifully arched eyebrows. 'Sorry?'

'Are you French?'

'*Oui*. You are English, and a pilot too, yes?'

Pete had nodded, and then winced as a sharp pain surged into the back of his head. Holding up a hand, he nursed the back of his skull. 'What happened?'

The woman had explained in broken English how two French boys had discovered him on the beach; not knowing whether he was English or German, they had decided to take no chances and hit him over the back of the head with a rock to be on the safe side. She smiled apologetically. 'I'm afraid they were, 'ow you say ...' she hesitated, 'a bit over-enthusiastic.'

'What happened to my dinghy?' said Pete. He looked around him as though expecting to see it close by. He was in what looked like the inside of a large wooden shed: in one corner there were tools for farming, and a large sheet covering what Pete assumed to be a tractor. 'I'm not in hospital ...' he said softly; then, looking at the woman in her pale blue tea dress, he added, 'And you're not a nurse ... are you?'

A woman standing behind the one he had been talking to giggled behind her hand. '*Combien d'infirmières portent des armes?*'

Frowning, Pete turned to his rescuer. 'I'm sorry, but did she just ask how many nurses carry guns?'

Smiling, the brunette nodded. '*Très bien!*' She glanced approvingly at the woman behind her. ''E can understand French, we 'ad better be careful what we say!' She slowly pulled a pistol from the pocket of her skirt.

'Blimey!' said Pete, much to the amusement of both women.

Sliding the pistol back into her pocket, she held out a hand. 'My name is Estelle Moreau, and this is my sister Marguerite.'

'*Je m'appelle* Pete Robinson,' said Pete.

''Ello, Pete. Are you wondering why two women with pistols 'ave you in this old barn?'

Pete beamed up at her. 'French Resistance?'

She nodded. 'We are going to try and get you back 'ome, but the place is crawling with Germans, so you must stay 'ere until it's safe, understood?'

Pete nodded enthusiastically. 'Golly, what an adventure I'm having. First I get shot down over the Channel and now this!'

'Makes you feel alive, *non*?'

'Very much so,' said Pete. He looked towards the door of the barn, which had opened a fraction.

Estelle followed his gaze. 'Ah, refreshments!'

An old man tottered into the barn, kicking the door closed with his foot. He swore at a black cat that shot across his path, nearly causing him to drop the tray he was carrying. He hurried over to Marguerite and handed her the tray; holding the peak of his flat cap between forefinger and thumb he nodded towards Pete, who waved an acknowledgement.

Marguerite placed the tray on a bale of hay beside Pete. He glanced hungrily at the food; he couldn't remember the last time he had had something to eat. There was a large chunk of cheese and a crusty bread roll as well as a dusty bottle of red wine. '*Bonjour*, I mean *merci*,' he said as he picked up the wine bottle.

'I think we speak English or we shall all get confused, yes?'

Having taken a large bite out of the bread, Pete nodded mutely as he watched Marguerite pour a large glass of wine and hand it to him. He took a long swig to help soften the stale bread. 'Do you have a plan for my escape?'

Estelle smiled enticingly. 'We do, but seeing as 'ow you find all this exciting I wonder if you would like to 'elp us carry out a mission?' She cocked an eyebrow. 'It will not be easy, and your life will be in danger, but if you succeed it will make a big difference to the war.' She smiled again. 'You will be an 'ero!'

Leaning back against his makeshift bed, Pete took another mouthful of wine. A hero! Now didn't that sound good!

'That was nigh on six months ago!' said Dana, tears pricking her eyes. 'You must've realised we'd all think the worst?'

'Of course I did, and if I could've got word out I would've, but Estelle said it would be too dangerous ...'

Dana's feelings of remorse were quickly turning to ones of resentment. 'Bully for Estelle. She wasn't the one worried sick ...'

'I know it was remiss of me not to—'

Dana snatched her hand from his and stood up to face him. 'Remiss?' Balling her hands into fists she thrust them on to her hips. 'Remiss is when you forget to wash your irons, or accidentally use someone else's boot polish by mistake, but that's not what you did, you didn't tell the people who love you that you were alive …' She pointed in the general direction of Liverpool. 'You didn't even tell your own father!'

'I can see you're angry …' Pete began only to be glared into silence.

'Well, ten out of ten for observation,' snapped Dana bitterly. She took a deep breath and let it out slowly, and as she did so, Pete sarcastically began counting to ten.

She raised her hand and brought it round until her palm connected with the side of his face. The noise resonated across the station. 'Don't you dare make fun of me!'

Pete held a hand to his face. 'I don't know what else to do—' He stopped speaking as a voice yelled out from across the yard; turning, Pete saw a man running towards him.

'What the hell's goin' on?' said Lenny as he arrived by Dana's side. He gave Pete the once-over, his eyes resting briefly on the pilot's insignia, before continuing: 'You all right, Dana?'

Nodding, she indicated Pete with an outstretched hand. 'Lenny, meet Pete Robinson.'

'Oh …' said Lenny as realisation dawned. 'Blimey.'

Pete raised an expectant brow. 'And you are?'

'Lenny Ackerman.'

Pete regarded Dana questioningly.

She looked at Lenny. 'Don't worry about me – I'm fine. Can you give us a minute?'

Lenny nodded. 'I won't be far away.'

Pete stared at Dana as Lenny walked away. 'You moved on fast …'

'You were dead' – Dana shot him a withering glance – 'but you knew I wasn't, so don't you dare try and take the moral high ground wi' me.'

Pete opened his mouth to speak, thought better of it and thrust his hands into his pockets. After a moment's silence, he nodded. 'You're right, apart from one thing: I didn't cheat on you with Estelle.'

Dana shook her head. 'And I didn't cheat on you; as far as I know you can't cheat on someone you believe to be dead.' Pete opened his mouth to speak but Dana was having none of it. 'I know about the letter your father sent you. Why didn't you tell me about it? And don't say because of me dad, because you got that letter before I even knew me dad were ill!'

Pete grimaced. 'I forgot all about your dad. Is he ...?'

Hot tears pricked Dana's eyes. 'He's dead, Pete, so not only did I lose you, but I lost my father too.' She shrugged off his attempt to comfort her. 'Too much water under the bridge, too many secrets ...' She shook her head. 'We never stood a chance.'

Pete rubbed the spot on his cheek where Dana had slapped him. 'I'd forgotten about Dad's letter, but you're right, I should've told you. I may not have kissed Estelle – or anyone else for that matter – but I guess I deserved the slap for keepin' you in the dark ...' Reaching down he took Dana's hand in his. 'I really did like you, Dana, don't ever think I didn't, and at the time I truly believed we might make a go of it, but I've changed a lot since I've been in France – or rather I've come to realise a few things.'

Dana looked at him curiously. 'Oh?'

'I want more than this.' He waved a vague hand around the station. 'I loved being part of the French Resistance, sneaking around in the dead of night, passing secret messages behind enemy lines ... it was thrilling, made me feel alive. I want more of that, so I'm going to ask if they can put me in for the special forces.'

'I can't say it surprises me.'

He shrugged. 'I used to think my father was the same as me when he was younger and that he'd changed as he grew older, but being in France made me realise that wasn't the case at all. We're two entirely different people, and that's why I'll never end up like him; it's not in me to sit around and watch life pass me by, and if he doesn't like it? Tough!'

'Have you told him you're back?'

'Not yet, that's next on my list.' He huffed a mirthless chuckle. 'He'll be made up when he hears we're not together.'

Dana had started to nod when she realised the time. 'Lenny and me are gettin' the bus' – she looked over to Lenny – 'I'd better gerra move on ...' Her expression softened as she looked back to Pete. 'I am glad you're home safe and well. Sorry about the slap.'

Pete laughed softly. 'Come on, I'll walk you over.'

Lenny looked at them expectantly. He knew Dana would never do anything to hurt him, but he had seen Pete for himself, and he was just as handsome and charming as he'd been described ... He smiled as Dana slipped her hand into his.

'C'mon, Lenny, we don't want to miss the bus.' Pausing, she nipped over to Pete and kissed him softly on the cheek. 'Welcome home, Pete.'

Sliding her hand back into Lenny's they walked towards the gate.

Sitting on the grassy knoll, Dana popped a chip into her mouth and savoured the taste of salt and vinegar. 'So this is what you call a romantic day out, Lenny Ackerman.'

Lenny, his legs stretched out in front of him, leaned on one elbow as he selected a chip. Making a wide sweeping motion with his arm, he indicated the view from where they sat. 'I'd rather be sittin' here lookin' out to sea than stuck in some stuffy restaurant somewhere, wouldn't you?'

Dana smiled, the sun warming her face. 'Beautiful, isn't it?'

'Sure is!' said Lenny.

Glancing down, Dana saw Lenny was looking up at her. 'Charmer.' She chuckled.

'Not guilty!' said Lenny. 'I wouldn't say it unless it were true, and you truly are beautiful.'

Dana felt her cheeks grow warm. 'Thanks for comin' to my rescue earlier.'

Lenny grinned. 'Not sure I were comin' to your rescue, not judgin' by the way you walloped him.'

She rolled her eyes. 'Don't remind me, although he did kind of deserve it, just a little bit.'

'Did you tell him about your bein' adopted?'

Dana shook her head. 'Seems irrelevant now.'

Standing up, Lenny leaned down to pull Dana to her feet. 'C'mon, let's go for a stroll on the beach. One of the lads who mans the pillboxes showed me a secret way to get through the barbed wire; it takes a bit of fancy footwork, but nothin' you can't handle.'

Lenny led Dana down to the beach where he examined what looked like an impenetrable wall of barbed wire. 'Aha! Here we go. Mind your head!'

To Dana's surprise he managed to pull the barbed wire to one side allowing the two of them to pass through unscathed. On the other side, Dana told Lenny to avert his eyes whilst she slipped her shoes and stockings off.

'You can turn back now!'

Lenny grinned. 'Like the feelin' of the sand between your toes?'

Dana beamed back at him. 'It's wonderful! Reminds me of when I were a kid. Me dad used to take me and Crystal on to Seaforth Sands for a gallop, before takin' him for a swim in the sea. When we'd finished me mam'd be ready with towels, a cup of tea and hot crumpets smothered in butter.'

'Did you ever go beachcombin'?' said Lenny.

She nodded. 'Dad was a real dab hand with a whittlin' knife; he'd find bits of driftwood and fashion them into toys for me to play with.' Bending down she picked up a small yellow shell. 'He used to make me bracelets out of cowrie shells.'

Lenny handed her a cockle shell. 'You can keep this as a reminder of our romantic day out. Probably best to check it's unoccupied first though!'

Giggling, Dana cupped the shell in her hand, before peeking inside. 'Empty! No, hang on ...' She tipped something out on to the palm of her hand. 'Of all the luck!' She beamed up at Lenny. 'Someone must've lost their ring ...' Her voice faded as Lenny took the ring from the palm of her hand.

'No they haven't; I've had it in my pocket this whole time.' He sank down on to one knee and gazed lovingly into her eyes. 'Dana Quinn, will you marry me?'

Dana stared at him in disbelief. 'Are you serious?'

In answer, Lenny slid the ring on to her finger. 'I've never been more serious about anythin' in my life. I love you, Dana, have done since the day I first laid eyes on you, whilst you were playin' at drivin' cars.'

Dana held a hand to her face to hide her embarrassment. 'I'm surprised you ever wanted to see me again after that!'

Standing up, Lenny cupped her face in his hands. 'That's why I knew you were the girl for me, no airs or graces; you may've felt silly, but you were unashamed of wantin' to do well, and I admired you for that.' He cocked an eyebrow. 'So, will you?'

Dana beamed as she admired the small band of silver that encircled her finger. 'Of course I'll marry you.'

Lenny slid his arms around her waist before kissing her softly. 'What do you think of your romantic day out now?'

'Patty knew!' squeaked Dana.

He laughed. 'So you can expect a million and one questions when you get back!'

Dana thought she was going to burst with happiness. 'Golly, how I love you, Lenny Ackerman.'

She felt his arms strengthen their embrace; leaning down he brushed his lips against hers. 'Good, because I love you too, with all my heart, my sweet cariad.'

READ
ON FOR
BONUS
CONTENT

Dear Reader,

When researching the lives of those who lived in Liverpool during World War Two, I find myself bowled over by the resilience, the bravery and the comradery of those who lived through the Blitz. It really was a case of one for all, and all for one. I have read many accounts of those who put their trust in the air raid shelters, as well as those who headed into the safety of the countryside, and it was whilst I was reading one such interview, that a photograph of a family standing outside a wagon caught my eye. Intrigued to learn more I read on. They were a family of Irish travellers who had lived in and around Liverpool during the Blitz. As they were Irish, I wondered why they hadn't gone back to the safety of their homeland, not only that but just how many travellers decided to stay in Britain during the war?

Eager to find out more I began to research the lives of the travelling community during the war years, and not only did some of them stay in Britain, a lot of them served in the armed forces. I was curious to know whether they faced discrimination, or if they were welcomed with open arms? And what would become of a family, when one or more of the children decided to stay and fight, if the parents wanted to return to the safety of Ireland?

Before I knew it Dana Quinn, the beautiful daughter of Shane and Colleen was born, and with her the trials and tribulations of life as a traveller in war torn Britain.

All I needed now was her beau, or should I make that beaus? Lenny and Pete, both of whom lived very different lives with opposite backgrounds. But who would Dana choose? The incredibly handsome Pete whom every woman wanted for herself, with his wealth and their shared love of horses, or Lenny, the man who taught her to drive, and kept her and her friends together?

As always I hope you enjoy reading *Liverpool Daughter* as much as I enjoyed writing it!

Love *Holly Flynn* xxx

VICTORIA SPONGE RECIPE

This is what my mother called a whisking sponge, and she made all different varieties, adding desiccated coconut to some, coffee or chocolate to others! All I know is they're incredibly easy to make and delicious to eat!

INGREDIENTS
115g self-raising flour
1 level tablespoon baking powder
115g soft butter
115g caster sugar
2 large eggs
1 teaspoon vanilla extract
A jar of your favourite jam
Icing sugar for dusting

METHOD
1. Prepare two sponge tins by greasing with butter.

2. Next pre-heat the oven to fan 170°C/gas mark 3.

3. Sift the flour and baking power into a large mixing bowl.

4. Add the rest of the ingredients and whisk until a smooth, creamy consistency.

5. Divide the mixture equally between the tins and smooth down with a spatula.

6. Place in the centre of the oven for 25 minutes, or until golden brown.

7. Leave the cakes to cool slightly before carefully turning onto wire cooling racks.

8. Once cool, spread with your favourite jam, and, if you're feeling particularly naughty, freshly whipped cream!

9. Sandwich the sponges together.

10. Lightly dust with icing sugar.

Voila!

Read on for an exclusive extract
from the second novel in the
Liverpool Sisters trilogy . . .

UNDER
THE
MISTLETOE

KATIE
FLYNN

OUT NOW

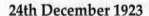

PROLOGUE

24th December 1923

Agnes McKinley pulled the large ring of keys from her skirt pocket and selected the one for the front door to the orphanage. As she slid it into the lock she paused momentarily, she could have sworn she heard a muffled grunting noise coming from the other side of the door as though someone was trying their best not to be heard. She pursed her lips. It'll be one of them nasty little brats, she thought bitterly, no doubt thinking that just because it's Christmas Eve, they can have themselves some fun, larking about in the snow, probably making themselves a snowman to scare one of us when we open the door, and now they're trying to sneak in unnoticed, well aren't they in for a nasty surprise! I shall smash their snowman to smithereens and cart them off to see Mrs Ancrum, that'll teach them. Seizing the brass handle she whipped the door open and shouted 'Gotcha!' To her surprise instead of looking into the upturned face of one of the girls, she found herself looking at the balding head of an elderly man, who was stooped over something on the top of the snow covered concrete steps. Hastily standing to attention he stared angrily at Agnes, who had turned her attention to the bundle which lay on the steps. Bending down she tweaked the blanket to one side. Eyes narrowing, her jaw flinched angrily.

'I don't know what you think you're doing, but you can ruddy well take it with you!' Standing up she thrust the baby toward the man who backed away.

'Nothing to do with me.' he spluttered.

Glaring at him, she indicated the thick snow which carpeted the ground. 'Well whoever dumped her here, must've flown away, 'cos yours are the only footprints in the snow!'

He glanced at the footprints which led to the front door, his eyes darted wildly around before fixing Agnes with a steely glare. 'Whoever dumped her must've done it before it started snowing!' Giving her a look of disgust, he shook his head. 'Stupid woman.'

Furious that he had the audacity to call her stupid, when he was quite clearly lying, Agnes wrinkled her nose as though she had smelt something horrid. 'She's still bloody warm, and it's been snowin' for over an hour, so . . .' she hesitated as her words caught up with her. 'What do you mean, she?'

He gawped at her, his jaw flinching every now and then as he made to speak. But Agnes wasn't going to give him time to think of any more excuses.

'You can't just dump your unwanted baby like a sack of rubbish!'

His face puce with anger he struck the ground with the tip of his walking cane. 'She is not my . . .'

Tired of listening to his excuses, Agnes thrust the baby into his arms, causing him to drop his cane. He stared at her in disbelief. 'I – I . . .'

'I – I,' she mimicked, 'Now take your baby and bugger off before I call the police!'

At the mention of the police the elderly man's sharp little blue eyes bored into hers, and spittle began to form in the corners of his mouth. 'Don't you bloody dare threaten me!' he roared. Realising that raising his voice might attract unwanted attention, he took a couple of deep breaths before trying a different tack. 'Why are you making such a big deal out of it? This is an orphanage, that's what you do, take in unwanted children, what difference is one more going to make?'

She cast him a withering look. 'One more miserable mouth to feed? One more bed to provide? One more unwanted brat to clothe? Oh no,' she said in mocking tones, 'one more won't make any difference!' She paused, something had been bothering her about the man and she now realised what it was. Placing her hands on her hips she stared at him accusingly. 'You've got a cheek, you're not even from around these parts yet here you are dumping your rubbish on our doorstep,' cocking her head to one side she rubbed a thoughtful hand over her chin, before clicking her fingers, 'you're a Scouser! A posh one,' her eyes travelled

from the gold wedding ring, to the Homburg hat which adorned his head, to the black woollen tailored coat, finishing with his highly polished oxford shoes, 'Doesn't look to me as though you can't afford a child, so I reckon you got some poor tart pregnant, then fetched her up here where no one knows either of you so she could give birth before your wife or your posh pals found out,' seeing the look of utter fury which crossed his face, she nodded smugly. 'I'm right, aren't I?'

He strode past her without replying and placed the baby on the steps, despite her protests he descended the stairs and picked his cane up off the ground.

'Oi!' Agnes cried out, 'don't you ruddy well ignore me you fat old . . .' she fell silent as he spun round and thrust the handle of the cane inches away from her nose.

Agnes went cross-eyed as she stared at the extremely heavy looking elaborate silver handle which looked as though it could cause her serious damage. It was in the shape of a cobra's head, its fangs bared, its neck frilled, it weaved back and forth in front of her eyes. He spoke through gritted teeth. 'Don't you ever speak to me like that again or I'll crack your head like a walnut . . .' without moving his cane he pushed his hand into his pocket, and pushed a fistful of notes into the middle of her chest, causing Agnes to stagger back slightly. Staring at her with utter hatred and contempt, he adjusted his hat, which had slid to the back of his head, and straightened his coat.

Some of the notes fell to the floor. He glanced down at them. 'Pick them up!'

Her mouth dry, Agnes did as he instructed.

Taking a step back from Agnes he brought his cane back by his side, although she noticed his fingers were still tightly curled around the stem. As Agnes stood up, the money clenched to her chest, he stared at her swollen belly, before fixing her with a look of disapproval. 'You have the audacity to judge me, when you're clearly with child, yet I see no wedding band?'

'But I'm not giving mine away.' Agnes said quietly.

'Well more bloody fool you!' he said hotly before turning on his heel and stalking off into the night.

Thoroughly shaken up from her ordeal Agnes stared down at the baby in her arms. 'I reckon you're not more than a few hours old, yet look at the trouble you're already causing.' She glanced at the retreating back of the old man. 'Not often I say this, but you're better off without that as your father.' Sighing heavily she made her way inside. The money and baby still tightly clutched to her chest she tried to shut the door, but she had too many things in her arms. Placing the baby on the floor, she pushed the money into her bodice when a sharp voice caused her to jump.

It was Mrs Ancrum who ran the orphanage, and she did not look happy. 'Agnes McKinley! What on earth are you doing?'

Fearing she had been caught red handed, Agnes hastily pulled her hand out from her bra, scattering notes everywhere. Before she had chance to explain, Mrs Ancrum had crossed the floor and was picking up the money, her eyes flicking toward the baby, she stood upright and waved the money in front of Agnes's face. 'Well?' She glanced at Agnes' bosom and held her other hand out, 'Hand them over!'

Shamefaced, Agnes began pulling the notes out from her bodice. When she had handed the last note to her employer she bent down and scooped the baby into her arms as she gabbled her excuses. 'I wasn't nicking the money, only I couldn't hold the baby and lock the door at the same time, so I thought . . .'

Mrs Ancrum looked at her with feigned surprise. 'You thought the baby belonged on the floor and the money in your bra!'

Agnes, her eyes rounding, shook her head. 'No! That's not it at all! The key was in my pocket, and my hands were too full . . .'

'So? Put the money on the floor and keep the baby in your arms, just goes to show . . .' snapped Mrs Ancrum. She stopped short, she had been so surprised to catch one of her employees

trying to conceal a considerable amount of money in her bodice, the fact that the same employee was in possession of a new born baby hadn't registered. 'Where did this come from?' she said, taking the baby in her arms.

'Some feller dumped her outside . . .' Agnes explained what had happened, hoping that once the other woman heard her tale she would not only believe what she had to say but sympathise with her predicament. Unfortunately for Agnes, Mrs Ancrum was still regarding her with unbelieving disapproval.

'How convenient!' she regarded Agnes through suspicious eyes, 'no witnesses to back you up, just a fistful of notes and a baby at your feet.' She glanced at Agnes's stomach. 'That amount of money would prove pretty handy with a baby on the way.'

Agnes swallowed hard. Why couldn't Mrs Ancrum see that she was telling the truth? A flicker of doubt entered her thoughts. The other woman was right, it was a lot of money, had she not been caught would Agnes have handed it over? With no witnesses, it would have been very easy for her to keep the money. She lowered her gaze. 'It's true,' she mumbled beneath her breath.

Mrs Ancrum shook her head. 'I know someone left their baby, and according to you they left her a considerable amount of money . . .' her face remained impassive, 'or did they pay you to turn a blind eye?'

Agnes's mouth hung open. 'That wasn't it at all!'

Mrs Ancrum raised a questioning brow. 'Wasn't it? How am I meant to know what really happened?' her eyes rested on Agnes's pregnant belly. 'You're going to struggle for money when the baby's born, especially after I turned you down for that pay rise you requested.' She glanced at the fistful of notes in her hand. 'A tidy sum like this would tide you over for a considerable time.' She shook her head fervently as Agnes tried to protest, 'I can only go by the facts, and I saw you shoving the money down your bra.' She glanced at the baby who was sleeping peacefully. 'Stealing from a baby!' her nose wrinkling

with distaste and she fixed Agnes with an icy stare, 'I should give you your marching orders . . .'

Agnes burst into tears. 'P – please don't! I swear I wasn't taking the money, I'll do anything it takes, but I can't bring up a baby on me own, especially with no job . . .' she glanced around the walls of the hallway, before fixing her employer with pleading eyes. '. . . and this is my home, I've got nowhere else to go!'

Mrs Ancrum drew a deep breath. 'As I was saying, I should give you your marching orders, but I shall be lenient under the circumstances.'

Sagging, Agnes held a hand to her forehead. 'Thank you, Mrs Ancrum, I promise I won't let you down.'

'You'd better not!' snapped the older woman. She held the baby toward Agnes, who stepped forward to receive the child. 'You say the child's a girl?'

Sniffing loudly, Agnes nodded.

'Then take her to the nursery, she shall be named Jessica Wilson after the founder of Greystones.'

Agnes nodded briefly before leaving the room. She glanced down at the baby in her arms, who was beginning to stir. 'You've nearly cost me my job as well as my home, Jessica Wilson.' A fluttering sensation in her tummy reminded her of her own unborn child. 'My baby's not going to be a Jessica Wilson, 'cos I'd never give her up . . .' she hesitated, '. . . but I would've had no choice should Mrs Ancrum have given me the sack.' A hollow feeling began to rise in her throat as the enormity of her narrow escape sank in. She glanced at Jessica with a look of angry disapproval. 'My baby's going to be a Bonnie, or a Billy.' She pushed the door to the nursery open with her foot. 'Welcome to Greystones Orphanage, Jessica Wilson, your steppin' stone to Barn Hill.'

THE BRAND NEW NOVEL FROM THE *SUNDAY TIMES* BESTSELLER

Liverpool, 1922

Olivia Campbell appears to have the perfect life. However, behind closed doors she lives in constant fear of her abusive father, and has no support from her mother.

Longing for love and affection she begins a relationship with Ted, a young lad who works in her father's factory. But her family disapprove of the relationship and forbid them from seeing each other.

When war comes to Liverpool, Olivia seizes the opportunity to leave behind her unhappy life and join the WAAF. There she meets a fellow trainee, Maude and the two embrace their newly found independence. Soon Olivia meets the handsome Ralph, and all thoughts of Ted are brushed aside. Until he returns to her life with some shocking news that turns her world upside down . . .

AVAILABLE IN PAPERBACK AND EBOOK

Enjoy the best of the

KATIE
FLYNN

Springtime Collection

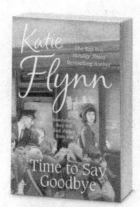

Katie Flynn
The Top Ten
Sunday Times
Bestselling Author
Time to Say Goodbye

Katie Flynn
The Top Ten
Sunday Times
Bestselling author
Sunshine and Shadows

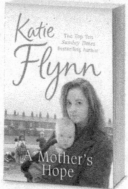

The Cuckoo Child
KATIE FLYNN

Katie Flynn
The Top Ten
Sunday Times
Bestselling Author
A Mother's Hope

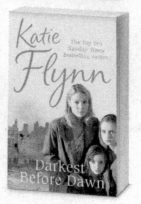

The Top Ten Sunday Times Bestselling Author
Katie Flynn
The Liverpool Rose

Katie Flynn
The Top Ten
Sunday Times
Bestselling Author
Darkest Before Dawn

KATIE FLYNN

If you want to continue to hear from the
Flynn family, and to receive the latest news about
new Katie Flynn books and competitions,
sign up to the Katie Flynn newsletter.

Join today by visiting
www.penguin.co.uk/katieflynnnewsletter